SUSAN JOHNSON

Brazen

The Library Of
Elaine Lepage,

BANTAM BOOKS

New York   Toronto   London   Sydney   Auckland

BRAZEN

A Bantam Book / November 1995

ISBN 0-553-57213-X

Published simultaneously in the United States and Canada

*Bantam Books are published by Bantam Books, a division of Bantam Doubleday Dell
Publishing Group, Inc. Its trademark, consisting of the words "Bantam Books" and
the portrayal of a rooster, is Registered in U.S. Patent and Trademark Office and in
other countries. Marca Registrada. Bantam Books, 1540 Broadway, New York, New
York 10036.*

PRINTED IN THE UNITED STATES OF AMERICA

RAD   0 9 8 7 6 5 4 3 2 1

Brazen

1

"No, darling," Kit Braddock murmured. "I *have* to sleep—"

A heated kiss silenced his dissent, and for a lengthy interval only the faint sound of lapping waves floating in through the open portholes broke the stillness. Then, sighing, he gently pushed the seductive woman away. Setting her at a safe distance, he dropped back into a sprawl amid the tangle of bedsheets, his tall, lean body dark against the white linen. "The race starts early," he said, gazing up at the siren kneeling at his side, his smile pale in the moonlight. "Be sensible," he cajoled.

"Wales's crew does all the work," she countered, her voice minutely fretful, her tumbled golden hair framing a pouty face.

"Not tomorrow. They're going to need help sailing against the *Meteor*. I also have to be polite to royalty all day," he added, stretching his large frame, the fluid ripple of muscle vivid in the gilded light of moonbeams. "And *that's* damned tiring."

"This won't take long."

Kit smiled broadly. "We all know the measure of your orgasmic speed, Saskia—but, sweetheart, it's really getting late."

At that precise moment, however, Cleo's warm mouth began tracing a slow gliding progress over the tanned firmness of his thigh with the ultimate focus of that journey reacting in a predictable way.

Noting his instant response, Saskia triumphantly smirked.

A wet tongue languidly slid up his rising erection, and he softly groaned as exquisite pleasure inundated his senses. Glancing down at the dark-haired woman resting between his legs, then up at the clock on the teak-paneled wall, he swiftly debated carnal urgency against the practicalities of time.

"Just once more . . . ," Saskia softly purred, her eyes half-lidded, anticipation stirring her blood, her gaze on the rigid length of Kit's penis slipping in and out of Cleo's mouth.

A third woman rolled closer on the large bed, her plump breasts swelling against Kit's shoulder. She was small and lithe, and when she raised herself slightly to touch her lips to his ear, the silken heat of her body slid up his arm. Her voice was no more than a seductive resonance in his ear, her tantalizing words reminding him of the night they'd outraced the pasha's yacht near Cyprus.

Lust flared through his body at the memory.

"Just a few minutes more . . . ," the Ceylonese beauty whispered.

His shadowed eyes swept the lush trio, their scented flesh fragrant in his nostrils, their naked charms incarnate womanhood.

He'd raced more than once without sleep, he thought. And, he decided, royalty would just have to be content with a less energetic guest . . . three hours from now.

Shutting his eyes, he shifted slightly to absorb the fierce jolt of pleasure convulsing his body, Cleo's training in the pasha's harem cultivated to excite every sensitive nerve . . . and obliterate cerebral concerns.

The race vanished from his thoughts.

Even the sound of waves faded from his ears.

Until sometime later when Cleo lifted her head.

Kit's eyes opened, and surveying his lovely companions, he said with a grin, "Now, then, darlings . . . who's going to be first?"

2

The ball at the Royal Yacht Club was raucous and heated—more so than usual, for the Prince of Wales's three-hundred-ton racing cutter *Britannia* had won against the kaiser's radically designed yacht *Meteor* that afternoon. Even had the prince not loathed his posturing nephew, the win would have been cause for celebration. But defeating what was reputedly the priciest yacht in the world was the sweetest of victories.

His Royal Highness had been celebrating since the finish line had heaved into view and the decibel levels at the Royal Yacht Club indicated England's pride and elation.

But two people escaping the din and tumult had taken refuge on the starlit terrace.

The Countess de Grae was struggling to maintain her composure against the pressure of tears welling in her throat and eyes. She never should have come to Cowes, despite the Prince of Wales's invitation; Cowes always reminded her of Joe. How many summers had she sailed with Joe Manton? Too many to forget all the memories. And while she understood Joe's need to marry now that he'd inherited his title, his marriage to Georgiana last month had left her feeling adrift, bereft of a dear friend.

Leaning against the stone balustrade, Kit Braddock was contemplating the distant tranquillity of his yacht moored far out in the harbor. After having sailed with the Prince of Wales on the *Britannia* that day—and after having drunk more than his share of celebratory toasts the last several hours—the peaceful hermitage of the *Desiree* lured his weary spirits. Inhaling deeply, he drew in the cool night air, the sharp tang of the sea breeze, refreshing after the cloying heat of the ballroom. He could see his stateroom lights twinkling across the water. Would it be possible to slip away unnoticed?

Tomorrow he raced against the Italians and French. His American-built ocean racer was expected to win. He smiled. Of course he'd win; his yacht could outrun anything on the seas. But some sleep wouldn't be out of order. . . .

When he first heard the muffled sobs, his immediate reaction was to ignore them.

It was late.

He was tired.

And weeping women invariably meant trouble.

But the closeness of the sound surprised him; he wondered that he'd overlooked her presence. That's what came of living the idle life of leisure during the London season, he noted. One lost one's fine edge playing the gentleman.

Angela de Grae preferred not to embarrass herself before the man who had been paying court to her best friend's daughter the past fortnight. Kit Braddock would have been distinguishable by his formidable size alone even had the moonlight not disclosed his distinctive features. Charlotte had glowingly described the rich, handsome American yachtsman who'd charmed his way into her young daughter's heart. Angela was to have been formally introduced to Priscilla's beau tonight—if she'd been able to withstand the brittle gaiety inside. How damnably awkward. Maybe the man would pretend not to have heard and go away. The countess dearly hoped he would.

The woman's scent struck Kit as a swirl of night air eddied across the secluded corner—an intense attar of rose—separate from the Asian lilies and climbing rugosas cascading over the terrace wall. The fragrance struck a vaguely familiar chord somewhere in the indecipherable recesses of his mind.

Then he heard a small sniffle.

And silently swearing, he debated his limited options. Would it be ignominious to cut and run? Had he been recognized? How could he possibly offer solace to some unknown woman? Lord, he disliked crying females. But ultimately good manners and an inherent courtesy prevailed, and when, with a suppressed sigh, he turned and moved toward the sound, his polite smile was in place.

The figure of a seated woman materialized from the mottled shadows of the turreted wall, very near indeed to where he'd been standing. "Could I be of some assistance?" he quietly said.

When the countess lifted her head, a streak of moonlight caught and shimmered on the pale tips of her fashionably curled coiffeur, framing the perfection of her face in a platinum halo.

For very good reason Angela de Grae had reigned as a recognized beauty for so long, Kit thought with a sudden stabbing clarity. She was undeniably breathtaking. Even with that sadness in her eyes.

When she gently shook her head, the renowned Lawton diamonds swung from her earlobes. "It's just a touch of melancholy," Angela murmured. "Fatigue, no doubt, after a very busy season. And the noise inside . . ." She shivered in delicate revulsion.

"Would you like an escort home?" Kit queried. Gossip was rife concerning Major Joe Manton's sudden marriage and the consequences to his long-term love affair with the countess. Her need for privacy was understandable. And then he suddenly recalled why the attar of roses had nudged his memory. The countess had been wearing the same perfume when he'd briefly met her years ago at Biarritz, where she'd been on holiday with the Prince of Wales.

"How can we leave? Bertie's still here," she replied with a small sigh. No one could precede a royal guest.

Kit's eyes shone with mischief. "I *could* lower you over the balustrade, and we could *both* escape."

Her mouth quirked faintly in a tentative smile. "How tempting. Are the festivities wearing thin for you, too, Mr. Braddock? We were supposed to meet formally tonight," she graciously added. "I'm Angela de Grae, a good friend of Priscilla's mother."

"I thought so," he neutrally replied, thinking her gracious not to flaunt her celebrity as a professional beauty. Her photos sold in enormous numbers in England. "And, yes, 'worn thin' is a very polite expression for my current mood. I'm racing early tomorrow, and I'd rather sleep tonight than watch everyone become increasingly drunk."

"Champagne *is* flowing in torrents, but Bertie is pleased with his victory. Especially after losing to his nephew last year."

"Willie deserved his trouncing today. He should have been disqualified for almost shearing off our bow on the turn. But at the moment I'm concerned only with escaping from the party. If I'm going to have my crew in shape in the morning, we're all going to need some rest."

"Do they wait for your return?" The countess's voice held the smallest hint of huskiness, an unconsciously flirtatious voice. "Priscilla doesn't know, of course." Although Kit Braddock referred to his female companions as "crew," reportedly he kept a small harem on board his yacht to entertain him on his journeys around the world.

"She's too young to know," he casually replied, "and rumor probably exaggerates."

The countess took note of the equivocal adverb, but she too understood the demands of politesse and said, "Yes, I'm sure," to both portions of his statement. It was very much a man's world in which she lived, and though her enormous personal wealth had always allowed her a greater measure of freedom than that allowed other women, even Angela de Grae had at times to recognize the stark reality of the double standard.

"Well, then?" His deep voice held a teasing query.

"I'm not sure my mopish brooding is worth a broken leg," Angela pleasantly retorted, rising from her chair and moving the small distance to the balustrade. Gazing over the climbing roses, she swiftly contemplated the drop to the ground. "Are you very strong? I certainly hope so," she quickly added, hoisting herself up on the balustrade and smoothly swinging her legs and lacy skirts over the side. "Although, Mr. Braddock," she went on in a delectable drawl, smiling at him from over her bare shoulder, "you certainly *look* as if you have the strength to rescue us from this tedious evening."

How old *was* she? he found himself suddenly wondering. She looked like a young girl perched on the terrace rail, her hands braced to balance herself. In the next quicksilver instant he decided it didn't matter. And in a flashing moment more he was responding to the smile that had charmed a legion of men since young "Angel" Lawton had first smiled up at her grandpapa from the cradle and Viscount Lawton had decided to overlook his scapegrace son in his will and leave his fortune to his beautiful granddaughter.

"Wait," Kit said, apropos her pose and other more disturbing sensations engendered by the countess's tempting smile. Leaping down onto the grass bordering the flower beds, he gingerly stepped between the tall stands of lilies, stopped directly below her, lifted his arms, smiled, and said, "Now."

Without hesitation she jumped in a flurry of petticoats and handmade lace and fell into his arms.

They both laughed amid the swaying lilies as he held her hard against him, like youngsters who'd joyously evaded authority—and then they suddenly went quiet, a volatile, urgent susceptibility stifling their breath. Heedless to circumstance, Kit's body responded to the impetuous sensation of desire while a rash answering heat coursed through Angela's blood. As he held her tightly, her slippered feet suspended in space, her small hands resting on his powerful shoulders, the countess found her voice first—because Priscilla Pembroke was enamored of this handsome young man, and because Charlotte was her very good friend.

"If you'd be so kind, Mr. Braddock, to set me down," she said, her voice pleasantly neutral.

He hesitated for the smallest moment, his life to date one of reckless disregard for convention. Her voluptuous body was pressed hard against his—against his swelling arousal—and he'd seen the startled, flashing heat in her eyes. He'd heard all the stories, too. She was a woman of great passion, lover to the Prince of Wales and others—Countess Angel, the great temptress of her age.

"You must put me down, Mr. Braddock. Priscilla wouldn't understand."

Mention of the young woman he'd been seeing lately served to curb Kit's less principled impulses, and he released his grip, allowing her to slide to the ground. "I hope she understands my abrupt departure," he casually said, ignoring the mild reprimand he'd been given. He smiled. "But winning the race tomorrow is important."

"Priscilla knows how men like to win, Mr. Braddock," the countess said with an answering smile. "She's a very sensible young girl."

"But not as beautiful as you," he softly replied, knowing even as he uttered the words, he shouldn't.

There was the briefest pause before she, as aware as he of incautious feeling, answered in a bland, courteous voice, "How flattering of you, Mr. Braddock." Moving away to a less intimate distance, she added, "I'll say good night now."

"Do you need an escort home?" Kit replied with a well-schooled politesse.

"No, I've only a half block to walk."

"Good night, then, Countess. Pleasant dreams."

"I never dream, Mr. Braddock." She was moving through the tall, stately lilies, the sumptuous flowers shoulder high to her diminutive size. "But thank you very much for saving me from a miserable evening. I'm in your debt." Turning, she smiled at him, then waved, her white kid glove pale in the shadowed night.

As she walked away over the velvety lawn, Kit found himself contemplating the enticing possibility of collecting that debt someday.

Someday when he was in a less politic mood. Or when he was less well behaved.

*W*hen Kit returned to his yacht, he found himself thinking of Angela de Grae numerous times in the course of the night. Each time that reality intruded into his reverie, and his gaze focused on the women in his bed—none of whom resembled the pale-haired countess—he always experienced a novel pang of regret.

Angela found herself unable to sleep when she arrived home. Standing on the balcony outside her boudoir, her gaze settled on the distinctive masts of the *Desiree* as it rode at anchor in the moonlight. She hoped Kit Braddock would win tomorrow, although her good wishes probably weren't required; everyone said the *Desiree* was going to take the cup this year. She suddenly smiled into the moonlit night as the realization struck her: For the first time in a month she wasn't overcome with melancholy.

Priscilla had found herself a remarkable young man.

3

By eleven the next morning, the Prince of Wales's guests were assembled for breakfast on the *Victoria and Albert,* his preferred residence at Cowes. The racing yachts were expected to clear the Needles by noon and make for the finish line. And the prince's guests had a perfect view from the decks of the *Victoria and Albert;* one need only look up from the breakfast tables scattered under the striped awnings.

"Isn't it fortunate we found a table away from that awful breeze?" Charlotte Pembroke, Countess Ansley said, waving a distasteful hand at the choppy sunlit sea.

"Since we're on the water, it's hard to avoid," Angela replied, smiling faintly at Charlotte's unsuccessful attempt to straighten the georgette ruffle on her daughter's neckline against the blustery wind.

"It *won't* lie down, Maman, and my hairdo's going to be ruined, too," Priscilla complained, tucking in a tendril of chestnut hair that had fallen from her fashionable upswept coiffure. "And the dreadful sun on my skin . . . ," she lamented, as if her mama might be able to arrest its shining beams.

"We needn't sit here much longer, darling. The racing yachts are scheduled to appear soon, and then we can go belowdecks out of this devastating weather."

While Angela had been a friend of Charlotte's for years, she was always amused at her fussy style of mothering. As for the weather, the morning couldn't have been more perfect: a clear blue sky above the sparkling sea, warm temperatures, the breeze pleasant. "Why not go below now if you'd be more comfortable?" Angela amiably suggested. "You needn't keep me company."

"We *can't* miss the *Desiree*'s finish." Charlotte's brows rose in delicate emphasis over the rim of her teacup.

"Kit would never forgive me," Priscilla breathed.

"His devotion to Prissy is charming." Charlotte had the smug look of a mother with an eligible bachelor securely in her net.

"He sends me the most gorgeous flowers. Huge, huge baskets—but, then, the Americans are always so lavish in their spending, and he's so *very* rich."

"Forty million a year," Charlotte said. While the aristocracy decried money as vulgar and beneath their notice, it was a constant topic of conversation: who had it; who didn't; who had expectations; who had cleverly made a fortune.

"And even if Kit's money is from trade—mines and shipping," Priscilla airily noted, "and he *doesn't* have a title, Maman says I can marry him if I wish. I think a Christmas wedding would be deevy. I could wear velvet and ermine with diamonds like snowflakes —Kit's company ships South African diamonds, too," she smugly noted, "and of course Grandmama's Brussels veil that every Pembroke bride has worn."

"Wynmere is so beautiful with snow." Lady Ansley pronounced the words with sufficient drama to cause Angela to look up from her creamed lobster, curious to see what would follow such theatrics. "The pristine countryside's like a fairy-tale set. So utterly *perfect* for young lovers."

"Has Mr. Braddock proposed?" Angela asked, her perception of Kit Braddock at odds with the Pembrokes. Idyllic concepts of devotion and young love didn't quite suit the adventuresome Mr. Braddock.

"Well . . . not precisely." Priscilla's large blue eyes in the perfect oval of her face narrowed slightly. "But Maman says he will, that's certain, because I'm the most beautiful deb this year, *everybody* agrees. So when I marry him, then Papa can have his new racers and stables and Maman will have Wynmere *all* redone, with the east wing redecorated for us. I could never think of living in the ghastly colonies. Do you think Baby May could be a flower girl at my wedding?"

"I'm sure she'd love to," Angela politely replied for her two-year-old daughter while wondering if Kit Braddock knew his wedding and future life were being arranged by this chit of a girl.

"Will Fitz be home from the Continent for the wedding?" Charlotte asked. "Your son would be perfect for one of the groomsmen." Her brows rose in searching query. "Or will he still be keeping his distance from England and that Manchester merchant's daughter who fancies him for a husband?"

"He wrote he'd be home next month," Angela replied. "And he's safe for the moment, since I offered Brook more than the Loftons did for Fitz's future coronet."

"But Brook continues to gamble." Charlotte's statement was in the way of question.

"Of course." Angela grimaced slightly, her husband's ineptitude at the gaming tables an ongoing expense for her.

"So the problem is only temporarily resolved."

"The immediate jeopardy of Fitz being sold off to the Lofton girl for the price of Brook's gambling debts has been averted. As for the future," Angela said with a sigh, "one can only meet each of Brook's monetary crises as they occur." Her husband was not only the bane of her life but a danger to her children, and she often wondered if she could continually protect them from his temper and greed. This last instance concerning her seventeen-year-old son had terrified her. Fitz had gone to visit his grandmother on her birthday and been coldly apprised of his coming engagement by his father. He'd ridden away from de Grae Castle in only his shirtsleeves, arriving at Easton exhausted and shaken the following day. She'd sent him abroad within hours, wanting him beyond his father's reach. And when she'd gone to Brook to negotiate her son's future, the price he was asking to release Fitz from the marriage contract was staggering.

"Brook has been a burden for you, darling," Charlotte bluntly retorted. "At least my Arnold isn't a spendthrift."

"Is it the Lofton heiress Fitz is avoiding?" Priscilla inquired. "The one whose papa owns a dozen mills and three banks and the best stud in the north?"

"The same," Angela said, surprised at the girl's definitive grasp of Reginald Lofton's assets. "Do you know her?"

"Heavens, no. She's pudding-faced and bourgeoisie. But you have plenty of money, so Fitz needn't really marry her. It's a shame there's not a son in the family."

"What if he were pudding-faced and bourgeois?" Angela quizzically inquired, unprepared for such a cool assessment of marriage by a young girl.

"He'd still be richer than Kit."

"Really," she softly uttered, astonished at such matter-of-fact financial auditing.

"Of course. The Lofton mills are the biggest in England, and their banks are involved in world trade, particularly South Africa."

"Priscilla is quite fascinated by business," her mother proudly interjected. "She and her father know to the penny everyone's worth."

A daunting thought, Angela considered, wondering if her own money would be safer from such avid scrutiny abroad. "So Mr. Braddock has reached the top of your eligible list because Lofton has no son."

"I could never marry a man who wasn't enormously wealthy," Priscilla succinctly noted. "And, after all, the arrangement would be infinitely fair; he'd be getting me for a wife." Her smile was sunnily self-assured.

"You must meet Prissy's Mr. Braddock. Why don't you come to Wynmere next week and meet her beau?" Charlotte cheerfully suggested. "Since we couldn't find you last night at the ball, you'll have an opportunity to see for yourself how charming the wealthy Mr. Braddock can be."

Angela had already discovered the agreeable extent of Kit Braddock's charm, and knowing that, she wisely excused herself. "I'm afraid I'm promised at the Oaks next week."

"With Wales, I suppose," Charlotte archly noted.

"You know how he likes old friends," Angela said, ignoring Charlotte's insinuating tone.

"How do you and Alice Keppel get along?" The Prince of Wales's mistress was a recent acquisition.

"She's a much better bridge player than I."

"At least *you* enjoyed Wales's friendship when he was young enough not to devote himself exclusively to bridge," Charlotte murmured with an irreverently raised brow.

"Bertie is always charming company. I'm sure Mrs. Keppel thoroughly enjoys their friendship." Despite Charlotte's prodding, she had no intention of discussing her past intimacies with the Prince of Wales.

"Joe and Georgiana aren't at Cowes, are they?" Charlotte asked, as if her mind had made the same connection as Angela's. It was common knowledge Angela had scandalously discarded the prince for Joe Manton.

"They're still in Europe." A soft constraint underlay Angela's answer.

"You raced with Joe last year, didn't you? Or did he race on your yacht?"

"We raced on his."

"Didn't you win some cup . . . the Queen's?"

"Yes."

"That silver one on the chinoiserie table in your sitting room? Do you still have it?" Lady Ansley posed, a faint sly smile curving her generous mouth.

"I didn't know you sailed." Priscilla interjected, astonishment in her wide-eyed gaze. "Don't you get wet and terribly windblown?"

Repressing her smile, Angela said, "You don't mind. It's great fun."

"Really? Well I should mind terribly—but, then, you hunt too, don't you?"

"My grandpapa liked to sail and hunt, so I learned very young to enjoy both."

"How very odd."

No more odd, Angela thought, than the practice of leaving young aristocratic girls like Priscilla largely untutored and uneducated. "It never seemed unusual to me," she calmly replied. "But we lived quite isolated at Easton when Grandpapa was alive."

"You and Kit have so much in common," Priscilla said. "He hunts, too," she went on, returning to her favorite topic other than herself. "You wouldn't think an American would be so refined. What a shame you're going to be at the Oaks next week."

"I'm sure I'll meet him soon. It sounds as though you've found a perfect beau," Angela kindly said, grateful for the disruption to Charlotte's interrogation about Joe Manton.

"We *could* all come to Easton the *following* week," Charlotte pointedly said with a grin, "if you'd invite us."

"How subtle," Angela replied with a faint smile. "But I'm sure Mr. Braddock would prefer doing something else. We live so simply at Easton."

"I'm sure he'd like to do whatever *I* like to do," Priscilla countered, the faintest petulance in her voice.

"You have a nicely tamed man."

"Since Priscilla *is* the most splendid girl out this season, he'd be an absolute fool not to be enamored," Lady Ansley asserted. "So are we invited, darling?"

As a friend of long standing, Charlotte was impossible to refuse. In addition, she had no subtlety when she wanted something. "If you won't be bored with our lazy schedule," Angela graciously acceded. "Easton has only country amusements, but Millie and Sutherland are coming down and perhaps Dolly and Carsons."

"Easton is always a jewel, darling, and no one entertains like you. It sounds as though you're having a cozy family party with your sisters. We'd love to join you."

Easton was Angela's country home, inherited from her grandfather. With her husband's estate distant from hers, they saw each other infrequently—a not unusual arrangement in aristocratic circles. Like many marriages based on practical and financial consider-ations, their union had evolved into one of strained civility and cool disregard.

"It's settled, then," Angela said while she consid-ered how best to dilute the inconvenient "coziness" of the gathering. Country weekends were notorious for flirtations, and though she didn't wish to misjudge Kit Braddock's intentions toward Priscilla, nor her own few brief moments alone with him, she would feel infi-nitely safer with several more people about. "I won-der," she queried, "if I should invite some guests more your age so you and your Mr. Braddock won't find the visit too dull?"

The silk violets on Priscilla's straw hat shimmered and bobbed as she vigorously shook her head. "I won't have you inviting Harriette Villiers or Fanny Frampton or any of the other debs," she hotly de-clared, "because they're nothing but little tarts. Every-one knows Fanny uses rouge and Harriette's own aunt says she's fast. Even Cecily, who puts on such inno-cent airs, lured Kit into the conservatory at Lord Al-bemarle's party, and I practically had to pull him from her clutches. I don't want the little sluts anywhere near him."

"Watch your language, dear," her mother warned. "What will Kit think if he hears you speaking like a common person?"

Kit Braddock struck Angela as devoutly unshock-able, but conscious of Priscilla's aversion to rivals, she suggested, "Why don't *you* send me a list of some friends you'd like to invite to Easton? Some who don't flirt," she added with a smile. Then, catching sight of the *Desiree* rounding the Gurnard spit with its rakish sails aloft and, even from that distance, its tremendous speed apparent, she was gripped by the familiar thrill she always felt at the sight of a fine ship. "The *Desiree*'s in the lead!" And even as she indicated the far-off roads east of Cowes, a cheer went up from the royal party seated near the rail.

"The Prince of Wales adores Kit." Priscilla pronounced each word with a priggish self-conceit, as if Kit Braddock's friendship with the prince was simply another measure of her own allure.

"Kit's always with the prince," Charlotte pridefully added.

"He must be amusing, then," Angela noted, her gaze shifting from the racing yachts to her companions. She knew Bertie didn't abide boredom.

"Oh, Kit's ever so droll. The darling can even make Papa smile."

A formidable feat, Angela thought. Arnold Pembroke had a dour, authoritarian temperament without a visible shred of humor.

"And Kit's helping HRH add to his racing stables," Priscilla declared. "They were at Newmarket together."

"Did you hear he brought Knolton's team the championship at Hurlingham last week?" Charlotte added.

"Charlie must have been pleased." But the image of Kit Braddock riding down the polo green at breakneck speed suddenly unnerved her—the sense of unrestrained power almost palpable. "Do send me your list of names," she quickly interposed, "as soon as possible." A houseful of guests would be added security against her quixotic feelings.

"I have a marvelous idea," Charlotte impetuously offered. "Why don't we bring Kit to Eden House to-night when we come to dine?"

"How *perfect,* Maman! Angela, you always have the most *wonderful* dinners with all the *best* people." Priscilla cast her most charming smile at Angela. "Do say we can!"

Everyone was standing at the rail by then, watching the *Desiree* close in for the finish, the French racer a thousand yards back, the Italians not even in sight. Only Charlotte and Priscilla seemed immune to the crackling excitement. Glancing at the sleek, graceful yacht slashing through the waves, Angela knew she couldn't refuse even if she wished, and at the moment she wasn't certain her answer would necessarily be motivated by politeness. From her vantage point, Kit's muscled form was clearly visible as he helped his crew work the sails. Nude above his white duck trousers, he was sleek with sea spray, his upper body glistening as if it were oiled, like a gladiator on display. A shock-ingly physical sight.

"Say yes, Angela. Please . . ."

It took a moment for Priscilla's plea to register in Angela's consciousness and a second more for her to find her voice. "Yes, of course. Mr. Braddock is wel-come if he wishes." His skin was deeply bronzed, she noted, her gaze drawn back to the conspicuous expo-sure of male virility. Then she noticed the women on deck. And she recalled the sensational accounts of his harem. No doubt obliging that number of women kept his body toned.

Kit Braddock was an excessively profligate man.

Even in an age setting new standards for profli-gacy.

Surely she had more sense.

—

*A*fter the requisite round of congratulations and celebratory toasts at the Royal Yacht Squadron Club, Kit received Charlotte's invitation to join them for dinner. Having taken the note outside to read, he smiled as he gazed at the lavender-scented message. How gratifying, he thought, to conclude his victorious day in company with the delicious Angela de Grae.

"Tell Countess Ansley I'd be pleased to join her and Lady Priscilla," he said to the waiting footman, folding the note and sliding it into his coat pocket.

As the servant exited the terrace, Kit drew in a deep, calming breath. It's only an invitation to dinner, he reminded himself, not an invitation into Countess Angel's bed, the thought of which did nothing for his composure. Swiftly sliding his fingers through his still damp hair, he stood motionless for a moment, his mind racing with tempting visions. Then, dropping his hands to his sides, he shook his fingers as though the irrepressible excitement strumming through his senses needed release. Steady, Braddock, he cautioned himself, you're too old for adolescent fantasies.

Relax.

It's just dinner, no more.

Then he slowly stretched and grinned.

On the other hand . . .

*Y*ou're in a fine humor," Saskia said with a smile, lounging on Kit's bed as he dressed for his dinner engagement. "And correct me if I'm wrong, but I detect something beyond the *Desiree*'s victory fueling your good mood."

"We've been friends too long, darling," Kit replied, tying his white tie with a deft expertise, smiling at her image in the mirror. "You can read my mind."

"She must be interesting to intrigue you so, which leaves out the dull-as-dishwater Priscilla Pembroke," Saskia murmured, her brows raised in artful query. "Tell me her name."

"The Countess Angel of fame, and I'm feeling very adolescent tonight. Do you remember your first time?"

"Of course. *That* excited," she purred. "How nice."

"Unfortunately, I don't think she's interested," Kit said with a rueful grimace as he ran two brushes over his sleek hair.

"Ah—but then again, you might be able to change her mind. . . ."

"Maybe, maybe not . . . I don't know," he said, dropping the silver-backed brushes onto the dresser top. "She's heard all the stories."

"About us."

He nodded and reached for his waistcoat draped over a nearby chair.

"Apparently the Pembrokes are willing to over-look the scandal."

"Money talks," he succinctly said, slipping his arms into the embroidered white silk vest.

"And the Angel isn't interested in your money?"

He shook his head as he buttoned the waistcoat. "Everyone's not as calculating as Priscilla's family. Be-sides, she has plenty of her own."

"Did you tell her we're all just friends?"

"I haven't had the chance to; I saw her only once, briefly, and she judiciously reminded me that she and Priscilla's mother are good friends."

"A distinct rebuff, darling."

"Exactly. But tell my libido that. She's been on my mind constantly."

"The notorious Countess Angel would appeal to you, of course. A woman who's always had her pick of men."

"Her reputation does have a certain tantalizing appeal."

"And what of your quest for a wife and a grandchild for your mother?"

His brows rose the smallest distance. "The two aren't related."

"Have you decided on the beautiful but stupid Priscilla Pembroke, then?"

"I haven't decided on anything, although until I met the countess, my plans seemed much more reasonable. She brought into focus Priscilla's numerous shortcomings."

"You apparently haven't been listening to me the last fortnight."

"While you, darling, haven't been subjected to my mother's loving but constant pleas for a grandchild. If I have to marry someone, at least young ladies like Priscilla understand the standard conventions. They trade their beauty or title for money; in turn they bear a required number of children to accommodate their husbands. It's a straightforward business arrangement. Which is precisely why I'm interested."

"Did you ever consider love?"

"No. Did you? I don't recall your marriage was based on romantical notions."

She grinned. "He *was* damnably rich."

"And old."

"Unfortunately . . . and cruel."

"Look, sweet, we're both practical people. When I met you in Java, you wanted passage out and I was happy to help, but in all the years we've known each other . . . and it's been a while . . ."

"Five years now."

"In those five years I've never heard you talk of love, so don't ask *me* to consider it as a requisite for my marriage. I wouldn't even consider marriage except my mother has her heart set on my marrying an English girl. She'd really like someone from Devon, her old home, but I warned her filial obligations extend only so far. If I was going to oblige her, she'd have to take potluck on the county."

"Not exactly a man in love," Saskia sardonically murmured.

"I prefer my bachelor life, darling, as you well know. And I don't see you searching out a husband."

"I don't have to with the generous sum you settled on me. Nor do any of us. Thanks to you." Kit had provided well-endowed bank accounts for his female companions, so their arrangement was one of mutual interest, not financial necessity.

"You've all been the best of company. It's my pleasure. Now, tell me, do you think Countess Angel will smile on me tonight or not?"

"Not with Priscilla there, darling. How could she?"

"Hmmm . . ." A faint frown drew his brows together. "So what do you suggest? Give me some of your astute female advice."

"Discard the prissy Priscilla."

"Some *reasonable* advice, sweet. Lord, I need a drink." Striding across the large stateroom, he lifted a decanter from its slot in a liquor compartment specially constructed to hold the bottles in heavy seas. Pouring a half glass of Kentucky bourbon, he dropped into a chair, stretched out his legs, lifted the glass in salute, and said with a smile, "To kind winds."

"Priscilla might look more interesting after a few of those," Saskia drolly noted.

"The countess surely will," he softly said.

"The woman is definitely on your mind."

His eyelids half lowered, and he dipped his head the faintest measure over the rim of his glass. "Oh, yes."

"Why?"

"I don't know. She's very beautiful, I suppose."

"Is she tall?" She knew Kit had a preference for tall women.

He shook his head.

"Is she flirtatious?"

He snorted. "Hardly. She gave me my congé."

"Perhaps she's a challenge."

He shrugged, then shook his head again. "No, it's not a game this time. It's . . . just . . . different," he slowly enunciated. "She's very small . . . ," he said, as if some explanation existed in those few words "And blond . . . very pale blond . . ." His voice trailed away for a moment, as did his attention, and Saskia contemplated a novel dimension to the Kit Braddock she'd known for five years. Perhaps she might get her wish, after all, apropos Priscilla. She'd hated watching him court the Pembroke girl for all the wrong reasons.

"So we won today," he said, rousing from his reverie, deliberately moving to more comprehensible topics. "Did you think we would?"

"Of course."

Kit grinned. "Me, too. Now we have a day off."

"Except for your social duties with the Prince of Wales."

"Another week or two, and then maybe I'll beg off from the Scottish shooting."

Which meant he might not propose to Priscilla,

after all, she pleasantly thought. Two days ago he'd planned on staying for the shooting. "Then next to New York?" she casually inquired.

He nodded. "And Newport later."

Was the Priscilla plan already jettisoned in his mind? she cheerfully mused, watching him drain the glass of liquor in one huge swallow. "You don't have time for another," she said, reading his thoughts. "You're going to be late if you don't finish dressing." Rising from the bed, she walked over to the armoire and took out his black evening coat. Holding it out for him, she teased with a grin, "Now, remember to be good tonight and mind your manners."

Setting his glass aside, he rose from the chair with a sigh. "I hate these complications."

"Leave your Angel alone, then."

Standing motionless for a moment, he seemed to consider. "But I don't want to," he softly murmured, moving toward the outheld jacket.

"I can tell," she calmly declared. *"Bon chance, mon ami."* Her smile held a special warmth for the man who had saved her life on the docks of Surabaja.

He grinned. "I may need your luck tonight," he said, sliding his arms into the sleeves. "I feel as if I'm sixteen."

"That in itself might tempt the sophisticated countess," Saskia lightly retorted, adjusting the jacket on his wide shoulders.

Turning around, Kit touched her chin lightly with a finger. "While Priscilla likes *older* men."

"What a shame. She'll have to find someone else."

"It's a thought, isn't it?"

"The first good one you've had since we arrived in England."

"Don't be shy with your feelings," he drawled.

"I've been the pillar of constraint since you first decided on this matrimonial venture."

"And I appreciate it," Kit quietly said.

"Go now," Saskia ordered, giving him a push toward the door. "Your countess is waiting."

4

The twilight in the large nursery at Eden House reflected the gold of the setting sun as Angela and daughter May, seated in the window nook facing the harbor, reread May's favorite story. Peter Rabbit was just about to get caught in Mr. McGregor's garden.[1]

"Wun wun! Wun wabbit!" Her large blue eyes wide with excitement, May quickly reached for the dog-eared corner of the page to turn it.

"Do you think he'll get away?" Angela whispered.

"Hurry, Mama," the child exclaimed, needing help with the glossy paper that slipped from her pudgy fingers.

"There." The next illustration flipped into view, and Baby May squealed with delight as Peter Rabbit slipped away under Mr. McGregor's garden gate. "And now he'll soon be home safe in his own little bed," Angela softly said.

"Gween bed, yike mine," May declared, beaming.

"Just like yours, darling." Baby May's bed had been specially designed to match the Beatrix Potter illustration.

"Me no sweep," she quickly said, shaking her head, intent on putting off her bedtime.

"We'll finish the story first."

"Me not sweepy."

"You don't have to sleep yet, sweetheart. But when you get tired like Peter Rabbit, then Bergie will tuck you in."

"Me sweep wit you."

"Later if you like. Mama has guests coming for dinner and I have to entertain them first."

"Bergie bring me yater."

"Bergie will bring you later," Angela agreed, giving her small daughter a hug. "And tomorrow we'll go down to the water in the morning."

"Me bring baby too," May said, holding her doll up by one leg. "She yike swim."

The door opened, and a young woman stood on the threshold. "It's eight o'clock, my lady," the nurse-maid said. "You wanted me to remind you."

"Mama has to go dress now, darling. Give Mama a kiss good night and then wake me in the morning."

"Erwy, erwy."

"As early as you like." And kissing her daughter good night, Angela rose in a flurry of azure lace and scent and walked through the adjoining door into her bedroom.

*H*er lady's maid was waiting, the gown she'd selected earlier laid out on the bed, her jewelry spread out on the mirrored top of the dressing table.

"Your guests will be here in half an hour, my lady. And if we have trouble with your hair in this damp air . . ."

"My guests can wait, then, Nellie. You needn't be anxious. This is a summer holiday, after all, and the prince won't be here, so we'll simply relax the rules tonight if necessary."

"But you know how the Marchioness of Belton complains if she doesn't eat on time."

"Should I be delayed, I'll have the footman see that her glass of champagne is kept full until I arrive downstairs. Sarah particularly likes the quality of my wine cellar."

"She'll be dreadful tipsy by the end of dinner."

"Isn't she always?" Angela replied with a smile as she seated herself before the dressing-table mirror. "But we're all used to Sarah by now. Let's do something casual with my hair tonight, Nellie," she went on. "I'm not in the mood for a head full of pins."

"Would you like the chignon with ribbons I did for the ball at Devonshire's last Christmas?"

"Perfect. White ribbons? Or green?"

"Green, my lady, with the sash on your gown."

And while Nellie brushed her heavy hair, Angela tried to convince herself that dinner tonight was no different from hundreds in the past. By keeping busy with May since her return from the race, she'd managed to suppress the enticing images of Kit Braddock insistently rising into her consciousness. She'd concentrate on the game she was playing with her daughter when they'd surface, tamping the unwanted memories. Granted Mr. Braddock was splendid and handsome, but she couldn't allow herself to be attracted. He was coming to dinner tonight as escort for Priscilla, as Priscilla's future husband, if the Pembrokes understood his attentions correctly. Regardless of his fascinating masculinity, he was outside the pale.

But she found herself flushed with excitement as she stood before her cheval glass for a final survey before going downstairs to her guests, her pulse trembling at her throat.

"You look like a dream tonight . . . ," Nellie said with a satisfied sigh. "An absolute dream."

Angela wore a Worth gown in damask rose chiffon, embroidered and beaded. The low décolletage of the gown was a simple vee of draped chiffon tied at the shoulders with ribbons matching the spring-green taffeta sash at her waist. Her flesh had a warm glow in contrast to the muted color of her gown—her bare arms and bosom, the slender curve of her throat, tinged with a blush.

Her pale golden hair framed her face in a froth of waves loosely constrained into a simple ribbon-tied chignon. Earrings of splendid baroque pearls were her only jewelry. She'd decided against the ropes of pearls lying on her dressing table. On such a lovely summer evening the fashionable excess of jewels required of every well-dressed lady seemed out of place.

"Have I kept them waiting long?" Angela asked, turning to check the small ormolu clock on the mantel.

"Only ten minutes."

Angela smiled. "In that case I needn't apologize."

*W*hen she walked into the large drawing room a few moments later, delicate, curvaceous, and so simply dressed every woman silently denounced her dresser, conversation momentarily ceased for the smallest breath-held hush. Then the most envious of the ladies quickly spoke to their companions again, feigning immunity to the Countess de Grae's fabulous beauty.

And the buzz of voices resumed.

But Charlotte Pembroke took note of Kit Braddock's swift, discerning survey before his attention returned to her daughter, and she decided it might be expeditious to see that he and Priscilla were left alone together sometime soon so he might propose.

An acceleration of the courtship, as it were.

Perhaps tomorrow night, when he came to their home for a small family gathering.

Moving into the room, Angela signaled her butler to begin announcing the order for the procession into dinner. As hostess, she entered the dining room first with the highest-ranking of her male guests, her old friend, Souveral, the Portuguese ambassador, followed by the others in a required protocol that distinguished between differences in titles.

Earlier, while arranging the seating at the table with her housekeeper, she'd deliberately placed Kit Braddock at the opposite end of the table. Charlotte, too, had been positioned several guests away to avoid any unwelcome interrogation. In her present disquieted frame of mind Angela preferred the most banal social conversation, and to that purpose she seated Souveral on her right and Violet Lanley on her left.

Her glance didn't stray past her immediate companions, nor did Kit indicate that he was aware of his hostess five people distant from him on his left. The room was awash with conversation and laughter, the candlelight lending an atmosphere of intimacy to the flower-decked table, light and shadow flickering over jewels and dazzling gowns. Soft-footed servants dispensed the numerous courses and wines with the discretion of a superbly trained staff. Potages were followed by hors d'oeuvres, relevés, entrées; rotis arrived in sumptuous variety, then entremets.

Kit noticed Angela ate very little. She only tasted the tomato-and-shrimp bisque. Waving away the hors d'oeuvres, she took a portion of pike à la Chambord but cut only two pieces and set them aside. The culotte of beef received a small shake of her head. She did eat the quail; he made a mental note to serve it to her should the occasion arise. And when the entremets arrived, the countess selected salad greens prepared with a dressing specially mixed at table side.

Moderation and discipline apparently maintained her superb figure, he decided, fascinated by another facet revealed. He wouldn't have thought her capable of constraint if even half the delectable scandals of her life were true. But then the desserts arrived, and his hasty judgments stood corrected as he observed her eat an apricot tart, a citron ice, and two cheeses with cherries. He should have known.

For some time Priscilla had been discussing the merits of her dressmaker over Worth, so Kit on her right had only to nod or agree at appropriate moments, neither of which interfered with the more pleasant diversion of watching Angela tuck into her array of desserts. On Priscilla's left, Lord Congreve, lecher that he was, actually asked questions of Priscilla, exerting his elderly charm to what purpose Kit couldn't imagine. Priscilla certainly wasn't going to fall into his bed, and as a married man, he wasn't an eligible suitor. But he diverted her attention, and for that Kit considered sending him a case of his favorite brandy tomorrow.

Apparently Souveral was offering Angela a choice tidbit of gossip because she laughed with genuine glee, and he wished he could see her laugh like that with him . . . at much closer range—preferably in his bed. . . .

"Mama says it's not necessary to spend a hundred guineas for a gown. This gown was only fifty and I'm very pleased."

Congreve immediately offered his sycophantic agreement while Kit, in turn, urbanely said, "It's very lovely, Priscilla."

"Think how much money I'll save you, darling."

Kit must have looked startled, because she giggled and tapped his cheek playfully with her fan. "Just ignore silly little me."

He definitely would, he thought, his current frame of mind worlds removed from any commitment to Priscilla Pembroke.

Into the small silence Congreve bluffly declared, "We men adore your silliness, Lady Priscilla—don't we, now, Braddock?"

"Always," Kit murmured, his smile polite.

"Now, tell me, my dear," old Congreve went on, "do you prefer your dressmaker to Doucet as well? His tea gowns are the height of elegance."

The man was definitely worth a dozen cases, Kit gratefully decided as Priscilla's monologue on female fashion resumed. Reprieved once again from his duties as dinner companion, he returned his gaze to his hostess.

Like a moth to the flame . . .

A very *hot* flame, as it turned out, for the sight of Lady Angela idly licking almond cream off a nougat candy she'd dipped into her dessert was mercilessly carnal to a man unused to restraint. As her tongue delicately glided over the nougat, he surveyed the minutiae of that progress with riveted interest. When a small dollop of cream collected on the tip of her pink tongue, he could almost taste the sweetness. A flaring heat spiked downward, licentious fantasies immediately filled his mind, and, shifting slightly on his chair to accommodate his swelling arousal, he watched her tongue slip back into her mouth, witnessed her savor the rich flavor of the confection, let his prodigal imagination run full rein as she swallowed the dollop of cream.

She was temptation incarnate, the enticing Eve of

every man's dreams, bathed in golden candlelight, her bare shoulders and arms lush, her plump breasts partially exposed in the deep vee of her décolletage, her features delicate in the luminous flame, like a Della Robbia madonna . . . save for her full, sensuous mouth—a decidedly unspiritual mouth. Captivated, he watched her lick the creamy residue from the nougat like a child leisurely consuming a sucker. Leaning back in her chair while her friends chatted around her, she seemed detached from the pulse of conversation. Was she aware of him watching her? he wondered. Was her lounging pose construed as sensual only to his susceptible psyche? Or was Lady Angel playing a teasing game of seduction?

Her eyes were half-lidded, her lashes indolently shielding her gaze, the slender hand at her mouth holding the candy graceful, languorous. Long moments later, having licked off all the almond cream, she slid the candy partially into her mouth and delicately nibbled on the nougat. Kit suddenly felt the indelible impress of her teeth as if they were devoted to his pleasure alone, the sensation hammering down his nerve endings with such intensity, he briefly shut his eyes.

If she was amusing herself, he thought on a suffocated breath, she played the game with exquisite skill. He could hear his pulse beating in his ears. And if any scruples of custom or decorum previously existed in his mind concerning his pursuit of the tempting Countess Angel, hot-blooded lust nonchalantly dismissed such paltry obstacles.

Her sense of duty or propriety to a friend be damned. He intended to have her. If not tonight— *soon.*

Look at me, he silently commanded, wanting to see an answering heat in her eyes, wondering if the notorious lady would be languorous in bed, too—or did she like her pleasure with excess? There had been talk of a relationship with the championship jockey, Lew Archer, so she didn't devote herself exclusively to aristocrats. How nice. Look up, my darling temptress, he urged, recalling the luscious feel of her in his arms, the fascinating provocation of her smile. And whether his message reached her or she'd tired of her detached reverie, her gaze suddenly lifted.

To meet his covetous eyes.

For an overwrought, tremulous moment they were alone amid the scents and sounds and glittering light.

Look away, Angela told herself. He was much too bold; he'd embarrass them both.

But she didn't, his eyes holding hers like green tiger's eyes, desire so palpable in their smoldering depths, a shiver fluttered up her spine. His auburn hair was touched with flame in the candlelight, and in that breath-held moment he struck her as irrepressibly dangerous. No rationale explained her sense of peril, but she felt unshielded and vulnerable under that audacious gaze.

He'd be impatient, she realized, as if he'd already entered her boudoir and was striding toward her, the unbridled lust in his eyes unmistakable. No circumspect courtier stared at her, but a sensational male animal. In hot pursuit.

Disquieted, she licked her lower lip, and he smiled faintly as if he knew what she was thinking.

She blushed at the impudent presumption in his brazen glance, and his smile widened with a cool self-assurance. Dipping his sleek head an infinitesimal distance, he acknowledged her patent response.

Her spine went stiff at his insolence. Good God, she wasn't some harem girl who turned docile at a man's command. She'd had her pick of men since she'd turned fifteen. But her fingers closed hard on the fan in her lap—as if self-discipline would save her from his undisguised hunger—and a fragile fan strut snapped under her clenched fingers.

Souveral looked down.

Kit's gaze flickered over her before he turned back to his dinner companions.

"I don't know how many fans I've ruined lately," Angela murmured, her voice taut with constraint and the prideful anger of a celebrated beauty. How dare he look away first.

"A shame, darling," Souveral blandly said, taking note of the color on her cheeks. "Let me buy you a new one tomorrow."

Forcing a smile, she shook her head. "No need, Freddy. I've dozens more."

"As you wish, darling." And turning to a footman offering a platter of pastries, he indicated his choice while Angela drew in a deep, calming breath. Her reaction to Kit Braddock was highly irregular, almost shocking in its intensity. Damn him and his insolence. Why was she responding so violently to a man she'd only just met?

"It's so annoying to play bridge with Wales when he constantly expects to win. Don't you agree?" Lady Violet pettishly said to Angela.

When she didn't immediately answer, Souveral, who rarely missed a flicker of an eyelash in society— nor had he in this instance—smoothly said, "Since you rarely play bridge, Angela dear, you'll have to agree that Violet has borne more than her share of Wales's lopsided play."

"Yes, Violet, how dreadful for you," Angela replied, her composure partially restored, grateful for Souveral's suave intercession, feeling less affected now by Kit Braddock's hunter's eyes. "I promise you no one need play bridge tonight."

"How comforting. Instead we can be entertained watching Charlotte trying to bring Priscilla's young man up to scratch," Violet amusedly said. "She's enormously heavy-handed. If I have to hear once more about Priscilla's expertise on the dance floor, or the story about her winning the prize for her watercolor of Lyme lighthouse, I swear I'll embarrass us all and scream."

"He's extremely wealthy," Souveral noted. "You can't blame Charlotte for trying. Wynmere *is* in need of repairs. And certainly we all understand the realities of marriage."

Violet grimaced. "Don't remind me." Violet was living on a generous marriage settlement that had been wisely set aside by her family. Her husband, Lord Dudley, in the meantime was systematically running through the rest of her fortune. As for the marquise, aristocratic Portuguese marriages were never for love.

"Do you think he's serious?" Angela inquired, curious despite herself.

"He?" The Portuguese ambassador raised one dark brow.

"Mr. Braddock." Her blue eyes meeting his were studiously without expression. "He's been with the prince a great deal."

As a favorite of the Prince of Wales, Souveral was always included in the heir to the throne's intimate circle. "Mr. Braddock never talks about women."

"Not even his harem?" Violet breathlessly queried.

"Particularly not his harem. But he did mention," the ambassador went on, observing Angela with a searching gaze, "that he was ready to acquire a wife."

"And Charlotte is selling the lovely doe-eyed,

pouty-lipped Priscilla to the highest bidder this season," Baroness Lanley snidely said.

"He doesn't strike me as a man too easily caught," the Marquise de Souveral remarked, tracing the stem of his wineglass with a perfectly manicured finger. "He's been sailing the world for at least a decade, indication of an independent man. And he's from the Braddock-Black family, who conduct themselves with a bohemian disregard for propriety. Their immense wealth, of course, allows such heedless behavior. You remember Hazard Black and his son Trey, don't you, Violet? They're frequent visitors to France. We saw them at Longchamps this spring. De Vec married a daughter, if you recall."

"Even though his wife had the whole of France's judicial system behind her and the Vatican as well." Violet smiled at memory of the delicious scandal.

"Not enough apparently for de Vec," Souveral blandly noted. "He's very much in the Braddock-Black mold. Audacious in the extreme." The ambassador's black brows rose faintly toward his bald forehead. "Considering Kit Braddock's past history and family affiliations, I'd say Charlotte may be overly optimistic about landing him for her daughter."

Inexplicably, the marquise's words cheered Angela even as a more prudent voice of reason reminded her that not only would a man like Kit Braddock leave devastation in his wake, but Charlotte *was* intent on gaining him for a son-in-law. So he was spoken for and, if it mattered, also too young.

As if his age were of any concern, she hotly reflected a second later. Or anything else about the presumptuous Mr. Braddock. Good God, she wasn't *interested* in a man with a harem. Period.

"On the other hand," the ambassador smoothly

advanced, "Charlotte might not be above some—er—unscrupulous methods to gain the advantage."

"Like Hortense did with her daughter and Lonsdale." Everyone knew the story of the young lord lured into bed and then "discovered" by the young lady's parents. "Personally," Violet said with a shrug, "I'm not so sure that would work with Mr. Braddock. He doesn't look like a man overly concerned with appearances."

"He *is* the only man I know who openly flaunts a harem. Perhaps you're right," Souveral calmly agreed. "So would you care to wager a small amount on whether Priscilla lands him? I think Charlotte is more than his match."

"Of course she isn't," the baroness emphatically declared. "And since I can use the money with Dudley robbing me blind, I'll bet a thousand guineas that Mr. Braddock wiggles free."

"Would *you* care to place a bet?" the ambassador asked Angela.

Her brows rose in mild disdain. "No, I certainly would *not*. Whether Priscilla and Charlotte are successful is irrelevant to me. Do you know how bored I am by all this frantic matchmaking every season?"

"Easy for you to say with your son only seventeen and the Grevilles likely to march him down the aisle without concern for your opinion. As for May," Violet went on, "you can afford to be indifferent to the matrimonial market for another sixteen years."

"They won't be sold on that block." Angela pronounced the words so softly, it struck both her listeners as extraordinary that such vehemence could be expressed in so delicate a tone.

"The voice of experience, no doubt," Violet gently said.

Without answering, Angela signaled for the butler,

and when he immediately appeared at her side, she said, "I think it's time for drinks and tea in the drawing room."[2]

As he bowed and murmured, "Very good, my lady," Angela rose from her chair and, smiling down the table at her guests, said, "Why don't we retire to the drawing room? The view from the balcony is wonderful this time of night."

Violet and Souveral exchanged glances as they rose to join their hostess, who was already moving toward the doors held open by two footmen. As they strolled together toward the drawing room, Violet softly said, "Her aversion to Brook and his entire family is almost an obsession."

"The man's abominable." Even spoken in an undertone, Souveral's loathing was marked.

"And he won't give her a divorce."

The ambassador sighed. "Even Bertie tried to exert influence." He shook his head. "De Grae threatened to name him correspondent."

"At least Dudley is just stupid and dull. De Grae can be frightening. She's had a constant struggle to protect her children from his savage temper over the years."

"He would have broken a weaker woman."

Violet smiled. "Certainly no one can characterize Angela as weak."

"Old Lord Lawton taught her well."

"So we should talk of more innocuous subjects than the marriage mart over tea," Violet gently said. "Particularly after this last episode with Fitz."

"Perhaps Mr. Braddock will entertain us with anecdotes of his race today."

"Would she like that?" Baroness Lanley softly queried, a faint smile gracing her face.

"You noticed, then."

"I've never seen her blush before. The man does have a conspicuous virility."

"A bit like Joe Manton."

"Not at all like Joe," Violet disagreed with a delicate snort of disgust. "You men perceive only such superficial attributes."

"How is he so different?"

Violet grinned. "For one thing, he has a harem."

Souveral laughed. "Besides that obvious distinction. They're both athletes; they both sail; I don't know if Kit hunts, but living in the unsettled west on occasion, I expect he does."

"Completely incidental," Violet drawled.

"Incidental to?"

"Mr. Braddock's seductive charm. You see, Angela and Joe were friends first. She misses that friendship most."

"They were lovers, certainly."

"Of course. But they grew up together on adjoining estates. The bonds that drew them together are quite different from Mr. Braddock's sensational physical appeal. She'll turn him down, of course. Because of Charlotte."

"Are you so certain he'll ask?" Souveral observed with a speculative smile.

"Granted, Mr. Braddock may not be in the habit of asking, with so many available women in his life, but Angela will rebuff him regardless."

"Really." The ambassador had his own opinion after the tantalizing exchange he'd witnessed at dinner.

"Trust me, Freddy. In the meantime, the progression of events should be entertaining. But whatever the outcome of Mr. Braddock's ardent pursuit, Priscilla certainly won't get him. And I shan't mind at all taking your money."

"If you recall, he *is* looking for a wife."

"He *thinks* he's looking for a wife," Violet replied, casting a smug glance at Souveral. "Men like Mr. Braddock never actually take that last fatal step. Eventually he'll just sail away again. Umm . . . smell the flowers," she murmured as they entered the drawing room. "Angela's homes are always so wonderfully scented."

The drawing room opened to the balcony overlooking The Solent, and the sea air drifting in through the French doors mingled with the heady fragrance of gardenias, sweet pea, and roses massed in large famille rose bowls. Angela stood at the open doorway, her gaze on the night sky.

Turning at their entrance, she said, "The stars are absolutely glorious. It's a shame we're all inside rehashing gossip. Again," she added with a sigh. "What a dreadful life." Her smile was strained.

"You'd rather be out on the sea tonight," Souveral noted.

"Wouldn't that be heavenly?" Angela breathed. "Instead," she went on with a small grimace, "we shall talk of banalities with great seriousness."

"Now, darling," Violet sardonically reproved, "Charlotte would disagree. Rather than banal, her plans to trap all that Braddock wealth are gravely important."

"Not to me," Angela softly retorted. "Oh, dear. How selfish that sounds. Forgive me . . . but I'm so restless." She clasped her fingers together tightly as if to hold herself together. "The season seemed so unbelievably long this year, and I shouldn't have come to Cowes." Her voice had quickened as if a storm seethed inside her. "Oh, lord, they're going to be here soon. Would you do me a favor, Violet, and pour tonight? I'm distinctly *not* in the mood."

"For tea or for everything?" Violet gently inquired, surveying Angela's white knuckles.

Angela made a small moue, abruptly unclasped her hands, and with a sketchy wave that encompassed the richly decorated room, said, "Look at this . . . we all have the same decorators; all our homes look alike; even our lives are pathetically identical." Although hers had changed substantially the last few years since she'd begun devoting more time to building and funding an agricultural college, and primary and secondary schools. "I'm so tired of the same people, the same conversations, the endless dinners, the utter tedium . . ."

"Why don't you escape tonight, just disappear for the rest of the evening?" the baroness kindly suggested. "Souveral and I will make your excuses and attend to the tea drinkers."

Angela hesitated, indecision etched in her drawn brows. "Would you mind?" she finally said. "For some reason I find the company more enervating this evening."

"Of course we don't mind. And it's not as though you won't be seeing everyone again tomorrow night at Charlotte's."

Angela softly groaned.

"You forgot."

"I forgot."

"Leave now," Violet coaxed, "before the others descend on us."

"You're sure?"

"Tell her, Freddy. You're so much more diplomatic than I."

"If you don't leave now, you'll be obliged to listen to the story of Priscilla's drawing prize again."

Angela grinned. "Exactly the incentive I need, darling. I'll see you tomorrow," she quickly declared, turning to exit the room through the connecting door to the library, narrowly eluding Charlotte and Lord Congreve, who were the first to arrive.

Delayed at table by Priscilla's recital of her presentation at court, Kit, Lady Wolcott, and Priscilla were the last to leave the dining room. After waiting in the library for several minutes to avoid any guests moving between the rooms, Angela was just slipping into her suite at the end of the corridor as the small party exited the dining room. And if Kit hadn't cast a bored glance down the hall while Priscilla and Lady Wolcott debated the length of their interviews with the queen, he wouldn't have caught a flashing glimpse of blond hair and rose chiffon disappearing from sight.

On entering the drawing room, he discovered why their hostess had retreated from her dinner party. "Poor dear has a dreadful headache," Lady Lanley explained, "so I insisted she leave us to our own devices. Angela promises to be in fine form for your dinner tomorrow night, Charlotte. Now, who wishes tea?"

And for a polite interval Kit answered numerous questions about his victorious race, drank brandy rather than tea, listened with desultory attention to the latest gossip, and more interestingly, speculated on the possibility of finding the countess alone in her rooms. The tables were just setting up for those who wished to play bridge when he recalled a previous engagement at the yacht club. "I promised Waring a survey of my sailing charts tonight," he explained to Charlotte and Priscilla. Certain the women couldn't accompany him, as the club was a strictly male preserve save for special entertainments, he'd judiciously chosen his venue.

"Can't someone else help Lord Waring?" Priscilla

protested. "I haven't seen you all day with that silly race taking all your time."

Her self-absorption always startled him. But in good humor, with more tantalizing plans entrain, Kit affably said, "I'm afraid Waring's depending on me, since I so recently sailed the course. And he's going to have some stiff competition with Harcourt tomorrow."

"Couldn't you stay just a little longer?" Priscilla affected a becoming pout.

"Now, darling," Charlotte interjected, "you mustn't be demanding." Her motherly advice was delivered with a gracious smile and the disquieting sense that the words "until after you're married" were left unsaid.

But in his present genial mood Kit ignored the scented deception, made all the necessary farewells, and took his leave. Animated by a sense of adventure, he stood in the quiet of the hall outside the drawing room and surveyed both directions. No servants. No sound. Nothing, he pleasantly contemplated, between himself and the doorway at the end of the hall.

Sliding his watch from his waistcoat pocket, he checked the time. Only eleven. He smiled.

Now to see if Lady Angela was in need of comfort for her headache.

5

Strolling down the carpeted corridor, Kit glanced at the sailing prints lining the walls, thinking Angela might enjoy seeing the Ruysdael he had in his stateroom. The storm-tossed seascape always reminded him of the transience and unpredictability of life. An icon, as it were, to his vagabond existence. How pleasant, he reflected, that the countess liked sailing—an unusual interest for a society belle—but, then, she was an uncommon lady in many ways.

As the last framed depiction of a marine scene slipped by, he stopped before the paneled door through which Angela had disappeared. Not pausing to question good manners or gentility—in terms of ladies' boudoirs the rules were flexible, he'd learned—he opened the door and stepped over the threshold. The small sitting room was subtly illuminated by silk-shaded lamps, decorated in rococo gilt and pastels and graced with the lovely Countess Angel in dishabille lounging on a chaise, her hair lying loose on her shoulders, her feet bare under the lacy hem of her dressing gown. Clothed in white with her pale hair gleaming, she was a luminous radiance in the shadowed cabinet.

Her voice, however, had the exacting intonation of reality. "I didn't invite you in," she said, closing the book in her lap and gazing at him with a challenging scrutiny.

"I wasn't sure I had the patience to wait for an invitation," Kit pleasantly said, shutting the door. "Do you really have a headache? If you do, I'm sorry."

"Would you leave if I said yes?"

He looked even more powerful framed by the graceful arabesques of the gilded door, she thought— dark, lean, half in shadow against the far wall, a forceful presence in her private rooms.

"Are you going to say yes?" Even leaning casually against the door, he conveyed a bold and potent energy beneath his elegant tailoring, as if a barbaric warrior stood at the gates.

A brief silence passed, the hum of indecision and possibility vibrating in the air.

Would he dare do more than breach the privacy of her solitude?

And how would she react should he try?

But she wasn't a timid ingenue uncertain in masculine company, she reminded herself. She was, in fact, more capable than most at keeping men in their place.

Her shoulder lifted in the merest of shrugs. "No, I don't have a headache."

An instant smile creased Kit's tanned cheek. "You just wanted to get away from me."

"You presume too much, Mr. Braddock. I scarcely know you."

"Perhaps we could become better acquainted," he quietly said. Pushing away from the door, he began moving toward a set of embroidered armchairs.

"I don't think so," she evenly replied. "And if you were a gentleman, you'd leave."

He stood very still for a moment, his gaze lazily surveying her. "Does that usually work?" he murmured, and without waiting for a reply, he resumed his course. Reaching a chair, he dropped onto the primrose brocade cushion, settled into a lazy sprawl, and gently said, "I'm not a gentleman."

"Look, Mr. Braddock," Angela quietly declared, placing the book in her lap on an adjacent table, "I won't pretend you aren't a fascinating man. Neither of us are disingenuous novices, but—"

"Ah—the iniquitous 'but' . . . ," Kit softly interposed. "Allow me," he murmured with a small smile and a faint inclination of his head, "to define all the debilitating reasons. First, we have Charlotte and Priscilla as major deterrents. Then, of course, your sense of friendship and duty as ethical considerations. Are we considering my poaching on the Prince of Wales's territory, or is that no longer of consequence? And we mustn't leave out your melancholy over Mr. Manton's recent marriage." When her brows rose in surprise, he went on with a brief smile, "Surely you know rumor has decreed you quite inconsolable. Have I covered everything?"

"Perfectly." Her voice was calm, as if starkly handsome men bent on seduction were common in her boudoir. "So you see how impossible any further friendship can be."

"Are you always so dispassionate?"

"Surely it can't matter much to a man with a traveling harem. You'll forget this sudden impulse of yours in a few hours."

"So cynical about men, my lady."

"I'm not eighteen, Mr. Braddock."

"Perhaps I could change your mind."

Angela smiled for the first time. "Really, Mr. Braddock, that's not very original."

"You've heard that too often."

"I imagine you were very young when I first heard it."

"How old are you?"

"Thirty-five."

"You were a mere girl when you married de Grae."

A mask seemed to descend over her face, all expression shut away. "I was seventeen," she said, her voice so chill, he wondered what the earl had done to her.

He knew they didn't live together, nor had they for years, but he hadn't realized how virulent was her dislike of her husband. "I'm sorry," he said, as if she'd confided all the merciless detail to him.

"There's no need, Mr. Braddock. I'm much more fortunate than most. But you can understand," she softly went on, "why I prefer not involving myself in your affairs. You'll be gone soon, I expect; Priscilla *is* a consideration, despite what you say; and, frankly, I can't see any advantage for me."

"You'd have a sailing partner for a time," he said with a grin.

"How clever of you, Mr. Braddock," she replied, her smile suddenly genuine. Had Bertie told him of her passion for sailing?

"Call me Kit."

"Why should I?"

"Your yacht isn't at Cowes this year. I'll take you sailing tomorrow."

"Umm . . . you know how to tempt me."

The husky purr of her voice stroked his senses, recalling the delectable lady he'd met on the terrace the night before. "I'll come for you at eight in the morning."

Swiftly rising from the chaise, she walked to the window in a flurry of white dimity and lace, nervously plucked at the curtain, quickly dropped it again, swiveled round to face him, and said, low and abrupt, "I can't."

"I've made no declaration to Priscilla," he placidly said. "Absolutely none. Nor do I intend to in the near future. As for Charlotte's friendship," he added, rising from the chair with a casual grace, "I'm only suggesting a sail on my yacht. In broad daylight. Bring a friend as chaperon, if you like." As he spoke, he moved across the small distance that separated them. He stood very close to her now. "Bring as many friends as you like," he murmured, touching her lightly on the shoulder with his fingertips.

"Please don't do that," she said, her voice no more than a whisper.

"The *Desiree* can outrun anything on the seas." His breath touched her cheek as he dipped his head close. "Let me show you."

He wasn't speaking exclusively of sailing yachts, she understood, forced back against the window by his nearness, the warmth of his body tangible. "You must leave," she urgently declared, averting her face from his heated eyes.

"Soon," he whispered, cupping her chin in the curve of his fingers, gently forcing her head back, exerting a delicate upward pressure so her mouth lifted to his. "I won't take long," he murmured, his scent filling her senses, fragrant, sensual, heated.

"You have to go," she breathed.

"I will," he said.

"Now."

"Right now," he whispered, lowering his mouth to

hers. And it seemed suddenly as if she'd waited aching aeons for the warmth of his lips.

He brushed a butterfly kiss over her mouth, a kiss of tantalizing promise and gentle persuasion, like a stolen kiss behind a choir stall in a church full of parishioners. She sighed—an intoxicating small sound of pleasure that did disastrous things to his sense of constraint. But he controlled his rash impulses, for the delectable Countess Angel was still uncertain, her mood wavering and capricious. Exerting the minutest pressure, he advanced another cautious degree, slowly parting the softness of her lips. With her chin held captive in his hand, his tongue invaded her mouth, twined with hers, then penetrated more deeply, demanding more, promising more. And Angela purred as a tremulous pulsing fluttered deep in the pit of her stomach—a schoolgirl response she hadn't felt in years. She hadn't expected such sensitivity from a man who walked in uninvited; she hadn't thought him capable of such acutely impressionable tenderness. It pleased her to be wrong.

The muted sound registered in Kit's consciousness as though she'd spoken to him and welcomed him in. His arousal swelled, a sharp-set lust overshadowed reason, and he impetuously considered taking her away and keeping her for himself alone. But even as the unprecedented impulse filled his brain, he shook away the unaccountable sensation. He had no need for ownership. On the contrary, he more sensibly noted as the momentary craving passed, he preferred his singularly unattached life. Reverting to more familiar ground, his talent at seduction well honed, he raised his free hand, slid his fingers through Angela's gilded hair until his palm rested on her temple. Lifting his mouth the merest hairsbreadth, he whispered, "Kiss me back, *mon ange*."

"I shouldn't." Equivocation trembled on her lips.

"But I want you to." As he wanted to bury himself deep inside her.

"And if I don't?" A touch of sulkiness colored her voice.

"Then I'll just have to wait here till you do," he said, wolfish and teasing.

He was an extraordinary man, she thought, gratified at his genial indulgence. She'd always reacted poorly to masculine authority. Touching his hands, she eased herself away, and leaning back sufficiently to see his face, she playfully murmured, "How long will you wait?"

"Humm . . ." His eyes shone with amusement. "Since I'm not racing tomorrow . . ."

"No, no . . . you'll cause a scandal if you stay that long." But her luscious smile mitigated her reproach.

"I'll hide under your bed," he said, roguish and quietly intent.

The thought of having Kit Braddock so . . . accessible sent a disturbing thrill flaring through her senses. But less reckless than he, she promptly acceded, "I'll kiss you once and then you *must* go."

"Good," he said, his answer carefully neutral. And releasing her, he stood waiting, his smile benevolent.

"Just one kiss now," she said, her lush undertone almost causing him to lose his practiced calm.

"Just one," he agreed, his deep voice velvet soft.

"I can't reach you." A hint of teasing gleamed in her sky-blue eyes, like a young girl trembling on the brink.

"Give me your hands." It pleased him that she'd forgotten enough of her qualms to find amusement in the game. And as she placed her small hands in his, he drew them to his shoulders and gently said, "Now, if you stand on your tiptoes, you can give me a kiss."

His strength was conspicuous beneath her hands, his muscles prominent, steel hard. He was strikingly large.

The final word spiked through her brain, triggering lascivious images. He *would* be large, a heated voice whispered, so *very* large, and for a shivering, lurid moment of unreason she wanted to feel him inside her.

He saw the instant flush color her cheeks and throat and slide down the ruched neckline of her robe. He could feel her breasts against his chest, and he wondered if they were blush pink, too, and waiting for his touch.

But he didn't move.

Because he knew better.

She took a deep breath to calm herself. It's only a kiss, she reminded herself. An innocuous, *single* kiss. Rising on her toes, she slid her hands over his shoulders, twined her arms around his neck, and said in carefully modulated tones, "Bend your head down, Mr. Braddock."

"Kit," he murmured.

"Kit," she softly said for the very first time. "I can't reach you."

You could reach me on a bed, he licentiously considered, but prudently repressed his thoughts. One step at a time for the extremely wary lady.

It was a lopsided game even between two experienced people, for Thomas Kitredge Braddock had a distinct advantage. With his unconventional living arrangements, he knew to the minutest degree the various stages of female arousal.

He was looking forward to the kiss.

Gripping her waist to steady her as she balanced

on her toes, he felt the froth of dimity slide on her skin. No corset or chemise or nightgown limited access to her voluptuous body, he heatedly realized. Only the elaborate boudoir confection, only lace and ribbons and gossamer silk.

When she kissed him, her mouth touched his only lightly at first, and breathless, he waited to see if there would be more. And when he felt her hands tighten at the nape of his neck, he smiled.

Her second kiss was lengthier. An enticing introduction, sensuous, lingering, fragrant with promise . . . and he was pleased to accommodate the tantalizing Countess Angel on her terms—or any terms.

"You're very polite," she murmured as her mouth lifted again, her gaze startlingly direct under her half-raised lashes.

"You're surprised."

She hesitated for the briefest moment and then softly said, "Yes."

He grinned. "I'm on my best behavior."

"And you're usually not?"

"I'm often not."

"Do your ladies mind?"

"Are you really interested?"

"A harem has a certain cachet; I'm intrigued."

"It's not a harem, but if it were, I'd be tempted to add you to it."

"Unfortunately, I'm too selfish to share."

"But, then, no one asks you in a harem," he gently reminded her, "whether you care or not." He'd also heard the stories of Joe Manton returning from his honeymoon in Paris to see Angela, and Kit wondered briefly who exactly was sharing with whom.

"Are you an authority on harem protocol?"

"No, but one of my friends is."

She knew he didn't mean a male friend; she knew it was one of his ladies. "Does she like you better?"

"Should we talk of Joe Manton or Bertie or Lew Archer? Tell me, do they like you best?"

"How well informed you are, Mr. Braddock."

"Kit," he murmured.

"Kit," she whispered as his mouth covered hers. And he didn't wait this time to be kissed, suddenly past all the mannered limits. She was lushly beautiful, she was half-naked in his arms, they were alone.

And he wanted more than a kiss.

Single-minded and intent, consummation a hot-spur craving, he slid his hands down her back, slipped his palms under her bottom, and pulling her close, he held her hard against the rigid length of his arousal.

She moaned against his mouth as a combustible heat exploded deep inside her. He was sensationally large. A delicious shock flared through her body, and she whimpered, a delicate, sensual sound of expectation and need.

"Don't let me interrupt such a charming scene." The sarcasm was indolently put, the Earl de Grae's soft drawl precise as a stiletto. One gloved hand still remained on the door latch, his flint-gray eyes dispassionately surveying the heated scene.

Angela's hands instantly dropped from Kit's shoulders, and she pushed away from his embrace. Standing very still, watching her husband with a scrutiny Kit had previously seen only in lethal skirmishes, she coolly said, "What brings you to Cowes?"

"I came over with Tarlington. He needed some fishing gear, and I wanted my gun that was left behind last year. Violet said you had a headache. This must be your doctor," her husband sardonically murmured, the hunting gun he held cradled in one arm, menacing adjunct to his mockery.

Eminently familiar with her husband's malevolence, she ignored his derision and calmly said, "I know how anxious you must be to leave for grouse hunting, but thank you for stopping by. Good night."

"No introductions, Angela?"

"No."

"Does he need your protection?"

"Everyone needs protection from you, Brook."

"I don't." Kit spoke very softly.

"He's very brave," the Earl de Grae gibed, readjusting the gun in the crook of his arm.

"Please, Kit, no," Angela softly said, placing a restraining hand on Kit's arm.

"He's a big man—but, then, you like them that way, don't you?" the earl insolently murmured, his gaze flicking over Kit's tall, athletic frame.

"I generally don't like small men," Angela smoothly agreed, "but, of course, there are women who do."

The earl, of middle height and slender, curled one well-bred lip. "How fortunate."

"Yes, I'm sure it is." Everyone knew of her husband's preference for young girls.

"I see the Blue Monkey is still keeping you company. Don't you tire of Souveral's toadyism?"

"If I cared to converse with you about my friends, Brook, or about anything at all, I wouldn't live at Easton. So please kindly leave. This is my house as well."

"I should see sweet Baby May before I go," the earl unctuously proposed.

"She's sleeping," Angela snapped. "I don't want her disturbed."

"Such defensiveness, my dear. Can't I see my daughter?"

"Not at this hour, Brook." Angela's voice was

brusque with temper, her eyes suddenly sheened with tears.

"My, what a tigress we have, protecting her cub. Did I tell you," he said with casual malice, "the Loftons called on me again?"

"We have a written agreement," she softly said. Angela had made certain her solicitor accompanied her on her trip to de Grae Castle. She knew Brook couldn't be trusted.

"It seems the Loftons' daughter is distraught." Her husband smiled, all sly cunning and deceit. "She's an only child," he murmured. "They've made a new offer."

"The document you signed is binding."

"Perhaps," he said, twisting slightly so the muzzle of the shotgun was pointing directly at her.

Kit stepped in front of Angela.

"You have your valiant Lancelot," Brook sardonically drawled.

Kit turned to Angela. "Do you want him to leave?" His voice was low, gentle.

She shook her head, the movement barely visible. The last thing she wanted was an excuse for Brook to pull the trigger. "I'm sorry you had to witness this," she softly murmured. She disliked so publicly airing her marital problems, and Brook armed was a distinct menace. "If you'll excuse me," she quietly said to Kit, hoping to defuse the encounter. "I suddenly do have a headache." And without a glance at her husband, she walked from the sitting room, closing the door into her bedchamber with an indelicate thud.

Followed by the sharp snap of the lock.

"She always has been difficult to control," the earl murmured, a half smile twitching his mouth, invariably assured of victory when he flexed his parental authority over his children. "Do you find her temper amusing?" he smoothly queried.

"I wasn't aware she had one."

"Then you must be very new. Angela's an emasculating bitch, if you wish forewarning. It's what comes from allowing women money and property rights." His voice had taken on a hard edge, his urbanity eclipsed by a bitter rancor.

The man was fighting a losing battle, Kit dispassionately reflected; Parliament had passed the Women's Property Rights Act[3] years ago. Glancing at Angela's locked door, he blandly said, "Since the countess has retired, I'll be leaving."

"No entreaties to dear Angela?" the earl gently taunted.

"I don't think so," Kit placidly replied, moving toward the door.

"She may relent," her husband said, not moving from his position before the exit.

"It's getting late."

"You're an American, aren't you?"

"Yes." Kit had come within two feet of Angela's husband. "And I'm in a hurry."

Brook Greville scrutinized the man towering over him and reacted sensibly to the repressed violence of his stance.

"She'll miss you," de Grae mocked, stepping aside.

"Perhaps some other time," Kit curtly said, then pulled the door open and walked out.

Sullen and exasperated, he *did* go to the yacht club, intent on drinking away his frustration. He'd been within moments of sharing the tempting Countess Angel's bed, and perversely, it galled him to find her husband so despicable. As if somehow she were responsible.

She wasn't, of course. He knew how heiresses were bartered off by their families. She'd been only seventeen.

Good God, de Grae must have been a nasty shock.

6

Angela didn't sleep that night either, but she was engaged in more productive endeavors than Kit's attempt to drink himself into oblivion.

She was busy arranging for her departure from Cowes. After having Baby May carried down from the nursery to her bedchamber, she spent the remainder of the night writing notes to her friends: Some were regrets for invitations she'd previously accepted; others were brief explanations of her change in plans. It had been a mistake to come to Cowes, and all she wished now was to return to the peaceful tranquillity of Easton.

Brook rarely came to Easton, so she was relatively safe from his spiteful venality. More important, Baby May was protected at the secluded Norfolk estate from the earl's uncharitable nature. And while Angela didn't overtly acknowledge she was running away from temptation, she did recognize that seeing Kit Braddock at Charlotte's tonight would be emotionally hazardous. She didn't wish to complicate her life further.

And Kit Braddock was too reckless a man.

—

*W*hen Kit entered his stateroom shortly after sunrise, he said only, "Forgive me ladies, but in my present churlish mood, I intend to sleep the day away. Alone." And dropping into a chair near the door, he silently contemplated his steepled fingers while his companions gathered their robes and disappeared.

As the door shut on the last woman, a stream of exasperated invective exploded into the silence as though at last he could give vent to his frustration. He was at once furious and indignant, resentful and sullen, and he wished for the thousandth time since last night that he'd wiped the insolent smile from the Earl de Grae's face.

Heaving himself from the chair, he swore again as he stripped off his jacket and jerked the studs from his shirtsleeves. His waistcoat joined his jacket on the floor, the diamond studs on his shirt front were pulled free in a single wrenching tug, his shirt was shrugged off and thrown like a missile at the Ruysdael over his bed. And he stood absolutely still in half undress, tamping the carnal need that no amount of brandy had obliterated.

Lord, she'd tasted sweet, and the feel of her in his arms . . . He clenched his fists against a powerful anger and need simultaneously filling his brain, the sensation so novel, he questioned whether he should drink so much in the future. He'd never been obsessed with a woman, so consumed by desire. As he stripped off his remaining clothes, he fought to subdue the disquieting sensation, finding brief solace in verbally consigning the world in general—and certain people in particular—to the uncomfortable nether regions of the world.

Then he fell naked onto his bed and instantly slept.

"*A*pparently the countess didn't favor him last night," Saskia commented as the ladies of the *Desiree* sat in the lounge, sipping their morning chocolate.

"Really, how could you tell?" Cleo ironically murmured.

"What countess?" a stately Nordic beauty inquired.

"The Countess de Grae," Saskia supplied. "Last night he was—in his own words—consumed with an adolescent passion for her."

"Doesn't she like men?" A young west-African woman, exquisite as a Benin sculpture, raised her perfect eyebrows.

"She mustn't if she turned Kit down." A slender Chinese woman Kit had first met in San Francisco pronounced her words with a distinct Western drawl.

"He'll need us, then, when he wakes," a buxom redhead said with a smile.

"We'll help him forget his countess," another woman softly murmured."

"And he's so . . . wonderfully insatiable after he's been drinking all night," the Ceylonese woman observed with a delicately arched brow. "We should all benefit from the countess's refusal."

A collective murmur of agreement drifted round the room.

"We can be grateful to the countess, as well, for Kit's sudden interest in someone other than the manipulative Lady Priscilla," Saskia said.

"Has he dropped the Pembroke girl?"

"Not precisely, but at least he's beginning to question her suitability."

"You've actually met her, haven't you?"

"We saw her on the Parade last week, and she would have been pointedly rude had Kit not been there."

"How did he respond?"

"He didn't notice her discourtesy. He pays her only the most superficial attention. Other than her function as possible brood mare for his children, he's largely indifferent to her. But with his new infatuation, perhaps his plans have changed."

"Don't forget he promised his mother an English bride."

Saskia shrugged. "The countess is English."

"And married."

"If you had seen him last night, you might wonder how much that matters."

"Of course it matters, Saskia," the Irish girl with the flame-red hair declared. "Divorce is scandalous. Besides, she won't even look at him, if you recall."

"How fortunate for us," Cleo softly drawled.

"Also, Kit's not exactly romantically inclined," the African woman reminded them. "If he's interested in the countess, it's not for marriage."

"True," Saskia said with a small sigh. "It's just that I so dislike that Pembroke girl. . . ."

Much later that morning, Kit was once again the topic of conversation, this time at the Pembrokes' rented villa, where Charlotte and Priscilla were breakfasting in a small room overlooking the sea.

When their light breakfast of tea and marmalade muffins had been served, Charlotte dismissed the serving girl, cast a glance at the door to see that it was completely closed, and carefully unfolded her napkin in her lap. Taking a sip of tea, she sat for a contemplative moment with the cup in midair and then, setting it back on the saucer, said, "I didn't like the way Mr. Braddock regarded Angela last night."

Priscilla looked up from her dissection of her muffin into four equal parts with a gaze innocent of understanding. "He didn't look at her. You must be mistaken."

"I'm not so certain I am," her mother murmured.

"For heaven's sake, she's your age. How could she possibly interest him?"

"Perhaps you're right, darling," Charlotte politely agreed, when she knew very well that the latitude of Angela's allure encompassed every man capable of breathing. "Nevertheless," she briskly went on, "I think it wouldn't hurt to give Mr. Braddock a private opportunity to propose. Tonight might be the perfect time, with only a few guests coming for dinner."

"Won't I have the tempting Angela for competition?" Priscilla archly quipped.

"Luckily, no," her mother bluntly retorted. "She sent her regrets. She's returning to Easton."

"There, you see?" Priscilla said, waving a portion of muffin at her mother. "If Kit had truly encouraged her, she would have come to dinner tonight to flirt with him. You've always said she adores handsome men," she smugly finished, and popped the marmalade morsel into her mouth.

"Listen to me, dear," her mother said with a sigh, an explanation of last night's heated gazes over dinner beyond her daughter's naive perception. "We don't have much time left. With the season over, Mr. Braddock may decide to leave very soon. However, with a little gentle persuasion, I'm sure he'll propose. So after dinner tonight you'll suggest showing him the orchids in the conservatory. At the same time I'll arrange for seating at the bridge tables, which should occupy our other guests and give you sufficient time alone with

Mr. Braddock to—er—encourage him in his proposal."

"May I let him kiss me?" Priscilla asked through a mouthful of muffin.

"Perhaps just a little . . . nothing too heated, mind you . . . but an obliging kiss or two wouldn't be out of place."

Swallowing, the young woman thoughtfully gazed at her mother for a moment before breaking into a deeply satisfied smile. "Then he'll have to marry me, won't he?"

"Generally, a gentleman understands his duty to a well-bred young girl, but it might be useful to wear your gown with the pearl-embroidered bodice."

"Because it's daring?"

"It's not precisely *daring,* but it *does* show off your wonderful bosom. And men like— "

"Big titties," Priscilla finished as she stirred sugar into her tea.

Momentarily stunned, Charlotte required a second to find her voice. "I *was* going to say feminine curves. Wher*ever,*" she starkly intoned, "did you hear such vulgarity?"

"The stable boys always whisper that behind my back, Mama. They're ever so bold," her daughter replied with a faint smile.

Charlotte's heart lurched. "If I ever see you so much as glance at one of those rough young men, Priscilla Pembroke," she said, her voice rising in horror and alarm, "I'll see that you're locked in your room for a month. *Do you understand?*"

"Of course, Mama," she calmly replied, her blue gaze unruffled. "Don't be alarmed. I never seriously look at a man unless he has scads and scads of money. I even had to tell poor Lord Everleigh that I couldn't dance with him very often. I said it ever so politely, but, Mama, you know as well as I do, that he's the youngest son in a family of ten. And no matter how handsome he is, he'll never be able to give me what I want."

The Countess Ansley released the breath she hadn't realized she'd been holding. "That's a good girl," she declared with heartfelt gratitude for her daughter's pragmatism. "Your papa always did say you were as sensible as he."

"Papa and I want those new stables, Mama, and you want the house redone. Why would I waste my beauty on a penniless man?"

"How clever you are, sweetheart. And Mr. Braddock is very far from penniless. He's one of those wonderful American millionaires with so much money they don't know what to do with it."

"And why shouldn't he spend it on me?" Priscilla cheerfully said.

"Why indeed not?" her mother agreed.

$\mathcal{K}$it arrived at the Pembrokes that evening in a pleasant humor. He'd slept for most of the day, which mitigated his pounding headache, and several hours of untrammeled sex with his feminine friends had pleasantly soothed his chafing temper. Also not to be discounted for moderating a fractious mood was his expectation of seeing Angela again.

But she wasn't there, he immediately discovered, because he asked the butler when he entered the house. The countess had returned to Easton, he was told with that bland haughtiness reserved for servants of the highest caste.

"When?" Kit bluntly inquired.

At which point he was treated to a fish-eyed look that would have reduced a man of lesser esteem to a puddle on the floor and told in gelid accents that such information was outside the purview of the Ansley household.

Kit's good cheer instantly evaporated; he took out his watch to check the time, decided three hours would be the absolute maximum for maintaining his civility that evening, and wondered with more than a fleeting interest: Where the hell was Easton?

None of which boded well for the Pembrokes' marriage plans.

Fortunately, dinner was blessedly short, for the food was tasteless in his mouth; each time the clock struck the quarter hour, he silently counted the chimes; he found it difficult to concentrate on conversation, and when dessert was over and Priscilla asked him if he wished to see the orchids in the conservatory, he quickly said yes, because he feared being trapped at a card table in the drawing room.

And if he'd not been so single-mindedly concerned with escape, he might have wondered at his rash, feverish interest in a woman who didn't wish to see him. But, then, he rarely questioned his own motives; he was essentially a man of action, as any of his acquaintances would attest. His only concern was that of achieving freedom from the Pembrokes' party; after that he'd see about the location of Easton.

"Sit down," Priscilla said, patting the space beside her on the ornate conservatory bench.

Her words registered in his brain as if on a time delay, with his thoughts elsewhere, so it seemed as though he were hesitating.

With the inherent instincts of a femme fatale, Priscilla offered added enticement to engage his interest. Leaning forward slightly, she allowed him a more unobstructed view of her splendid breasts. "Darling," she sweetly murmured, "do sit down."

When he rather absentmindedly sat, she decided a more explicit overture was necessary, and placing her hand on his thigh, she gently said, "There. That's better. I haven't had a moment alone with you all evening."

Instant warning signals flashed in his brain. With his preoccupation unrelated to immediate events, he'd not been aware of the proffered private view of her breasts, but her hand on his leg set off deeply rooted alarms. He knew the rules, even though he generally chose to ignore them, and no virginal miss put her hand on a man's thigh unless there was very good reason. "Are these the orchids?" he suddenly inquired, abruptly rising from the bench and moving to a display of pale-green petals hanging in spidery tendrils from a nearby tree. "Tell me about them," he said from a safe distance. "My ignorance of flowers is complete."

"I don't know anything about them, either," Priscilla said with a pretty smile as she stood. "I just wanted you to myself tonight," she murmured, moving toward him. "Do you think me utterly shameless?" she went on, advancing across the flagstone floor until her pearl-embroidered bodice touched his waistcoat.

The trap was so obvious now, he almost smiled, his estimation of the young Priscilla's ruthlessness sharply adjusted upward. "Now, what would your mother say," Kit softly declared, retreating a step, "to your disregarding the rules of propriety? I know my mother would remind me to be a gentleman."

"Pooh on that," Priscilla breathed, following him. "Mama lets me do what I want."

"I'm sure she doesn't," he pleasantly said, gauging the distance to the door. "And certainly your papa wouldn't approve. We'll look at the flowers some other time," he added, not yet ready to be coerced into marriage. "Come and play the piano for me," he politely suggested, backing toward the door. "I particularly like your rendition of Liszt."

"I don't want to play the piano. I want to kiss you."

After a decade of avoiding the marriage trap, Kit was adept at evasion. "There are so many people about," he genially said as his hand grasped the door handle. "We'll find some privacy later. Come play for me now." Standing in the open doorway, he was poised for flight. He might or might not marry Priscilla someday, but he certainly wasn't ready to make that momentous decision tonight. "Please?" he gallantly appealed.

With grudging ill grace and a pouty lower lip, Priscilla agreed. "Only if you'll turn the pages," she fretfully added.

"With pleasure," he agreed, catching sight of the porter in the hallway with a sense of relief.

She swept by him with an oblique pettish glance, and he followed her into the security of the drawing room. But before Kit managed to extricate himself from the Pembroke household a long, tedious hour later, he had a drumming headache, aching jaw muscles from forcing a smile, and an entirely new loathing for Liszt.

He needed a drink badly, he decided, and after walking the short distance to the yacht club, he said, "A bottle of brandy, please," to the first footman he saw on entering the club rooms. It was going to take more than one drink to rinse the distaste of Priscilla's puerile machinations from his mouth. Did the Pembrokes really think he'd agree to marry the young chit because he'd kissed her?

Dropping into a chair in a secluded corner, he leaned his head against the chair back, shut his eyes, and wondered if he had the nerve to marry a well-bred young lady, even to please his mother. Although his mother was precious to him, a marriage of convenience didn't have the same appeal that it had had even a few days ago. He'd have to actually listen to Priscilla occasionally, he supposed, if they were married, and he'd have to sit across the dinner table from her and perhaps the breakfast table. Lord, could he endure it?

You wouldn't be home much though, an inner voice soothed. Your wife would have to understand you spend months at sea each year. Marriage wouldn't be so great a burden on your life. Except for the children, he thought with a sinking feeling. Would he want to leave his children in Priscilla's care? Fortunately, the brandy arrived to interrupt further contemplation of such an unpalatable question. And following closely on the heels of the serving man, two of Bertie's friends arrived to keep him company.

Talk turned to sailing then, and Kit's unease over a future life with Priscilla was relegated to subconscious levels. Shortly after midnight Bertie walked in with Souveral, and the circle of drinkers around Kit expanded.

The Prince of Wales had never been given any royal duties by his mother, the queen, who jealously guarded her prerogatives, so his life was essentially a round of idle social pleasure. His coterie followed him from country house to country house, from London, to Cowes, to Sandringham, to Biarritz, Monte Carlo, Paris, Marienbad, depending on the season. He raced and hunted and dallied with women, enjoying the same aristocratic amusements as any noble. The only difference was the degree of his authority. One didn't refuse a royal invitation without good reason, and if the prince expressed a wish to visit a family house, he was obliged. So when he said to Kit later in the evening, "You're coming to the Oaks next week, aren't you?" it was in the nature of a royal command.

"I'm promised at Wynmere," Kit replied, recalling his previous agreement to visit Priscilla's home.

"Why not go there the following week?" Bertie heartily suggested.

"I think they've also made plans for that week," Kit replied, "although I can't precisely recall. I'm afraid I'm promised to the Pembrokes." It seemed as though he'd committed to the plans ages ago. Or perhaps only in a less irresolute mood.

"You going to marry the gel?"

"Perhaps."

Bertie's eyebrows rose in response to Kit's equivocation. "Postpone Wynmere. Tell them I insisted."

At Kit's hesitation Souveral quietly said, "The Countess de Grae will be down for the races."

The prince swiveled a glance between his good friend the ambassador and Kit. "Really," he softly murmured. "Well, then, seems to me the Pembroke gel can wait a week to see you, Braddock. Need you anyway, dammit, to help me with my racers. My trainer tells me I've a chance Winslow might take the Gold Stakes. Angela knows horses, too, better than most men. Did you know that?"

"No."

"Best female rider in England. Has one of the prime stables, too. An uncommon woman—but, then, I'm sure you've noticed."

"Yes."

"Some problem, Braddock?" the prince bluffly inquired, aware of Kit's reticent replies.

"No, no problem," he softly returned. "I'd appreciate it, though, if your secretary would send an explanation to the Pembrokes."

"Capital! Consider it done. You've brought me considerable luck on the track this season, Braddock. I need you at the Oaks, and I'll tell them as much."

The conversation turned to a discussion of horseflesh and the remaining races of the season. With all of the men owners of racing stables, disagreements over favorites were heated. Kit offered his opinion less often than did the others, his thoughts not entirely focused on the conversation. Did Angela know he was coming to the Oaks?

*W*hen he reached his yacht several hours later, he insisted on sleeping alone for the second night in a row. "We have to race tomorrow, and I'm dead tired," he'd said, not gruffly, like the night before, but there was no question of changing his mind. He was distinctly different, the ladies of the *Desiree* decided. What they couldn't agree on was what had made him so unsociable.

Had they asked him, he wouldn't have known, either.

Had they suggested the concept of unrequited love, he would have scoffed.

Love was a foreign emotion to Kit Braddock.

As was fidelity.

Angela de Grae inspired strong emotion, he would have admitted, but certainly neither of those.

7

The Oaks weekend had a full complement of Bertie's Marlborough House set. Since the prince's private secretary, Sir Francis Knollys, generally sent a list of preferred guests to a prospective host, a convivial group of friends was always assured.[4]

Joe Manton and Georgiana were present at their first country house party since returning from their honeymoon. When Angela saw them at lunch on Friday, Georgiana was cool, but Joe greeted her with his usual salutation of a hug and a kiss.

Of those who took notice of Joe's welcome to Angela, none had expected anything less. Angela and Joe's friendship was of long standing.

"We missed you at Cowes," Angela pleasantly remarked. "Someone else had to win this year."

"I hear an American took the cup," Joe said.

"Really? I didn't stay the entire time." So Kit had won; not that she'd doubted his ability.

"Do you have a horse racing here?"

Angela shook her head.

"Joe!" his wife called out from across the room.

"Tell Olivia about that new bistro in Paris. I can't recall the name."

Joe smiled. "Duty calls."

"Of course."

"Do you want to come out tomorrow morning for the horses' workouts? We could ride early or do some shooting before the others wake up and begin the slaughter."

"Georgiana wouldn't appreciate it."

"She doesn't like horses. Let me see you in the morning. Early," he softly added.

She saw the familiar heated look in his eyes, the tempestuous flame she'd seen so many times before. "I told you how I felt before your wedding and again when you came back from Paris during your honeymoon," she quietly said. "I understand why you married. But we're simply friends now, Joe. I don't want to involve myself in your marriage."

"I would have married you if I could. You know that."

"I know." Her voice was hushed. "But you're married to Georgiana, and I don't relish the role of Jezebel."

"Joe!" Georgiana was beckoning with her handkerchief.

"Hell," he muttered, quickly glancing across the room. "And you're wrong, Angela," he heatedly said, his eyes intent on her once again. "It's not over between us. It never will be. Come see me in the morning and I'll show you."

"She's looking daggers, Joe. You'd better go."

"I'll see you tomorrow morning."

He was the same, Angela thought, watching him walk away to join the group of women with his wife—intense, bent on his own pleasure, and yet, still, despite all the changes in their lives—that friend from her long-ago childhood.

*A*ngela went riding alone that afternoon, not wishing to join the ladies and their gossip, nor the men at the paddock where the horses were being readied for the race on Saturday. Bertie had specially asked her to come to the Oaks, so she couldn't refuse, but the familiar entertainments held less appeal than in the past. Her world had been gradually changing the last few years. May's birth had been a partial impetus; she simply wished to spend more time with her daughter. But the schools she was funding increasingly involved her interest, the contrast between that mission of education and her friends' frivolous pursuit of pleasure more striking as her commitment grew. The country lanes were peaceful, her favorite mount as glad as she to be away from the bustle of Morton Castle, and they stayed away too long. When she returned, the bell had already rung for tea.

A fixture of the country house parties, teatime was often the first opportunity for the men and women to meet during the day if the men had left early for shooting. It also afforded the women another opportunity to change clothes—in this case into their most alluring lace and chiffon creations that were designed to suggest a provocative dishabille, as though the ladies had just risen from their beds.

After rushing through her dressing, Angela arrived in the drawing room breathless, late, and determined to make certain she had an ironclad excuse for any future royal invitations. Alice Keppel was certainly capable of amusing Bertie, she thought, as were any number of other women. He no longer needed her in attendance.

But she graciously smiled as the prince waved her over.

"You're late, darling," Bertie gently reprimanded, a stickler for schedules. "But since you look stunning, we'll forgive you." Angela's celadon-green Doucet gown, a flourish of drifting chiffon and ribbon-festooned lace, was both ethereal and sumptuously sensual.

"The countryside was so pleasant, I rode longer than I should. How did Winslow run today?"

"He's in top form, absolutely top form—a stunning animal. And purchased thanks to Kit's advice. You remember Mr. Braddock, don't you?" the Prince of Wales pleasantly remarked, motioning with his beringed hand.

And for a flashing moment Angela couldn't catch her breath.

"Good afternoon, Countess," Kit politely said.

How had she missed him? she wondered; even though he was off to one side, he stood a head taller than the men around the prince. "Good afternoon, Mr. Braddock." With effort she controlled her sense of shock. He was to have been at Wynmere this week, not standing before her, starkly handsome in a black velvet smoking jacket that seemed to invite her sense of touch.

"I insisted Kit come," the Prince of Wales bluffly said, as if reading Angela's mind. "Needed him to help with Winslow."

"Is your horse going to win tomorrow, then?" she cordially inquired, sternly shutting away the tumultuous sensations Kit's presence incited. "I hear Hartley's racer might give you some competition," she added with a smile.

"We'll see about that, won't we, Kit?" the prince

cheerfully declared. "I might even have my second Derby winner in Winslow."

"He's fast and powerful," Kit noted, "and likes to run in the lead." His shoulder lifted in a small shrug. "It looks promising."

"Do you have a racing stable?" Angela asked when she shouldn't show interest in anything Kit Braddock did, when she should walk away from him and talk to the women across the room. When she shouldn't be wondering what it felt like to touch his hard body through silk velvet.

"I share some thoroughbreds with my brother-in-law and nephew. And some polo ponies."

"Have your horses won?"

"Often enough to make it interesting," he softly said.

"And profitable," the prince said with a chuckle. "He won half a million with his horse at Belmont last spring."

"The odds favored me," Kit modestly acknowledged.

"Have you raced in England?" their host, Lord Morton, inquired.

"Not recently."

"But this year his stable took two firsts at Longchamps," the Prince of Wales interposed.

"I didn't think American thoroughbreds were that good." Joe Manton's voice held a hint of challenge.

"Occasionally we get lucky," Kit affably replied. "I only hope Winslow will be as fortunate tomorrow," he added, deflecting Joe Manton's deprecatory comment, deciding Angela's lover must have heard of his interest in her.

"Hear! Hear!" Bertie said, smiling through his cigar smoke. "To victory tomorrow," he offered, raising his glass of brandy.

A dozen glasses were lifted to the future sovereign and then quickly emptied just as the bell chimed announcing the next interval—dressing for dinner.

*A*n hour and a half later, when the guests converged near the dining-room doorway, Angela discovered she was to be escorted into dinner by Kit.

"You arranged this?" she coolly inquired in a hushed undertone.

"I suspect Bertie did," Kit quietly said.

"And what of Wynmere?"

"Bertie didn't want me to go."

"I didn't think you so docile, Mr. Braddock."

"You don't know me very well, Countess. On occasion," he said with a smile, "I can be infinitely docile."

"How fascinating." Sarcasm melted through her voice.

"Not as fascinating as you in this provocative crimson gown," he murmured, his green eyes amused.

"I deliberately left Cowes, Mr. Braddock."

"I know that."

Her brows flew upward.

"You're *not* the first lady I've kissed." His dark lashes indolently drifted downward, and he gazed at her with a lazy, half-lidded look. "You just have too many scruples."

"While you have none."

"You're right," he agreed, unabashed. "Which is probably why I'm still alive."

"Did you kiss the wrong woman at some point?"

He smiled. "Are you curious?"

"Of course not. Ah, finally," she murmured as the couple in front of them moved forward. And, placing her hand lightly on his arm, she smiled up at him and said, well-mannered and bland, "Lady Morton has a marvelous French chef."

"Just like home," he amiably replied, as capable as she of artifice. He wasn't in a hurry; the weekend had just begun.

*D*inner was sumptuous and lengthy. Angela deliberately devoted her attention to her other dinner companion, so Kit conversed through the first two courses with Lady Hareswood, who particularly liked to discuss her Hareswood beagles. He learned of their breeding and bloodlines in great detail before she was eventually drawn into conversation with Lord Gordon on her right. At which point he allowed himself simply to sit back and enjoy the enchanting sight and sound of the Countess de Grae.

She and Lord Villiers were comparing their hunting guns and local gunsmiths of note. It always surprised him that a woman of her size was so competent in the sporting field, although he cautioned himself against such prejudice; both his mother and sister were of modest height and eminently qualified in many areas perceived as male preserves. Maybe it was Angela's fair coloring that lent her such an air of delicacy, as if she were a fragile maid.

But she was eating tonight, he noticed, in a decidedly indelicate way. She ate the sole Alice as though she thoroughly enjoyed each morsel; the partridge and noodles with foie gras disappeared in short order, while the second remove, lamb noisettes with artichoke hearts and peas, seemed a particular favorite of hers, for she had a second serving. Fascinated, he wondered if her remarkable appetite extended to other areas of her life as well.

When Lord Villiers was engaged in conversation

with his neighbors on his left, Angela ate in silence for some time, intent on her lamb chop. Kit was drinking more than he was eating, the repast at teatime more than adequate for his evening meal. He felt remarkably content, like a child who'd just been given a much-coveted toy. Her perfume surrounded him, her bare shoulder and arm and tantalizing décolletage just inches away, the sound of her voice pleasant in his ears.

"You're not eating," she said, turning to look at him at last. "May I have your filet of beef?"

"You're eating enough for both of us, and yes, you may," he replied with a teasing warmth, moving his plate closer to hers. "I thought you ate only desserts."

She looked up, query in her gaze, the filet suspended midway to her plate.

"At Eden House," he explained. "You ate only dessert."

"It was hot that evening," she simply said, setting the beef down.

"And you eat meat only when it's cool?"

She smiled. "You're a curious man, Mr. Braddock."

"Kit," he said, smiling back. "I won't take advantage of you if you call me by my given name."

"Am I being juvenile about this?" She was neatly cutting the filet.

"Not juvenile, just overly punctilious."

She looked up at him. "I should embrace your prodigal dissipation instead?"

"Nothing so rash, perhaps." He grinned. "Although I do subscribe to a certain degree of discretion."

"Really. You surprise me." Her lacy lashes lifted over wide blue eyes. "And where exactly do you practice this discretion?"

"Anywhere you wish," he softly murmured, heated promise nicely blended with challenge in his voice.

"And if I won't?"

"I'm devastated, of course." A faint smile played on his mouth.

"Why don't I believe that?"

"You're too cynical."

"While you're too charming."

"How can you be certain what I am if you don't try?" His query was quietly put, his expression suddenly without drollery.

Setting her knife and fork on her plate with such suddenness the ringing clang drew attention, she found herself the unwonted focus of several gazes.

"Did the beef disagree with you?" Kit asked in a conversational tone that carried.

"I'm not sure," she neutrally said, smiling at those guests who seemed especially intent, like Joe Manton and the prince.

"Some fresh water, perhaps," Kit suggested, and without waiting for an answer, he motioned the footman forward.

"How kind of you, Mr. Braddock."

Both were highly skilled in cultivated politesse, and before long the curious had returned to their conversations.

"I'm sorry," Kit quietly said when the others were no longer observing them. He sighed. "That's what comes of speaking with sincerity."

"Something unusual for you?" Angela's voice was sardonic again; she didn't wish to be touched by his presence *or* his sincerity.

"No." He studied her for a moment, the teasing mockery erased from his eyes. "I came here only to see you."

"I wouldn't have come had I known you were here."

"But you're not indifferent. You can't say you are."

"Lord, Kit," Angela softly murmured. "This is impossible. You must recognize that. Please."

"Because of Joe Manton?"

"No!"

"Are you sure?" He could understand if she was still in love with him.

"Yes. I made it clear to him I wouldn't interfere in his marriage. He's aware of my feelings—not that it's any of your business."

"Good," he tersely said, as though they'd signed the last signature on a long-negotiated treaty.

"No, it's not good," Angela heatedly retorted. "Nothing *about* this is good." Her voice lowered to a luscious growl. "My life is content."

"Whatever you say," he gently replied, but he was pleased. She looked glorious with her cheeks flushed rosy pink.

"You've wasted your time coming here, Mr. Braddock," she pointedly said, signaling for her wineglass to be refilled, "although I'm sure several other women here would be more than pleased to oblige you."

"I can enjoy the racing if nothing else," he pleasantly said, ignoring her critical observation. "And the viscount's wine cellar's not to be discounted as an attraction," he added, watching Angela take an unladylike draft of wine.

"You're much too smooth, Mr. Braddock."

"And you're much too proper, Countess . . . on occasion," he gently added.

"It won't happen again," she said, understanding perfectly.

"Would you care to make a small wager on that?"

"You'll lose."

"Maybe I won't. Say, five hundred pounds."

"For what time period?"

He liked the sound of that; perhaps she wasn't saying no altogether. "This weekend."

"I'm sure I can withstand your appeal that long."

"In that case you'll be five hundred pounds richer."

"Extra money for my school," she briskly declared. "You have a wager."

"Starting now," he gently said.

*A*fter dinner, as the guests strolled down the enfilade of rooms toward the Gibbons library, where the viscount and his wife had arranged for after-dinner activities, Kit drew Angela aside—to give him an opinion on the Turner seascape in the sitting room ahead, he politely murmured to her companion. And had he not tightly grasped her hand, Angela would have refused.

"It'll just take a moment," he gently added, with a smile for the dowager Lady Lambeth at her side, ignoring Angela's unobtrusive efforts to disengage her hand.

"Go on, gel," the dowager said with a twinkle in her eye. "If I was fifty years younger, Braddock, I'd go myself."

"I'd be honored anytime, Lady Lambeth," Kit replied with a grin. "Redheads have always appealed to me."

"Now, there's a charming rogue," she cheerfully said, patting her dyed red curls. "Come have tea with me sometime in Park Lane and we can compare stories."

"With pleasure," Kit promised. "Now, if you'll

excuse us . . ." Tightening his grip, he pulled Angela through the archway into the small room housing the magnificent Turner painting.

"What do you think you're doing!" Angela resentfully exploded, visibly struggling against his hold now that others couldn't see.

"I need a kiss to get me through the evening," Kit murmured, not breaking stride, tugging her into the alcove where the golden seascape resided.

"You're mad! What if someone comes in? What if—"

He'd intended his kiss to be more gentle; he'd meant to kiss her only once and release her—to simply remind her of their heated feelings that night at Cowes. But the moment his mouth touched hers, nicety lost its tenuous grip, as did rational thought, and he briefly wondered whether she'd scream if he carried her upstairs to his bedroom. Her voluptuous body was pressed down the length of his tall frame, her back arched in his embrace, her initial struggles subdued beneath his savage kiss.

He ate at her mouth, craving the taste of her, wanting all her sweetness. Suddenly lifting her higher, he fit her more conveniently against his rampant erection, a willful, arbitrary act unhampered by discretion.

She tried not to respond to such blatant demand. But he was rock hard, enormous, unyielding—his impatient passion feverishly arousing. Without preliminaries, he was taking up where he'd last left off, intent on coming in with or without her invitation. And she couldn't pretend she hadn't thought of him a thousand times since Cowes, her own desire only repressed —never nullified. Suddenly her hips moved seemingly of their own accord, pressing into his hardness.

He groaned deep in his throat, so she felt as well as heard the intoxicating sound; his hand slipped lower, pulling her closer still, and he quickly decided the secluded alcove would do as well as his bed.

"Don't move," he murmured as his mouth lifted from hers. "I'm going to shut the door."

"Someone might come."

"I'll lock it."

"Kit, please, no—"

His mouth blotted out her appeal with a restless impatience, and when she should have taken affront, instead she felt a delirious heat burn through her body. She clung to him, wanting what he wanted, on fire to feel him inside her. Lacing her fingers through his hair, she made a fist around his heavy silken waves and pulled. "Tell me I'm not going to regret this," she breathed, as his head lifted and their eyes met.

"Never," he whispered, his voice ragged with a suffocated intensity. "Believe me."

"They have to be here somewhere," a female voice declared, the sound coming from the hallway, drifting through the opened doorway into the Turner alcove.

Kit swore.

"It's Olivia," Angela murmured, breathless and tense in his arms. "She's after you . . . in case you haven't noticed." Taking a deep breath, she said more calmly, "And I've just been saved from my own deplorable lack of constraint."

"I like your lack of constraint." Kit's eyes were hot with desire.

"Darling," Angela softly reproved, "you like *any* female." In a cooler, more temperate mood now, she was grateful for Olivia's salvation. "But thank you for . . . the pleasure."

He understood her abrupt reversal, but he knew, too, how readily she'd responded. "Let me see you tonight."

Angela sighed. "I wish I could."

"I can make you change your mind," he said with a faint smile.

"I don't think so. . . . *Olivia!*" Angela shouted. "We're in the red room looking at the Turner! Good night, darling, Kit," she softly said, sliding from his embrace. "And you might like Olivia," she added with a grin. "Rumor has it she's quite insatiable."

"Thank you for the information, but my current interest is in blond countesses."

"Ah . . . there you are," Olivia Manchester said as she entered the room. "I told Florence you couldn't have gone far. Since when have you been interested in art, Angela?"

"Mr. Braddock explained Turner's technique so well, I was enthralled."

"The countess is an apt pupil," Kit drawled.

"Would you explain some of that . . . technique . . . to me?" the dark-haired duchess softly inquired.

"Perhaps after tea. Right now I'm ready for a cognac."

"Do join us in the drawing room, ladies, and you must tell Mr. Braddock all about Lexford's experiments, Olivia. The duke has a penchant for agriculture," Angela sweetly declared.

"Really."

"While I have a penchant for lovely men like you," the Duchess of Lexford murmured.

"There, you see?" Angela dulcetly purred. "You have something in common already."

"Would you like a cognac, too?" Kit blandly inquired of the two women standing in the doorway as if they'd been speaking prosaically of the weather. "Allow me to escort you," he said, not waiting for an answer, already moving toward the hall.

—

$\mathcal{V}$ery soon after entering the drawing room, a group of men gathered around Angela. She held court with flirtatious ease, laughing, smiling, teasing by turn, comfortably onstage in a familiar role. She deliberately encouraged the male adulation, intent on warding off any further privacy with Kit.

Not inclined to pay homage to the countess in such a throng, nor join the serious bridge players at the tables near the fire, nor be seduced by the Duchess of Lexford, Kit politely excused himself from the multitude after a time and retired to a quiet corner where he could drink in peace. But he'd not considered his position as eligible bachelor or the extent of the female guests' fascination.

He'd already been thoroughly discussed by them at tea in terms of his accessibility, his stark good looks, his fascinating history of sexual adventuring, and before long he found himself the center of attention in a cluster of beautiful women.

Their conversation was rich with innuendo and less subtle questions concerning his female crew. He responded to both with a charming urbanity and evasion, determined to remain aloof from their flirtatious advances. Aware of the amorous rendezvous prevalent at country house parties, he circumspectly avoided their seductive overtures. The Countess de Grae, he thought, glancing at her amid her fawning courtiers, was the only lady at Morton Castle to engage his carnal interest.

"Ride in *our* carriage to the races tomorrow," the young Marchioness of Berwick cajoled, her voice lush with enticement.

"Come with us instead," Olivia Manchester offered. "Lexford is so dull, he'll be sleeping before we leave the driveway."

Her message was blatantly clear, although Kit wondered whether her elderly snoring husband might blight an amorous interlude. "I'm afraid I'm promised to Bertie's group," he politely replied. "It seems I'm here this weekend as professional trainer to Winslow."

"Or professional stud . . . ," the comely Lady MacLeish purred.

"Clarissa! What will Mr. Braddock think!" The young marchioness was new at the game.

"I hope he'll think of me first tonight, darling," Clarissa murmured with a provocative wink in Kit's direction.

And so it went in the course of the evening, the amorous game of advance and retreat a delicious amusement for the idle young ladies. The object of their desires saw it more as an evasive maneuver requiring equal parts diplomacy, facile charm, and finesse. But Morton's cognac helped blur the fine edges of the truth, so no one left unhappy.

Kit locked his bedroom door that night against any invasion of pursuing ladies—a decisive aberration in terms of his previous country-house habits.

And in so doing, he turned away Clarissa, Olivia, and the neophyte adulteress, the Marchioness of Berwick.[5]

8

The day of racing began early, with the carriages brought round directly after breakfast, and following a short period of disorganized chaos, all the guests were comfortably seated in the appropriate vehicles. After an hour's ride through the bucolic countryside, cool, green, and limpid under a cloudless blue sky, they reached the small country track with its stands overlooking a racing flat framed by low-rising hills. The Prince of Wales's party had been given the only box at the track, a small area quickly filled with his guests, servants, and a smattering of local officials.

After the country magistrates and councilmen offered short and occasionally awkward speeches of welcome, the prince and his aristocratic guests settled into the intimate clubbism and familiar pleasures of the races. During the course of the day, Angela and Kit often found themselves in close proximity, whether in seats watching the races, at lunch when everyone stood elbow to elbow enjoying Viscount Morton's elaborate picnic fare, or occasionally in the same conversational group.

Angela wore primrose-sprigged muslin, for the August weather was hot, and Kit thought her even more beautiful in the simple girlish gown. He'd seen her only in evening dress before, or in her elaborate dressing gown, their couturier origins conspicuous. Today her wide-brimmed straw hat and unornamented gown had the look of a country dressmaker.

The other ladies, in contrast, looked overdressed in their silk gowns. And Angela genuinely liked the races, Kit discovered, her eye for prime horseflesh well trained. She bet heavily, too. It surprised him at first, although it shouldn't have, he decided on further reflection. She had an unfettered self-reliance, unlike conventional females of her class. Perhaps that distinction more than any other was what attracted him.

In the flux and flow of social intercourse among the country house party sharing such limited quarters in the reserved box, Angela learned more of Kit, too. He'd only recently turned thirty and was indeed in England looking for a bride—although he quickly clarified that he'd undertaken the mission only to please his mother; whether he chose a bride was still moot. He'd inherited his vast fortune from his father and had already gone through five sailing vessels in the past decade—some exchanged for swifter, better designs, others replaced when he'd lost yachts to savage storms.

When he talked of his favorite waters off the South China Sea, his imagery was so enchanting, Angela found herself wishing she could sail them, too. But she primarily listened when Kit spoke of his peripatetic travels, her own life very ordinary in comparison, her round of idle leisure amusements notable only for their enervating wastefulness.

And whether close at hand or from a distance, she found his vital energy as fascinating as his rakish beauty. He moved with a deceptively languid power, as though his galvanic strength had been refined by an intrinsic animal grace. And beneath his well-tailored country tweeds and twill, the unmistakable presence of a modern-day buccaneer remained. Even in repose, he exuded a barely leashed force, and Angela found herself frequently contemplating the glorious possibilities of Kit Braddock uncurbed.

The thought was no more than abstract speculation, she quickly reminded herself, like admiring Rembrandt's magnificent use of light or the stark beauty of a storm. But a warm flush stole through her senses whenever he smiled at her. And while she consciously refrained from responding to his very personal smile, she couldn't deny its potent affect.

Several hours later, after chilled champagne had been dispensed to mitigate the summer heat, and a lighthearted gaiety enlivened the ambience of the prince's party, Angela overheard Olivia say to Kit in flirtatious reproach, "Darling, your bedroom door was locked last night. Who was the lucky lady?"

While his answer, brief and muted, wasn't audible, Angela experienced an unexpected flurry of jealousy, followed precipitously by an irrepressible mental image of Kit making love to another woman.

No! she impetuously thought, a curious sense of possession jolting her; he should have belonged to her last night. But seconds later saner reason prevailed, and forcing aside the graphic images in her brain, she reminded herself that regardless of the fact that Kit Braddock struck her libido like a hammer blow, he was unsuitable. For beyond the numerous and obvious obstacles to any relationship between them, she took issue with the sheer quantity of women in his life. Last night in the drawing room was no exception.

Although apparently it wasn't Olivia who had captivated Kit's attention.

But when they found themselves momentarily alone sometime later, after the Viscountess Morton had been drawn aside into a heated conversation concerning a young actress recently married into the nobility, Kit was well mannered and decorous.

"Does Belle Bixtin's coup annoy you as well?" he mildly inquired.

"Nigel was fortunate to find such a pleasant wife," Angela replied. "I find all this outrage silly. Many peers have ancestors who were once on the stage."

"You have democratic ideals?"

"You find that so strange?"

"In this company? Yes."

"I do, regardless. Will Donegan win this next race, do you think?"

"No."

"No? So sure?"

And taking his cue from the countess's obvious lack of interest in discussing her politics, they spoke then only of the upcoming races. Both capable of a disciplined courtesy, they urbanely discussed Morton and Joe's chances of taking a first and agreed that Winslow might bring Bertie his second Derby winner in as many years. The conversation was impersonal and curiously detached, as though they were speaking in the third person or through a pane of glass, until Kit said, "Did you sleep well last night?"

Angela swiftly glanced around, the intimacy in his query flagrant, like his piercing gaze.

"No one heard," he quietly said. "No one's looking. Answer me."

It took her perceptible seconds too long to say, "Yes, I slept perfectly."

His glance turned assessing for a moment, but

when he spoke, he offered no challenge. He said only, deep and hushed, "I didn't sleep at all. I was thinking of you."

"I imagine you say that to every impressionable lady."

"Are you impressionable?" he softly asked, ignoring her slur.

"You're years too late." But her voice trembled at the end because he'd moved a step closer.

"Come to my room tonight or I'll come to yours," he said as though her replies didn't matter. "No one will know. My word on it." He spoke earnestly, without his habitual teasing mockery.

"Am I supposed to simply say yes to such bluntness?"

His shoulder lifted in the minutest shrug, but his eyes were grave. "I'd like that."

"Did the lady last night?"

Brief surprise showed in his gaze.

"Am I not supposed to ask?"

"No, of course not." But he didn't answer.

"I overheard Olivia. Am I scheduled to be your Saturday-night entertainment?" A light sarcasm frosted her words.

He smiled, the gravity instantly erased from his gaze. "Are you jealous?"

"Not of anyone here, I assure you."

"Not even the beautifully naive Marchioness of Berwick?"

How discerning of him, she resentfully thought, to understand the envy such young beauty could generate. "No, not even her," she coolly lied.

"Personally, I find such undiluted sweetness wearying," Kit said. His mouth quirked into a wolfish grin. "I prefer a difficult, enigmatic woman like you."

"How flattering," Angela sardonically murmured, "but you still haven't answered my question."

"I slept alone," he said, not pretending to misunderstand. "I didn't know you cared."

"Maybe I don't."

"And maybe that equivocation was worth my trip to Morton Castle," he whispered.

It felt for a moment as though he'd intimately touched her in sight of everyone, and as a rising heat pulsed through her body, she said with obvious effort, her voice taut with emotion, "I don't know what to do . . . about you and . . . my unconscionable attraction. About your—"

"Why don't I wait for an invitation?" he softly interposed.

"I don't— Look," she said with a small sigh, "there won't be an invitation."

"I'll wait anyway."

"You shouldn't."

"Did I mention I've been sleeping alone since you left Cowes?"

"Please," she bluntly reproached. "You're a man with a harem, and I'm not a grass-green girl."

"Nevertheless, it's true."

His answer startled her. "This novel celibacy is all for me?" she incredulously inquired.

"I'd like to say no." He sighed. "Believe me, I don't understand any of this. I don't even know what I'm doing here, but I couldn't stay away. And the word 'celibacy' is a real stumbling block for me, so don't ask me any more troublesome questions. Do you think anyone would notice if I tossed you over my shoulder," he queried, his grin reckless and rakish, "and made for the nearest carriage?"

"Are we changing the subject?"

"Definitely."

"Well, then, if I could ignore the world and live by feeling alone," she replied with an answering smile, "you'd be welcome to try."

"A pleasant prospect, Countess. Do you prefer being on the top or bottom?"

"You shock me."

"Do I really?"

"Everything about you causes me disquiet."

He laughed. "How damnably refined you are. Something considerably stronger than disquiet has disrupted my life since we met, darling," he said with a rueful grimace, "and I'm not real sure I can talk it away. Although considering our public venue and all these local officials who are more easily shocked than Bertie's cosmopolitan coterie, I suppose I'd better behave. Why don't you come watch the races with me, and I'll see what I can do to ease your apprehensions and my frustration?"

"And if you can't?"

Then we'll face them in bed, he thought, but he said instead, "Maybe we're taking this too seriously. How can it hurt to enjoy each other's company?"

"You know people will talk."

"About me? I'd never step foot outside if I worried about that, and surely, Countess, you must know they've been talking about you for most of your life."

"So I'm exaggerating this all out of proportion."

"Exactly."

"And you're just another of Bertie's guests."

"See how easy it is."

"And I don't have to fear for my reputation with you."

His brows quirked in teasing speculation. "Am I obliged to answer?"

She smiled. "You're honest, at least."

He grinned. "And you're damned intriguing,

Countess Angel. Come make me happy and watch the races with me."

How could she refuse such an engaging smile?

The remainder of the afternoon they spent away from the stands, watching the races from the turf, leaning on the track rail in companionable friendship, discussing the merits of the thoroughbreds, cheering on their favorite horses and jockeys, betting occasionally and winning.

They talked of sailing and hunting and breeding horses; Kit spoke of his yacht with a passionate intensity. And when Angela mentioned May once, he said, "I like children. My sister's been telling me for years I should have some of my own."

"So you're perusing the marriage mart in London this season."

His shoulders restlessly shifted as he leaned on the rail. "It's very off-putting."

"And foreign to your disreputable way of life."

"Sometimes such blatant merchandising of women seems more disreputable to me."

Angela changed the subject then, her own feelings on marriage too raw. She mentioned a young boat designer in Plymouth who had recently come to her notice. And before long a new race began.

The pleasure they took in each other's company didn't go unnoticed that afternoon. More than one spectator in the Prince of Wales's box kept watch on their activities.

"Damn her," Olivia muttered as she stood with Clarissa MacLeish, gazing down at the two figures cheering on Winslow's long-legged stride to the finish line. "As if she doesn't have enough men already."

"He's too young for her, too," Clarissa noted, pursing her mouth in a tight, resentful line.

"Apparently she doesn't agree with you," Olivia grumbled. "Nor does he, from the look of things."

Several yards away from Olivia and Clarissa's vantage point, Georgiana and Joe Manton watched Winslow take a runaway first in his race. "Darling, look at Angela and that American," Georgiana said to her husband, her voice uncharitably gloating. "They're hugging each other after Winslow's win. I think she's taken a fancy to him."

"Really? I didn't notice," Joe casually replied. "Wales is certainly going to have cause for celebration tonight. His horse outran the field by six lengths." While fully aware of the couple at the track rail, Joe Manton had no intention of discussing Angela with his wife. But he took silent umbrage at Kit Braddock's attention to the woman he still regarded as his personal property. And his scowl deepened as the afternoon wore on.

"So, Souveral . . . will our American win the fair maid?" the Prince of Wales softly drawled sometime later, after he'd accepted all the congratulations on Winslow's victory and the following race had begun.

"He seems intent on pursuit," the ambassador replied, his gaze still on Angela and Kit. "Then again, Angela has become wearied of amorous amusements, I'm told." He shrugged. "So perhaps the young Priscilla will have him, after all."

"The Pembroke gel can't prevent his wooing our lovely Angel."

"Spoken like a true patrician, Your Highness. But now that the countess has become such an attentive student of W. T. Stead, her views toward pleasure may have altered somewhat."

"Don't talk to me of that radical firebrand,

Freddy. His damned talk of democracy will ruin this country. He counsels Angela *only* on her women's school. *Nothing* more."

"Ah, yes, of course, her school," Souveral diplomatically agreed. "I'd forgotten." If the queen and her son chose not to accept the rising strength of the working class, he surely wasn't going to educate them to the changing reality of the world.[6] "Then again, as an American, perhaps Kit's democratic ideals will appeal to Angela should his charm fail to win her."

"To hell with politics, Freddy. He'll have her, mark my words," the prince emphatically declared. No woman had ever refused His Royal Highness, despite his short, pudgy bulk, and though he was considerate of all his amorous partners, he didn't pretend to any equality between the sexes. His preference was for pretty, voluptuous women who understood their sole role was to charm.

"So, then . . . the only question remaining is . . . when," Souveral softly murmured.

"Fifty guineas says he has her tonight," the prince said.

"Really, Your Highness. She's a friend."

"No need to be squeamish, Freddy. Discretion, of course, and all that. Just between you and me, after all. Come, come."

"If you insist, Bertie. Fifty guineas says he doesn't." The ambassador knew Angela better than the prince, who never saw beyond a woman's beauty and her ability to amuse. "And fifty more that he leaves Morton Castle in a sullen mood."

"Never, Freddy." The prince smiled broadly. "Just look at them."

—

*A*fter the carriages had returned to Morton Castle, after Kit and Angela had spent the greater part of the journey back acutely aware of each other despite the company of Olivia and Lexford in their carriage, after the ladies and most of the men had returned to the castle, those remaining accompanied the Prince of Wales to the paddocks to see that the horses were properly settled for the night.

In the bustle and activity of unloading the racers in the stable yard, Kit and Souveral stood to one side, away from the melee of horses, owners, trainers, grooms, and jockeys.

"He loves to win," Souveral observed, the prince's jovial mood obvious as he talked to his trainer.

"Don't we all?"

Kit's drawl held an undercurrent of intensity that caused the ambassador to say softly, "She's very different from what she was even a year ago."

"Meaning?" There was no need to inquire of whom Souveral spoke.

"She's questioning her identity, her class, all the amusements in her past."

"That explains her wavering restraint. It appears my timing's unfortunate."

"Don't take it personally. Her new iconoclastic perceptions probably induced Joe Manton to finally marry, too.

"Did she cut him off?" A blunt, noncerebral query.

"Perhaps emotionally," Souveral blandly replied.

"And he cared?" Kit noted with a masculine disregard for philosophical sensibilities.

"She's a very independent woman."

"But provocative despite that defect," Kit said with a grin.

"Your interest is unmistakable."

"So?" The single word was infused with a lazy indifference.

"So I'd be cautious of Mr. Manton. Although his wife was heartened by Angela's response to you, I don't think Joe appreciated your poaching on his territory."

"*His* territory?" Kit's eyes narrowed slightly. "The man's greedy."

"Just a friendly warning. He's very jealous."

"Then he should have married her."

"The English are less prone to divorce than the Americans."[7]

"In that case he'll have to get used to sharing."

"So Bertie was right, after all. He was sure you'd prevail."

"Not yet, Souveral," Kit softly said, "but I always get what I want."

"So does Angela," Souveral gently replied.

*K*it wasn't expecting Joe Manton's challenge so soon, or perhaps not at all, despite Souveral's warning. It took him by surprise.

The party from the stable yard was walking back to the castle through the hushed golden haze of the setting sun, the trailing procession strung out in haphazard groups along the curved path dissecting the parkland. Their voices were muted by the vast, open space, fragments of their words and conversations drifting away into the stillness of early twilight, the peace of nature overwhelming.

Those in the lead were just beginning to ascend the gentle grassy incline leading to the drawbridge when a heated voice coming from behind Kit murmured, "Stay away from her."

There was no question who was speaking. Slowing

his stride, Kit glanced over his shoulder, and as Joe Manton came abreast of him, he calmly said, "You relinquished rights when you married."

"You're wrong."

"That's not what I understand, but I'll ask the lady again."

"I don't care what she says. I'm telling you to stay clear of her."

"And if I don't?"

Their voices were no more than a murmur as they strolled toward the portal to the castle, two large men of equal height, neither in the habit of retreating.

"You'll answer to me if you touch her." Joe Manton's black brows were glowering slashes over his eyes.

"If I touch her, it'll be at the lady's request."

Joe's expression went flint hard. "You can't have her."

"No, I think it's you who can't have her. Your recent marriage apparently altered your status," Kit mildly said. "But I sympathize with your feelings of ownership. She's a magnificent woman."

"Isn't your harem enough?" Joe growled.

"Isn't your wife?" Kit pleasantly retorted. "Ah, there she is now," he said, catching sight of Georgiana waving from the portcullis gate. "She's waiting for you. But you're still newlyweds, aren't you?" Kit added with a bland smile. Knowing that Georgiana's husband had left her in Paris during their honeymoon to make a flying trip back to Angela, Kit suspected the wife would keep Joe on a very short leash at Morton Castle.

Returning his wife's wave with a briefly raised hand, Joe muttered, "See that you keep your distance from Angela." And lengthening his stride, he moved past Kit.

It should be an interesting evening, Kit reflected, watching Georgiana run toward her husband. A besotted lover intent on retaining Angela's favor, a new wife, proprietary and watchful. And the legendary Countess Angel—all in the same intimate group.

9

If not precisely interesting, the evening turned out to be charged with emotion, none of a particularly positive nature unless one considered Olivia's high spirits relevant.

During the interval before dinner, Angela had mentally renewed all the reasonable arguments against any involvement with Kit, and she studiously avoided him. He gave her high points for evasion, but Joe stayed near her, and she'd also had considerable practice with hordes of men constantly in hot pursuit. A sobering thought, he decided, as he lounged in the drawing room after dinner amid the social banter, watching Angela across the room, drinking more than usual, responding to conversation directed at him with brief or monosyllabic answers. Feeling deeply frustrated as he slowly emptied a cognac bottle, he surveyed the women around him and wondered why he didn't find them more appealing—which thought further irritated him. Silently damning the Countess de Grae's uncommon appeal, he poured himself another drink.

Angela excused herself early that night, for the

strain of appearing uninterested when Kit Braddock's powerful presence seared her senses inevitably took its toll. Her head pounded, her facial muscles ached from forcing a smile, and if she had to make another amusing remark, she'd choke on the words. Not a single person in the room, save the man she couldn't have, interested her. And after a lifetime with these vacuous people, she had little patience for their gossip.

As Angela left the room, Olivia relaxed against the gold damask cushions of an ornately carved settee. Her only rival of note had left the field. Her elderly husband, who always retired early, was dead asleep by now, while Kit, looking moody and sullen sprawled in a Jacobean chair of sturdy enough proportions to support his large frame, was drinking himself into a black temper.

How deliciously perfect, she contemplated, intent on discovering the ardent tempests behind that sullen intensity. She preferred violence with her sex, and she rather thought if Kit was to continue drinking like that, he might oblige her.

$\mathcal{V}$ery late that night she rapped on his bedroom door. Although not the first woman to approach his room that evening, she was the only one with a message guaranteed to gain her entrance.

"It's Angela," she said.

And when the key turned in the lock and the door opened, she softly said, "Angela's not coming, so you might as well fuck me."

"I'm being entertained already," he said, lifting the brandy glass in his hand, "by this."

"I'm much better," Olivia softly said.

Still dressed in his evening clothes, although his tie and shirt collar were loosened, Kit surveyed the sultry, dark-haired woman clothed in a sheer apricot-colored dressing gown.

A second passed, then two.

"You'll enjoy yourself," Olivia whispered, slipping the single bow at the neckline open. "I'm very inventive." Shrugging the soft silk from her shoulders, she gazed up at him as the diaphanous gown drifted to the carpet.

Kit's half-lidded gaze slowly assessed her, from her smoldering dark eyes downward in a leisurely appraisal. Her heavy breasts were pinked with arousal, her waist was so narrow he could span it with his hands, and her full hips reminded him of the flaunting sexuality of Eastern sculpture. He inhaled deeply, his handsome features utterly without expression, his stance motionless, indecision taut in the quiet hallway. Then, exhaling slowly, he said, "Why not?"

*B*loody hell, he thought as he strode down the hallway a long time later. He never should have let her in. And if he hadn't been half-drunk, he wouldn't have. Lord, he disliked cruel, ferocious sex.

He walked for miles over the carefully manicured acres of parkland, trying to escape the distaste of his encounter with Olivia. Frustrated and angry, with recriminations and resentment looping through his brain and no temperate logic to explain or blunt the turmoil, he found himself eventually blaming Angela for ruining the tranquillity of his libertine life. But then his uncurbed desire would surface, and he'd swear into the cool night air. Or worse—memories of Olivia would reoccur, and he'd wonder at his lack of judgment, drunk or not. The pendulum swing of emotions fluctuated and floundered, pitched and rolled, until he finally decided he had to have more sense than to allow one woman to alter his existence so radically—a woman, for Christ's sake, who'd allowed him only a damned *kiss*. Good God, he wasn't fifteen; he must be losing his mind.

To hell with her, he thought as he stalked across the wet grass, the rosy light of dawn beginning to rise over the horizon. Just to hell with her!

$\mathcal{A}$ngela was standing at her bedroom window, restless after a sleepless night, when she first caught sight of Kit in the distance, coming up from the river flats, his hair gleaming red in the sunrise.

After a tortured night of longing, she watched his approach to the castle with the minute scrutiny of a jealous lover. Where had he been? she wondered. And with whom? Could he actually have spent the night alone? Was it possible to believe his outrageous claim of celibacy? Could she allow herself to care? Contradictory emotions jostled in her brain—suspicion, anxiety, hope, all in tumultuous disarray.

But as he neared, she saw the disheveled state of his clothes, took note of his stockingless feet, realized the discolored steaks on his white shirt front were *blood*! Olivia, of course, she instantly realized, recognizing the blatant hallmarks of her amorous style. And an incomprehensible fury exploded inside her.

He was a liar, she raged, and she was like a gullible young girl with her first lover. Betrayed, deceived, seduced by his consummate charm. Damn him, she bitterly thought, tears stinging her eyes, and damn Olivia, too, for finding him so accessible.

He suddenly disappeared from sight, swallowed up under the shadow of the massive walls, and she stood with her cheek pressed against the coolness of the window, monstrously betrayed, miserable, utterly defenseless against her perversely obstinate desire.

For she wanted him still, despite all the women in his life, despite Olivia's bloody souvenirs, despite every practical admonition of a rational mind. How strange it was to fall victim to a man who had no feelings beyond a transient passion. How ironic when she'd always affected the same pose.

Breakfast would be an ordeal. Olivia would preen, and she would be obliged to watch *them* together— exchanging intimate glances, speaking to each other in that arcane code of lovers, making plans under the pretense of bland conversation to meet each other later. But a confrontation was inevitable in the incestuous group at Morton Castle, if not at breakfast, at lunch or tea or dinner, so she might as well steel herself to go down to the morning room and confront all the billing and cooing now. This was the last day of the weekend, after all; she could survive a single day.

*K*it was already in the breakfast room when she arrived, although she offered no sign of recognition Buffet tables lined two walls, their polished surfaces covered with an extravagant array of hot and cold foods displayed on the famous Morton gold plate. She would take a small portion from the breakfast menu, she determined, find an out-of-the-way table, eat as quickly as possible, and immediately return to her room. In the milling array of guests up early to share breakfast with the prince before he attended church— a rigid custom he never altered—passing unnoticed was a possibility.

And if not for Bertie's interference, she might have succeeded in her plan. But the prince called her over to his table in so loud a voice, she couldn't feign inattention. He noisily made room for her beside him, forcing Alice to move her chair, calling for a footman to bring fresh tea. And when Angela finally sat down, it took a few seconds more to greet the other guests at the table. The Mortons looked country hale and hearty, Alice Keppel always was immaculately dressed and smiling, and when Angela gazed across the table at the last person in the small company, Kit gazed back at her and said good morning without expression. His eyes were shadowed with fatigue, two raking scars streaked his cheek, and the stark imprint of teeth mutilated his neck.

Her stomach tightened at the sight of Olivia's conspicuous marks. If there'd been any doubt, there was none now. He looked ravaged from his night of dissipation. And fresh anger overwhelmed her.

"Are you coming to church with us?" the prince asked.

With effort she forced her mind to absorb the question, classify it, form an appropriate answer, as if the inquiry had been infinitely complex instead of the simplest of queries. She finally replied, "Not this morning," and then paused, unable to process a plausible excuse.

"Angela wasn't feeling well last night, Bertie. I'm sure she'd rather rest," Alice Keppel kindly intervened.

"Are you sick, my dear?" the prince asked, concern in his voice.

"Nothing serious," she replied. "I've been tired since the season began."

"You always do too much," Bertie chided.

"Force of habit after all these years," Angela dissembled. "I'll rest at Easton next week."

"See that you do, darling. We can't have you under the weather when the Scottish holidays are almost upon us."

"I'll be fine," she said, smiling with effort.

And then Alice graciously distracted Bertie's interest by asking a question about Winslow's condition that morning. Thus encouraged, Bertie settled into a prideful narrative replay of Winslow's victory the previous day. No longer required to do more than look attentive, Angela forced herself to eat so she could quickly make her excuses and leave. It was much more difficult than she'd thought to sit across from Kit, trying to ignore what had happened last night when the debauchery was branded on his face.

He scarcely moved from his lounging posture. With his head resting against the chair back and his eyes half-shut, he seemed almost dozing. And he didn't eat, although he'd drink some ice water occasionally or speak briefly when prompted by the prince to verify some point concerning the race. The Mortons hardly spoke at all, but Bertie was used to holding court, and he required only an audience.

Just as the prince was concluding his account of the race, Olivia swept into the breakfast room, stood for a moment just inside the entrance, looking decadent in scarlet-red charmeuse, and then made directly for the Prince of Wales's table. On the way she stopped intimately close to Kit's chair, her hip brushing his arm, and gently touching his scarred cheek, she softly said, "Poor dear, you're hurt."

"I'm in a hellish mood this morning, Olivia," he murmured, shifting in his chair so she wasn't touching him.

"But still handsome as sin," Olivia whispered with a flagrant familiarity. "Are you coming to church with us?" Her seductive purr lent a perversely unchaste implication to the simple question.

"No," Kit muttered, and suddenly rising, he shoved his chair back with a harsh scraping sound that sliced through his pounding head like a knife blade. Wincing, he said on a small exhalation, "If you'll excuse me," and bowing to the table at large, he added with patent mendacity, "I've some matters to attend to."

"What a very *remarkable* man," Olivia enthusiastically proclaimed, dropping into Kit's vacated chair in a cloud of heavy perfume. "Doesn't it seem Americans have this extraordinary *animal* energy?"

The Viscountess Morton turned an unbecoming shade of red while her husband nervously cleared his throat, Olivia's overt sexuality at breakfast indecorous to country gentry far removed from the scandal and glitter of the Marlborough House set.

"Now, Olivia, mind your manners," Alice Keppel chided. "We're not in Mayfair."

"I'm sorry," Olivia murmured, affecting a wide-eyed innocence. "Did I inadvertently say something racy?" Her glance swung across to Angela, and she smiled with benign triumph. "It's just that I'm in such a glorious mood," she cooed. "Did everyone sleep well?"

No answer was required to such gratuitous gloating, nor did anyone care to chance further enlightenment apropos Olivia's good spirits.

The prince inquired of the viscount whether the fishing was good in the nearby river. The viscount gratefully responded to a topic with which he was comfortable, and Angela counted the minutes until she could escape Olivia's boastful presence.

Kit left the castle before lunch with polite regrets to the prince and his hosts for his abrupt departure.

Olivia sulked the rest of the day.

Angela found an excuse to leave on the evening

train, and when she arrived at Easton the following day, a letter from Kit was in her mail, posted from London.

A five-hundred-pound note fell out when she unfolded the single sheet of cream paper.

You win, Countess, he'd swiftly scrawled, his handwriting slashing across the pale paper with graphic force. *All good wishes to your schoolgirls.*

He hadn't even signed his name.

10

Kit had no intention of going to Easton the following week. He told Priscilla so when she mentioned their planned visit.

"I'm afraid I'll be busy," he said. They'd both come up to London, and over a luncheon at the Ritz that Priscilla had cajoled him into attending, she was doing her best to convince her elusive suitor to join them at Easton.

"Maman says you could go sailing there. Angela has her yacht moored on her estate."

Kit glanced at Priscilla's mother four tables away, deep in conversation with a friend. He shouldn't have agreed to lunch, although he'd answered Charlotte's invitation in a weak moment early one morning when he was more hungover than usual—a common occurrence of late. "I wish I could," he lied, "but I've banking appointments in the City that will keep me occupied."

"You could come on Saturday," Priscilla coaxed. "Bankers don't work on Saturday."

"It's a possibility," he said, because he didn't want to continue the argument.

"Oh, I just know you'll come! And we'll have the dearest time. Angela's house just reeks of history, not to mention her restored medieval monastery and her darling bird sanctuary. She even has cooing love-birds," Priscilla flirtatiously added.

"Did I mention I saw a bauble at Asprey's this morning I thought just perfect for you?" Kit said, intent on diverting her attention from further conversation about Easton. "If your *maman* has time after lunch, I'd like her opinion on it."

"For *me*!" Priscilla exclaimed, all thoughts of Easton instantly obliterated. "Tell me what it is!"

"The manager told me a maharani once owned it. It's a simple little bracelet, but the pearls are superb."

Now, Priscilla knew as well as Kit that presents to young maidens were restricted to inexpensive trinkets —but pearls were at least girlish enough, and a brace-let was less intimate than some other item of jewelry. And the cachet of a maharani's estate denoted a costly piece—all elements suitably contrived by Kit to make the gift acceptable as well as desirable. It was a delib-erate choice on his part. He perceived it as a going-away gift. The *Desiree* had been ready to sail since early in the week.

*A*s far as Angela knew, the Pembroke ladies and Kit were scheduled to appear; she'd not heard differ-ently from Charlotte, who had been hopeful Kit would agree at the last minute. So Angela arranged her guest list accordingly, intent on filling her house with people so no opportunity would arise where she'd be alone with Kit. Although if their last meeting at Morton Cas-tle was any indication, he'd already lost interest.

Her half sister, Millie, and her brother-in-law, the Duke of Sutherland, arrived first on Thursday morning, followed closely by her half sister, Dolly, and her husband, Carsons. They were all in a festive mood, and after the usual overflow of luggage her sisters traveled with was settled in their rooms, the small family party gathered for luncheon.

When Angela mentioned the number of guests expected, Millie said with surprise, "I thought you were done with large parties. You swore after the last one for Bertie you'd never again have so many boring people about."

"Humor me, darling. I'm insulating myself against Charlotte, Priscilla, and Priscilla's beau. After the endless season I'm not inclined to serve as duenna. With so many others around, I won't be obliged."

Millie paused with her salad fork in midair. "Charlotte still hasn't brought that rich young man to the altar?"

"Not last I heard," Angela replied, thinking of Olivia's nail marks.

"Charlotte's girl was with a gorgeous red-haired man at the Ritz a few days ago," Dolly said. "Would that be the prospective bridegroom?"

"It sounds like Mr. Braddock." So Kit was still seeing Priscilla, Angela thought. Why did it surprise her? He was a practical man; he needed a bride. Like most men, he viewed his amorous activities as separate from that search.

"If he's her suitor, he didn't look very attentive."

"For heaven's sake, Dolly," her husband disputed. "Why would he look attentive over lunch at the Ritz?"

"If he was truly in love, he would," she sweetly countered.

"It seems Mr. Braddock is selecting a bride to please his mother," Angela indicated, "not for love. His mother's anxious for grandchildren."

"Good luck to Charlotte, then," the duke said

with a chuckle, breaking his bread in two. "He must have a stableful of deb brood mares to choose from. But count me out as chaperon to the young miss. You *women* can protect her virginity. I expect that's the basic item for sale in this arrangement."

"Edward," his wife admonished. "You needn't be so blunt."

"We're only family here, darling." He grinned, reaching for the butter. "I promise not to mention it over dinner."

*W*hen Charlotte and Priscilla arrived Thursday afternoon, however, they came alone.

"Mr. Braddock has business in London he can't postpone," Charlotte stiffly intoned as she stepped down from the Easton carriage that had conveyed them from Angela's private rail station.

She needn't have invited twenty more guests, Angela immediately thought.

"*I* need a hot bath," Priscilla petulantly said as she followed her mother down from the carriage. "The train was absolutely black with dreadful soot. Even in our private compartment. Maman is going to write to the rail company and complain first thing tomorrow."

Angela searched Priscilla's luxurious traveling ensemble of turquoise silk for any indication of dirt. "How terrible for you," she pleasantly said, acting the hostess with undisturbed serenity, despite the fact that not a smudge was in evidence. "I'll see that you have hot water immediately."

"You have *crowds* of people here," Charlotte said with surprise as she stood on the gravel drive, viewing the large company on the croquet lawn.

"Just a few friends, darling. I thought you and Priscilla might like to be amused. Freddy came specially to see you, Charlotte, and Sutherland particularly asked to sit near you at dinner," Angela said with a smile.

"Oh, Sutherland is such a dear charmer. I feel more refreshed already. Come, Priscilla, we must see to our toilettes."

*D*inner was festive. Angela loved Easton, and without the emotional constraints of Kit's presence, she thoroughly enjoyed her role of hostess that evening. Essentially a house party of family, her immediate relatives were augmented by a score or more of cousins plus Freddy Souveral, who had been a friend to her even before Bertie.

Her cook had prepared a full range of favorite foods served at Easton for decades, each course reminiscent of long-ago family dinners, and as was the custom on informal occasions, silly toasts were the order of the day, with Sutherland leading off in an extemporaneous poem to Angela's pet toucan. He set the sportive mood, and each toast that followed added to the raucous atmosphere. But before the rowdiness escalated into full-scale mayhem, Millie temporarily quieted the merriment by proposing a toast to their beloved grandfather, who had nurtured and improved Easton and passed it on to another generation.

During the brief lull inspired by each relative's poignant memory of the old viscount, Angela's butler approached her with a message. A man was waiting to see her in her study, he quietly said. He wouldn't give his name.

"He says he's a friend, my lady," Ridgely murmured.

"Is he a local man?" she asked, rising from her

chair. As the largest landowner in the county, she was often petitioned for help, even at odd times like this.

"I don't recognize him, my lady."

"Very well, continue serving. I'll be back directly." And with a swift explanation to Freddy and her sister Millie, Angela left the room. With dessert served next, dinner was almost over. Her absence wouldn't disrupt the remainder of the meal.

The gaslights had been turned on in her study, but shadows enveloped the far corners, and surveying the large chamber from the threshold, she saw no sign of a man. But when she walked into the room, a tall figure rose from a chair near the window and advanced into the light.

A stifled cry stung her throat and she stopped in rigid disbelief.

Kit was dressed in rain-soaked riding clothes, his boots mud-spattered, his hair darkened with moisture.

"I tried to stay away," he said.

"Don't say that," Angela whispered, her heart beating so loudly the sound hammered in her ears. "Priscilla and her mother are in the dining room," she breathed in horror.

"They won't see me. I'm staying at the Golden Hart in Easton Vale."

"You can't be here!" she repudiated. "I've a houseful of guests. There are people everywhere."

"I'll wait till they go."

"No one's leaving until Sunday."

"That's only three days."

"Oh, God," Angela murmured, reaching for a nearby chair to steady herself.

In two swift strides Kit was at her side, his arms

sliding around her, gently holding her upright. "I shouldn't have surprised you."

"Olivia's marks are almost gone," Angela incongruously whispered, when she should have told him to go, when she should have broken away from his embrace, when she shouldn't have felt such joy at seeing him.

"I'll pay penance for that night. I felt like hell about it."

"I'm losing my mind," she whispered, her hands reaching up to stroke the cool dampness of his cheeks.

"Mine's been gone for weeks," he softly said, pulling her closer. "Do you know how hard it's raining out there?"

His smile was exactly as she remembered, instant and warm and so intimate, he made her feel as though he'd never smiled at anyone else before. "You need dry clothes," she murmured.

"Or no clothes," he softly said.

"What am I going to do?" Her plea was underlaid with sweet promise.

"I'm not the one to ask, because my answer hasn't changed since that first night at Cowes."

"While I've been saying no."

"For what seems a very long time," he gently said.

"I filled the house with guests to save me from you."

"I could have told you it wouldn't work."

"I can't send you out in the storm."

"Good."

"You're not going to help me resist, are you?"

"I don't think so. It's five miles to Easton Vale, the roads were miserable; I'm serious about this."

"Now comes the question I shouldn't ask."

He grinned. "But you're going to."

"What of Priscilla?"

"I'm not going to marry her."

She could have said "Are you sure?" but she didn't want to know.

"I'm sure," he said, as if he could read her mind. "Are you happy now?"

She smiled up at him, jubilant and glowing. "I can't remember when I've been happier."

"I suppose you tell all the men that." He had his demons, too.

"I've never been happy before, not like this," she quietly said. "Only with my children, and that's different."

"I'm keeping you," he declared with a heart-stopping smile.

"I'll let you," she answered, recklessly opening her heart.

They were like artless children in their joy, these two people who had done and seen and heard so much. The possibility that new experiences existed should have been beyond their imagination. But this was bright and shiny new.

Like holding untarnished hope in your hands.

Or kissing your true love for the first time.

Or finding happiness in a world of wasted lives.

"Tell me what to do," she whispered, clinging to him, her gaze lifted to his great height, the sounds of revelry in the dining room distinct. "Dinner's almost over. I have to go back."

"I'll wait till Sunday."

She shut her eyes briefly, took a deep breath as if she were suffocating, and said in a heated rush, "I can't wait."

"Then I'll see you later this evening," he softly replied, willing his voice to a calmness he wasn't feeling; he'd been wanting her a very long time.

"Not here." She was tense in his arms, her voice a flutter of apprehension.

"Tell me where. Anywhere."

A contrary spark flashed in her eyes. "Are you always so accommodating?"

"I'm never accommodating. I've been traveling since morning to get here, I'm wetter than hell, and you don't have a reason in the world for jealousy."

"I shouldn't believe you."

"You should. Now, tell me where and I'll be there."

After all her misgivings, after the legions of women in his life, after Priscilla and Charlotte and her decision to protect herself against him with a multitude of guests in her house, she breathlessly said, "Wait for me at Stone House." And in a rush of words she gave him directions to the medieval monastery she'd restored on her property.

"Tell them a friend of your bailiff's stopped by," he said as her gaze nervously swung to the clock on the mantel, "and the problem with the road to Easton Vale will be fixed in the morning."

She stared at him for a moment, her expression indefinable, tentative.

"I had time to think of an excuse for you while I was waiting."

All her uncertainties came flooding back; he was so glib and faithless.

"I've never ridden through the rain for a woman before," he softly murmured.

"Am I that transparent?"

"You've been resisting me so long," he gently noted, "I'm beginning to recognize the signs." His smile was sweetly chaste for a man of his reputation. "And I'm not leaving Easton now that I've found you."

"Tell me about Priscilla again. I have to go back in there and face her."

"I had lunch with her on Tuesday."

"My sister saw you."

"Did she say I looked bored?"

Angela smiled faintly. "She said you looked inattentive."

"I told Priscilla I was leaving for America very soon and with her mother's blessing bought her a parting gift."

"That magnificent pearl bracelet Priscilla's flaunting."

"That one. So she knows I won't be proposing."

"Thank you," Angela whispered.

"Thank me later," Kit said with a grin. "Now go, before someone comes looking for you and finds you in this compromising position." Releasing her, he gave her a gentle push toward the door.

She turned back at the threshold. He was standing quietly watching her. "I'm so glad you came," she murmured.

His smile flashed white in his bronzed face. "You couldn't keep me away."

11

The rest of the evening passed in a blur, although Angela answered when spoken to, poured tea, and listened with seeming attentiveness to the conversation, danced with Freddy and her brothers-in-law when Dolly decided to play her favorite waltzes on the piano, and caught herself staring at Priscilla on numerous occasions as if trying to decide what Kit could have seen in such an uncharitable nature. She even managed to sit still through two hands of bridge with her cousins from Sussex without making any drastic blunders. But when the party broke up shortly after midnight, and Angela stood in the hall wishing everyone good night, she wondered how she'd managed to get through three hours without any recollection of events.

She was actually trembling as she watched the last guests ascend the stairway, unconsciously counting the steps until the distant figures disappeared down the hallway. Then she turned and swiftly walked across the large entrance hall to the front door. "Tell Nellie I'll be staying at Stone House tonight," she said to the hall porter, who was at his station near the door. "And if you don't mind, I'll borrow your umbrella," she added.

"Likely should have a cloak fetched," the old man familiarly said. "The rain's blowin' mighty fierce."

"No need, Pen," she replied to the old retainer, who had worked at Easton all his life. "It's not cold."

"If'n you say so, my lady," he said, moving past her to open the door, knowing she often stayed the night at her retreat. "But keep to the east side of them old beeches, and you'll have some protection from the wind."

"I promise," Angela said with a smile as she released the latch on the large, utilitarian umbrella. Stepping into the night, she shivered not from cold, but from a flaring excitement.

The rain blew and swirled around her as she ran down the path to Stone House, the wild storm as tempestuous as her passions. Holding the umbrella like a shield against the wind, she hastened toward the man who'd tantalized and enticed her imagination for weeks. Her silver tissue gown trailed in a damp, silken stream behind her; the rain-drenched skirt clung to her legs as she splashed through puddles, soaking her silver satin pumps. But she scarcely noticed the wet, so heated were her senses; she thought only of her destination and the man who waited there.

The beeches planted in a great sweeping line by some long-ago ancestor towered above her, their ancient limbs creaking in the storm, their leaves rustling and stirring in the wind, swaying sentinels to her hurried passage. Leaning into the buffeting gusts, she wondered if Kit would actually be there or whether she'd only imagined his presence at Easton House.

His startling appearance tonight suddenly seemed unreal—the innocuous postdinner entertainments the familiar reality instead—not the reckless buccaneer of a man standing in her study.

Then she saw the lights in the distance and she smiled in the darkness and rain.

He was there.

He was waiting for her.

Happiness had a name.

*H*e must have been watching for her because the door opened as she approached the low garden gate. Lamplight spilled out into the night, illuminating the cobbled walk, and Kit swept through the portal, crossing the porch in two long strides. Wearing only breeches and an open-necked shirt, with his feet bare, he looked like one of her tenant farmers, and she thought how pleasant it would be if he belonged to Easton and to her. But he had none of the deference of a family retainer; he took the steps in a flying leap, ran to meet her, took the umbrella from her, and swept her up into his arms.

"I didn't know if I could wait much longer," he murmured, striding toward the house. "Tell me you missed me," he said, grinning down at her through the rain. "I've been going crazy waiting; I was about to come find you. Did everyone finally go off to bed?"

"Finally," she said with a blissful smile. "And, yes, I missed you terribly. The evening seemed endless."

"Are you tired?" he asked as he moved under the protection of the porch roof, his voice suddenly altering, touched with concern.

Smiling, she shook her head, her feelings impossible to describe, weeks of anticipation and longing, skittish anxieties and nerves willingly jettisoned without a qualm.

Her hair was pale in the darkness, riotously curled

from the moisture, her joyous face more beautiful than he'd remembered. "Maybe you *should* rest," he gallantly offered, as if she'd not responded strongly enough to convince him, her drenched body cool against his skin. "Come sit by the fire," he added as they entered the house.

Gazing through the archway into the small parlor, Angela saw a glowing fire on the grate, Kit's boots and jacket drying near the hearth, a bouquet of roses on a table beside the sofa. "You've picked roses," she said, looking up at him, delight in her eyes, the scent of the Paul Neyron roses fragrant in the air.

"Bertie said you liked roses."

"How chivalrous," she teased, "and on a night like this."

"I had three hours, seventeen minutes"—he swiftly tipped his head down to look at the plain leather-banded wristwatch he always wore—"and twenty-two seconds on my hands," he answered, grinning. "Now, why don't you sit by the fire and I'll find a towel to dry you?"

"I don't want to."

His gaze turned searching.

"I don't want to sit down," she softly clarified.

"I wasn't sure," he said. "You see how I'm trying to behave."

"Now that you're here, you mean," she dulcetly murmured.

"And probably only marginally even now," he said, his lashes drifting downward so he gazed at her from under their dark fringe. "There's a fire upstairs, too."

For a moment the only sound in the shadowed foyer was the rhythmic dripping from the umbrella he still held in his hand.

"I'd like to go upstairs," Angela whispered, the

simple words taking on momentous significance in the hushed entryway.

Placing the umbrella on a richly carved console sculpted centuries ago by some pious monk, Kit briefly surveyed the stairway before them as though silently debating the possibility of ascent. Then, returning his gaze to her, he quietly said, "This hasn't happened to me before. I find myself . . . susceptible—"

"—to feeling?"

He nodded. "The rules seem different."

"Perhaps we're both novices tonight."

He shook his head. "I'm too jealous of every man who's ever looked at you."

"As I am of the ladies in your life." Green-eyed, she begrudged them his affection.

"I'll send them away." A month ago such a promise would have been incomprehensible.

"Then there aren't any more men," Angela impulsively replied, this woman who'd always basked in male attention. "Come see my bed."

As Kit walked toward the stairway, she lightly touched his cheek with a brushing fingertip. "You needn't carry me."

"I find myself wanting to," Kit said, his grin boyish. "I feel like a bridegroom."

"Wouldn't that be nice?" Angela murmured, finding the thought so pleasing, she questioned her sanity. She'd not viewed marriage with favor for years.

"Terrifyingly nice," Kit qualified, his dark brows mildly elevated.

Angela laughed. "Such uncertainty. Should I take offense?"

"No, because I'm very certain of one thing, at least."

"Yes," she softly replied, knowing that the world could be crashing around her and she'd want him still.

He moved up the narrow staircase swiftly, as though her weight were incidental, and when he reached the top of the stairs, he had to duck slightly to pass under the lintel, his head almost brushing the low ceiling as they passed down the hall. How wonderfully large he was, Angela thought with a shiver of heated longing—and how audacious. Who else would boldly appear in the midst of her house party?

"Tell me about the paintings on your bed," Kit said, well mannered and urbane, striding down the shadowed corridor.

"How leisured and cool you are," Angela murmured, his striking sensuality in sharp contrast to his politesse. "What if I'm in a hurry?"

He smiled. "We'll talk about it *after* you show me your bed." Stopping outside her bedroom door, he nudged it open with his foot.

Light spilled out into the hallway, illuminating Angela's perplexed expression. "You're serious."

"I like to watch you," he said, setting her down just inside the threshold. "I'm not going anywhere." He leaned his broad shoulders against the doorjamb and lazily crossed his arms. "Give me a history lesson."

His casualness intrigued her, and his calm assumption that he intended to stay in her life.

"They look like tempera paintings," he noted with a nod in the direction of the lavishly painted bed, as if prompting a reluctant student to recite.

Glancing up, she cast him a searching look. "Will this take long?"

"It doesn't have to. I saw your bed when I came up to light the fire and found it richly"—he smiled—"dare I say flamboyantly—decorated. It suited you, I thought. The paintings are superb, by the way. I particularly like the orchard scene."

"You're very strange."

"Because I don't instantly make love to you?"

"No, because you're actually interested in the paintings."

"They're unusual. That style of book illumination on a bed is unique. And," he said with a cheerful grin, "I'd like to know something about the busy brotherhood of monks depicted, since they're all going to be watching us tonight."

"Will they really?" The novel thought raised her eyebrows.

"If you were nude before me, believe me, I would," he said, amusement rich in his eyes. "Are they fourteenth century?"

She shook her head. "Twelfth century. It was a miracle the bed survived in such remarkable condition."

"The book of hours perhaps made it useful."

"As did the calendar of months with all the local customs of the season portrayed," she added. "Those might be fourteenth century, so you have a very refined eye."

"I know." His green gaze swept down the sumptuous curves of her body clearly revealed beneath her clinging gown, the wet silver tissue no more than a delicate film over her flesh.

"If you're very good, I might let you lie on it," she playfully offered.

"Since I *am* very good," Kit replied with a wolfish grin, "I'd be happy to oblige you."

"Immodest man."

"After I get you out of those wet things, you can judge for yourself."

His smile delighted her. "Will that be soon?"

"I was thinking yes. History lessons make me amorous."

"How nice. I'll tell you of the Dominican brothers who built Stone House while you unhook this soggy gown." And turning her back, she smiled at him over her shoulder. "You don't mind playing lady's maid do you?"

"I'll make an exception tonight."

She swung around so quickly, his hands were left suspended in midair. "Do you ever do anything for yourself?" Although a man with a harem by definition wouldn't have to—and she knew it.

"What do you mean by 'anything'?" he carefully said, taking note of the displeasure in her voice.

"I mean sexually," she explicitly said.

He hesitated, the myriad replies coming to mind not likely to soothe her temper. "Is there a correct answer to this question?" he gently asked.

"Just tell me." Her hands were clenched at her sides, her gaze direct and heated.

"I said I'd send them all home." His deep voice was mild.

Her rigid posture relaxed and she ruefully smiled, the temper gone from her eyes. "I'm sorry. It shouldn't matter so much, but it does."

"I understand," he quietly replied, "because I want to *own* you, and not graciously or benevolently, but with the most barbaric intent."

"I know. I was contemplating how pleasant it would be if you were my dependent at Easton."

The faintest smile creased his tanned cheek. "This ownership could be a problem."

"You'd know about ownership, wouldn't you." Her voice had taken on an acerbic bite again.

"They're friends. Don't get angry again," he said,

touching her fingertips gently. "I'm sending them away."

Angela sighed. "This is very unusual for me; I'm asking too much of you."[8]

"No, you're not," he simply said, folding her hand in his.

The small room under the eaves held a cloistered ambience, offering warm sanctuary from the storm outside, hermitage, as well, from the fashionable beau monde and all the obstacles and impediments that world could impose.

"You might find me very hard to get rid of," Kit murmured, pulling Angela close.

"How perfect," she murmured, gazing up at him. "Because I like the idea of you at Easton."

"As your stud in residence?" His voice was sportive, but he was watching her with an unusual gravity in his eyes.

"For that, of course," she agreed, sliding her finger over the sensuous curve of his lower lip. "But also because you've brought great joy to my life."

"Would I have to learn how to farm?" he teased.

"I *could* keep you at Easton as my personal secretary," she facetiously responded.

"How personal?"

"*Very* personal."

"In that case, I'll take the job, my pretty little countess," and dipping his head, he kissed her very gently and chastely as if sealing their bargain.

"Now, my lady," he said with mock deference, "I'd be remiss in my duties if I didn't suggest you remove that wet gown. You're going to catch your chill."

"But that's why I have you."

"Exactly. So turn around and we'll begin our pleasant association." He worked unhurriedly, stop-

ping occasionally to kiss her scented neck or cheek or
pale shoulder while she took the pins from her tumbled hair and dropped them to the floor. Their movements were executed with a familiar, languid intimacy,
as if their roles were familiar and they'd done this a
hundred times before. When the gown was unhooked,
he slid the silk tissue from her shoulders where it hung
damply, stripped the clinging material free, and dis-
posed of the dress over a chair back.

"Thank you, Braddock," she said, and sliding her
hands up his chest, she balanced on tiptoe and kissed
him.

"My distinct pleasure, my lady," he modestly replied, quietly unmoving, his gaze blandly neutral.

"Am I paying you well enough, Braddock?" Angela playfully inquired, tracing a proprietary finger
down his corded throat.

"Oh, yes," he softly said, his eyes holding hers for
a salient moment. "I'm the envy of your staff."

"You don't mind my personal attention?"

"No, ma'am."

"Do the maids miss your—er—company now that
I've taken you away? I've heard you were quite in demand below stairs."

"I couldn't say, my lady."

"So modest, Braddock."

"Yes, ma'am. You're shivering, ma'am, from your
wet petticoats."

"Don't you want to talk about my maids, Braddock?"

"No, ma'am. If you come closer to the fire, I'll
take those wet things off." And without waiting for
her reply, he guided her nearer the hearth, where he
untied her sodden petticoats with swift expertise.

"You seem to be very competent," Angela noted,

devoid now of petticoats, warmed by the fire and Kit's closeness.

"I was well trained, my lady."

"How fortunate for me. Give me a kiss, Braddock, so I can judge for myself."

"Where, my lady?" he mildly inquired.

"You're a cheeky young man."

"Some ladies have preferences, ma'am."

A flush of anger warmed her cheeks; she was never immune to his past. "Kindly keep such references to yourself, Braddock."

"Yes, ma'am. Do your aristocratic lovers follow your orders, too?" He was as thin-skinned as she.

"You're impertinent," she snapped.

"But you want my cock anyway," he quietly said, hot-tempered at the thought of her passionate eagerness and all the men who had loved her.

Her blue eyes flashed. "I could have you sent away."

"But you won't," he said. "Now, come here," he softly ordered, "and I'll kiss you on your haughty mouth."

"You damned arrogant—"

"—stud?"

As if the word had triggered her optic nerves, her gaze fell to the blatant evidence of his arousal, bulging under the skintight chamois of his riding breeches.

"What do you think, Countess?" he lazily drawled. "Does it find favor in your eyes?"

Her body had turned liquid at the sight, his enormous erection stretching the leather from his crotch to his waist.

"Come closer, darling. Touch it."

"You're very brazen," she murmured, but she took the hand he held out to her, and when he placed her palm on his pulsing hardness, she shivered. She'd never seen such a formidable length and thickness or felt one as stiff. With trepidation she reached for his belt.

"Perhaps, my lady, we should get to know each other better first," Kit said with a wicked grin, gently restraining her hands.

"That won't be necessary." Pulling backward, she struggled to free herself from his grip.

"You're sure, now?" he murmured, holding her effortlessly. "You're not interested in conversation?"

"I'm sure," she said, a flush of passion pinking her flesh. "I don't want to wait."

"Should we take this off, then?" Kit murmured, releasing her hands, tracing a lazy finger over the rigid boning compressing her tightly laced waist.

"I don't care if it's on or off," she whispered, her body pulsing with carnal urgency.

"What tantalizing eagerness," he whispered, circling her small waist with his hands. "What if I make you wait?" His palms slid upward over the constricting satin and lace, then higher to caress the pale mounds of her ripe breasts balanced and quivering in lacy half cups stretched taut under their weight.

"You can't," she breathed, her eyes half-shut against the exquisite sensation of his hands on her breasts.

"Will you climax without me?"

"I'd rather not."

"That sounds like a yes. How easily aroused you are, Countess," he softly said, lightly pinching her jewel-hard nipples through the sheer blue lace.

"It's been a very long time." Her voice was barely audible, so pronounced and absorbing was the throbbing between her legs, the hard pressure of his fingers spiraling directly downward to the pulsing core of her body.

"How long a time?" A new authority colored the softness of his inquiry, his fingers tightened harshly; he was no longer playing her game.

"Weeks," she whispered, almost swooning from the sharp, delirious sensation.

"How many weeks?" An intemperate, jealous question.

Her eyes were half-closed, her breathing a light panting rhythm, the world eclipsed by heated sensation.

"How many weeks?" he curtly repeated, beset by demons he couldn't control, his fingers cruel.

"Since . . . before Cowes," she managed to reply, the last word dying away in a breathy whimper.

"Then you shouldn't have to wait any longer," he gently said, the sting suddenly gone from his voice, his fingers unclasping from her smarting nipples, his hands moving to close tenderly on her shoulders. Turning her so he could reach the laces at the back of her corset, he deftly untied the silk cords and stripped them away while she stood inundated with desire. When he lifted the lacy garment, she spun around and melted against his body, her hands shaking as she reached for the buttons on his shirt.

"Wait," he softly commanded, forcing her hands away, placing them firmly at her sides. "Stand still."

Trembling, breathless with need, she obeyed as he undid the tiny pearl buttons of her brief chemise, pulled it off, untied the blue silk waist ribbons of her drawers and, holding the loosened ribbons between his slender tanned fingers, maintained just enough pressure to hold her last piece of clothing in place. "This seems an occasion," he gently murmured, gazing at her quivering with desire, her lush body half-nude, the most alluring woman in all of England waiting for his touch.

"I hope you didn't spend a long day of travel to make a speech," she whispered, her gaze flame hot.

"Just a short one." His voice was mild, as though he were unmoved by desire.

But his tight riding breeches left no doubt of his physical response, and tantalized by the riveting sight, Angela restlessly reached over to stroke the velvety leather strained tight over his erection.

"Marry me," he said, letting the ribbons slip through his fingers, watching the sheer drawers slide down her legs, her nudity tinseled by the golden firelight.

"Maybe I will," Angela whispered, measuring the ostentatious length of him with a delicate fingertip. "If you please me."

"Ummm . . . incentive," he murmured, lifting her away from the dimity and lace puddled at her feet, setting her down again. "I'll have to think of something gratifying."

"This will be gratification enough," she purred, stroking her palm down his hardness.

"Unbuckle my belt," he softly decreed as he slid a cuff button free, the warmth of her hand compelling.

When she responded with haste and competence, he found himself momentarily rankled at her proficiency. But he was swiftly reaching the point where nuances of resentment lost out to more fundamental urges, and critically intent on burying himself inside the delectable Countess Angel, he cast aside lesser objections. Stripping his buttons open with a rough tug, he shrugged out of his shirt. "I'll do that," he curtly said, and brushing her hands aside, quickly unfastened his leather breeches.

He heard a small, breathy "Oh," as he stripped the tight chamois from his hips and thighs and swiftly rolled the supple suede down his legs.

"Is that a yes to my marriage proposal?" he roguishly murmured, standing upright, familiar with that initial female reaction.

"*Definitely* a yes," Angela dulcetly murmured, touching the quivering tip arched against his belly, the violent throbbing between her legs matching the pulse beat in the sharply conspicuous veins of his penis. Tracing his erection in a languid downward motion, she felt her body open in welcome as if her fingertips were vetting agent for her brain.

"Will I fit?" he whispered, sliding his hand between her thighs. "Do you think you can take it . . . all?" he softly inquired, slipping one finger into her pulsing cleft.

"I'll try," she breathily responded, the words half-swallowed as he slid a second finger inside. And gently stroking, he measured, probed, slowly forced entry deeper and deeper until her breathing changed and she clung to him, overwhelmed by torrid desire.

"Are you ready now?" His drenched fingers were answer enough, but he wished to have her tell him. "Are you?" he quietly repeated.

"I want this," she finally answered on a small caught breath, touching Kit's splendid arousal. And bending, she licked the full-stretched head with her tongue.

His fingers slid from her body. "It's yours," he whispered, watching her gently stroke his glistening length as if gauging how much she could swallow, bringing added dimension to his arousal.

"Oh, my," she uttered in fascinated admiration as the rigid shaft grew under her hands.

"We're fond of you," Kit said with a faint smile.

She looked up, her own smile playful. "I think I'll lock you away in a monk's cell, darling, and keep this all for myself."

"And maybe I'll let you," he softly replied.

"Would you be difficult to control?"

"Impossible, I think."

And for an unprecedented moment in time, Angela considered keeping a man for more than a transient diversion. "Then I must enjoy you while I can," she flirtatiously murmured, reverting to familiar patterns, and dipping her head, she took him into her mouth.

He hadn't known what he'd expected, but the sensation was so shockingly good, he knew the feeling would be forever etched in his memory. And he wondered if this is what came from waiting so long for a woman one fancied.

His hands moved to cradle her head as his hardness slid deeper, and when she sucked with both skill and paralyzing energy, his eyes shut fleetingly, a soft groan lodged deep in his throat, and he stood utterly still, defenseless against the fierce pleasure. Holding him solidly in her hands, she moved after a time, so he rested even deeper against the back of her throat for a searing passage of time and then, swaying backward, partially released him, his sleek flesh wet from her mouth. Leaning forward again, she drew him back into her mouth, ultimately settling into a heart-stopping rhythm, the pressure of her warm mouth and tongue and slender fingers so intense and riveting, the entire focus of his life was momentarily in her hands. She was very, very expert, he vaguely thought in the minuscule fragment of his brain not entirely engulfed by rapt, soul-stirring sensation.

But moments later, quivering on the orgasmic brink, Kit abruptly eased away, pulled Angela upright, and, gripping her hand, hastily drew her toward the bed. Falling in a sprawl onto the linen coverlet, he quickly tumbled her forward, catching her easily as she fell. After he gently lowered her atop him, they met at long last after weeks of denial and pursuit, flesh to flesh, heart to heart, salacious lust to lust.

For the briefest seconds she lay on his hard-muscled body, her small form dwarfed by his size, her skin pale against his bronzed flesh, her blond tresses spread in silken disarray over his arms and shoulders. Then, beset by a savage urgency, he swiftly rolled her beneath him.

"At last," Angela breathed.

"Forgive my brusqueness."

"I'm not looking for courtesy."

He took in a calming breath. "You shouldn't say that."

"I mean it."

His eyes went shut briefly, and when he gazed at her again, pitched flame shone in their green depths.

"I've wanted you from that first night at Cowes," she whispered, feeling then as now as if, in some hurtling, cosmic scheme, she was meant to mate with him.

"I don't want to hurt you," he whispered.

"You won't," she promised. He was poised above her, about to offer her all she craved. Burning with feverish need, sleek with readiness, her thighs spread open in welcome, unsated and greedy, she was frantic to feel him inside her.

"You're sure."

"Yes, yes." And clutching his powerful shoulders, she tugged at him to bring him closer.

He couldn't refuse; no man could have, and when he moved, she felt his hardness breach her heated, throbbing tissue.

Triggering a sudden stinging terror of recall deep inside her psyche. "Wait!" Angela cried, panic-stricken. "Wait, wait, wait, *wait*!" And pushing Kit away with fear-induced strength, she scrambled out of reach. "I can't get pregnant," she breathlessly said, distancing herself against the painted headboard, the monks at eventide prayer peeking over her shoulder. "I forgot," she ambiguously said, trembling.

Sprawled on his back in stunned surprise, Kit blankly gazed at her. He was dying, he thought, clenching his fists momentarily against the explosive violence of his feelings. Drawing in a deep, restraining breath, he tried to stabilize his confounded senses, and in as mild a voice as he could muster with his brain still in ramming speed and his libido conceptualizing the word "rape" for the first time in his life, he panted, "I won't . . . climax inside you."

"But what if you do?" Angela fearfully whispered. "You might, and then . . . oh, lord," she groaned, overcome with self-reproach. "I forgot, I never forget, I never do, I never, *never* do," she incredulously breathed, her hands planted hard on her thighs to control their tremor, her spine stiffly erect, her agitation patently visible. "Just wait . . . ," she softly pleaded, her voice a small smothered sound, and sliding off the bed, she flew to the armoire, threw open the doors, pulled out a drawer, and began frantically pawing through it.

Nightgowns and lingerie fell to the floor in disarray as she wildly searched through drawers, systematically tossing their contents aside. By the third drawer Kit's breathing had returned to something near normal, his heartbeat had subsided to a less erratic rhythm, and his orgasmic urgency had diminished to manageable levels. With his mind no longer completely inundated by the deluge of libidinous desire, he was better able to appreciate the present captivating view. Just short feet away, precisely at eye level as he lay on the monk's bed, was the lush and secular splendor of Angela's pink bottom, deliciously displayed in all its blushing beauty as she bent over the low drawers. "Could I help?" he murmured, his attention riveted on the pouty lips of her vagina.

"I'm looking for a Dutch cap,"[9] Angela replied, exasperation fluttering through her voice. "There should be one here somewhere; there should be more than one, dammit. You appeared so suddenly, it never occurred to me—well, *that* did of course," she qualified, "but the practicalities didn't, and I know there are some here." Throwing several more items onto the floor, she glanced at him over her shoulder. "I get pregnant if a man even looks at me, so bear with me. I don't suppose you're anxious to become a father tonight." And turning back to an unemptied drawer, she wrenched it from the armoire and upended it onto the needlepoint carpet.

Of course she'd use contraceptives, he realized as he surveyed the disordered jumble of clothing on the floor; she'd be a fool not to. But more selfish, sharply personal motives took issue with Angela de Grae's sensuous affability and the fact that she kept a supply of Dutch caps on hand in this isolated cottage. Not just one, but several, he moodily contemplated. How the hell many did she need? he wondered, suddenly experiencing the sensation of countless other men in the firelit room.

But only seconds later cooler reason intervened, and he reminded himself that Countess Angel was, after all, a woman renowned for her passions and seductive allure; the cachet of temptress had intrigued him as well. He hadn't expected her to be virginal. Still, despite all, he brooded with a perverse illogic extraordinary to a man of his licentious repute; he wished to be the only man in her life—not just tonight, but last night and last month and last year.

"Hallelujah!" Angela softly exclaimed, extracting

a small green leather pouch from within the silky environs of a lingerie drawer, and spinning around, she smiled enchantingly. "This won't take long," she murmured. "I just have to find some—ah, here it is," she said, lifting out a small glass jar from the purse. "And now if you'll excuse me for a moment . . . this is slightly awkward."

"Let me do it. All the *Desiree* women use Dutch caps."

She suddenly went motionless, her smile disappeared, her eyes took on a coolness. "Fuck you," she softly said.

"And hopefully very soon," he lazily drawled. "Tell me—how many men have slept in this bed?"

"When it comes to records, Mr. Braddock, I feel sure I'd lose to your saturnalian instincts. I generally like men one at a time."

"Generally?" he inquired, a noticeable growl underscoring the word.

"Almost always," she sweetly replied, not inclined to satisfy his possessive impulses with the very mundane truth. "So if you're looking for a virgin, you're looking in the wrong place. And I wasn't the one who traveled all day from London,"—her brows rose marginally—"for a fuck."

"I think you annoy me." His dark brows were drawn together in a scowl.

"What a shame," Angela murmured, "when I still find myself fascinated by your very large cock."

An absolute silence fell in the small bedchamber, even the crackle of the fire in the hearth momentarily hushed as if the sudden tension had smothered the physical properties of flame.

Kit lay dead still on the monk's bed, his green gaze coolly measuring.

"It's five wet miles to the Golden Hart," Angela softly said.

"I could stay here out of the rain and *not* fuck you."

"Is that a challenge? You might lose."

"I won't lose."

"You lost at Morton Castle."

"I wouldn't tonight."

"What a damned waste," Angela said with a smile. "You have the most glorious erection. Although I expect you hear that all the time."

Kit's mouth twitched for a moment in involuntary response, and then he laughed in genuine amusement. "You're the first, darling, to compliment me so bluntly. But thank you," he said with a smile. "And forgive my bad manners," he went on, his smile lighting up his eyes. "I haven't acted like a sullen adolescent for a very long time."

"My seventeen-year-old son has the same charming sulk when he doesn't get his way."

It took him a moment to digest her casual remark. She wasn't a mother in his mind. She was a Salome, Delilah, Venus; she was the focus of his lust. "You shouldn't have a seventeen-year-old son," he softly noted.

"But I do."

A small silence descended again, their restored intimacy marred.

Then Kit suddenly shifted in his lounging pose as though he'd reached a decision. "Give me that," he said, holding out his hand for the green leather case she held.

"You're sure, now?"

He looked at her standing nude and lush on the cabbage-rose needlepoint rug waiting for his answer. Reason didn't enter the equation as he contemplated his reply, nor did anything resembling logic. Angela de Grae was the antithesis of all he'd come to England looking for; she was neither virginal, nor young, nor unmarried. She was a woman of passion, never at a loss for an ardent suitor; she was the mother of two children. She was someone else's wife.

"I'm sure," he quietly said.

12

"You don't have to do this," she ambiguously noted as she approached the bed.

He wondered briefly if she was referring to an issue beyond the immediate prospect of intercourse. But then she held out the leather case, and he blandly said, "I don't mind."

"The procedure can be indelicate."

"So can a pregnancy."

"How nice you are, Mr. Braddock," she said, sitting on the bed. "I expect that special charm of yours partially accounts for all the women."

"This is new," he said, ignoring her reference, taking out the small rubber cervical cap.

"Are you surprised?" She'd moved closer to where he lay propped on one elbow, examining the device.

"Pleased, and don't ask me why. I don't know."

"I know I want to feel you inside me."

"We agree on everything," he said with a grin.

"Everything carnal."

"It's a start." He was smiling broadly. "We can reach agreement on the less important issues later.

Now, *mon ange,* if you'll just put your sweet body on these pillows, I'll see what I can do to accelerate this process."

Taking the rubber cap out of the case, he unscrewed the top on the small jar, dipped his finger into the ointment, lifted out a dollop of spermicide,[10] and began spreading the white cream inside the Dutch cap.

"How proficient you are."

He looked up, thinking if anyone should be nettled, it was he. "Doesn't Bertie do this?" he neutrally asked, controlling his temper.

"Not as deftly." Mockery flavored her words.

"I've probably had more practice," Kit lazily replied. "But then again—" He shrugged with Gallic irony. "Should we compare records?"

"I don't know what I'm doing here," Angela pettishly murmured.

"You mean you don't care to admit what you're doing here, *mon ange.* We're both here for the same thing." And replacing the jar lid, he shoved it back into the leather pouch and set it aside. Delicately placing the greased Dutch cap on Angela's stomach, he said, "Don't move," and rolling over on the bed, he reached down to the floor for his shirt in order to wipe his fingers.

As he picked up his shirt, a small golden ball lying beneath was exposed. It must have fallen from the drawer Angela had upended, and then rolled under his shirt, he decided—and despite an immediate cautionary injunction to restraint, his temper flared.

Closing his fingers around the golden sphere, he rolled back into a sitting position on the bed and, holding the gleaming ball delicately between his thumb and forefinger, sardonically said, "Would you like to use this too?"[11]

"I don't think we'll need it," she coolly answered.

"You're right." His voice was brusque and conclusive, but he held it still, twirling the shiny globe lightly between his fingers. "Perhaps you use this with smaller men."

"My life is my own."

"Yours and all the gossips."

"Then ask them about that. I'm not about to discuss it."

"Show me how it fits."

"No." But the thought excited her.

"There should be another one. Should I find it?"

"No," she said again, because he was too moody already, and if he looked, he'd find more than another gold ball.

"What else is there?" he murmured, as if reading her mind.

"Nothing," she lied, his formidable size suddenly taking on ominous proportions.

"These little monks have seen a thing or two, I don't doubt," he softly said, his gaze swiftly raking the painted headboard before returning to her face. "Do you ever feel inhibited?"

"I'm not religious."

"Just sexually active."

"Like you."

His smile was without humor. "That much?" he murmured.

"It wasn't meant literally. I'm not in your class, Mr. Braddock. Would you rather call this off?"

"Not at all. On the contrary . . ." His smile was wolfish. "I look forward to the diversity of your interests." And leaning over, he gently spread her legs and slipped the golden ball between the moist lips of her vagina. "We'll start with this," he said, delicately stroking her pouty labia so she felt the solid shape of the precariously lodged sphere. "Lie still now, or you'll lose the sensation and this, too," he added, touching the Dutch cap lying on her stomach.

"I should say no," she whispered, the aftermath of his touch still tingling through her senses, the cool metal warming in her body.

"But you can't," he accurately noted. "Wait for me now," he smoothly murmured, knowing she would, knowing he wouldn't let her leave should she wish, and rising from the bed, he walked over to the door and locked it.

"You needn't do that," Angela said.

"Just in case," Kit quietly replied, his tone of voice authoritarian despite its mildness, his powerful body large in the intimate dimensions of the room.

"No one will come." He walked like a predatory animal, she thought, watching him cross the room to the bed.

"I know that."

And the obverse need for a locked door sent a frisson down her spine. But she wouldn't allow her fear to show, and she said instead, imperious and direct, "Are you dangerous?"

"Not to you."

"I'm relieved," she sarcastically observed.

"Not yet, *mon ange,*" he pleasantly said, "but you will be."

"Such arrogance."

"Hardly. You're so primed, darling, even Bertie, inept as he is, could bring you to climax."

"You *are* arrogant."

"I've seen our exhibitionist heir to the throne in action in the brothels. It's an observation only, but"— his smile was as audacious as his sizable erection— "you'll find *me* more satisfying."

The bed dipped under his weight, and for the first

time Angela found herself glancing at the faces of the monks painted on the footboard of the bed, almost expecting their eyes to be trained on her. For in terms of shameless effrontery, she felt sure Kit Braddock was not only accomplished but inspired.

"Now, then," he conversationally said, lying down beside her. "Let's see what we can do about ending your long period of carnal inactivity. You shouldn't have to wait for weeks," he murmured, trailing a finger slowly over her collarbone as she trembled beneath his touch, her senses inflamed, a tantalizing excitement possessing her body. "You're almost distraught." His voice was lazy and low, his slender fingers tracing a path downward over the fullness of one breast, stopping to gently caress the taut crest of her nipple.

She shuddered at his touch, so near to orgasm after all the titillating sexual play, she could almost feel his words drifting over her flesh.

"We'll save this for later," he said, lifting the creamed cap from her belly, reaching across her to place it on the bedside table. "You're hot," he whispered, easing back into his lounging posture at her side, her skin degrees warmer than his. Bending his head, he licked at her nipple, the wetness cool for a moment only until his lips closed over the turgid crest, and just as he exerted pressure with his mouth, so she felt the exquisite heat slide downward, his fingers slipped inside her and he pushed the golden ball upward, past her velvety folds and slick tissue, plunging it so deep, she screamed with the exquisite pleasure. And just as her heated cry died away in a lingering fragment of sound, he pressed upward a small distance more into the shuddering, gorged recesses of her body, and she felt her orgasm begin.

"No . . . ," she whimpered, wanting him in-

stead, wanting to feel the ultimate, unparalleled sensation.

"You can't stop it, *mon ange,*" he whispered,
shifting his position, his breath warm on her cheek.
"Kiss me now, so I can feel it, too." And as the thrilling rapture exploded within her, she felt his mouth on
hers, gentle, soothing, indelibly sweet.

Sometime later, when her eyes opened to Kit's beguiling gaze, she whispered, "I wanted *you.*"

"Your body was impatient," he pleasantly said, at
his ease beside her, lounging on one elbow.

"You're very seductive," she murmured, smiling
up at him, all rosy pink and flushed.

"*You're* very small," he softly said, sliding his palm
over her mons.

The weight of his hand ignited a flurry of lambent
heat, and reaching up for him, she laced her arms
around his neck and pulled his head down for a kiss.
"I haven't even felt you inside me yet, and I feel sublime," she purred, kissing him with an engaging happiness. "You have to stay," she murmured as she
released his mouth. Her blue eyes were aglow with
passion.

"I will."

"You have to stay a long time."

"A very long time," he softly agreed.

"I've never tingled like this in my fingers and toes;
I'm shaking because I want you so—look," she said,
both wistful and enticing, sitting up abruptly, holding
out her small hands.

She looked very young in the firelight, her pale
hair a ruffled halo of curls, her cheeks flushed, her
long-lashed eyes wide with appeal.

"I like you trembling for me," Kit whispered,
lightly touching her hands.

"Don't make me wait any longer," she pleaded.

His own sensations were unique in this secluded house miles from where he should be. And while he couldn't deny his lustful need for her, Countess Angel stirred other feelings equally intense. "I'll never make you wait," he softly murmured, bringing her fingers to his lips. And then, moving from his reclining pose, he gently lowered her onto the bed and reached for the Dutch cap.

"I can't look," she whispered, shutting her eyes.

He laughed. "How chaste you are. The monks are even blushing."

Her eyes snapped open, and she scanned the nearest painted scenes.

"They don't *really* mind, darling," Kit said with a smile, completely at ease with the small rubber cap balanced between his fingers, as if he were always nude in her bedroom, ready to accommodate her.

"I shouldn't be so self-conscious."

"At least not with me," he softly said, charmed by the tender girl beneath the celebrated inamorata.

"I'll try not to."

"You could keep your eyes open," he teased.

She made a small moue. "Must I?"

"Try," he gently said.

"You're enchanting, you know," she murmured, her mouth curving into a glorious smile. "I'm absolutely intent on keeping you."

He grinned. "Then I'll expect an increase in wages."

"Anything," she expansively replied. "As long as I can have that."

"How nice," he pleasantly murmured, his gaze following hers to his pulsing erection. "We're in accord."

"Do you think my guests would miss me for a few

days?" she whispered, her attention absorbed by Kit's beautifully endowed sex.

"You can't afford the scandal, *mon chou*," he gently noted, feeling oddly protective of her, as if she were too vulnerable in her passions, and ironically, for a man of his dissolute appetites, he was the voice of reason. "But they won't miss you tonight," he soothed. "Now, lift up a little," he said, "and we'll put this pillow under your bottom."

She felt the pulsing begin deep inside her as though his softly spoken directive had turned on a libidinous switch. And when she felt the pillow slide beneath her and he murmured, "That's a good girl," she would have willingly ordered her guests out of her house to have the promise in his voice fulfilled.

He helped her settle comfortably on the white lace-trimmed cushion, smoothing her thighs open with a warm palm, adjusting her legs so she was offered to him resplendent and flaunting. And with smooth finesse he extracted the golden ball from her vagina. "I'll find the other one and have you wear them for tea one day," he quietly said, placing the sphere coated with her secretions on the bedside table. "And I'll watch you come while we drink our tea."

"Could I have you afterward?" The timbre of her voice was diffident.

"Of course, that's why I'm here at Easton. To see that you're always orgasmic and filled with sperm. So we need this inside you," he said, holding up the Dutch cap. "Look, now, I'm going to put it in." And leaning forward, he delicately parted her labia. "Can you see?"

Ensconced on a sea of lacy pillows, like a pampered harem beauty, she felt as though she were in a fantastical world of voluptuary feeling, rich, raw, and so acute, she could only nod to his question.

"You seem to be ready for intercourse," he murmured, his fingers covered with her pearly fluid.

"Please put the cap in," she breathed, all sensation focused in the pulsing core of her body.

"Even while you're looking?"

She nodded, frantic for him.

"And then what, my lady?" he softly asked, watching a drop of translucent white liquid slide over his knuckle.

"Then make love to me. Hurry, please. Or give the cap to me and I'll do it myself." She no longer cared about awkwardness or decorum, so desperate was she to feel him.

"I'll do it. In your impatience, you might not insert it properly, and you could become pregnant with my child." His voice dropped to a husky murmur. "We wouldn't want that, now, would we?"

A fevered thrill coursed through her, a fierce and inflammable wanting so reckless, she shivered.

"You wouldn't stay," she whispered, her eyes wanton blue.

"You don't know that." His deep voice held an irrepressible heat, a kind of madness infusing his soul.

"No . . ." A whisper of agony.

Her lamentation like a knife blade of cold reason to his confounded senses.

"Hush, darling," he soothed, selfish pleasure too long his raison d'être for reckless feeling to hold sway. "It's only play."

It was voraciously more to the beautiful woman who until tonight had always regarded lust as delicious but never desperate. "Kit, I'm dying," Angela implored, her hips moving in irrepressible, feverish yearning.

Would she take him without the protection of the Dutch cap? he wondered, intemperance briefly appropriating his mind. Was she so hot, she'd willingly risk all? And for a moment, the violence of his need to possess her completely overwhelmed reason, and he understood why so many men worshiped at her feet. He was no exception to her provocative appeal as she lay before him with her thighs spread and her sweet cunt unabashedly wet in welcome, her dainty form strangely titillating, her froth of platinum hair almost doll-like in its silken splendor, the girlish image enough to satisfy the palate of the most jaded rake. But her full breasts and narrow waist, the soft curves of her hips and thighs were flauntingly female, overlaying the childlike image with a flagrant sensuality. As if Meissen had crafted a salacious version of their precious shepherdess maids.

And he couldn't resist the celebrated Countess Angel any more than other men could turn away from such ripe, fulsome sexuality in rut.

Nor would he chance paternity on a brute whim.

So with speedy dispatch and the proficiency of much practice, he slid the Dutch cap up her sleek passage, easing it into place with his middle finger, adjusting it swiftly with a sweeping fingertip around the rim so it rested snugly over her cervix.

Then, pulling the pillow away from under her hips, he settled between her legs with the smooth facility of confirmed habit and, guiding the head of his erection, entered her. Cautious of her diminutive size, he eased forward slowly.

Until she gasped.

And only half-sheathed, he lay still inside her while she clutched at his shoulders, delicately impaled, quivering between pleasure and pain.

He kissed her gently then, young-boy kisses, soothing kisses, warm, forbearing kisses, until he felt the reluctant tissue yield and melt around him. She sighed sweetly as he glided forward a small distance more, surrendering to the luxurious ravishment with a soft, delicious moan. With discipline and infinite care, he slowly moved in and as gently out again in a prudent, repetitive flux and flow, stretching her, exerting pressure sideways at times, insinuating his enormous length into her tightness gradually until he was completely embedded at last. And stretched deliciously taut, tantalized and overpowered, she shuddered under his hands.

"Am I hurting you?" he whispered, buried to the hilt, quiescent.

Her arms tightened around him in answer, and he dared to move, withdrawing slowly and then as slowly driving full stretch into her.

She whimpered.

He hastily withdrew.

"No, no," she breathed, raising her hips, drawing him back, the pressure of her hands forceful. "There, there-oh-there," she whispered as he sank back inside her.

She was wet and fiery hot around him and yet so tight, he continued to move with discretion, not allowing himself to thrust forward with any force. He found the restraint itself oddly erotic, as if her fragility accentuated the intrinsic power of his erection, as if she were in carnal bondage to him.

And for the first time in her life the most exalted, desired beauty of her day tamely yielded herself completely to a man, enslaved by the delicious sensation of ravishment heating her body to tinder point. Almost faint from the agonizing delirium, she willingly served as receptacle for Kit Braddock's flagrant sex.

"More," she begged, her nails scoring deep into his back, her body so flame hot she could no longer

distinguish individual sensations from an all-encom-
passing need for consummation.

For a second Kit debated his response, not sure he
was capable of unlimited restraint.

"Please, please, please . . ." Her voice was hysterical.

Another second passed, then two as he struggled
to curb his overwrought libido.

"Kit . . . ," she softly wailed.

Perhaps he'd been celibate too long, or then
again, maybe he'd never been celibate enough.
Quickly bracing his feet, he took a small futile breath
of restraint, grasped her shoulders, and whispering
"I'm sorry," recklessly plunged forward.

Her wild cry echoed in the monk's chamber under
the eaves, but in the grips of his own savage compul-
sions, he moved by instinct alone, unhearing, driving
in over and over again, penetrating without caution or
constraint, each stroke driven by the entire force of his
lower body.

"Oh, God," she whimpered as the killing pleasure
hammered her senses, as her orgasm burst through her
mind and nerves and quivering hot center of her body.
"Oh God, oh God, oh God . . ." The feverish beautiful agony spread, unfolded, stretched in excruciating
ecstasy.

The little monks would appreciate her piety, Kit
drolly thought, a faint smile flickering over his counte-
nance as he heedlessly plunged deep inside her again,
his own style of savage epiphany overwhelming his
senses. Shutting his eyes, he ignored the harsh cut of
Angela's nails in his back, disregarded her breathless
cries echoing in his ears, and, meeting her violent climax, poured out great convulsive rivers of sperm,
finding glorious surfeit at last in Countess Angel's
temptress body.

—

*M*oments later, still agitated and restless, his breathing as turbulent as his emotions, Kit brushed Angela's mouth in a tender kiss and, lifting himself away, sprawled facedown beside her.

"Oh, my God," she whispered, horrified at the sight of blood on his back. "You're bleeding."

He opened his eyes at her exclamation and, turning his head the minimum distance to see her, smiled in reassurance. "It's nothing."

She began to move. "I'll get some water to wash—"

In a flashing movement he stopped her, the flat of his palm hard on her stomach. "I'm . . . fine," he murmured, his breathing still ragged.

She was no different from Olivia, she thought, overcome with remorse. "I'm so sorry," she said, regret liquid in her voice. "I feel terrible."

His head moved in faint negation as he lay on the pristine-white linen trying to catch his breath, his sweat-sheened body gleaming in the firelight. "You don't . . . feel terrible," he faintly replied. Her soft flesh beneath his hand was warm and heated, triggering unquiet, susceptible emotions, his desire for her still rampant. His palm slid downward, over her blond silken curls, then lower until the heel of his hand cupped her sperm-wet labia. "You feel . . . luscious."

Her eyes went shut as though closing off the exquisite sensations from the world, and she groaned, luxurious pleasure seeping languidly upward from the inexorable pressure of his palm.

"Do you still want me?" he whispered, gently massaging the sensitive flesh.

"Always," she whispered, not understanding her

sense of utter submission, only feeling the heated sorcery.

His fingers slipped inside her, and she shuddered as a raw, acute ecstasy surged through her body. It was too soon, she was too sore, then limitless bliss melted through her senses, and trembling, she forgot all else but the gratifying enchantment.

She was incarnate sensuality, he thought, a tropical heat of a woman, eternally receptive. And he wanted her with an uncurbed appetite, as if he'd not just climaxed moments ago, as if her lubricated passage sleek around his fingers were a magnet to his intemperate desire. Gently withdrawing his fingers, he slid them damply up her body, touched her mouth gently so she opened her eyes, and softly said, "I'm coming in."

"I can't say no." A tremulous bewilderment echoed in her words.

"You're not allowed to say no," he murmured, his eyes like green fire, and he moved quickly between her legs, his erection so rigid and aroused, he wondered whether she was indeed some magical temptress.

Without preliminaries, he drove in.

Her cry this time was one of genuine pain.

And he fell away instantly, her tightness unmistakable.

"How can I want you . . . even now," she whispered, gazing up at him as he balanced above her, her pulsing body blithely immune to the limits of her tender, swollen flesh.

"You can't," he gently said, leaning down to kiss her tenderly. "I won't let you." And rolling onto his back with only a transient twinge of pain, he gathered her into his arms. "I'm here for more than tonight," he murmured, adjusting her comfortably against him

"Tell that to my unbridled lust. I'm addicted."

"I'll indulge your addiction later, *mon ange*. Do you think I want you to be in pain?"

Tucked under the curve of his arm, his large, warm body comforting, she wanted to say, "Let me stay here always," the feeling extraordinary, unprecedented for a woman who valued her independence above all things, the rare emotion so intense, she felt shakily close to tears. Biting her bottom lip, she tried to repress the wetness welling in her eyes, thinking how embarrassed she'd be, thinking too about the transience of love affairs and all the wasted lives she knew. But the rare measure of contentment she felt in the arms of this man, who was notorious for the number of women in his life, also gave rise to her tears. The absurdity of her feelings, like those of a lovesick young girl. She could no more stay with him than fly to the moon.

The firelit room blurred before her eyes.

And the first tear spilled over.

He noticed immediately, the wetness cool on his skin, and shifting her in his arms so he could see her face, he softly said, "How badly are you hurt?" His brows were drawn together, his eyes were filled with self-reproach. "I knew this was going to happen. You should have pushed me away, you should have stopped me—"

She touched his troubled brow. "I didn't want you to stop," she gently said. "I'm not crying because of that."

He went very still. "What did I do?"

"You didn't do anything except make me feel more pleasure than I've ever felt before."

His shadowed gaze was puzzled. "That's why you're crying?"

She nodded, tears suddenly streaming down her cheeks in a flood.

He gently wiped away the wetness with a corner of the sheet. "You're not sad?"

She shook her head and cried harder.

Lifting her into his arms, he swiftly rose from the bed and, grabbing the coverlet half-draped on the floor, strode over to a chair near the fire. Sitting down, he arranged her in the folds of the quilt so she was tucked in warm as a baby, wiped her tears again, and holding her close, said, "If you tell me, I'll solve whatever's making you cry."

"You . . . can't," she whispered in a hiccupy breath.

He bent his head so she saw the intensity in his gaze. "I can do anything."

"You can't change . . . the world."

"I can change a lot of it."

She shrugged in a small, futile gesture and, brushing her eyes with her fingers, purposefully said, "I'm better." She took a deep breath. "Men dislike crying women. Forgive me."

She could have been an actress, he thought, so sudden was her transformation, but he detected an intrinsic resilience beneath her casual disclaimer. As if the young girl inside her was remembering childhood remonstrances of accountability and good breeding.

"You were crying the first night I met you," he reminded her.

"How embarrassing it must have been for you."

"Only at first."

"You see."

"But this is different."

"It isn't, though." And despite her sternest admonitions, she couldn't keep her lip from quivering.

"It is," he gently said. "Even if you've avoided me and all the repercussions until now."

"There won't be any repercussions."

"There will be. I'm not in the habit of casually asking women to marry me."

"Please, Kit, don't make me cry again."

"So you know this isn't just another . . . heated liaison."

"Of course it is," she resolutely said. "What else could it possibly be?"

"I don't care if you're married."

"Maybe I do." She could see the hundreds of disapproving Lawton faces going back into history, her mother's in the forefront, and of course the ultimate blockade—Brook.

"Then I'll change your mind."

She sighed. "How nice it would be if it were that simple."

"Leave it to me," he simply said, and smiled.

His smile could banish the gloom from the entire world, she thought. It could almost make her feel as though he were right. "Let's argue about this impossibility some other time," she said with a tentative smile, testing her restored composure, anxious to avoid a deadlock issue. "And since we *are* involved at the moment in a 'heated liaison,' I'd like to discuss that instead."

"What would you like to discuss?" he pleasantly said, willing to accommodate her conversational shift. "You're not entirely capable of a heated *anything* right now, darling."

" 'Entirely,' perhaps, is the operative word, Mr. Braddock," she replied, her voice rich with innuendo.

"Ah . . . you mean some less uncomfortable alternative."

"Would you mind? I have this overwhelming addiction to your touch, your body, your exquisite competence. And despite even floods of tears, my carnal urges are unquenched."

"It looks as though I'm going to have to stay *real* close to you, Countess," he said in a lazy drawl, "seeing as how you have these unquenchable desires and I'm jealous as hell."

"They're only for you."

"Pardon me," he said, infinitely polite, "if I'm slightly suspect."

"You don't believe me?"

"Let's just say you've built a distinguished reputation, and it hasn't been for needlework." His smile was delectable.

"No one else ever mattered."

"Thank you," he softly said. And at least for that moment he wanted to believe her.

And before long Angela was quenching a portion of her insatiable desire for Kit Braddock as she lay on the bed enjoying the talented ingenuity of his mouth and tongue and fingers on that part of her anatomy too swollen and tender for more strenuous activity. Just looking at him kept her passions burning high, or more aptly, the tantalizing sight of his permanently aroused erection *and* his well-trained skills brought her to climax twice more before she said, "How unselfish you are. Let me now."

The sun was beginning to lighten the morning sky when he died away into her mouth for the last time, and drawing her up to lie on his chest, he kissed her wet lips. "Come away with me," he softly said.

"And if I do?" How could she even think such a thought? she wondered as her words echoed in her ears.

"I'll make you happy."

"I'd like that. But—"

"No *but*'s this morning," he genially said. "Only *yes*'s and submission."

"Yes, then, yes, yes, yes, yes, yes." Unalloyed joy shone in her eyes.

"I'll make Baby May happy, too."

"Please don't get serious."

"Then I won't tell you when I'm serious."

She ruefully smiled. "Then I'll survive knowing you," she quietly said.

*H*e washed her before she left, like a perfect lady's maid or a perfect lover, taking caution with her tender bottom, gently drying her, helping her dress in a fresh gown from her wardrobe tucked under the eaves. And admitting his lack of competence when it came to coiffeurs, he politely handed her the pins as she put up her hair.

"I don't mind doing my hair if you do everything else," she teased as he stood beside her in front of the mirror.

"My pleasure, ma'am," he replied with a dazzling grin. "Come back soon."

And he walked her to the border of the main grounds, standing with her at the end of the beech allée as the sun rose in glorious splendor over Easton's facade. He kissed her good-bye under the old towering trees, a lingering, gentle kiss that had none of last night's torrid passion.

"You have to go," he whispered at last.

"I have to go."

But neither moved.

He broke away first, setting her from him and turning her toward the house. "Go," he said, "before I keep you here forever."

"I'll come back as soon as I can," she promised, gazing at him over her shoulder. He was barefoot in the dew-wet grass, and half-undressed as he'd been last night, and so elegantly beautiful and powerfully masculine, she understood why legions of women loved him.

"I'll be here."

She turned twice to wave at him, and when she turned the third time, he'd disappeared.

But he watched her until she entered the house.

13

Slipping in through a terrace door, Angela returned to her room, changed into a nightgown, and slept briefly before her daughter came in for breakfast. When May left with Bergie to go down to the stables for her morning pony ride, Angela said to Nellie, "Tell Millie I'm going to sleep late but I'll be down for luncheon." It wasn't unusual for ladies at a country house party to stay in their rooms in the morning; her absence wouldn't be remarked on. "Wake me at eleven," she added. "I'll bathe and dress then. I think the peach organza with the tucked bodice will do nicely today. Isn't it a gorgeous morning, Nellie?"

"It's a lovely day, my lady. But it's always lovely at Easton."

"Isn't it, though?" Angela said with a sigh of contentment.

"Now, you get some rest, my lady. We don't want any dark circles under your eyes." Nellie had been personal maid to Angela since her adolescence, and she treated her with the familiarity of a longtime family retainer.

"I'm *really* happy, Nellie," Angela blithely declared, tossing her peignoir onto a chair. "It's a wonderful feeling."

"It is indeed, my lady," Nellie cordially agreed, pleased to see her mistress in such high spirits. The entire staff wished her more happiness; her dreadful marriage was often discussed below stairs, particularly on those occasions when the Earl de Grae would appear to cause havoc in the household. "Now, you shut your eyes, and I'll close your curtains and see that no one disturbs you until eleven."

*W*hile Angela slept, Kit was on his way back from the inn in Easton Vale, having ridden there directly after Angela had left. He needed a bath and a change of clothes among other things, and he would have found it impossible to sleep anyway. The early-morning ride was refreshing, the scented air smelling of fresh-cut hay, the temperature pleasantly cool in the shaded lanes. Easton was situated in beautiful country, he thought, gazing out over the bucolic farmlands stretching away into the distance. Peaceful and untouched, as if time had passed it by.

After stabling his horse in the meticulously restored stable block, he strolled through the kitchen garden and entered the house from the back. Although the kitchen was empty, he discovered a steaming loaf of bread on the table, and a pot of tea in a knit tea cozy beside it, along with a stoneware jug of strawberry jam he dipped his finger inside to taste. He'd already found the well-stocked larder before he left, not sure if he should eat at the inn. Apparently a discreet staff saw to the upkeep of Stone House.

A fire had been freshly laid in the parlor, he noted, as he moved through the first-floor rooms on his way to the bedroom to deposit his traveling bag. The umbrella was gone from the hall console, replaced by a bouquet of delphinium and lilies. And when he opened the bedroom door, the disordered room he'd left short hours ago was immaculate. He wondered what had happened to the golden ball on the night table.

Dropping his bag onto the chair by the door, he walked over to the newly made bed, the lavender scent of fresh bed linen fragrant, the lace-trimmed pillow covers new and unwrinkled, the coverlet embroidered in daisies today, not bluebells.

Curious, he began pulling out the armoire drawers, searching for the golden ball. He found it in the second drawer on the right, along with its lost partner, both gleaming clean and ready for use. He found, too, as he continued looking through the drawers, a multitude of sex toys, each carefully wrapped in white silk. And with a measure of annoyance he wouldn't have been able to explain satisfactorily, he took them all out and lined them up on the dresser top.

Angela de Grae certainly wasn't the usual inhibited Victorian wife.

*A*fter being wakened at eleven, Angela first retired to her dressing room to remove the Dutch cap. With alarm, she discovered it had been partially dislodged, and a sinking feeling settled in her stomach as she slipped it out. Kit was too large, she was too small, and a twinge of panic assailed her, for she knew she wanted to make love to him, not just now, but every minute he was at Easton—the extent of her desire beyond anything she'd ever known. Beyond reason and prudence—all-consuming.

They should use condoms[12] as an alternative, but

she didn't have any, the cervical cap having always been her contraceptive of choice, since she preferred being in control of her own future. And she couldn't ask one of her servants to go to the village chemist for condoms—if he even stocked them. Damn!

Walking into her adjoining bath, where Nellie waited with her hot tub, she debated the limited choices at her disposal that weekend. She wouldn't even see Kit until tonight, so this evening would be hindered. Kit could go to the chemist on Saturday, but whether he'd be able to purchase condoms in a sleepy little village was moot and not her area of expertise. Sinking into the soothing water, she closed her eyes and wished her problem away. But the seriousness of the consequences continued to plague her mind. She couldn't risk getting pregnant. Brook had been dangerously difficult about her last pregnancy. And if he hadn't known without a doubt it was his—as he did, for the events of May's conception were horrific—she would have been in grave danger.

He was obsessed with family bloodlines, the Greville heritage a point of honor with him. How strange, when he had no honor. But, then, Brook wasn't entirely rational, as she'd learned too late. Married at seventeen to a man her mother and stepfather had selected for her, pregnant a month after the wedding, she'd discovered the first Christmas season of their marriage, when she was already heavy with child, that her husband had a streak of cruelty her father-in-law calmly referred to as Brook's "unfortunate appetite."

Arriving home a day early from a dress fitting in London that long-ago Christmas, she'd found him whipping a young maid, the screams from his bedchamber too violent to ignore. She'd fainted at the sight that met her eyes when she'd opened the door.

And when she'd packed and left that very night, neither her family nor his had seemed surprised by his actions. She'd felt as though she'd been a human sacrifice sent forth in ignorance by both families.

And when she threatened to divorce him, she discovered she didn't have sufficient grounds. She could sue him only on the grounds of bigamy or severe cruelty. Conversely, with the prevailing double standard, if Brook chose to divorce her, she risked never seeing her child. Her solicitor had also explained to her that the law allowed her husband to imprison her, if he wished, to force her to cohabit with him. Newly in charge of her fortune now that she was married, she'd been shocked at the limited range of a wife's freedom. But ultimately her wealth had protected her and her marriage settlement—a fixture of all aristocratic marriages—and the fact that women's property rights were newly won in Britain's Parliament. So she'd bartered her freedom for a large yearly payment to the Grevilles.

But one was never completely secure against Brook. And his family couldn't always control his conduct.

So she was vitally concerned about a pregnancy; she always had been.

$\mathcal{L}$uncheon was served on the terrace, the weather perfection, the last days of August sunshiny, indolent days—the sleepy aftermath of a heated summer. The alfresco meal had the colorful display of a stage set, beautifully dressed women in all the hues of the rainbow, lavish arrays of food and flowers spread down the long linen-draped table, laughing conversation and sparkling wine.

And a hostess at the head of the table who outshone the sun.

"Does she use rouge and paint, Mama?" Priscilla petulantly asked, gazing at Angela's glowing good looks, her toilette of peach organza accentuating her pale hair and blushing complexion.

"It's the cut of her gown, darling," Charlotte commented. "It has a schoolgirl simplicity. And Worth's fabrics are so dear, they make any complexion radiant." But beneath her casual disclaimer, Charlotte scrutinized the dazzling image of their hostess, more fair and comely than usual. Could it be the golden sunlight?

"The rest did Angela good," Millie remarked to her sister, who sat beside her at the opposite end of the informally arranged table.

"She's always happiest at Easton," Dolly said.

"And safe from Brook."

"At least safer." Dolly signed. "He's such a cruel man."

"You'd think he'd come to a brutal end soon with all his dissolute activities."

Dolly leaned closer to her sister. "Carsons tells me he was found in some stew in Seven Dials trying to buy a young girl," she whispered, her eyes round with horror. "Can you imagine! Someone called a constable, there was a terrible blowup, his solicitor came to take him home, and everything was hushed up as usual."

"Sutherland thinks Angela should force the issue of divorce, but I told him she's in actual danger from Brook. He doesn't understand, of course—but, then, he doesn't really know Brook."

"I feel so sorry for her."

"Apparently you don't have to today," Millie reminded her. "She's in fine spirits."

—

*A*fter luncheon the party went off to a variety of pursuits—croquet, lawn tennis, riding, bridge—and Angela left to spend some time with May.

"Go boat wide," May insisted when Angela arrived in the nursery, the small lake on Easton one of the young child's favorite haunts. "Peter Wabbit go too."

So they set off down the path to the lake hand in hand, discussing who was going to row the boat.

"Me, me, me!" May insisted, her piping small voice filled with elation. "Let me!"

"Should we take turns?"

"No, me! Mama sit wit Peter Wabbit."

"I'll help if you get tired."

"Me no tired." The little two-year-old vigorously shook her blond curls. "Me no tired no more ever."

"I'll just rest, then," Angela said with a smile.

"You sweep. Me row."

And it was settled.

The lake was placid as a mirror, the small boat of immense pleasure to May, who proudly rowed them around in circles five feet from the shore. When her little face was red from exertion, Angela coaxed her into releasing the oars briefly and spelled her for a short interval. The routine was repeated several more times until May tired of the exercise and Angela rowed them back to shore.

As the small boat slid up the grassy embankment and May scrambled out, Angela's eyes lifted to follow her daughter onto the shore, and she saw Kit standing quietly in the shadows of a towering cypress.

He was dressed in croquet whites as if he'd just come off the lawn in front of the house. And she thought him perfectly beautiful in white linen trousers and shirt.

He didn't move until she beckoned him forward, and as he walked out of the cool shadows, he said, "I was content to watch you."

"While I'm only content eating you alive," she whispered, touching his arm lightly in lieu of throwing herself at him.

"Later," he murmured with a smile before sliding a glance toward May. She was intently digging a hole with a stick in a muddy depression a few yards down the shore. Turning his smile again on Angela, he quietly said, "Do you like my disguise?"

"You are perfectly house party. A fixture in the background."

"I came prepared."

"Did they feed you?"

"They?"

"The Stone House staff."

"I didn't see anyone to ask, but I'd already found the larder, and fresh bread and tea appeared as if by magic. Discretion apparently is their byword."

"I prefer not having staff under foot."

"I imagine you do," he softly said. "I found all the toys, nicely washed and put away."

"Please, Kit, don't start. You don't own my past."

He gazed out over the lake for a moment as though some answer to his grudging resentment existed in its placid depths. "You're right," he quietly said on a small exhalation. "Another Worth gown, I see," he pleasantly added. "His elegance is unmistakable."

"Friends?" she whispered, touching his fingertips gently.

"Of course." His hand curled around hers briefly,

and his smile warmed her heart. "Now, am I going to meet May?"

Angela introduced Kit as a friend, and within moments Kit had joined the young child in her play, helping her scoop away a channel through the squishy mud to let in water from the lake. Then they both worked on the construction of a dam wall for their new pond, discussing with great earnestness the best way to build it while Angela sat nearby and served as sounding board for all their ideas.

"He know lots, Mama," May exclaimed, patting the soft mud with vigor. "'Bout bwilding stuff. You real dood," she added, looking up at Kit with a smile.

"He is, isn't he?" Angela agreed, enchanted by the sweet picture of play. Brook would never have considered playing with the children. Nor would any of the aristocratic men she knew. And struck with a sudden small melancholy, she realized how much she'd missed of simple happiness in her opulent world.

"Come help us, Mama," Kit cheerfully coaxed. "We'll let you add this last section of dam, won't we?" he declared, looking to May for sanction.

"Here, Mama," May offered, indicating the portion with her muddy hand. "It's weally fun."

And when Angela joined them, she found herself transported to another world, the feel of the cool, wet mud delightful, the play lighthearted, the rare sense of family so different from the normal structure of her life. And when she lost her balance as she was reaching to stabilize her newly built dam wall and accidentally brushed against Kit, a warmth of extraordinary proportions filled her soul.

"Careful, Mama," he murmured, steadying her with the back of his hands that were still clean, his inflection on the appellation fraught with sensual undertones.

"I don't think I can be," she whispered, an instant rush of desire melting through her body.

"You have to," he softly said, carefully setting her away. "I think we're ready to sail some boats on this pond," he added in a conversational tone. "Have you ever built a boat, May?" he asked, snapping a small twig in two.

"Show me, show me!" Her attention was immediately focused on his activities, and she sat very still, watching him tie a small mast together with a long blade of grass.

After splashing their hands clean in the lake—a lengthy amusement in itself for Baby May—they sailed tiny twig boats with leaf sails on their pond, the diversion entertaining child and adults for so long that Bergie came looking for her charge.

Kit saw her first as she crested the rise between the house and the lake. "I should go," he quietly said.

"There's no need," Angela replied, placing her hand on his arm to keep him from rising.

"Another discreet servant?"

"They all are. Aren't yours?"

He grimaced. His were, of course, for all the obvious reasons that weren't supposed to apply to women, he thought moodily, with that streak of convenient masculine bias. "I thought this was supposed to be a man's world."

"It mostly is."

"Not mostly enough, apparently," he grumbled.

"I adore your jealousy."

"I hate it," he muttered.

"Bergie!" Baby May shrieked, catching sight of her nursemaid. Scrambling to her feet, she ran toward the young woman. "Come see! Come see! I's havin' fun!"

"She's just like you," Kit said, smiling at the sight of the toddler racing away to meet her nanny. "Enthusiastic."

"I'm like her when I have reason to be. You're one of my few reasons." She touched his hand as it lay on the grass, her wet fingerprint streaking the back of it.

"How long do I have to wait?" he asked, his voice subdued.

Angela glanced up the hill where Bergie was lifting May into her arms. "Probably till tonight."

"I like that 'probably.'"

"I *should* go back to my guests."

"Then again . . ." Kit murmured, husky and low.

"I almost came to you before lunch. The next three days are going to be"—she took a steadying breath—"very difficult."

"It sounds as if you need a rest this afternoon," Kit softly said.

"I shouldn't," Angela whispered, her gaze drifting down his chest to the juncture of his thighs.

"Just a short rest," he suggestively murmured, aware of her interested gaze. "Nobody would even miss you."

"Maybe they wouldn't," she tentatively replied, a warm flush pinking her cheeks.

"It's up to you," he said, his voice velvety soft. "Now here they come, Mama," he quietly added, his lush undertone suggestive of all the sweet fecundity of motherhood. "Take a deep breath."

And the following few minutes passed without any outward indication of the intimacy between Angela and Kit, thanks in large part to Kit's well-mannered urbanity. He helped May show Bergie how the boats sailed and then spoke to the young nursemaid in her native Swedish, asking her how she'd happened to arrive at Easton.

The young girl blushed and stammered at first, but Kit quickly put her at ease, and when she left some time later with May, she shyly waved at Kit and bid him *adjo* ("good-bye").

"How do you know Swedish?" Angela asked when May and her nanny had gone, curious at his fluency.

"I spent some time in Stockholm."

"An unusual place to stay," she said with a trace of mistrust.

"I had a friend who lived there."

"A female friend, no doubt."

"No. Is that better?" He didn't mention that Uma on the *Desiree* had helped refine his accent.

"Tell me about him."

"You don't trust me." His grin was lighthearted and shameless.

"Not for a second. Tell me."

"I met Harald in Tahiti; he was writing an article for a Paris art publication on Gauguin's last work. Since he was about to set sail for his home in Stockholm, he traveled with me. I was bound there to set up a small trading office. Is that satisfactory, my lady?" He sardonically finished.

"You actually work?"

"I own a moderate-sized shipping line."

"So Charlotte said, but that doesn't mean you necessarily participate in the business."

"Why wouldn't I?"

"Many men don't."

"If they're sensible, they do."

"Do you have other trading offices?"

"A few," he modestly said. Twenty-two at last

count; his first was in Macao, now moved farther inland to the more lucrative market at Canton.

"You surprise me."

"Because I work?"

"Because you don't give the appearance of work."

"My months at sea aren't exclusively for pleasure; the Eastern market, particularly, is volatile. I spend a lot of time in Asia. The burgeoning market in Africa is extremely profitable as well."

"Do you speak Chinese?"

"Five dialects, not nearly enough, but my manager at Pearl River is the consummate linguist; I rely on him to interpret the subtleties."

"I'm astonished." How different he seemed; how insular her own life by comparison. "Do you know Cecil Rhodes? He's a dear friend of mine. I spent my Scottish holidays with him last year."

"We do business from time to time. As an American with our own history of British colonialism, I have my misgivings about beneficent colonial rule, of course, but he's definitely made lucrative inroads into South Africa."

"He's become *very* wealthy."

"Wealthy enough to be Bertie's friend," Kit said with a quirked smile. The Prince of Wales allowed a select few millionaire businessmen into his circle despite the queen's old-fashioned reproaches about vulgar backgrounds. Bertie found that the ready availability of their financial resources far outweighed their common blood.

"Like you."

"Like me. But I haven't given him any money, nor will I. He has plenty enough for someone who simply breathes every day."

"You find a leisured life distasteful?"

"Only if it's taken seriously. I believe in working for a living."

"Is it enough to run an estate?" she provocatively said.

"If it's well-done," he succinctly answered.

"My grandfather taught me to take care that Easton thrived."

"With good results, it seems."

"I have two schools and a small sewing establishment for young women. My agricultural college for both men and women will open soon." She spoke with a spirit of pride.

"Bertie told me."

"He thinks I'm silly."

"Bertie doesn't understand social change."

"I had him talk to my friend W. T. Stead about the goals of the Socialist party, but Bertie was only polite."[13]

"I know."

"He scoffed, I suppose."

"Well, let's just say Bertie considers women principally as . . . diversions."

"While you don't?"

"Sometimes; not always. In your case, definitely not."

"How smoothly sweet you are, Mr. Braddock."

"Call me Kit," he said with a grin.

"I remember when you first said that."

"In your boudoir at Cowes."

"I wanted you very much that night."

"I could tell."

"And I thoroughly dislike Olivia, damn you."

"I share your aversion, darling, believe me."

"But you couldn't resist."

"I was deeply frustrated."

"Could I use that excuse some night?"

"As long as it's with me."

His tone of voice sent a shiver down her spine, the finality, the flat assertion, the sense of future she dared not think of. "Please kiss me," she whispered, because she wanted to wipe away the terror of the unknown, of the future they could never have. Because she could have him right now this minute, and the rest was too sad to contemplate.

"Someone might see."

She looked around and then, leaning close, touched her lips to his.

"You're reckless," he murmured, sliding his hands under her arms. "That must be why I love you." And rising, he pulled her to her feet.

"Say it again. Tell me you love me." A young-girl tremor quivered through her voice. She'd never wanted a man's love. But she did suddenly with fool-hardy desperation.

For a flashing second it seemed as if she could hear the grass grow, so silent was the lakeshore, and she wished to reclaim her foolish words.

"I love you," Kit quietly replied without inflection, simply and plainly. "I've never said that before," he softly added.

"Nor have I."

"You have to tell me, then. It's only fair."

"I don't know if I can."

"You don't know if you love me?"

"I don't know if I can say it."

"De Grae ruined so much for you."

"Yes," she whispered.

"Tell me you love me later," he gently declared. "I know you do."

She nodded, her eyes filled with tears. Those tears

made him want to kill de Grae for whatever he'd done to her.

Sliding a hand under her legs, he swung her up into his arms and held her close. "To hell with your house guests," he murmured. "You're coming with me."

14

He talked to her of May on the way back to Stone House, how clever she was, how articulate for a two-year-old, how pretty and vivacious, like her mother. He spoke of his trip up from London, too, and of the people he'd visited during the days after Morton Castle, his voice soothing, his manner comforting, never asking or expecting an answer, his monologue intended only to distract her from the melancholy of her thoughts.

And much later, as he carried her through the orchards behind Stone House, his praise for her restoration project warming her heart, Angela lifted her head from his shoulder and kissed his cheek. "Thank you," she said. "You always make everything better."

"Keep it in mind, darling," he replied with a smile, ducking his head under a low-hanging bough. "I can fix anything."

"Even my life?" Sorrow vibrated in her voice.

"Particularly your life, *mon ange.*" And he stopped for a moment under an apple-laden tree to kiss her. "Don't you know that's why I'm here?" he murmured when his mouth lifted from hers. "To make you happy."

"And doing a very fine job of it," she softly said.

"We try," he modestly declared with a thoroughly immodest grin.

Seconds later he pushed open the kitchen door and let them into the cool silence of the house. "There," he quietly said. "This is better than your house party. No one needs entertaining. Except me, of course," he added with a faint grin. "And I'm extremely easy to please. Let me make you a cup of tea," he suggested, placing her carefully on a sturdy chair near the table, her spirits, he thought, in need of reviving.

"You know how?" Her eyes looked huge in the sun-dappled interior.

"You don't?"

"No one ever showed me." An heiress from the cradle, kitchens were an unknown world.

"Then pay attention, sweet." And in a brief time he placed two cups of tea before them and sat down opposite her as though he'd been at home in her kitchen all his life.

"You amaze me," Angela said, the simple pleasure of watching Kit enough to cast away gloom.

"Isn't this better than your drawing room?"

"Infinitely. You're here." She felt an overwhelming contentment. "What am I going to do when you go?"

"Come with me, of course."

"You're a very impractical man."

"And you've been living in this sheltered world too long, *ma petit*. Now, drink your tea and then I'll give you a present."

Her eyes lit up. "I love presents."

"You're supposed to say something deprecating or at least ingratiating," he mockingly teased.

"Where is it?"

"That's not quite what the etiquette books suggest," he said with a grin, thinking her so much more charming than the Priscillas of the world who go through the pretense of refusal as they're stripping the jewelry from your grasp.

"There—I drank my tea." She briskly set her cup down.

"My lord, I didn't know you were so greedy."

"You didn't?" she noted, a teasing warmth in her voice.

"Well, about presents." He held out his hand across the worn wooden table. "Shut your eyes."

She did instantly as a child would and put out her hand, and he smiled, always charmed by the openness of her spirit.

She followed him, with her hand in his, through several of the downstairs rooms, and when he said, "You can open your eyes," she found herself in the room she used for an estate office. "Over there," he said, pointing at a small envelope on a table near the window.

She'd expected jewelry or some bibelot, the usual gift a man gives a woman. The small cream envelope looked mysterious lying on her writing table as she approached. It was addressed simply "Angela" on the outside, without endearment or flourish, in a hand she recognized from his previous note. She looked over at him before she picked it up, wondering if his expression would hold some clue, but he only smiled faintly and said, "Open it."

There was no waxed crest on the back; he hadn't even sealed it. She pulled out a small card with Kit's full name engraved in plain type on the front.

"Thomas Kitredge Braddock" suited him, she thought, sliding her finger over the raised print; it sounded solidly male. Lifting the flap, she read the note, his swift scrawl filling the small card.

> *A small present for the pleasure of your company. A Henry Watson design and rebuilding of the* Shark.
> *With love,*
> *Kit*

He'd given her a staggering gift, an American-millionaire kind of gift, she thought, all the stories of extravagant largess suddenly personalized. "It's wonderful," she softly said, running her thumb over the word "love." "But I can't accept it," she added with a small shake of her head. "It's too much." The cost of having the young Plymouth boat designer redo her yacht would be scandalous.

"Consider it a betrothal gift," Kit casually said. "I'm having the *Desiree* redesigned, too. I told him we'd be down to talk to him in the next fortnight."

"When did you tell him this?"

"I decide this morning. I telegraphed him; he telegraphed me and I him, et cetera, et cetera, although I'd already gone to talk to him after Morton Castle. Things were nicely stirred up at the railway station in Easton Vale this morning."

"You're too extravagant."

"We could race together when our yachts are finished. Have you ever been in the waters off Brisbane?"

She set the card down on the table. "Kit, we have to be sensible about this." She spoke in that polite, persuasive tone used with young children asking for the impossible. "I can't accept such an expensive gift, even though I adore your thoughtfulness. And I can't race with you in the outbacks of the world. I simply can't. Nor is there a betrothal, no matter how you tease."

"The *Shark* will run five knots faster when it's refurbished, maybe seven," he said as though she'd not mentioned major obstacles to his plans. But a man who'd staked claim to twenty-two trading depots in countries throughout the world wasn't likely to see a divorce as a hindrance. Nor a husband.

"You're not listening to me."

"I'm listening, darling. Just *think* about using Henry Watson. You don't have to decide right now. Discuss it with him when we go down to see him about the *Desiree*."

"You're asking too much of me," she quietly said. "I just want to make love to you. I can't change my entire life."

"Fine," he calmly said, shrugging as he did, with the merest lift of his shoulder. "Where would you like to make love?"

"Are you angry?"

"No, of course not. I know I'm asking a lot; what with aristocratic family tradition and society's conventions—"

"—and the fact that I'm married."

"Look, darling, I don't want to upset you, but you don't have a marriage."

"Kit!" she wailed.

He put up his hands in conciliation. "Let's not talk about this anymore. Come here," he cajoled, his voice low and hushed. "I haven't held you for at least ten minutes, and I'm going through withdrawal."

"Are you going to be reasonable now?" she said, gazing at him through narrowed eyes.

"Not completely," he pleasantly replied, immune

to her chastisement. "I thought I'd have you show me how some of those playthings upstairs operate."

"And if I don't want to?"

"How much time do we have?" he asked, ignoring her response.

She glanced at the small brass clock on the table and softly groaned. "I have to be back for tea."

"How long?"

"Maybe an hour. Oh, lord," she softly exclaimed. "Why is everything so complicated?"

"Smile, darling," he cajoled. "You're taking this all too seriously."

"And you're here to remind me it isn't serious."

"It's only a game, darling." One he intended to win, but he knew the advantages of a strategic retreat.

She smiled. "An amorous game."

"There," he said, smiling back at her and holding out his hand.

He kissed her in the office, and often as they slowly moved down the hallway, and with more difficulty on the stairs, although he was resourceful, and when at last, breathless with laughter and heated desire, they stood in the doorway of the bedroom, he stopped her from unbuttoning the tucked bodice of her gown.

"No," he softly said, holding both her hands in one of his. "Leave it on. There isn't time."

"You promised," she whispered, her body flushed with passion.

"I will."

"But you can't climax in me."

"I won't."

"I wasn't planning on seeing you this afternoon. I haven't a Dutch cap."

"I know."

"And you'll go to the village for condoms today?"

She'd explained between kisses on the stairs the magnitude of her problem.

"First thing afterward."

"Am I talking too much?"

"Not at all," he said with a grin. "I'm not easily distracted."

Her gaze fell to his erection lifting the pleated white linen of his trousers. "Can I have this now?" she whispered, touching him.

"Soon," he replied. "Look at this first." And guiding her over to the dresser, he said of the array of objects laying on white silk, "Pick one."

"I don't want to."

"I will, then," he calmly said as though her refusal were irrelevant, and reaching out to select a small tortoiseshell dildo, he slid it into his trouser pocket.

"These are all from a long time ago," she explained, not certain of his mood.

"I know. Humor me. And then the maids will have something to talk about tomorrow."

"They don't talk."

"Oh, yes, they do."

"How are you such an authority?"

"You don't want to know."

"It's something brazen, I suppose."

"Democratic, I'd say. Now, stand here, Angel," he said, indicating a position in front of the cheval glass, not about to discuss his particular experiences with maids and mistresses.

"You certainly charmed Bergie," she petulantly said, always nettled by his history of indiscriminate womanizing.

"I'm not going to talk about it," he calmly said, moving her with a gentle pressure on her arm until she stood before the mirror. "Now, lift up your skirts."

She hesitated, even as his directive stirred her

senses, his voice softly abrupt, commanding without undue volume, his eyes lazily half-lidded as though he were a casual participant.

"You don't have much time," he murmured, "if you want satisfaction." He turned his arm slightly to look at his watch.

"Will I have a turn to give orders?" she queried, raising her chin contentiously.

"No," he said, restive under his conflicting emotions. "Not with me." No one had a collection like the one on the dresser without using it, and contemplation of that fact put him out of temper. "Lift your skirts now, or you'll have to wait for me until tonight."

"Maybe I don't care."

"Or maybe you care *too much* about sex," he coolly said, touching the tips of her nipples prominent and visible beneath the delicate peach silk of her gown. "Or do these," he murmured, flicking the taut crests softly with his fingertips, "indicate indifference?"

"I'm sorry if I'm too sexual," she said, the aftermath of his touch trembling through her body as though he were individually caressing each heated cell.

"Sometimes I'm sorry, too." A lazy smile appeared on his handsome face. "But not right now. Come, darling," he softly ordered, indicating with a gesture of his hand that she raise her skirt.

And she obeyed because she wanted him. As she had this morning even as she'd left him, or when she'd slept or bathed or listened to her guests' idle gossip at lunch, or later at the lakeshore, and now with such raw longing she would have willingly done more than pull her skirts aside.

"Stand still while I take your drawers off," he calmly said as though he hadn't noticed her breathing had changed. And she held her skirt and petticoats

bunched at her waist, prey to an overpowering need
for him so wanton, no rationale existed to explain its
shocking violence. And she wondered inflamed, yet irrationally quickening at the disagreeable notion,
whether all the women he knew felt the same way.

His fingers were cool at her waist untying the rib-
bon to her drawers, as though his feelings were dispassionate while her skin was hot with feverish wanting.

And if she weren't so in need of him, she might
have taken issue with his detachment.

When the bow was undone, he let her drawers
slip down her legs and, dropping to one knee, lifted
her slippered feet one at a time to free them from the
lacy undergarment. Peach lace garters held up her
white silk stockings, and a lush expanse of tantalizing
thigh gleamed above her stocking tops. And higher yet
blond silken down and the delectable curve of her
hips and stomach.

"Look at yourself," he quietly directed, gently
stroking her mons hair. "See how beautiful you are,"
he murmured. And leaning forward, he kissed her
silken curls.

The erotic image in the mirror was distinctly pri-
meval male, purposeful, seductively resolute, in pursuit, Kit's auburn hair dark against her naked flesh, his
broad shoulders and athletic body barbaric in their
strength. Irrepressible need overwhelmed her mind,
flame-hot desire seeped inward from the heated pressure of his mouth, and when his tongue slid into her
pulsing cleft, her knees went weak at the flood of pleasure. His hands came up quickly to steady her, his
palms solid and strong on her thighs, and holding her
firmly, he delicately licked her clitoris with finesse and
consummate skill and such gentleness, she thought
him magically capable of climbing into the very heart
of her psyche.

"There, now," he said, easing away and rising a few moments later after she'd dreamily climaxed into the heat of his mouth. "Is that better?"

"In comparison to just about everything, yes," she softly sighed.

He laughed at her unguarded candor. "How easy you are to please," he said.

"And how well you do it," she faintly murmured, a luscious lassitude warming her senses.

"You can please *me* now," he gently said, kissing her cheek as she watched him in the mirror gracefully lean down to reach her.

"Anything," she whispered.

"This is very small," he noted, sliding the dildo from his pocket. "You'll hardly notice it," he murmured, slipping the polished head partially inside her. "Can you feel that?"

Her vaginal muscles contracted, anticipation instantly aroused, the word "penetration" suddenly flame hot in her blood, as if her mind were serving as seductive procuress for her senses.

"Answer me, darling," he murmured, sliding the cool instrument in another small distance. "Tell me how this feels."

It took a lingering moment to speak with the focus of her mind on nonverbal sensation, but she managed at last to articulate "Wonderful," in a delicious small sound, thinking too how good he smelled, like a shower-drenched forest, some unconnected portion of her mind finding favor with him quite separate from the carnal love she was feeling.

"Are you ready, then?" he unnecessarily said as her hips moved in heated response to the partially inserted dildo, and he slid it into her sleek passage, pressing it so deeply inside her, the small horned object disappeared entirely.

She pressed her thighs together to intensify the ravishing delight.

"Let me," Kit whispered, sliding his hand between her legs, slipping his fingers inside enough to exert pressure on the dildo. "You need me to help you, don't you?"

"Yes," she breathed, the sound drifting away because he knew how to move the small object in the most enticing rhythm, knew exactly where she was most susceptible to feeling. And she began to climax very soon again, as if she were no more than yielding flesh to his expertise, as submissive as his harem women, whom she pretended to scorn, as slavishly dependent on his touch.

She embraced him afterward, shameless in her affection, and pulling his face down, she rained sweet, ardent kisses on him. He was blissful enchantment and spectacularly indulgent to her, and she didn't care about anything but the delicious happiness he brought her.

And before long her grateful kisses turned seductive, the sway of her hips took on a bewitching rhythm, her murmurs were softly pleading. "I want to feel you, darling Kit. You promised . . ." A melting kiss, a small sigh of longing, her hand on his moving it over her breast. "Please, please, please," she implored.

"Soon," he promised, caressing the fullness of her breast, wanting to possess all her glorious abandonment for himself alone. "Walk with me in the garden first. You'll like the feel of this," he lightly pressed his hand between her legs, "when you walk." He wished to see her among her flowers, under the warm sun, in a public venue, knowing beneath the precious Worth gown and handmade lingerie, knowing deep inside her was the small tortoiseshell dildo he had put there, and she was moment by moment on the brink of orgasm. And only his.

"No," she protested, "not now, some other time," and grasping his hand, she began tugging him toward the bed.

"Now, if you were bigger, you could say no," he lightly noted, sweeping her into his arms.

She gasped at the stabbing pleasure as the dildo pressed deeply inside her, the solid strength of Kit's arm secure against her bottom.

"Feeling better?" he murmured, exerting pressure with his forearm against her pouty cleft.

She couldn't speak for a moment with the lush heat melting through her body, but when the stabbing pleasure had settled into a less breathless pulsing, she licked the lobe of his ear and softly said, "Will you lie with me in the grass?"

"My pleasure," he whispered, moving down the hall, kissing the tip of her nose. "And a dozen other places as well."

"Because you're staying," she sweetly murmured, logic always relegated to distant outlands when she was in his arms.

"Because I'm staying," he agreed, beginning to descend the stairs.

"Forever and ever . . ." She loved to hear the sweet, impossible words.

He smiled at her artless delight. "Always and always," he whispered.

She kissed him for his gratifying response, and he stopped at the bottom of the steps to kiss her back.

She clung unreservedly to him, her arms twined tightly around his neck, her gartered legs exposed with her skirts trailing over the newel, their kiss heated—in all a licentious display to meet Violet's startled gaze as she stood outside the glass-paned front door. "Angela!" she shrieked.

Kit went still, Angela groaned, and Violet shouted in a dangerously carrying voice, "I see you clearly, darlings, so you might as well let me in!"

Carefully setting Angela on her feet, Kit smoothed her skirts down with a swift competence. "Are you all right?" he gently asked, her cheeks flushed from her arousal. And when she didn't immediately reply but held on to his hand for support, he quickly said, "I'll tell her to leave."

"I will."

But her voice trembled and he said very low, "Let me."

"No." Violet could be tenacious as a bulldog.

He stroked her back lightly, a soothing gesture.

"Don't touch me," Angela whispered, a flurry of desire rushing through her body from his brushing fingers.

His hand dropped away instantly.

"I want you too much," she explained so softly, he had to strain to hear the words.

"Are you going to manage?" His voice was gentle.

"Yes," Angela said with a quick, calming breath. "At least I think so." And straightening her skirts with a brief shake, she began to walk to the door. After two short steps she stopped. "I can't," she breathlessly said, on the very verge of climax, the friction of the dildo on her engorged tissue riveting.

"Don't move," he said, walking toward the door.

"Please, Kit." She clenched her fists at the throbbing intensity between her legs. "I'll talk to her."

He glanced back at her quickly, his hand on the doorknob, inclined to handle their unwanted visitor himself. Their eyes held for a moment. "Your call," he softly said, and opened the door.

"How cozy you are," Violet exclaimed, sweeping through the door in a blur of primrose lawn. "Hello, Mr. Braddock; darling Angela, you look flushed," she said with a friendly indiscretion. "It must be the summer heat."

"I hope you have some very good reason for coming here," Angela quietly said, the pulsing deep inside her distracting, her voice sounding as though it struck her ears from some great distance.

"Of course I do, darling. I saved you from Priscilla, who was about to bring several of your guests to view your rose garden. I told her since you often rest in the afternoon at Stone House, it might be prudent if I went first to verify whether we'd be disturbing you. And we would have, I see. You may thank me."

"Thank you. Now go."

"You don't care to join our party, Mr. Braddock?" Violet sweetly inquired, turning her attention on Kit, who was intently watching Angela.

It took him a flashing second to answer, and when his gaze swung to Violet, she didn't wonder that Angela was flushed; incandescent sexual heat shone from his green eyes. "My presence would be awkward with the Ansleys," he briefly replied.

"I hear you're going back to America."

"I'm not certain."

"Priscilla seems to think you are."

"I told her I was." He no longer even made the pretense of polite regard; his eyes were trained on Angela.

"I see," Violet softly murmured. "Will you let Angela come back for tea?" she pleasantly asked, wondering at her friend's unusual reticence and Kit's marked concern.

"Go, Violet," Angela muttered. "Just go."

"Do enjoy yourselves, darlings," Violet cheerfully

declared, Angela's mysterious behavior of no consequence to her good spirits. She was a much richer woman for her afternoon's walk. She couldn't wait to tell Souveral.

Immediately the door closed on Violet, Angela said, almost fainting for him, "If you make me wait a second, I'll never speak to you again."

He recognized the explosive fever in her voice. "I'll do my best, Countess," he said with a smile. "Hold on."

It took him two seconds to lock the door and two seconds more to pull the curtains across the windows facing the courtyard. Then he carried her into the parlor so she needn't walk, lifting her under her arms and moving carefully so as not to disturb the dildo unnecessarily.

She was quivering slightly in her feverish need as he lowered her facedown over the nearest table. Setting the lamp on the floor, he lifted her skirts, nudged her legs apart into a splayed position with his knee while he quickly unbuttoned his trousers. Swiftly extracting the dildo, he gazed for a fraction of a second at the enchanting sight of her curvaceous bottom and dewy-wet cleft, and he wondered briefly who needed whom more in this hot-blooded relationship—the thought of fucking himself to death in that sweet, scented body a very real possibility.

"Kit." The small sound was striking in its naked entreaty.

He entered her immediately, gliding into her with less difficulty than the night before, her pliant flesh stretched from their previous encounter. With only a minimum of resistance he plunged forward and submerged himself hilt-deep.

She was wildly eager, her hips and bottom swinging back impatiently to meet him, stirring restlessly as he withdrew, her whimpers indicating gratification as he drove in again. She gripped the table edges as the rapture mounted, as his erection slid in and out of her with a powerful driving force.

He heard her first small cry, felt her orgasmic flutters begin, watched her sigh and collapse beneath him in the swift, feverish abandonment he was beginning to recognize.

How sublime he was, she thought, luxuriating in a warm, heated bliss inundating her senses—and how gorgeously large . . . she moved the minutest fraction to experience the sensation of being filled completely. If he stayed, she mused with hedonist self-indulgence, she could have him inside her whenever she wished, in daylight or at night, before breakfast or during breakfast, she genially contemplated, a lustful ripple stirring her gorged vagina.

He felt the faint flutter as if he were attuned to her innermost longings, and he moved inside her, penetrating an intense, small distance deeper.

Angela moaned in exquisite response, her body addicted to his sensual enchantment, gratified beyond any previous memory of pleasure. "Don't ever leave," she whispered.

"I like it here," Kit murmured, his hands gripping her waist firmly, his fluid penetration and withdrawal ravishing her senses. "I'll be staying." And he serviced her that afternoon as if he were indeed her stud in residence, solicitous of her pleasure, sensitive to the nuances of her arousal, expert at provoking her most violent sensations.

Fully clothed except for his rampant erection rhythmically visible on the withdrawal stroke, he might have been a house guest surveying some bibelot on the table had someone walked into the parlor. Only on closer observation would the bibelot turn out to be Easton's beautiful hostess with her skirts tossed up over her creamy behind.

And her wanton sensibilities panting on the cataclysmic edge.

Kit's grip tightened as the inevitable shudders coursed through her body, and he buried himself deep inside her with enchanting precision.

Short minutes later another flaring climax quivered through her body with a shocking intensity, and oversensitive after so many violent orgasms, she grew faint from excess.

At which time Kit decided the lady was at least temporarily sated, and he allowed himself release.

As promised . . . outside her body.

Moments later he glanced at the clock, wiped his semen from her lower back with a handkerchief, gently drew her skirts down as she lay prostrate on the tabletop, and with courtly good manners helped her to stand.

Placing her hands carefully on the table for support, she leaned against the solid piece of furniture, breathless and flushed and utterly replete. "You remembered," she softly said, deeply relieved.

"While you forgot," he replied with a small smile as he buttoned his trousers.

"I'm utterly mindless with you. You're ruining me."

"Come back tonight," he quietly said, "and I'll ruin you some more."

"I find my slavish devotion to your touch . . . unnerving."

"It's not as though I haven't made a few changes in my life, *mon ange,*" he gently said. "We're both subject to our passions. Although I've a modicum more discretion," he went on with a grin. "Did you like your sensible fuck? Not a hair out of place, not a button or bow undone. Hardly a wrinkle in your frock."

She smiled, luscious and sweet and fully sated. "Do you have other kinds as well?"

"Come see me tonight," he softly said. "I'll show you my repertoire."

"Can you die of this ecstasy?"

"I don't think so," he said, smiling faintly. "But we could try."

15

Violet was waiting for her after tea. Not that Angela hadn't been expecting her after having warded off her sly looks and innuendo for the past hour while her guests discussed their leisured afternoon activities.

"Don't you just adore knowing something little Priscilla doesn't know?" Violet said, falling in step with Angela as she exited the sun-drenched drawing room. "She's such an irritating young girl."

"You weren't particularly subtle in your questions," Angela noted, glancing down the corridor to see that no other guests were about. "Charlotte didn't appreciate your pointed inquiries into her daughter's marriage plans."

"I was curious. I should think you would be, too, considering your Mr. Braddock was so recently in the running for the position of banker to Wynmere."

"He's not *my* Mr. Braddock," Angela punctiliously corrected, although the possessive sound of the phrase flashed pleasantly through her mind.

"It rather looked as though he was this afternoon. Or at least he's temporarily in your net," Violet added with a gracefully arched eyebrow. "You have to tell me everything. He's the most gorgeous male animal I've ever seen, so I want to know each luscious detail. We'll send Nellie away and have a nice chat before dinner."

"He's extremely nice," Angela carefully said, for the first time in their long friendship not certain she wished to confide in Violet.

"It must be love, darling." Violet's gaze held hers knowingly. "How wonderful for you."

Angela sighed. "Don't be flip this time, Violet. I can't bear it." And her eyes suddenly filled with tears.

"Darling," her friend softly exclaimed, gently touching Angela's arm as they passed down the enfilade of rooms in the old Jacobean house. "I wouldn't ever if you really care. My lord, if anyone deserves any happiness after your torturous years of marriage to Brook, it's you."

"Which marriage is the problem, of course."

"He's serious?" Violet's eyes were wide with shock; Kit Braddock didn't appear to have a serious bone in his body.

"I don't know. He says he is."

"Good God, what of his harem? I'm sorry, I shouldn't ask," she immediately apologized, "but he's not exactly a pillar of virtue. Can you possibly believe him?"

"Probably not," Angela replied with a rueful smile.

Violet's brows rose into her hairline in agreement. "At least you haven't lost all your senses."

"I'd like to believe him, though. He offers happiness so charmingly."

They'd reached Angela's suite of rooms, and just before entering, Violet said, "If you don't mind, I *will* send Nellie away. She's sure to worry if she thinks you in danger of losing your mind completely."

Angela smiled. "Do you think me that far gone?"

"I'm sure it's only temporary, darling. But I've never seen you near tears for a man before."

And once Nellie had departed, Violet said, "Sit down and listen while I try to talk some sense into you."

"I'm not sure I want to listen," Angela replied, dropping onto a small gilded chaise some Lawton had brought back from a Venetian tour. "I've never been so happy."

"He's going to break your heart," Violet asserted, sitting down with a graceful flounce of her lavender silk skirt. "The man is a veritable legend with women. His whole family is; all the Braddock-Blacks are imbued with a conspicuous seductive appeal. Even while Kit was supposedly courting Priscilla, he was rather systematically going through London's entire roster of flirtatious married ladies and leaving them entirely satisfied, I'm told. Not to mention his duties to his harem, which one can only assume he fulfilled. Why him, darling? Of all people?"

"I understand all the obvious problems, Violet," Angela said, restlessly adjusting the position of a book on the table beside the chaise. "I talked myself out of him a dozen times in the past weeks. And until he appeared last night during dinner, I thought I'd safely put him out of my life."

"The interruption wasn't your bailiff with a road problem?"

"No."

"And you fell into his arms."

"Yes," she quietly said.

"You were a challenge to him; you realize that,

don't you?" Violet admonished. "Women don't refuse him."

"Perhaps I was. I don't know him well enough to judge."

"You're not going to do anything foolish, now, are you?"

"I don't think so."

The baroness tipped her head to one side and gazed critically at her friend. "That sounds very equivocal."

"Because it is," Angela softly admitted. "My emotions are in the most wretched turmoil."

"You'll be careful, at least," Violet cautioned. "Brook isn't getting any easier to manage. The rumors of his vices are becoming more blatant. And you know how he reacted to the gossip of you and Joe Manton a few years ago."

"I won't forget." Nor would she ever—Baby May the direct result of his brutal violence.

"He really should be put away."

"His family won't agree. They never will."

"You heard about the Seven Dials incident."

"Dolly told me. How very frightening for the young girl. There's something in his eyes of late," Angela murmured. "Have you noticed? Baby May's terrified of him."

"Do you sometimes wonder about the state of our parents' minds when they married us off?" Violet curiously posed, a mild frown marring the smoothness of her brow.

"I think they considered it primarily a business decision," Angela replied, having asked herself the same question any number of times over the years. "My stepfather's priority had to do with giving as little as possible to the Grevilles in dower money. Mother saw only the glory of the Greville coronet and lands . . . our family were mere viscounts. And I was relieved not to have to marry the queen's hemophiliac son. She'd been quite intent on the match."

"While I thought Dudley had a nice smile."

Angela shrugged. "What does one know at seventeen?"

"Not what we do now, darling, so don't be taken in by another charming smile. You know I truly wish you happiness—lord knows, I wish *myself* happiness —but, sweetheart, of all people Kit Braddock isn't the man to offer you that commodity. That's all I'm saying. I just don't want you to be brutally hurt by a disreputable rogue."

"I know," Angela quietly said. "I've thought about this at great length. Don't worry unnecessarily; I shan't offer up my heart like a green girl."

"In that case, darling, enjoy the pleasure," Violet advised with a playful grin. "I'm sure he's extremely competent as a lover. Just don't let him add you to his harem."

"I won't." Nor did she divulge the extent of her feelings for Kit. Violet wouldn't understand. She didn't understand herself.

"He'll keep you awake tonight, I suppose," Violet murmured, her tone arch and insinuating.

Angela smiled. "I certainly hope so."

"You're going to be very tired tomorrow, darling, and still saddled with a houseful of guests. Why not succumb to a mild summer cold?" she suggested. "Nothing overly serious, of course—just enough to allow you to rest during the day."

"I'll see, Violet. In only one more day everyone will be leaving."

"And at least the nasty little Priscilla didn't get him."

"I'm so glad for him," Angela softly said. "She wouldn't have made him very happy."

"She won't make anyone happy unless they like to talk about her exclusively—her dresses, her hair—"

"—her fine artistic talent," Angela drolly murmured. "Although marriage may not offer her what she wishes, either," she went on in a subdued tone. "Neither you nor I knew enough at that age to stand up to our families."

"As if it would have done any good. They would have locked you away until you'd consented."[14]

"Do you know anyone who's truly happy?" Angela quietly asked.[15]

"How did we get onto this melancholy subject? Of course I don't, nor do you."

A small smile appeared on Angela's face as she lounged in her frothy tea gown on the chaise in her boudoir. "So I shall enjoy him immensely, Violet, while I may."

"And well you should. Kit Braddock doesn't strike me as a man who will tarry long."

"I won't be down for breakfast."

"And I'll keep your guests away from Stone House. Have you told your sisters?"

"No. If Kit decides to stay a bit longer, I'll tell them. But who knows?" She shrugged her silk-clad shoulder so the large beaded peony, artfully arranged by Mr. Worth's expert hand, shimmered in the sunlight. "His reputation precludes any notion of permanence."

"A sensible approach, darling."

"Haven't I always been sensible about my life?" Since the shocking denouement of all her girlish dreams shortly after her marriage to Brook, she'd arranged matters to minimize emotional trauma. It wasn't always easy, with Brook's periodic assaults into her existence, but by and large she viewed the world through reasonable eyes. Like so many of her peers in loveless marriages, she understood the maxim of family duty and even more the volatile threat of her husband's irrational mind.

"With the exception of occasional lapses like Mr. Braddock," Violet prompted.

"Yes," Angela agreed, her smile a flash of delight. "He's definitely a lapse in judgment, but so very accomplished that one forgets his charm is the result of much practice."

"Well, enjoy yourself in the meantime."

"I intend to," she sweetly replied.

*W*hile Angela was serving her guests tea and debating the sincerity of Kit's actions with Violet, Kit was on a dutiful mission for condoms and about to enter the establishment of the village of Easton's only chemist.

Two elderly ladies carefully scrutinized him as he passed them in the doorway, even turning once they were outside the shop to peruse him more closely. When he waved at them through the window, they quickly went on their way, but he was reminded of the lack of privacy in small villages.

He waited for the chemist to finish measuring out some arsenic for a man who had the appearance of lesser gentry. His tweeds were well made but not of the latest fashion, nor had his graying whiskers been au courant anytime these last twenty years.

"Damned moles are eating all my bulbs, damned if they aren't, Jeffreys. I'm going after them before they wipe me out."

"This should work, Mr. Capshaw," the shopkeeper said, wrapping the powder in a paper twist.

"I've heard of good results from the ladies in the garden club." He set the packet on the counter with a flourish.

"You can wait on the gentleman here, Jeffreys. I'm not sure I don't need a thing or two more if I can find my list." And the country squire began slapping his pockets as if the crackle of paper were his means of discovering his list.

"Can I help you, sir?" the chemist asked Kit, dusting off his hands on his canvas apron, taking in Kit's fashionable riding garb with the appraising eyes of a man who went home with a wealth of local gossip for his wife each night.

"I'd like some condoms," Kit said. "Whatever you have."

The slapping of pockets abruptly ceased; the chemist looked Kit over even more carefully, as if memorizing details for his wife. "Do you have a special brand in mind?" he smoothly inquired.

"Show me what you have," Kit casually replied, long past the point of being intimidated by anything so benign as village curiosity.

"Visiting around here?" the country gentleman inquired, moving nearer the counter so he could observe the transaction more closely.

Kit turned to him, his gaze bland. "Just passing through."

"Nice bit of horseflesh outside," the man commented. "Almost looks like some of the countess's stable."

And Kit realized he was in one of those quiet corners of England where any stranger was immediately noticed because so few outsiders ever had reason to journey there.

"You must be one of her house party. She often

has the prince to stay, you know. You're an American, aren't you?"

He wasn't certain which question to answer first and how exactly to answer it. The truth would never do, of course. "I'm just using one of her horses," he ambiguously said. "For a day or so. We hunted together with the Quorn," he added, hunting generally of interest to country gentlemen. He preferred not discussing her house party.

"Best hunting pack in England, they say," Mr. Capshaw said. "The countess can hold her own with any of 'em."

She obviously was an object of pride for the locals. "She's a fine rider," he neutrally said.

"Best female rider in England, they say," the chemist respectfully said. "Read it myself in the *World* right under her picture with that new bloodstock she bought from out Araby way somewhere."

"Been here before?" Mr. Capshaw inquired, gazing at the intaglio ring on Kit's left hand, the Chinese script on the green gemstone catching the light from the windows.

"No."

"Staying around here?"

"Perhaps. I'm not sure."

"Where are you from in America?"

"San Francisco." That was safe, at least. "I'm in a bit of a rush. The condoms?" he suggested, interested in abbreviating the catechism. Unlike most instances where only his reputation was at stake and he could be as rude or brusque as he wished, here in Angela's village a faux pas could put her at risk of damaging gossip.

"Just have a few," the chemist said, but when he sorted through a nearby drawer, he came up with a handful.

"That's fine," Kit said, taking out an assortment of bills from his pocket.

"Which one do you want?" After a cautious glance at the door, the shopkeeper spread the packets out on the counter.

"I'll take them all."

"Well, now . . . er . . . have to tally up the separate amounts," the chemist stammered.

"That's not necessary," Kit replied, dropping a large bill onto the counter and scooping up the packets with his other hand. "Keep the change," he cordially said, slipping the collection into his pocket, and with a dip of his head to the two men, he strode from the shop with Easton village's supply of condoms.

"Must be a mighty busy fellow," Capshaw said with a wink at Jeffreys.

"And a mighty rich one, too. Look at this bill he left," the chemist said, holding a fifty-pound note in his hand.

"I expect anyone riding the countess's bloodstock must have plenty of money. Her half sister married a duke, and she and the prince are personal friends. An American, though. Wonder if he's one of those millionaires buying himself a country estate over here?"

"I'll ask Mrs. Jeffreys to ask her nephew's wife, who has a cousin who's a parlor maid at Easton. Man like that one. She'd remember him."

16

Anxious to leave before her last guest was seen off to bed, Angela took Violet's suggestion and complained of a cold when the evening became too tedious to bear. She ostensibly went up to bed early only to descend one of the back staircases minutes later to exit the house through one of the servants' entrances.

She ran like an eager child intent on play, feeling as lighthearted, too, crossing the shadowed lawn in a swift dash, her diamanté tulle gown sparkling in the silvery light of the moon. The beech allée shimmered in the moonlight like a gleaming pathway to the man she loved, and she laughed out loud, so jubilant were her spirits. She was blessedly free for the entire night, Kit was waiting for her, and tomorrow when she woke, only twenty-four hours remained before her guests would depart.

Then she'd have him for herself alone.

She felt giddy at the prospect, not at all sensible, as she'd professed to Violet.

"You sound cheerful," Kit murmured, coming up from behind and scooping her into his arms.

She screamed at his sudden appearance, then laughed again and threw her arms around his neck. "I'm dizzy in love," she joyously declared, "and you're astonishingly good at ambushing ladies in the night," she teased, kissing him lightly on the cheek.

"Only one lady," he corrected, carrying her effortlessly down the gravel walk. "What took you so long?"

"Everyone's still intent on cards or drinking or playing the piano. Did you know Priscilla is absolutely terrible on the piano?" she cheerfully added.

"I had the misfortune to hear her one night. I shall never be able to listen to Liszt again."

"Ummm, you're so darling," she murmured, leaving a line of butterfly kisses down his cheek. "Did you know you're darling?" she merrily inquired, licking his earlobe.

He'd been told that once or twice before, but he said, "No, never," with a perfectly straight face and added in a lush undertone that immediately set her carnal urges on full alert, "What's it like to have sex with a woman dizzy in love?"

"Ask me later—I don't know—but I think 'excess' is the operative word. Have you ever been fucked to death?" she softly asked.

"I'm glad I rested this evening." His smile held a wicked impertinence.

"You're definitely going to need your strength," she sportively agreed. "Do you think it's the full moon?" she mused, gazing up briefly at the brilliant sky. "I'm full of lust."

"I don't think so, because I experienced the same sensation this morning, this afternoon—"

"—at lunch, at dinner, I know. I hope you don't have any plans outside of Easton for a while."

"I've canceled my schedule."

"So you're completely at my disposal."

"Completely."

"What a lovely word when you say it like that."

"And after your guests leave on Sunday, consider yourself at *my* disposal," he softly said.

"Except for Baby May," she quickly interjected.

"Except for her," he agreed.

He carried her into the cottage and up the stairs and into the small bedroom under the eaves. And when he set her on the monk's bed and she saw all the condoms spread out on the coverlet, she said with the sweetest of smiles, "You remembered."

"I always remember. You pick the first one. Personally, I prefer the condom with the queen's portrait on it," he said with a grin.[16] "So very patriotic."

"Do you think it might seem a bit strange—to be making love with the queen?"

"Don't say *with* the queen, darling. The thought is enough to make one consider abstinence."

"Even if I were lying here waiting for you?" Angela teased.

"I'd have to really concentrate," he murmured. "The Hanovers aren't known for their good looks."

"While the Braddocks definitely are."

"Thank you," he modestly said, looking murderously handsome leaning against the bedpost in riding boots, breeches, and shirt, all lithe power and splendid bone structure, his heavy auburn hair sleek and gleaming in the lamplight, his green eyes touched with a sensual wildness. "And the Lawton family tree has offered up the most beautiful woman in the world."

She'd heard all the superlatives so many times before, but when Kit spoke the graceful words, they suddenly mattered. "We're very lucky," she said, happiness inundating her soul.

"We are," he quietly agreed, leaning down to

brush a delicate kiss across her mouth as she sat cross-legged on the bed. "Now, pick one or you're going to be made love to without any protection. I'm impatient. It's been five hours."

"Five and a half," she meticulously corrected with a small flirtatious smile.

"I have a feeling these aren't going to last long," he mildly said, gazing at her with half-lidded eyes. "And then you're going to have to trust me."

"You can't get more?" The faintest panic resonated in her words.

"Not in Easton. This is it; I bought the entire supply while evading a multitude of questions in the process. Some old gentleman recognized your bloodstock."

"I suppose Jeffreys was inquisitive."

"Very."

"Oh, dear." But then her mind veered from the possible ramifications of Jeffreys's curiosity to the more serious consequences of insufficient condoms. "This is all we have?"

"It's not a problem."

"Maybe for you it's not." It was an overwhelming problem for her.

"Once these are gone, I won't climax in you—trust me."

She looked up at him from under her lashes. "Surely that must be the most reckless and overused sentence in the history of man."

"In my case it's true. But suit yourself," he calmly said. "I can ride over to Easton Vale tomorrow or the next day and buy some more."

"The shops are closed on Sunday."

"Darling," he softly said, sitting down beside her. "You're beginning to sound as though this is your first time. Let me reassure you. Although I've been making

love to women for many years, I've purposely never
had any children. I'm probably more careful than you
are. How's that? Can we close this discussion?"

"You can be that certain."

"Yes." He'd been a tall and coltish sixteen, on
tour with his tutor, when the pretty Duchess Dumont
had taken him under her wing that spring in Paris.
And in the course of those genial weeks, she'd
schooled him in a comprehensive and artful variety of
sensual pleasures, among them the critical act of withdrawal, a polite courtesy every civilized Frenchman
practiced.

"I should believe you," she nervously said.

"Please do."

"It's harder for a woman to be casual about . . .
the consequences."

"It's not as though you have a dozen children. For
a woman who claims to get pregnant if a man looks at
her, you must have found some solution."

"But the cervical cap doesn't work with you . . .
and me . . . you know it was displaced, oh hell," she
exclaimed. "I hate all this."

Falling back onto the pillows, Kit folded his arms
behind his head and shut his eyes. "Wake me up," he
said with a faint smile, "when this issue has been resolved to your satisfaction."

"Don't you dare ignore me," she fervently protested, tumbling on top of him and throwing her arms
around his neck, "when I'm distraught and nervous
and anxious for my life and so madly in love," she
whispered, "I'm going to die."

His arms came up to hold her first and then his
eyes opened, and his voice, when he spoke next, was
strangely quiet. "What do you mean 'anxious for your
life'?"

"It's nothing." She didn't want to talk about her marriage and all the impossibilities it occasioned.

"You're not worried so much about a pregnancy as what would happen if you became pregnant, aren't you?" An essential gravity underscored his words. "Talk to me about this."

"If you must know," she said, because his gaze was so serious, she knew she couldn't deflect his interest with some frivolous response, "Brook was very difficult about my pregnancy with May."

"Is she his child?" It was common after the requisite heir was born for aristocratic husbands to overlook additional children who bore no resemblance to them. He wasn't necessarily asking a tactless question.[17]

"Yes."

"But he didn't believe you."

"Not at first."

"What did he do at first?" he quietly asked.

She didn't answer, but he saw the flicker of fear in her eyes.

"He hurt you, didn't he?"

"Yes."

"You're lucky the baby wasn't harmed," he softly said, thinking Brook Greville deserved to be hurt, too.

"I'm very grateful she wasn't."

"She's adorable. You're very fortunate."

"Oh, Kit, don't make me cry," she whispered, her mouth trembling, her eyes bright with tears. "What good does it do to talk about any of this?" What good did it do to think about the past or the future when all she had was the moment?

"I'm sorry, Angel," he murmured, holding her close, gently stroking her back, offering comfort and solace. "I won't bring it up again, I promise," he kindly said. "And you won't become pregnant. My word on it."

"Thank you," she said on a small, sad sigh. "Now I love you even more."

"How much more?" he lightly said, gazing down at her as she rested on his shoulder, his smile redolent of heady sensuality, intent on distracting her from her morbid memories.

"Mountains more and whales more and all the tea in China more." She was smiling again.

"I love *you* more than the *Desiree,* even more than my mother," he playfully added.

"She wouldn't like me," Angela said, thinking how unsuitable she'd be to a fond mother who wished her only son to marry well.

"She'd love you because *I* love you. She's very smart, and she doesn't care about convention—as you can well imagine," he added with a grin. "Considering my life—or hers, for that matter. She wasn't married to my father, she told me a few years ago. He was already married. Like you. They met at the opera, of all places. My father, Mama said, had no appreciation for music. She was a concert pianist. But they fell in love anyway . . . and then he died before I was born."

"I'm sorry," Angela gently said, thinking how terrible it must have been for his mother.

"I feel I know him anyway," Kit declared. "Mother always talked of him as though he were alive. She's very artistic, slightly mystical, and prone to be overprotective."

"Not that it did any good, I'm assuming, with you," Angela said with a smile, knowing his life had been lived on the edge for years.

"You'll like her," he simply said. "Everyone does. But how will *your* friends react to me?" he lazily queried. "What did Violet say? She must have had a comment or two after seeing you in half undress this afternoon."

Angela wiggled slightly upright, rested her arms on his chest, and gazed at him with mischievous eyes. "She told me to beware particularly of your seductive charm."

"And you didn't listen to her."

"Time enough for that when you leave me," she flippantly replied.

He frowned. "You're impossibly hard to convince. Don't you know any sincere men?"

"Pardon me if I don't automatically put you in that category."

"People change."

"Then I know one sincere man now."

"How very cynical you are, *mon ange*."

"One learns, darling," she said with delicate emphasis. "I was fifteen when I was first appraised for the marriage mart, although at the time I wasn't aware I was being judged. Disraeli, who was very old but still a dear friend of the queen, invited me to a play. I was honored and filled with trepidation, but he put me at my ease; he had enormous charm. I found out years later that I was being vetted that evening as a possible consort for the queen's son, Prince Leopold. And I've had occasion to discover many times since that men rarely treat beautiful women with sincerity. There's always some motive to their interest. I'm not necessarily disturbed by the fact, only aware of it."

"I'll change your mind."

"I look forward to the process. Will your sexual prowess figure in the methodology?"

"No."

"I want it to," she softly said.

"All right."

"My, you're accommodating," she murmured.

He smiled. "I think someone said that to me once before."

"I don't think anyone *ever* said that to you before." Her gaze was coolly intense.

"You're right," he instantly replied, his voice sweet with accord. "I must have been thinking about something else. Tell me what you want."

"I want something from your amorous repertoire."

"Something romantic?"

"No, something wildly carnal," she said, all glittering sumptuous beauty.

He laughed. "You *are* a greedy little wanton."

"Only with you." Her voice was a whisper.

"I like the sound of that," he said, his words plain as the lucid green of his eyes. "And you can stay all night, can't you?"

"For hours."

"There's always your toy collection," he softly drawled.

"No, absolutely not," she hotly disputed. "I forbid you. You always get angry and resentful and sullen, and I can't change my past. Tomorrow I'm throwing that all away."

"I already did," he quietly said, watching her intently.

"Good," she simply said. "You saved me the trouble. Now, take your clothes off," she abruptly commanded, pushing herself up from his chest, hitching her diamanté and midnight-blue tulle gown up so she could straddle his hips, beginning to unbutton his shirt. "You talk too much."

He smiled at her charming demand and the restoration of her cheerful impudence. He disliked seeing her unhappy. "You undress me and I'll undress you and then we'll see if we can think of something to do to pass the time," he softly said. "Would you care to see the rose garden in moonlight?"

They made love that night in the monk's bed first because neither could wait long enough to make their way to the rose garden. And they used the condom with the queen's face on it. Between the intrinsic religiosity of the monk's bed and Victoria's philosophical presence hovering in the air, a certain beguiling cachet of God and country was imparted to the act.

"I feel so damned righteous," Kit breathlessly murmured afterward, stripping the condom off as he lay panting beside Angela. His grin flashed white against his tan. "It's a new and decadent feeling for me."

"Please throw away that damned portrait thing," Angela whispered, her breathing agitated. "I kept thinking of the way she eats—ugh."[18]

Kit laughed. "I won't show you the next one."

"No, don't. They're much too imaginative."

A packet with a strange dragon on the silver tissue served their purposes next in the rose garden, although Angela prudently refused to look at it. The air was cool that night, but their bodies were so heated, they would have melted the snow at the poles. And later as he lay in the dew-wet grass, with Angela sitting impaled on his erection, Kit murmured, "Mr. Jeffreys said you were the best female rider in England." He smiled as she moved up slowly so she could feel the full splendor of his length and then slid down again with exquisite attention, squirming slightly at the last in order to take him in completely. "I'd say at least the Continent, too," he added in a teasing whisper, her unabashed sexuality enchanting.

She tried to hit him then, but he was quicker and caught her hands lightly in his. And while she sputtered about all the women he'd bedded and how dare he compare her to them, he pinioned her hands at her hips and, covering them with his, held her hard on his erection while he told her he was only teasing, he wanted only her, he needed only her, he adored only her, each word punctuated with a delicate thrusting emphasis that added greatly to her understanding.

And sometime later, after she'd expired in gratifying ecstasy, he said, "Do you believe me now?"

"I'm convinced," she blissfully agreed.

They strolled to the stables after a time because the horses had begun nickering at the sounds from the rose garden, and after feeding apples from the orchard to the three mounts Angela kept at Stone House, they made love in the sweet-smelling hayloft. They both picked hay from their hair on the way back to the house and kissed and giggled and thought separately and together how wonderful love was. For two people who'd always only played the game, the revelation was staggering, the feeling having overcome them slowly in the past days and weeks, finally revealing itself completely that night in all the fullness of its glory.

"I don't know how it happened," Angela whispered toward morning as she lay in his arms before the fire. "But I'm very glad I love you."

He knew how it had happened, this man who made it a point of going after what he wanted, but he said only, "I'm *more* glad. Tell me how many hours."

She looked at the clock on the mantel. "Twenty-eight," she said. They'd been playing the game all night. "Until Easton is empty of guests."

"And then what?"

"Then I can make love to you anytime I want."

"Or anytime *I* want."

"Yes," she whispered. "Particularly that."

*H*e walked her back to the terrace door at sunrise while she nervously scanned the gleaming windows of Easton for possible curious faces.

"Relax, darling. None of your guests would even consider rising this early." He gently squeezed her hand in reassurance as they passed under the arched gate into the terrace garden. "And I'll be gone in a few minutes."

"I don't want you to," she irrationally said, fretful of his leaving and the long day of politesse before her.

"I'll stay if you want, but you'll have hell to pay with the Ansleys. I don't give a damn, but you have more scruples. Do you want me to stay?"

She sighed. "No, not in the rational part of my brain that's still marginally functioning. Just tell me I'll survive another day."

"You will," he softly asserted, bending to kiss her gently on the cheek as they reached the glass-paned door. "Why don't you bring Baby May to visit this afternoon if you can get away?" he offered. "We can show her the new kittens in the stables."

"She'd love that. You'll be there, now?" A kind of panic settled in her stomach at the thought of his leaving her; she knew someday he'd leave her for good.

"All day, all night, whenever you come."

"I never thought love was so desperate," she whispered.

"It's frightening, isn't it?" he quietly agreed. "But I'm glad I found you at the yacht club that night."

"It seems ages ago."

"When we both had different lives. You're cold," he abruptly said, gathering her in his arms as she shivered.

She'd felt a sudden terror at the thought of their

very disparate lives—impossible lives to reconcile. What was she going to do when this was all over? How would she survive the sorrow?

"You're tired, Angel," Kit soothed, his body warming hers, his strength comforting. "You haven't had much sleep lately. Rest today if you can and I'll see you tonight instead."

She shook her head.

"Well, go rest now. You can sleep for a few hours this morning."

"You'll be there this afternoon?"

"Anytime."

She smiled up at him, his blanket assurance balm to her fears. "May and I will come to see you."

"Perfect," he said. And he kissed her gently as though he knew her spirits were more fragile this morning. Then he said very, very softly, "I'll be waiting," and walked away.

She watched him traverse the garden and cross the parkland, not wanting to lose sight of him. Pressed against the terrace door, she stood with tears streaming down her face, wondering why life was so unfair, why she didn't deserve to have him for her own. Then his figure disappeared behind the yew hedge that marked the border of Stone House, and he was gone.

The glass panes felt cold beneath her hands, and she shivered in the morning air, self-pity and sadness overwhelming her. She was thirty-five years old, she thought, and even now she wouldn't be allowed happiness, as much a prisoner of her caste as her most lowly cottager. Brook wouldn't permit a divorce. He'd not only threatened her and her children, but Bertie himself, while her mother had always been staunchly opposed, reminding her that the scandal would spread as high as the throne itself. The Prince of Wales had barely survived the Mordaunt scandal[19] when he'd been forced into court as a witness, the dishonor humiliating and shameful for the royal family. He'd been actually booed in the streets afterward.

So there was no hope for her—nothing, at least, that wouldn't be death defying and heedless. She was helpless to change her life, she despondently thought.

But a few moments later she took herself to task as she'd often done over the years when obligations and duties required discharging, and wiping away her tears with the back of her hand, she squared her shoulders and stood up straight, her mother's voice in her ears. "Life is duty. People depend on you." And driven by the obligations of civility, she entered her house because she had another day yet to entertain her guests.

She did sleep a few hours that morning and survived the prattle and frivolous gaiety of lunch only because she knew she could escape soon with May. Kit was in the stable yard with the kittens when they arrived, and if anyone had wished to charm May, a better amusement couldn't have been devised. She was ecstatic at the sight and clapped her hands in glee. Kit had made some kitten toys with string and bits of straw, and before long May and the fuzzy kittens were tumbling about on the grassy verge of the yard under the watchful eyes of the mother cat, Angela, and Kit.

"Look! Look!" she'd periodically shout when a kitten would pounce on the toy she held on a string. And she'd squeal with delight at the tug-of-war that would ensue, feline and toddler equally bewitched by the game.

When the kittens finally tired of play, Kit invited them in for tea, made and served with his smooth efficiency and competence.

"Don't tell me you made these," Angela softly

224   S U S A N   J O H N S O N

teased, indicating the plate of cream cakes, one of
which her daughter was demolishing before their eyes.

"I went into Easton Vale this morning. The baker
recognized your horse, too. You have no anonymity in
these parts."

"Easton Vale?" she murmured, their eyes meeting
over the blond head of her daughter.

"They didn't have what you wanted," he quietly
said. "So I exposed myself to their village chemist's
grilling for no good reason. I'm sorry. But the bakery
was quite good." He grinned. "The ride over wasn't
completely wasted."

"Oh, dear."

"You're going to have to rely on me."

She gazed at him keenly across the scrubbed pine
table. "A dilemma," she murmured.

"Only for you."

"Mama, want nother," May piped up, waving at
the plate of cakes. "Me hungry."

By the time Angela had helped her daughter to
another cake, the discussion had turned to May's
question-and-answer format about kittens. Could she
play with them again? Why wouldn't the mother let
them come out to play soon? If she waited a long, long
time would they play with her?

They decided instead on a ride down to the dock
where the *Shark* was moored, because May liked
Mommy's big boat. She rode with Kit, keeping up a
steady stream of chatter from Stone House down the
country lane to the dock on the estuary to the sea.

It turned out they stayed longer than they planned
because May found her toy box in her cabin while Kit
was intrigued by the style of the *Shark*'s steel rigging
and the navigation instruments Angela had recently
purchased. She showed him the new sextant and compass and how they functioned. Interested in buying

some for himself, he tested the line of collimation at several adjustments on the sextant and operated the deflector on the compass at a number of settings. They spoke of the routes they'd sailed and the best times of year to navigate the cape and the Strait of Gibraltar and the North Atlantic. They agreed on the styles of rigging they preferred, on the splendor of the seas at night, they agreed that racing was possibly the most exciting phenomenon in the world. The harmony of spirit and substance was simple and genuine, their conversation so animated at times, bliss was palpable in the air.

Looking up suddenly to see the sun beginning to set over the marshy landscape, Angela hastily said, "Heavens, I have to go."

"I'm sorry," Kit apologized, lost in the congenial conversation and unaware himself of the time. "It's my fault for keeping you. Do you think they've sent out the alarm?"

"No, but I'll ride directly back to the house with May."

"And I'll see you tonight."

"Very late, I'm afraid. I'll have to be dutiful tonight."

"I understand."

When May was finally coaxed away from her toys, she insisted on hugging Kit before she was lifted into the saddle. "Kiss, kiss, kiss too," she cried, and deposited a wet kiss on Kit's cheek.

And as he waited to wave them off, May screamed from her mother's lap, "See you morrow. Member!"

"I won't forget," Kit replied, his smile all grace and beauty.

"Thank you," Angela softly said, her gaze holding his. "Thank you for everything."

———

*W*hen Angela arrived at Stone House after midnight, Kit said, "I've a fire in the parlor and chilled champagne. Come sit with me for one drink first." And she fell asleep in his arms within minutes, as he knew she would, the last few days exhausting, her delicate vitality unable to withstand so many sleepless nights. He was more familiar with carouse in his dissolute life—days without sleep weren't unusual.

Moving carefully so as not to wake her, he wrapped her warmly in a quilt, moved the champagne bottle closer, and settled comfortably on the sofa. He leisurely drank the champagne while he watched her sleep, charmed by her vulnerable beauty, fascinated by the fathomless love she inspired in him, deeply touched by his need for her.

How quickly his life had altered, he mused, his first sight of her that night at Cowes forever sealing his fate. After having roamed the world tasting pleasure with careless self-indulgence, scornful of love and permanent attachments, there she was suddenly and he was bewitched.

He'd called it other things at first, too long a man with a licentious past to recognize love easily. But perhaps he'd known from the beginning and had only, finally, to face it. He smiled into the burning embers. Saskia was right.

He began planning their future in the shadowed parlor of Stone House, arranging all the necessary details carefully in his mind, beginning with the lawyers. He'd need the very best to free Angela from an unstable brute of a husband, especially with the current state of England's divorce law. There was her son, too, away on holiday in Europe, she'd said. How would he respond to the altered state of his family? He ticked the issues off one by one, reconciling all the steps against the cautions he was sure to receive from his lawyers and bankers. But he didn't care what it cost; he'd make that clear to them. He wanted her free of the Grevilles.

He wanted her free to marry him.

When the sun was fully up, he lazily stretched his cramped muscles and woke her with a kiss. "They're leaving this morning," he whispered.

She came awake with a start, smiled, murmured, "Good news," and shut her eyes again.

"They'll want you to see them off, darling," he softly said, smiling at her lingering drowsiness. He'd never seen her wake before; she reminded him of a sleepy child. "Or shall *I* say your good-byes?"

She sat bolt upright, looked around to get her bearings, and then said with a luscious smile, "I plan on having you help me, darling, but not with that."

"Would my appearance at the leave-taking be considered a social blunder in your circles?" he teased.

"Actually, I'm afraid Priscilla might toss you into her carriage and make off with you."

"Not likely while I still have breath."

"Would you have actually married her?"

He shrugged. "It seemed a reasonable option at the time."

"How cold-blooded that sounds."

"Don't talk to me of marriages of convenience, *mon ange,*" he gently said, "or we'd have to compare degrees of cold-bloodedness, wouldn't we?"

"My apologies, of course," she immediately said. "You're right, you're always right"—her eyes sparkled with mischief—"and I'll make it up to you this afternoon. Is that suitably contrite?" she mockingly inquired.

"Contrition in any form whatsoever from a lady of

your, shall we say, demanding temperament, staggers the mind." His crooked smile matched his ruffled hair. "I'll definitely wait this afternoon to discover my reward."

"You didn't make love to me last night."

"You fell asleep."

"You should have wakened me."

"We've plenty of time."

"What a glorious prospect," she joyfully murmured.

"So you should leave now."

"Kiss me first."

"Go *right* now," he firmly declared, lifting her from his lap. "Or you won't make it home to see your guests off," he softly added, rising himself and stepping away a safe distance. Never one to deny his carnal urges, he wasn't sure he was capable of simply kissing her. She was all warm and drowsy and imploring, not exactly the right combination to cool his ardor.

"Won't you kiss me?"

"No. This is all new to me, darling . . . this unselfish virtue. I'd rather not."

"Do I have to wait until this afternoon?"

"I'd suggest it."

"Think of me?" she flirtatiously purred.

He gazed at her through narrowed eyes. "Get the hell out of here," he growled, not often so selfless.

She grinned and blew him a kiss before she ran from the room.

And he took a cold bath that helped only marginally.

17

Sunday afternoon began a blissful idyll of blind hope, glowing happiness, and unfettered love. Angela came for him at one, she and Baby May and Peter Rabbit, and they all walked back together to Easton. The servants were all waiting on the drive as though the master had come home, and they greeted him with courtesy and smiles as she wished them to, he didn't doubt. They walked in her parkland, and she showed him her well-run estate with pride in her accomplishments. He saw the new agricultural college with the several buildings almost complete, the primary and secondary schools she maintained for the village, the sewing business she'd established for young women who were too frail to work with their families on the land—the one for which she'd been accused of coddling her tenants by the conservative press. He met the tenant farmers, too, and their wives and children, who all made a fuss over Baby May.

May had decided he should carry her on their expedition, and she fit into his arms with the same natural state of perfection as her mother. They walked

miles that afternoon in their tour of the estate, stopping once for tea at her steward's cottage, where the
men talked at length about threshers as if they'd been
lifelong friends.

"Do you like it?" Angela asked as they strolled
back to the house, Baby May asleep in Kit's arms.

"It's a model estate; I've never seen better, but
you know that, don't you?" he replied, smiling at her.
"A countess who farms. I'm impressed."

"I'll show you the rest tomorrow. But we'll have
to ride."

"I'd like that. I've some plantations on Java. I'll
show them to you some day."

She touched his arm in answer and smiled up at
him. "It seems as if you've always been here."

"Get used to it," he said. "I intend to stay."

*I*solated at Easton, they lived in a dream world the
next fortnight, making love, being in love, talking of
love, obsessed with the rare, quixotic, hotheaded, and
devastating splendor of their feelings.

They rose early because May did, and Kit had always liked the mornings best, regardless that in the
past he'd often greeted the day still in evening dress.
And they contented themselves with the simple
rhythms of a country day. They helped with the har-
vests of hay and oats, Kit surprising the farmers by
pitching in and coaxing Angela to participate as well.
And they made a daily visit to the carpenters working
on the buildings for the agricultural college, each new
bit of progress a delight to Angela.

Often in the evenings after May had gone to sleep,
they rode along the shore road and watched the moon
rise over the misty marshlands, the sense of solitude

both grand and sublime, nothing of the outside world intruding on their contentment.

They frequently sailed the *Shark* with a minimum crew, up the east coast and down again, Angela showing her off one day in a high wind, the sails all aloft and screaming as they raced south to Dover.

One night she told him of the father she'd never known, a tall, auburn-haired man, a colonel in the Blues, headstrong, self-willed, she'd said, known for his athletic skills and splendid horsemanship. Never on cordial terms with his own father, he'd died when she was three.

"I've always identified with him," she said as they lay in her bedroom at Easton. "Perhaps because my mother and I are so different. And my sisters, too, although I love them dearly. My sisters were blue-eyed darlings of circumspection and neatness, while I was always being chastised for my wild escapades."

"I think I recognized your sweet impulsiveness that first night at the yacht club," Kit murmured, sprawled on the bed beside her. "Who else would have jumped ship so readily?" He lazily turned his head and smiled at her. "I just knew I wanted to taste that wildness in bed."

"And self-indulgent, I agreed. My sisters would have continued to refuse your advances."

"Lucky for me you couldn't resist," he said, all cheeky impudence and a luscious smile.

"Lucky for me you didn't mind riding through the rain to Easton."

"And you felt sorry for me because I was wet."

"What I was feeling for you, darling," she unabashedly admitted, fresh-faced and glowingly nude, "had nothing to do with pity."

"I know." He grinned and, rolling over swiftly, covered her with his body, resting his weight lightly on his elbows. "I was thinking," he murmured, his mouth only inches away, "since it's been—what? ten minutes or so?—since we last made love . . . perhaps, possibly . . . maybe . . . you might be interested in renewing this incredible sexual bond—"

"I thought you'd never ask," she said, malapert and delectable, "and since I've been taking advantage of you for most of the evening . . . I was trying to be less demanding."

He laughed. "Don't worry, I know how to say no."

"Do you really?"

"I'm sure I do in theory."

"But you never actually have," she softly challenged.

He paused for a moment, debating a tactful response.

"Be honest."

"Of course I have," he lied.

Her flagrant smile was touched with merriment. "That's the right answer."

He grinned at the playful sport. "Now you can answer one for me." He delicately licked the curve of her bottom lip. "How deep do you want it?" he whispered.

$\mathcal{T}$wo days later near sunset, Angela and Kit were ensconced in large wicker chairs on the terrace, watching May wheel her doll perambulator at great speed up and down the slate pavement, when a man came down the drive. He was carrying a valise, although from their vantage point he was too distant for them to distinguish features. Then he walked from the shadows of the great lime trees, and the sun caught in the gold of his hair. "Fitz!" Angela cried, recognizing her son.

Coming out of her chair in a bound, she ran down the stairs to meet him.

"Fit me bruver," May said, coming to stand beside Kit's chair. "He like me," she matter-of-factly declared.

"Your brother's been on holiday, hasn't he?" Kit said.

"He back now. He bring me present." And as they waited on the terrace, May went on at length about the kind of presents her brother had promised her in his last letter.

Beaming, Angela came back arm in arm with a tall, slender young man. "This is my son, Gordon Fitzroy," she said to Kit, who was standing with May at the top of the stairs. "Fitz, a friend of mine from America has been staying with us. Say hello to Mr. Braddock."

The men shook hands, the young man's smile reminding Kit of his mother's.

"You won the Queen's Cup, didn't you?" Fitz said. "Ronnie Lennox said your racer is prime."

"I've got Watson in Plymouth adding a new fin keel to my yacht now. When it's finished, he guarantees I'll have the fastest racer on the seas. You'll have to come down and see it."

"Thank you, sir. I'd like that." He stood very straight, his eyes almost on a level with Kit's.

"I hope you have May's present," Angela interrupted, trying to restrain May, who was tugging at her brother's valise.

"How many do you want?" the young man inquired, turning to smile at his young sister.

"Lots and lots!" May squealed, jumping from foot to foot, her curls bouncing.

"Come look, then, moppet," he said, ruffling her

hair. And setting the suitcase down, he kneeled to un-
latch it.

The distribution of presents was accomplished
with much laughter and shrieks of delight from Baby
May, while Angela accepted her first edition of the
letters of Racine with warm appreciation.

"I found it at Galantarais—you know that shop in
Paris, Maman, where you always want to buy everything. Père Forney remembered you and said you
wanted this."

"I did," she said, stroking the soft worn leather.
"It's perfect."

And over dinner they heard of his travels in Germany and France, of his traveling companions' antics,
of the friends he'd visited in both countries. "Auntie
Vickie sent you a present, too, but it's in my luggage at
the station," he said referring to the dowager Empress
Frederick of Germany in familiar terms. The English
ambassador in Paris had introduced him to several
young ladies, he said, and he'd danced with them all at
a summer ball at the Duc de Gramont's. "But they
don't like sailing much," he'd added, as if that were
his criteria for acceptance.

So they all went sailing on the *Shark* the next day,
a festive, hospitable time, with the sea such a source of
pleasure to them all, and when they came back very
late, the moonlight was so brilliant, the marshland was
like silver tinsel stretched to the horizon. Fitz carried
his sleeping sister back to the house, taking over his
familiar role. He helped tuck May into bed, trading
quips with Bergie like a teasing relative, asking about
her family, inquiring of her niece's birthday party,
keeping harmony with her in a Swedish lullaby as May
dropped back to sleep. And then they'd retired downstairs for tea and drinks, and afterward, as Fitz kissed

his mother good night, he offered Kit a warm good
night as well, like a cordial host.

He seeemed older than his years, Kit thought,
watching the young boy mount the stairs, the estrange-
ment of the de Grae marriage no doubt a cause of
Fitz's early maturity. But he was less than a year from
his majority, Kit reminded himself, so perhaps not so
young, after all. Hell, Kit recalled, he'd made his first
trip to China at that age.

_A_t breakfast the next morning after Angela and
May had disappeared into the library to search for a
book describing the small medieval church with the
knight's tomb they were going to see that day, Fitz
carefully set down his knife and fork, cleared his
throat, and, gazing across the table at Kit, said, "If you
don't mind my asking . . ." He coughed slightly,
raked a hand quickly through his pale hair—obviously
ill at ease—and then with visible determination
plunged forward. "I was wondering, sir, what your intentions are toward my mother."

His face had flushed slightly, and his hands laced
together on the tabletop were clenched tight. He was
protecting his mother, Kit realized with quiet amusement.

"That is . . . you see—Maman's never had anyone stay with her . . . ," Fitz uncomfortably went on.

"For so long," Kit softly interjected.

The young boy nodded, his gaze holding Kit's
with direct clarity.

"I've asked your mother to marry me," Kit said.
"But she's been evasive, citing societal and family
pressures. I'd marry her tomorrow if I could."

Fitz let out an explosive sigh. "That's good news,"

he impetuously declared and then smiled with boyish elation. "She likes you, I can tell."

"Yes, I think she does," Kit replied with a faint smile. "You'll have to help me convince her to make some changes in her life."

"You mean de Grae."

Kit nodded, not sure how candid he could be with the man's own son.

"I don't like him, sir. He doesn't deserve Maman."

"I agree," Kit said, his question answered. "But we must convince your mother."

"She doesn't really take advice from me. Although she always listens," Fitz quickly pointed out, his loyalty evident.

"I think it's hard for mothers to believe their children ever truly grow up. My mother has me here in England looking for a wife. Astonishingly—and I'm a lot older than you—I couldn't refuse her."

"Couldn't refuse whom?" Angela asked, walking back into the room with May, the book in her hand.

"My mother and her quest for a grandchild."

A blush colored Angela's fair skin. "What are you two talking about?"

"Mothers in general. How we find them adorable. Right, Fitz?" Kit said with a broad grin and a wink.

"Yes, sir," the young boy replied, his eyes lighting up with a mischievous, companionable glow.

"So are we off to see this tomb?" Kit genially inquired. "Tell us about it."

They drove through the fall countryside to a small church at Capel Green, the autumn weather sunny and mild, the open carriage allowing them to bask in the warmth of the sun on their sight-seeing jaunt.

When they reached the simple stone structure, built by a Norman knight a decade after the first landing at Hastings, they admired the ancient stained-glass windows and the marble effigies of the knight and his lady, their graceful forms lying in perpetual rest atop their tombs. Fitz liked the battle scenes depicted on the west window best; May thought the posies in the lady's hands clasped on her breast so lifelike, she touched them several times, certain they were real.

Kit found himself moved by the sense of tender affection and attachment in the inscriptions on the vaults. The knight and his wife had lived long lives for their day, the lady preceding her husband in death by less than a year, as indicated by the dates on the monuments. Beneath the sinuous drapery flowing over her ornate casket, the inscription "Our beloved, we are desolate in our loss" was inscribed on the lady's tomb. And the entwined initials of the husband and wife were wreathed in wild roses delicately carved from the white translucent marble.

The knight hadn't been a young man when he had died. He'd been a dozen years older than his wife, and he must have loved her very much, for he'd had carved on his sarcophagus the words "There is joy in seeing you again."

Kit held Angela close for a moment in the cool interior, thinking how fleeting life was, how little time one had in the great continuum of humankind before plans and hopes and dreams no longer mattered.

"They loved each other, didn't they?" she softly said, her face lifted to his.

"Like us," he murmured, tightening his hold on her waist. "And if we live as long, I can love you for decades more."

"I'm happy only with you."

He nodded, thinking what a close thing it had

been that night on the terrace of the yacht club. How he'd almost walked away.

At that moment in the small church built so long ago, bathed in the limpid light of the colored windows, they felt akin to the knight and his lady, as deeply in love, filled with hope and joy, grateful in the shadow of the ancient tombs to have found each other.

But then May came running up, shouting in excitement about a falcon on a headstone outside, and the world suddenly intruded.

"She's such a quiet child," Kit teased, his gaze on May's small figure racing back outside.

"She'll have to find someone like you when she grows up. Someone not interested in demure women."

"I like demure women."

Angela's brows rose. "Really?"

"Did I say from a distance?"

"Thank you," she said with a grin. "You have such charm."

"Whatever it takes to keep you happy, Angel." His smile was sunshine bright.

They spent some time in the graveyard, admiring the falcon first and then the other sculptures adorning the tombstones, reading the inscriptions, seeing the family histories of the small parish unfold over the centuries. And when they drove into the nearby village for luncheon later, they sat at a table set outside on a terrace shaded by a huge old oak.

The servant girl was chatty and vivacious, telling them much of the local history as she served them a luncheon of cold chicken, hot beef and kidney pie, with fresh new apples from the orchard behind the inn. They had apple tart, too, with fresh cream and mugs of locally brewed ale, and when they relaxed after their meal, she brought the children twists of taffy. Fitz wasn't sure for a moment whether he wasn't too old to accept the childishsweet, but the pretty servant girl said with a lovely smile, "Come now, young master, sweets for the sweet."

He took it with pleasure then and gave her a gold sovereign for her smile, so she stayed for a time and entertained them with stories of the celebrated knight and his lady.

"The knight's lady was blond, they say, as fair as the gleaming sun. Like your lady and your children," she added, looking at Kit. "You're outnumbered by towheads," she went on with a smile.

"Maybe the next one will have my coloring," Kit said with a grin directed at Angela.

She turned pink.

Fitz's gaze darted quickly between his mother and Kit.

And May said, "Me want more taffy," ending a potentially embarrassing situation.

But later that night, when Kit had gone upstairs to respond to May's fifth request for a drink, Fitz said to his mother as they sat in the small drawing room overlooking the east lawn, "You should think about getting a divorce from de Grae."

Angela was momentarily startled by her son's comment. "It's not that simple," she ambiguously said. There was no point in alarming Fitz when he was powerless to alter his father's behavior.

"Some people get divorces."

"It's a possibility," she evasively replied. Brook had threatened the children, herself, and Bertie were she to file for divorce, so such a course was a very remote possibility in her mind. She had too many people to guard from her husband's violence and sense of revenge.

"If you did, we wouldn't have to ever see him again," Fitz declared.

"A pleasant thought, isn't it?" Angela said.

"You do like Kit, don't you?"

"Very much."

"He likes you, too, I know."

"Are you matchmaking?" Angela teased.

"He wouldn't hurt you like de Grae."

A small silence descended on the room as they both recalled the harrowing memories.

"No, he'd never hurt me like that," Angela softly replied, though a twinge of melancholy invaded her soul when she thought of the pain she'd endure if Kit ever left her, as she knew he eventually must. He couln't stay in England indefinitely.

Nor could she so easily divorce her husband, despite her son's hopes.

*B*ut during the following days, unpleasant possibilities were set aside, and the small family group dwelt happily at Easton. Kit had had his ponies and polo gear sent up from London, and he and Fitz spent their mornings practicing in the pasture near Stone House.

Kit was tutoring Fitz in the basic skills, and they'd set up a makeshift field with goals so he could learn the necessary speed and distance equations, the degree of power needed on the mallet to drive a ball down the field, the sharp turns that were a requisite to success as a player. And one on one they crossed and recrossed the pasture, sometimes slowly as if choreographing a languid ballet, stopping and discussing each move—other times at an all-out gallop, whooping and shouting in jubilant high spirits.

It was a time of deep contentment as Angela watched her son enjoy the friendship of the man she loved, and she and May would often sit on the porch at Stone House, overseeing the activities on the polo field. The two men would join them for lunch, and after serving the food, the servants were dismissed, leaving them alone in the cottage.

Kit preferred eating in the kitchen so May could make tea for them—an accomplishment of great pride for her. She carefully counted the spoonfuls of tea into the teapot and accepted the grown-ups' help only when lifting the boiling kettle of water. She knew exactly the length of five minutes on the clock, and when she poured the tea into everyone's cup, she beamed.

And no one said "Milk or yemon?" with such charm.

Fitz, too, grew in assurance under Kit's warm regard, his life to date devoid of a male role model. He smiled more and laughed; he could even joke about his near engagement with a playfulness very different from the alarm he had experienced when he'd left England in July.

"Get used to it," Kit had teased. "You'll have to evade a host of pursuing women before you finally find the one you love." And he'd smiled at Angela with such affection, she forgave him for all the pursuing women in his past.

"The women I could manage," Fitz said with a faint smile. "It's de Grae who's terrifying." His brows drew together—a familiar reaction to his father's name.

"Your mother and I will see to de Grae," Kit had calmly said. "You're years too young for marriage."

And the boy had visibly relaxed, Kit's presence offering a powerful sense of security.

After lunch Angela and May went upstairs for May's afternoon nap, and over the remains of a lemon curd dessert, the men talked of Fitz's school term due to begin. They compared anecdotes on school bullies and schoolmasters, on boyish larks that hadn't changed much from those of Kit's generation. Kit said, "Do you have enough spending money? As I recall, mine was always gone before the term ended."

"Maman's generous," Fitz replied. "The trustees replenish my account when it gets low."

"*My* mother believed in teaching a practical frugality." Kit smiled. "That's when I first learned to gamble."

"Can you show me how to shuffle the cards like you did last night—in that sweeping arc?"

"It takes a bit of practice. I'll show you how to keep track of your opponent's hand, too. That's even more useful. An old gambler in Rio taught me."

"You've been everywhere, haven't you?" Fitz said with a sigh of longing.

"Almost . . . although there are places I wouldn't recommend visiting a second time." Lounging in his chair, Kit looked the country gentleman in tweeds and riding pants, far removed from the dangerous haunts that momentarily pervaded his mind.

"Take me with you sometime." Fitz's eyes were aglow with interest.

"I'll take you all with me, just as soon as your mother brings herself to disregard those rules of society constraining her."

"I saw him beat mother once," Fitz quietly said, his statement discordant, the sudden necessity to divulge his feelings evident in his trembling voice. "He picked her up and threw her across the room. One minute she was standing, and the next she was sitting on the floor." His face was tight with pain. "She told me to go. I should have helped her."

"Don't blame yourself," Kit murmured, reaching across the table to touch Fitz's white-knuckled hand pressed against the tablecloth. "De Grae's to blame. No one else."

"I should have helped her," the boy repeated in a whisper, his gaze downcast.

"You were a child," Kit gently said. "Your mother didn't want you hurt, too."

"I hate him," Fitz whispered.

"You and I can protect your mother now. She'll be fine."

Fitz's gaze came up and met Kit's clear green eyes. "I'm glad you're here."

Kit nodded. "So am I."

Fitz stayed another week before leaving to meet friends for a walking tour in the Lake Country, a last short holiday before fall term began.

"He liked you," Angela said after he left. "He said you were good for me."

"A perceptive child," Kit murmured, smiling at her across the breakfast table. "He's very much your son," Kit added, "so naturally I liked him, too."

"He has the Lawton looks, don't you think?"

"Very much. He's handsome and well-mannered, and most important, a skilled sailor," Kit said with a grin. "You did well, Maman."

"He's all I had for many years," she quietly said.

"Now you have me as well," he offered with the open warmth she thrived on. "And speaking of this fond attachment, I'd like you to come to London with me. I have two meetings I can't avoid."

"I don't know," she equivocated. "I might be unwise. Someone could see us."

"Stay at my flat. You'll be incognito there. I have to meet my banker about some shipments coming in from China. A day, maybe two, and we'll come back to Easton."

"I *could* stop at my shop in Bond Street and see if

my manager needs anything new from the sewing school at Easton." Angela's shop specialized in trousseaux, and with her vast acquaintance in the peerage, the skills of the girls at her sewing school were much in demand. As in the case of her agricultural college, she'd been criticized for opening a business. Trade was considered déclassé by her friends. But ever practical, she considered the opportunity to provide work for her tenants more important than social strictures.[20]

"It's settled, then. Could we leave tomorrow?"

"For just two days? I don't want May alone too long."

"Two days," he promised.

18

 When they arrived at Kit's flat in St. James the next day, Kit's butler greeted them with unusual reserve. For a moment Kit wondered whether Whitfield had suddenly acquired piety and was objecting to Angela's presence. But considering he had taken care of his employer's London home for several years in an atmosphere of highly irregular conduct, Kit rather doubted it. He was about to question his butler's behavior when Whitfield murmured as he was helping Kit off with his coat, "Miss Saskia is here, sir."

Kit hestitated at the unexpected news. He'd thought the women had all departed some time ago.

"These vases are similar to the ones in the dining room at Easton," Angela was saying, admiring the Ming vases on the foyer table.

"Take them back with you," Kit offered, his mind racing, the potential for conflict imminent. Perhaps explosive, he mused with disquiet, the sound of high heels clicking on parquet suddenly distinct.

"Whitfield, I can't find that ledger in Kit's desk. Johnston needs it for—" Startled and dismayed, Saskia abruptly checked her progress at the sight of Kit and Angela. The last she'd heard, Kit had planned on staying at Easton for some time. "I just came back . . . for the Pearl River ledger," she said, her voice faltering and restrained. "The warehouse manager . . . needs it. Whitfield, get my cloak."

"Never mind, Whitfield," Kit murmured. His friendship with Saskia was of long standing, and her diffidence was disturbing to him. "Angela," he said, drawing her forward, hoping she was in an understanding mood, "I'd like you to meet Saskia Vanderwael. Saskia, the Countess de Grae."

She *is* small, Saskia thought, gazing at the petite woman at Kit's side. "My pleasure, Countess," she politely said, feeling very large suddenly and vastly de trop. "Forgive me for intruding."

"Good afternoon, Miss Vanderwael," Angela cordially replied, surprised at the woman's grace, not surprised at her beauty. "And you're not intruding. I'm sure Kit is interested in the ledger, too. Didn't you come into the city to take care of your business?" she added, gazing up at him with a smile.

"Thank you, yes," he gently said, relieved by Angela's amicable response. "Whitfield, we'll have tea and drinks in the study. Come, ladies," he went on, taking Angela by the hand, smiling at Saskia.

The flat was large, high-ceilinged, decorated to meet a bachelor's requirements in subdued blues and browns and greens, with velvet and leather chairs and sofas, and prints and paintings of sailing.

They walked through the reception rooms and then down a hallway to a large study at the back that overlooked a garden bright with fall chrysanthemums.

After seating Angela, Kit proceeded to show Saskia the leather-bound volume tucked away in a bottom desk drawer, and they immediately fell into a

lengthy discussion of the merchandise being unloaded
at the Chelsea warehouse.

She's stunning, Angela thought, observing Saskia
as she pointed out various items on the ledger pages to
Kit. Tall, slender, with enormous dark eyes and superb
bones, her gown of cranberry wool couturier, her
golden hair dressed in the latest fashion, Saskia was as
elegant as she was knowledgeable about shipping,
from the sounds of the conversation—the swift recital
of prices and weights and customs duties esoteric and
professional.

How long had she known him? Angela wondered,
their rapport so obviously harmonious. She'd say
something and he'd finish her sentence, or he'd bring
up a point and she'd be nodding halfway through his
sentence. He laughed once and she smiled in agreement and said something in a language Angela didn't
recognize. Chinese, perhaps.

But when the butler brought in the tea tray a few
moments later, Kit immediately broke off the discussion and came to sit beside Angela on the small green
leather sofa, putting his arm around her in full sight of
the manservant and Saskia. "Excuse us, darling," he
said, smiling down at her as though he'd newly discovered he loved her. "I've been worried about that ship-
ment, but all is well."

"Thanks to Johnston," Saskia noted, lounging in a
large club chair with the comfortable informality of
someone familiar with the flat.

"Thanks to you as well," Kit countered. "Remember to pay yourself a bonus for those Tang sculptures
you talked me into bringing out of Shaanxi. Saskia has
an eye for art," he added, turning to Angela. "She's
very good."

And an eye for handsome men as well, Angela
thought. But she felt oddly benevolent to the lovely

woman who had known Kit for so much longer than she. Saskia was leaving him at Kit's request, and understanding her own love for him, Angela responded to her rival with compassion rather than jealousy.

They drank tea and then champagne, talked of the work being done on the *Desiree,* of their activities at Easton. Saskia had made plans to settle in Paris; they discussed at length the various neighborhoods with good apartments. Then, glancing at his watch, Kit said to Angela, "I should see Chambers before the bank closes. Would you mind if I was gone for a short time?"

She didn't; she understood, good-natured and obliging. And he kissed her softly and rose to leave.

Setting down her glass, Saskia stood as well.

"Please stay if you wish," Angela said to her. "If you have business to conduct here, I can find something to keep me busy."

"You *could* check those invoices against Johnston's numbers, Saskia," Kit suggested. "If you want to," he politely added, cautious about the two women's feelings.

"If you don't mind, I'll just stay for a minute," Saskia replied. "I haven't found the bales of Thai silk listed, yet I recall seeing them somewhere."

"Fine; I'm gone. Good-bye, darling. Ask Whitfield for anything you wish. Thank you, Saskia . . . again." And with a wave he strode from the room.

As Saskia began moving toward the desk, Angela quietly said, "Do you love him?"

"Not the way you do."

"How is that?" Angela spoke even more softly, Saskia's response oddly unnerving for its lack of inflection.

"You love him too much." Standing behind the desk now, she leaned her fingertips on the leather top and added in a kindly tone, "He's in love with you the same way. Don't be alarmed."

"I can't help it. I wish I could."

"You can do anything if you want to, Countess. But I understand," she ambiguously said, not sure she wished to be confessor to Kit's true love.

"How long have you known him?" Angela inquired. "Forgive me for asking, but I know so little about him other than the most superficial facts." She wished, too, with apprehension, to hear about their relationship.

"I met Kit five years ago in Java," Saskia replied, her tone measured, cautious of revealing too much. "He saved me from thugs my husband had hired to kill me. We're very good friends."

"But you're more than friends, too," Angela softly prompted.

"We were until he met you. Then we were all pensioned off," Saskia noted with a faint smile.

"I have this strange feeling I should say I'm sorry, when I'm not."

"You needn't blame yourself. It was Kit's decision, not made, I'm sure, without profound consideration. And we were all with him by choice. He's made us all quite wealthy, you know. A decided advantage in this world, as you're well aware," Saskia quietly added. "I hope it works out for you."

"Why do you say that?" The temperate moderation of Saskia's words had a disquietingly prophetic sound.

"Because he's going to want everything from you. He loves you that much. And I'm not certain the Countess de Grae can give him all he wants."

"Perhaps I can." But a problematic tentativeness ruffled the serenity of her reply.

"Then everything will be perfect," Saskia politely

answered, overlooking the tenor of Angela's response. "And I'll be happy for him because I *do* love him, but not desperately, like you." She lightly brushed the desktop with her fingertips and then smiled faintly. "My sojourn in Java took away some of my heart. I didn't know that could happen, but it did."

"I'm sorry. Husbands can be very difficult."

"Even dangerous."

"Yes, that too."

"I made some inquiries about your husband when Kit decided to pension us off," Saskia said, her voice suddenly earnest. "I'd watch your back."

Angela shook her head. "I don't want to think about it."

"You may have to eventually."

She sighed. "I know."

"Kit's very competent. One doesn't survive Macao in the days he was there and the South China Sea without battle scars."

"Oh, please," Angela nervously said, "don't even suggest such a thing."

"I'm sure it won't come to that," Saskia cordially said.

"How morbid this conversation has become," Angela said with a small smile. "Everything is much less complicated at Easton."

"How nice for you. Have you been sailing?"

And their conversation turned on a pleasant, less personal note as the women discussed their love of the sea.

*K*it talked Angela into going to dinner that night. He'd engaged a private room at Kettner's. No one saw them enter, but the young Marchioness of Berwick, waiting in a queue at the door for her carriage, caught a glimpse of them as they left. She couldn't wait to tell Olivia the next morning. She rang her so early, Olivia's maid was reluctant to wake her mistress.

"Just wake her!" Grace Albright barked. "This instant!"

"She has him," the marchioness wailed when Olivia groggily answered the phone. "I saw them last night at Kettner's. He's so-o-o gorgeous, and she's, well, you know she always looks stunning, and he was handing her into a carriage and I just wanted to scream."

"Good God, what time is it? And who the bloody hell are you talking about, Grace?"

"Who *cares* what time it is?" the marchioness bitterly retorted. "The woman snared him just as you said she would, and it's not fair because she already has a thousand lovers—"

"Angela," Olivia softly said, recognizing the description, suddenly fully awake. "Don't tell me she was with Kit," she curtly queried.

"Of course she was with Kit. Doesn't she get every man in the entire world?" the marchioness heatedly replied. "Starting with Bertie, who practically followed her around like a puppy for years."

"Are you certain it was Kit?" Olivia's voice was brusque; Grace was flightier than most. "Tell me what you saw."

"I'm *certain,* Olivia," she snapped. "Do you think I'd call you at eight in the morning if I wasn't? How can you mistake Kit Braddock?" she indignantly said. "He looked so beautiful, so sinfully male, I wanted to cry, especially when I had to sit next to Sidney afterward, who's afraid of guns and horses and a thousand other things. It's so *damned* irritating," she exasperatedly went on, "seeing them together, and Kit was practically carrying Angela out to the carriage, he was so solicitous. How does she *do* it?" The marchioness's voice had risen to shrewish levels. "She's fifteen years older than I am; she's older than *he* is."

"They must have had a private room." There was no point in debating Angela's appeal.

"I imagine they did. I'm sure they *needed* a private room."

"Lawton House is closed," Olivia declared, less interested in their sexual activities, which were a given, than in the possibility of thwarting Angela's liaison. "She must be staying with him."

"Could we pay a call on him? I'd love *any* excuse to see him."

"He wouldn't be home to us even if we did call. Let me think for a moment."

"I don't want her to have him, Olivia!" Grace wailed. "Once men fall in love with Angela, they never look at anyone else."

"Is Brook in town?"

"Sidney mentioned him yesterday. He has been here; Sidney said something about a temper tantrum Brook had at the club over a meal—or was it a hand of cards? I wasn't listening; Sidney's so boring."

"Wasn't the dowager Countess de Grae at Agnes's dinner the other night, with her two plain daughters?" Olivia observed. "If they knew of Angela's new beau, *they* could tell Brook. You know, since Joe Manton, de Grae's been very strange . . . or maybe he's always been strange," she concluded. "In any event, I doubt Kit's interested in a serious contretemps with an irate husband."

"You're *so* clever, Olivia," Grace joyfully cooed. "Then poor Kit would be in need of consoling, and we could offer him our sympathy. Don't you just get a shiver thinking of him?"

What Olivia experienced thinking of Kit Braddock required a man or masturbation to satisfy; she was long past the girlish shiver. And Kit had been much on her mind since Morton Castle, his particular proclivities in terms of savage sex intoxicating to recall. "He does have a special charm," Olivia softly agreed. "So why don't I dress, you come fetch me, and we'll call on the very proper and righteous de Grae women?"

The dowager Countess de Grae was gracious when Olivia and Grace arrived on a mission ostensibly having to do with charity work. Her two daughters were less welcoming; they had none of their mother's charm or looks, favoring their father instead.

The ladies spoke of the weather first, all agreeing the fall was unusually mild. The dowager poured tea with the refined manners of another more proper age while her daughters cast each other searching looks. They were suspicious of anything the Duchess of Lexford espoused. And she and charity were such an obvious mismatch, they wondered what had really prompted her visit.

The paintings at the Royal Academy showing were discussed next, and all commiserated on Lord Leighton's recent death. The charity work, when it eventually rose in the conversation, had to do with a hospital needing funds for a new wing, and as the daughters suspected, Olivia was vague on the details. But the dowager promised to donate to the project, and smiles were exchanged all around.

"Have you seen Angela lately?" Olivia casually asked, accepting her second cup of tea with a cordial smile.

"Not since shortly after Maman's birthday in July," the eldest sister, Gwendolyn, replied. "She's busy at Easton with her building and schools." Her tone suggested something less than approval.

"She and Brook can hardly be civil to each other," the younger sister interjected, a caustic edge to her voice. "Her visit to de Grae Castle threw everything in such disarray. She even brought her solicitor, as if she needed legal counsel to step inside her husband's home."

"That's enough, girls," their mother admonished, as if they were youngsters instead of forty-year-old matrons with children of their own. "Angela and Brook have agreed to disagree and it's not our affair." The dowager, aware of her son's wickedness, had always sympathized with her daughter-in-law, although she was unable to offer her more than tacit support. The late earl had been a man of violent tempers, as well.

"I saw Angela at Kettner's last night," Grace exclaimed, unable to contain herself any longer.

"How nice. I understand their chef is excellent," Angela's mother-in-law pleasantly said.

Casting a swift, glowering look at the impetuous marchioness, who didn't have enough sense to lay the proper groundwork to their revelation, Olivia noted in a suitably troubled tone, "She was unfortunately in the company of Mr. Braddock . . . that rich American who keeps a harem aboard his yacht. An escort, I'm afraid, of highly questionable taste."

"Is he not a personal friend of the prince?" the dowager asked.

"Maman, how can you always defend her?" her eldest daughter protested, her mouth drawn into a grim line of disapproval. "The man has a *harem*!"

"I'll thank you to refrain from reproving me, Gwendolyn," her mother quietly said. "Have your husbands gone off to Scotland for the hunting?" she urbanely inquired of Olivia and Grace. "It seems so many of the men have left London now."

"Archie hasn't hunted in years," Olivia politely replied, understanding the conversation about Angela was closed, realizing, too, that the dowager was a staunch advocate for her daughter-in-law. "I'm afraid he's too old."

"A shame when you're so young and vibrant yourself," the dowager blandly remarked, her smile gracious. Everyone knew of Olivia's penchant for young men.

"I wish *Sidney* would go hunting," the marchioness fretfully declared.

"Perhaps you should take up the sport," the dowager suggested, smiling at the young girl who had married a man with nothing to recommend him but his wealth—a not uncommon occurrence in their class. "You meet such interesting people at the hunts. Angela hunts to hounds all winter and finds much pleasure in the activity."

The late earl had always disapproved of Angela's hunting, not thinking it at all ladylike; the dowager had thought her wonderfully independent.

"Is Brook hunting?" Olivia asked, intent on sowing her seeds of discontent elsewhere if the dowager proved unproductive to her plans.

"Yes, he just left; he so enjoys shooting things," his mother neutrally said. "May I get you more tea?"

Grace was fidgeting like a schoolgirl, and Olivia wondered how she thought to interest Kit Braddock with such a lack of sophistication. But at least the girl gave her an opportunity to leave. "I'm afraid Grace has organized our schedule rather tightly today. We're to see several others on our charity mission." She rose. "But thank you so much for your contribution, and give our regards to your family."

———

She's starting again, Maman," Gwendolyn exploded, the moment their guests had left. "Has the woman no shame? I can see why Brook so despises her. She has absolutely no discretion."

"Since you never see Angela, I don't understand how her activities are of any concern to you, Gwendolyn. As for Brook, you're ignorant of much in his life; Angela has cause."

"Cause to take lovers with impunity?" her daughter Beatrice righteously inquired.

"Cause for more than that," their mother quietly said. "You know nothing of their marriage. The subject is closed."

But the two sisters wrote to their brother, telling him of Angela's appearance at Kettner's with Kit Braddock, and when the slaughter of grouse was over in Scotland, he traveled south to Easton to see his wife and daughter.

He was looking forward to the encounter with quickening expectation. It was as if something had immutably altered in their relationship when he'd beaten Angela over Joe Manton's blatant indiscretions. And he'd often thought of that night and of her cringing terror with pleasure. He'd never seen Angela submissive before; she'd been an imperious heiress, an independent woman of great beauty and presence, even at seventeen. After spoiling her completely, the old viscount had made a mistake leaving his fortune to his granddaughter, his father had always said. And he agreed.

Brook wondered if Angela would cry out again if he was to beat her. She hadn't until the very end last time. The violence had aroused him, as it always did, her sobbing fear bringing his lust to fever pitch, and he'd taken his pleasure in her as was his husbandly right. Perhaps he should have beaten her years ago, he thougtfully deliberated, and she wouldn't have treated him with such contempt.

A pleasant possibility to look forward to.

But on a more prosaic level, his trip to Easton served another purpose. His gambling debts had reached that point again where he could no longer go to his estate trustees for funds. The Earls de Grae, while of ancient heritage and noble birth, hadn't had the advantage of owning acres rich in coal or iron. Nor had his early ancestors had the wherewithal to marry city heiresses like the Lawtons, who brought in vast tracts of London real estate with their dowries. His marriage to Angela had in fact been a means of bolstering the de Grae finances. So she could give him some of her lavish stores of money to pay off his debts, he resentfully thought, always deeply insulted that she retained control of her fortune. Because she was his wife, her wealth should have been *his*.

19

Brook Greville arrived at Easton two days later, asking directions of the servants as he entered the house, finding Angela in the nursery reading to May.

"How sweet a picture to return home to," the earl sardonically said, leaning against the doorjamb, all evil intent and rudeness.

At the sight of her father, May, who was sitting in Angela's lap, laced her small arms around her mother's waist and clung tightly to her.

"Do you want something?" Angela kept her voice calm with effort; he was looking at her with covetous eyes.

"Can't I come and visit?"

Instead of answering, Angela turned toward the other door into the nursery and shouted, "Bergie!"

"She looks more like you every day, Angela," her husband disdainfully noted. "Are you teaching her how to be an heiress, too?"

"We have two children, Brook. Fitz shares my fortune."

"He's very like you, too, my dear. How do you do it?"

"By behaving like a normal parent. Oh, here you are, Bergie," she said, relief flooding through her senses, her need to protect May preeminent in her mind. "May will be going for a walk now. Take her sweater in case it turns cool."

"Come here, May. Let Papa hold you," Brook softly said, tapping his leg as if he were calling a dog.

Eyeing him warily, May tightened her grasp on her mother.

Pushing away from the door, the earl stalked into the room, his eyes glittering strangely. "I'm your father, you stupid child," he wrathfully declared, and stooping down, he jerked May from Angela's arms.

May screamed, squirming frantically, her little arms and legs flailing, her back arched against her father's brutal hold, her cries a frightened, piercing shriek.

Lurching to her feet with pounding heart, Angela shouted, "Put her down!" her voice sounding shrill in her ears. Flying at him, she raised her fists to strike him.

He suddenly dropped the young girl as though he'd grown tired of the game.

Scooping May into her arms, Angela held her close, then swiftly moved toward Bergie, who was standing terrified in the dressing-room doorway, and handed her daughter to the nursemaid. "Take her to Stone House," she quietly said, and shoved them out of the room.

Whirling on her husband, she uttered in a deadly quiet tone, "Don't ever do that to May again. Don't ever touch her again, you monster. And get out of my house or I'll have you thrown out."

"By your new lover?"

"By him or one of my other lovers," she contentiously spit, "you loathsome, despicable man."

"What other lovers?" a voice from the doorway softly inquired.

"He's jealous," Brook snidely remarked, turning to see Kit standing quietly at the door. "Does he think he's alone in your affections, my dear?" he mockingly inquired. "Should I start listing all your lovers?"

"At least they're not eight-year-old girls," she responded with contempt.

"Who was the first?" he theatrically mused, ignoring her rebuke. "Charlie Beresford? His wife became so angry, she wrote to the prime minister," the earl derisively noted. "Unfortunately, the prime minister wasn't much help; he wanted Angela himself."

"Angela and I compare our lists," Kit softly said, his voice chill beneath the velvet tone. "I don't recall you being on hers," he gently said, his powerful frame filling the doorway, the box of special cream cakes he'd brought for May still in his hand. "I don't think she likes you," he added, curt and brusque, the lazy mockery gone. "You should go."

"Are you here for the duration, then?" De Grae was dressed in black, his form still trim at fifty, but he had a poisonous look, like a menacing viper.

"Something like that," Kit murmured. Stepping into the room, he placed the box of cakes on a play table. "And I think in future Angela would prefer you not arrive unannounced."

"I don't want you ever coming back," Angela said, her voice hard and cold, her hands clenched at her sides to keep herself from trembling. "Easton is mine and you're not welcome."

"That seems pretty plain, de Grae," Kit mildly said, having moved between Angela and her husband, protecting her.

"Gwendolyn wrote me about you," the earl drawled, unheedful of his dismissal, his own obsessions of more import. "You fuck all the women, I hear."

"Not all of them. Not your sister." It was an insult.

"He must be a change for you, Angela. This one doesn't fall prostrate at your feet, does he?"

"Nor does he beat me, Brook."

"You deserved it." The hostility in his voice was like a knife blade.

Kit moved so swiftly, Angela's response caught in her throat, her words changing to a stifled scream.

Picking up Brook bodily, Kit held him at arm's length with his feet dangling above the floor, and he said in a voice of implacable certainty, "If you ever touch her again, de Grae, I'll kill you."

Then he tossed the earl away as if disburdening himself of something noxious.

Although he fell heavily, Brook scrambled instantly to his feet, his eyes malevolent and fanatical. "You can't watch her every second," he said with hellish delight.

"Get out," Kit murmured, "or I'll kill you now."

"You'll see me again, Angela," Brook whispered, turning briefly to gaze at his wife.

And he left then with a careless wave as though he'd stopped by only for a friendly chat, his footsteps echoing down the third-floor hallway, his eerie, tuneless whistle hanging in the air like dread.

"His sister wrote to him," Angela said, collapsing onto a nursery chair, trembling in the aftermath of his malignant presence. "Someone must have seen us in London."

"You shouldn't have to deal with him," Kit quietly said, coming over and sitting on the floor near her, gently touching her hands clasped tightly in her lap.

"I know. It's harder now . . . since I love you. I'm more afraid; I've so much more to lose. I might lose you."

"I'm not going anywhere. But you should divorce him. What's the point any longer . . . ?"

"Could we talk about this later?" All the ramifications of a public divorce and scandal overwhelmed her. She took a fortifying breath. "My mind's in tumult."

"Where did you hide May?" Kit asked with a smile, willing to give her time to sort out the complications. "She's missing the cream cakes."

"You're so lovely and normal," she murmured, lightly touching his windswept hair. "What would I do without you?"

"Take up with all your old lovers?"

"I love your jealousy—and no, never, never."

"Then I'll let you have a cream cake, too," he teased. "Let's go find May."

"I had Bergie take her to Stone House. Brook terrorized her when he tried picking her up."

"We'll distract her with something fun," Kit quietly said, rising and pulling her to her feet. "You carry the cakes and I'll carry you, and we'll talk only about pleasant things, like the presents I have for you and May at Stone House," he went on, handing her the box and lifting her into his arms.

"Where did you get presents?" Her surprise registered in her voice.

"In Easton Vale," he replied, exiting the room.

"What do they have in Easton Vale?" The local village had limited shopping.

"Well, pardon me, my sophisticated countess," he sardonically murmured, his eyes sparkling with amusement, "but there are many things in Easton Vale that appeal to three ladies I know. You'll just have to wait and see. I found something for Bergie, too."

"She adores you already. Now she'll love you forever."

"That's the general idea."

"Arrogant man." She hung on tightly as he descended the stairs in graceful leaps.

"It works every time," he declared, strolling down the second-floor corridor. "Ladies just love presents."

"You know too much about what ladies like," she teased. "I'm not going to let you out of my sight ever again."

"Nor I you." After seeing Brook again, he meant it. The man was dangerous.

*H*e'd bought them both new bridles for their mounts, red leather, silver embellished, their names beautifully engraved on the polished silver. And red leather vests to match, ordered a week ago when he'd seen one in the harness maker's window.

Bergie's gloves were lavender leather, scented and embroidered, and she blushed ten shades of red when she thanked him.

Later that day, after cream cakes and tea, after playful kittens and much laughter, after a peaceful dinnertime in the nursery with Peter Rabbit, the memory of the earl's visit had been tempered by the more familiar joy and contentment of their small family group.

But fragments of fear remained, and Baby May brought the incident up again when she was being tucked into bed. "Me 'fraid," she said.

"Mama's here, darling," Angela soothed. "You don't have to be afraid."

"Brook bad," the little girl emphatically declared. She never called him Papa.

"He won't be back," her mother said, glancing over at Kit, who lounged in a chair at the foot of her bed.

"For sure?" she tentatively inquired, clutching Peter Rabbit tightly.

"For sure," Kit answered. "Mama told him to go."

"Tanks, Mama," May whispered, her relief obvious. "Me sweep now."

And Angela and Kit sat with her until she fell asleep.

*Y*ou're going to have to get him out of your life," Kit remarked as they left the nursery. "De Grae's not only dangerous to you, but to May and Fitz."

"If Brook wasn't so unpredictable, a person could deal with him," Angela replied. "But he's threatened Bertie enough to alarm him. And the queen will be enraged if Wales is brought into court again as a correspondent in a divorce. It's so frustrating; Brook's impossible to deal with."

"Look, darling, you're going to have to work this out. I'm not going to tell you what to do. But de Grae is unstable and a real risk to you and your children. Think about that."

"I will, I do . . . I have for years."

"You'll have to make a decision soon. The *Desiree* will be ready to sail in a month."

"A month?" she whispered.

"Don't sound so terrified, darling. Surely a lady who can run an estate, raise two children, found a college, race yachts, hunt, and find time to enjoy some of the pleasures of life can make one more decision. You still have four weeks."

The month sped by, the leaves began changing, Fitz spent another week with them before going to Cambridge, May learned to read *Peter Rabbit* because Kit spent enormous time with her and she desperately wanted to read. He never once brought up the divorce again, and Angela almost came to believe she could be happy and in love without facing any unsolvable problems.

She clung to him like a young girl with a first crush, wanting to touch him a dozen times an hour, and he enjoyed her adoration and offered his in return. They both learned of tender devotion and winsome love and the benevolence of passion as adjunct to desire, a partiality they found more tantalizing when matched with love. This precious affection opened new dimensions and the deepest recesses of their hearts.

The explosion when it came was unexpected; they both presumed too much . . . or not enough.

It all began benignly, almost romantically.

They were having a drink in the library, dinner was over, May had been put to bed, a rich contentment inundated their senses. Sitting across from Angela, Kit was sunk deep in a leather chair, lean and handsome in evening dress, his long legs stretched out before him, his gaze warm and affectionate over the rim of his whiskey glass.

"I've never given you any jewelry," he said.

"You've given me so much more," she murmured, so deep in love, her heart ached. Curled up on the sofa with her legs tucked under her, she leaned against the sofa arm and smiled at him, her hair and gown pale in the glow of the lamps.

"I have something for you." And setting down his glass, he rose from the chair. Sliding his finger into his waistcoat pocket as he crossed the short distance to the couch, he drew an object from his pocket. "I didn't think I'd ever do this," he murmured with a quirked grin, dropping lightly to one knee. Gazing up at her with a beguiling gleam in his emerald eyes, he softly said, "Will you marry me and make me a happy man?" And drawing her right hand from her lap, he slipped a spectacular diamond ring onto her fourth finger. "That one's in the way," he casually noted, tapping her wedding band on her left hand. "So for now . . ." He smiled.

When she didn't answer, he looked at her for a moment and then sat back on the carpet, gazing at her with a mild bewilderment. "I think you're supposed to say something."

"Why can't we just leave it the way it is?" Her voice was no more than a whisper.

"Because," he said very deliberately, a new coolness in his eyes, "I don't care to share you."

"You won't have to."

He exhaled in a long, slow breath. "I am, though, regardless of what you say, and I don't like it."

"If I try to divorce him, who knows what Brook will do? He'll certainly implicate Wales."

"Who the hell cares?" he coldly replied, swiftly coming to his feet, intolerant of aristocratic custom.

"All the details of my life will be dragged through the papers. My children will suffer. My family would be mortified. The queen—" Her words came to a quiet halt under Kit's fierce gaze.

"I don't understand you people," he growled.

"You do what you damned well please, ignoring every social and moral convention—the only mortal sin that of disclosure. Why does it matter what others think? They know who you're fucking anyway!"

"Please, Kit. Try to understand."

"Understand what? That everyone lives a sham life, that nothing is what it appears, that only the first-born son is guaranteed a legal father? I'm having real trouble here."

"Maybe with time I could convince Brook to be more reasonable and—"

"I don't want to wait," he bluntly interposed. "Good God, Angela, you've been in this miserable marriage for eighteen years. How much longer do you intend to delay the inevitable? Just sue for divorce."

"I wish it were that simple."

"It is if you want it to be." Each word was a grating, harsh denunciation.

"I'm sorry," she whispered.

"No, I'm sorry," Kit murmured, his voice taut with restraint. "I thought you actually loved me. I didn't realize I was just another diversion in your smoothly run and discreet—I use the term loosely—life of amorous play. But all the men at least keep life interesting, right?"

"There haven't been enough to say 'all,' " she refuted, bristling at his implication. "And how dare you censure me—a man with a harem?"

"A *former* harem, thanks to you," he curtly noted. "But it's been pleasant having been added to your short list, Countess," he added with a silky smile. "A definite experience. Will you let your husband beat you again in the interests of maintaining this acceptable facade for your mother and the queen and your public?" Towering above her, he stood like an avenging angel, militant and wrathful, derision plain on his face.

"If I were a man, I could divorce with impunity—but, then, we both know it's a man's world, don't we?" She didn't need a reprimand on conjugal relations from a man of his intemperate habits.

"And you've learned to manipulate it nicely, haven't you?"

"I survive," she said, thinking how little he knew of the harsh necessities of her life. "My fortune helps. But *you* know about the merits of wealth," she quietly went on. "We both understand the extent of its power."

"That's it?" It was as though he hadn't been listening.

"I can't divorce him unless he agrees. If he decides to fight me in court, it could be dangerous to me personally, to the children; he could ruin the Prince of Wales."[21] She'd been trying to make him understand that for weeks.

"Thank you for your hospitality, then." His gaze was brutally cold.

"Thank *you*," she softly said. "For your friendship."

"I don't want to be friends."

"I know."

Kit looked at her for a moment more, his expression unreadable, and then, with a curt nod, he strode from the room.

She sat numbed for a very long time, not wanting to move, hoping with the flimsiest pipe-dream fantasy that he'd come walking back in and take her in his arms and make her sadness disappear.

But she'd seen the coldness in his eyes.

And even in her most wishful dreams, she couldn't erase that look from her memory.

When she finally left the library hours later and went up to her room, his clothes were gone, along with his two leather satchels and his boots from under the chair in the dressing room. He'd forgotten one ivory comb; she found it lying on her vanity table where he'd left it the night before, after combing her hair. And he'd missed his leather jacket tossed onto a chair in a shadowed corner of her room.

She put the jacket on, rolling the sleeves up clumsily, hugging it closely to her body, the scent of his cologne surrounding her, wanting desperately to leave everything and go with him to Brisbane or Madagascar or to a cottage in Maine. And then she sat down by the fire in the chair he always sat in and cried great oceans of tears because she couldn't go anywhere with him.

And all her happiness was gone.

In the morning Bergie told her Kit had come up to hold May for a moment before he'd left. "Is he coming back soon?" the young girl asked. He'd said he had to leave on some business.

"I'm not sure," Angela replied, wondering what she was going to say to May when he didn't return.

Wondering if the desolation filling her soul would dissipate in a thousand years.

Kit had written a letter to Fitz from London trying to explain his leaving:

Your mother doesn't want to consider a divorce now, and I can't convince her otherwise. She envisions numerous unsolvable problems with society. I don't see these problems as insur-

mountable, but she's lived with these people all her life, and I haven't. You might understand better than I.

If there's anything I can ever help you with, don't hesitate to call on me, or if you feel the urge to see China someday, I've always room for another passenger on the Desiree. *I'll leave Chambers's address. He can find me anywhere.*

Keep the ponies. You're getting to be a good polo player.

Fondly,
Kit

20

In the coming days Angela busied herself on the estate, rising early and working until late into the night, trying to obliterate her pain with constant activity. She began hiring teachers for her college and working with them to set up a curriculum, asking her tenant farmers for input as well. They had meetings upon meetings; she took notes and organized them when she couldn't sleep in the middle of the night. Fitz came home once and consoled her with his presence, although she could tell he missed Kit almost as much as she. May had stopped asking for Kit a dozen times an hour; she asked only a dozen times a day. But at the end of the first fortnight after Kit had walked out, Angela's life had fallen into a manageable routine because she filled every hour of the day with activities. And when she couldn't sleep at night, she read farm reports from her steward—a sleeping potion of sorts.

She felt strong enough to go into London during the last days of the month. Her bankers needed an update on the amount of money she was pouring into her college. Their letters had become insistent of late.

—

*K*it was dealing with his loss in a more active fashion. He was still in London, waiting for some contracts on real estate he'd purchased, waiting as well for Henry Watson to finally finish the *Desiree*. He'd allowed him to install a new, more powerful engine, and some of the parts had been delayed. So while he filled his days with business, as was a pattern with him, his nights were spent in London's exclusive brothels in an endless round of sport.

He was drinking more than usual, and on the rare occasions he attended some society function, when he was approached by ladies looking to renew a past amorous acquaintance, he'd politely say, as if he were discussing the weather, "I'm sorry. I promised my mother to abstain from sex."

He didn't, of course, but he didn't care to *talk* to women; he wanted only to fuck them, and the brothels offered him that opportunity. So he started his nights at a club, and then, after drinking and gambling until he was suitably drunk and in need of a woman, he'd repair to one of the numerous luxurious houses of pleasure and pick out his companion, or companions, for the evening.

He was generous with his money and his talents in bed, so he was well loved by madams and ladies alike. By the end of the month he was on a first-name basis with every courtesan of note in London.

Saskia hadn't left the city by the time he'd returned, hot-tempered and wrathful, from Easton, so she was staying with him in his flat. But he wasn't sharing her bed; he teased her one morning, when he'd come home at daybreak still roaring drunk, that he'd lost his taste for women outside of red velvet chambers.

"Fucking you would be like fucking my sister," he softly added, patting her gently on the arm as she helped him out of his topcoat. "I can't do it, darling," he cheerfully said, kissing her lightly on the cheek. "Have you thought of Madame Centisi's? I hear she has fine-looking studs for ladies of wealth. Take it out of petty cash, sweet. The cash box in my study is full." Leaning against the wall for a moment, he shut his eyes. He was tired, he was tired of being tired; he was tired of looking for Angela in every woman he fucked.

He exhaled, opened his eyes, and with a gaze so lucid Saskia wondered at the abrupt transformation, he smiled and said, "What do we have for papers to sign this morning? Chambers was supposed to send over the abstracts late yesterday."

"They're on your desk."

"Just give me a minute to change. Could you ask the cook to make me some coffee? Strong. Very strong." He grinned. "And don't look all motherly like that. I'll survive very well without her."

But he wondered if he really would at those times when he found himself alone, even briefly. Angela would fill his mind, the memory of her smile, her scent, the feel of her skin, her luscious cry of pleasure when she climaxed, when he was buried deep inside her . . . And then he'd come alert with a start and ruthlessly crush the memories, sweep them away, discard them where they belonged on the rubbish heap of impossible dreams.

*W*hen Angela came to town, she planned on staying no more than three days. One day for her bankers, one to see her friends, and one set aside for relatives who were convinced she was moldering away at

Easton, since she'd not been seen in society since August.

The bankers were difficult, as usual, not inclined to approve of her plans to help her tenants so lavishly. They subscribed to the theory that paying people a living wage and housing them in comfort was spoiling them beyond all necessity. The poor liked to be poor, they would say; it was their place in society, they would smugly add as they sat across from her, fat and well dressed and living in luxury.

"I don't need your approval," she would ultimately declare after politeness and courtesy had been dispensed with and they were scowling like so many unhappy piglets. "Simply write the bank drafts and have them ready for me tomorrow. Thank you, gentlemen, for your time." And she would leave them prognosticating a dire future for one who so little understood the God-given right of the wealthy to rule.

She saw Violet first the next day, because she missed her most and because she wanted someone to talk to about her misery.

"He's still in town, you know," Violet revealed, before she'd even walked completely into the drawing room.

There was no point in feigning ignorance. "I thought he'd gone some time ago," she said, sitting down.

"Mr. Braddock's trying to set new records in the brothels, rumor has it."

"How out of character," Angela sardonically replied.

"He's not pining away," Violet softly said, watching Angela carefully, "if you were hoping for that."

"I really don't have any hopes at all," Angela said with a small sigh. "When I told him I couldn't marry him, I knew everything was irrevocably over. He gave me this," she added, lifting her hand. She hadn't had the heart to take off his ring; it was a last link, if nothing else—a reminder that he'd loved her once.

"How absolutely gorgeous," Violet exclaimed, leaning over to touch the huge diamond. "Everyone's going to want to look at it. Did you know he bought the ring from Cartier? Lucy and Margaret heard of it when they shopped there the day after his purchase. The clerks were all abuzz. He spent fifty thousand pounds by telegram."

"I can't wear it, then." She had forgotten how small her world was.

"Wear it with friends. I find the gesture enormously romantic. Lucy's dying to see it. I told her you were in town. And she's sympathetic; she had to give up Drew last year because her husband threatened to divorce her."

"I *wish* Brook would divorce me. I'd *pay* him to divorce me."

"You've tried that, of course."

"More times than I can remember. No one in his family has ever divorced, and Brook is very dogmatic about it. Although my mother-in-law should have— she had reason enough. But she's too sweet and old-fashioned and willing to endure. She's the only one in the family who's truly decent."

"Maybe he'll die."

Angela laughed. "You sound exactly as you did at eight, when you wished your nasty governess to expire at age thirty."

"At least Brook isn't that young."

"So I should be hopeful."

"You seem to be surviving your loss," Violet noted, pleased to see Angela could still laugh.

"It's not as though I have a choice, now, do I? And surely you and I have learned how to survive unhappiness. We could write a manual on it. Which morbid thought reminds me I have to see mother tomorrow. I hope she won't grill me. I'm not in the mood for moralizing piety. If Brook wasn't so dangerously certain to implicate Bertie in court, and if I didn't fear for the children, I'd sue for divorce and damn the circumstances. Damn mother's pious rules of life, too."

"One would hate to be the one to topple the throne."

"How was I to know when I was twenty that years later I'd rue the day Bertie looked my way?"

Violet shrugged. "How could anyone have known?"

They commiserated on the unfairness of life, but both knew how useless self-pity was, and before long Violet moved on to the latest tidbits of gossip, hoping to raise Angela's spirits. When Lucy and Margaret came in shortly after, Lucy dropped into a chair in a crisp rustle of taffeta and immediately said, "You absolutely have to say yes. It's going to be the greatest fun. Margaret has talked me into it and you'll just swoon. Tell them, Margo."

"I've heard of the most delicious place," the Countess of Bensenhurst declared. "It's all very exclusive and refined, and no one will ever know we've gone."

"Madame Centisi's," Violet offered.

"How did you know?" Lucy asked. "She's just opened."

"She just opened on Half-Moon Street. Ask me about Chesterfield Way."

"You've been there?" Margaret was all eyes.

"Years ago, before Andrew began amusing me."

"Well, you have to go again," Lucy insisted. "I

promised Margo I'd go, and you have to come along for moral support."

"What exactly is Madame Centisi's?—although I think I can guess," Angela murmured, curious despite her somber mood.

"It's all plush silk, purple I'm told," Margo added with a wicked wink, "with gilded mirrors and fine wines—"

"—and devilishly handsome men who'll do anything you ask them to," Lucy interjected, her voice all aflutter.

"No, thank you," Angela immediately demurred. "I'd be embarrassed to pick out a man, not to mention telling him what I wanted."

"But that's the fun," Lucy fervently maintained. "You can order these gorgeous men about for the price of a new hat."

"There's a certain attraction to the concept," Violet sportively noted. "Seeing how we have so little control in many areas of our life."

"Violet," Angela admonished. "Don't even consider it. Besides, you have Andrew to order about."

"But he's out of town hunting," Violet murmured.

"She's going to go, Margo. Look at that gleam in her eyes. Didn't I tell you she would?" Lucy brightly avowed. "Now all we have to do is convince Angela that one little night in a respectable brothel won't send her into the burning flames of hell."

"If I was worried about the flames of hell, darlings," Angela said, "I would have lived my life very differently."

"There. You see," Lucy briskly said. "Then why not go? How else will you have the experience? Look on it as an experiment, all scientific and psychological. Haven't you read Havelock Ellis and Dr. Freud?[22]

Maybe you have some hidden desires you've been repressing."

Angela and Violet exchanged glances, just as they'd done countless times in the past, their shared confidences the basis of a warm, enduring friendship.

"You see, darling," Violet softly said to Angela, raising her eyebrow delicately, "you're obliged to go along to show your respect for the new science of psychology."

"Really?" she said. "Would that be what I was doing?"

"Absolutely, Angela, and you'd be having fun in the bargain," Lucy implored. "You have to come along. We'll drink some champagne first so you won't be going there sober."

"It'll be good for you," Violet quietly said.

And for a moment Angela wondered if this entire scenario had been planned for her benefit.

"Don't look at me like that," Violet protested. "I was planning on a dull dinner at Watley's."

"You're sure?" Angela suspiciously queried.

"Tell her, Lucy. Did I know about this?"

"She couldn't have, Angela. Margo just told me on the way over, and my coachman must have thought we were planning something illicit with all our whispering and giggles. Which reminds me, we'll have to hire a carriage tonight. I don't want any word of this going back to Charles."

"As if he'd notice," Violet blandly said, knowing Lucy's husband had just set up the brightest star of the Roxie music hall as his newest mistress. "So why don't we meet here at nine," Violet briskly said, "and I'll have the chilled champagne and a hired coach at the ready."

21

Kit's evening began like every other evening of late, with dinner at his club and gambling afterward. It was only ten o'clock, he noticed, glancing at the clock in the card room, and he was bored already—with the conversation, with his run of luck, with the whiskey he'd been drinking since five. Watson had better have the *Desiree* fitted up soon, or he was going to expire of ennui.

When a man said "May I sit in?" sometime later, Kit barely looked up, his heavy-lidded gaze indolent. But he did survey the man with slightly more interest when he saw who it was. And he decided Joe Manton was drunker than he.

"Does everyone feel lucky tonight?" Joe inquired, swaying slightly before sitting down, motioning for markers with a negligent wave. "Some days are just damned fine, aren't they?" he proclaimed, smiling broadly.

"You're in good humor, Manton," one of the men declared.

"Had tea at the Ritz with Angela," he said. "She'd put anyone in a good mood."

"Back in London, is she?" The young Duke of Carnaevon inquired. "Thought she was busy in the country with her schools and building projects."

"She's tired of it," Joe said, looking directly at Kit with barefaced conceit. "She came into town for some entertainment."

"Thought I heard from my wife that Georgiana's off to the Rutlands for the weekend," an old gentleman said with a roguish wink. "Damned fortunate timing."

"She'll be gone for a week," Joe said, a boastful, overweening smile indicative of his plans.

"It's my deal, I think," Kit lazily said, sliding up from his lounging sprawl and reaching for the cards. "Why don't we raise the stakes and make this interesting?"

Kit had honed his skills in the gambling dens of Macao, where one's life often hung in the balance over a hand of cards, and he was nimble-fingered, accomplished, and difficult to beat. Before long Joe Manton was calling for new markers.

Then Binky Wootton joined the game, half-drunk himself, and immediately launched into a tantalizing bit of gossip. He'd been exiting a sporting house frequented by aristocratic young bloods when he chanced to look down the street at a carriage debouching several ladies in front of Madame Centisi's. "And who do you think I saw?" he asked, arranging his cards in his hand with a smooth flick of his fingers, gazing at them with weighty deliberation.

"Your wife?" his friend the duke sardonically inquired.

"She doesn't have that much energy," Binky replied without looking up. A handsome young rake, Binky had been obliged to marry beneath him when his father gambled away the family capital.

"Just so long as she gives you an heir along with her money, my boy," an elderly gentleman said, "a husband can overlook her father's brewery."

"My *père*'s words exactly," Binky casually observed, discarding two cards. "Now, as for the fascinating ladies on their night out," he went on, his wife not of interest to him in person or otherwise, "although, naturally, they were all veiled, one was Charlie's wife—I recognized her sable cloak. I couldn't distinguish two of them, but the fourth one's hood caught on the carriage door as she was alighting, and the distinctive fair hair of the Countess de Grae was unmistakable." He let out a low whistle. "I envy the bucks at Madame Centisi's their night's play."

"Amen to that, Binky. Can't say I wholly approve of this damned equality, though," another man said.

"Wouldn't mind if my wife spent some of her money there," Binky drawled. "Would rid me of the damned obligation."

"Hear! Hear!" Joe raffishly exclaimed, lifting his brandy glass to the table at large before draining it.

"Ain't been married that long, Joe. Tired of the ball and chain already?" one of the players sportively inquired.

"Don't know that men are made to be husbands," Joe Manton brusquely growled.

"Have to marry sometime. That's the rub," the duke muttered, his marriage to his cousin prompted by the necessity of keeping the fortune in the family.

"You planning on marrying soon, Braddock?" Joe drawled, his swaggering insolence mocking. "Heard you ordered yourself a fine diamond engagement ring."

Kit gazed at him for a contemptuous, glittering second, provoked by more than Joe's crowing triumph, outraged by the charade of Angela's life. Ill-tempered and sulky, he gruffly said, "She's all yours, Manton. Yours and England's and her husband's, of course . . . we mustn't forget him. That's how it works over here, doesn't it?" he churlishly went on. "Everyone just muddles along." And tossing down his cards, he abruptly stood, knocking over his chair in his explosive rising. "I wish you pleasure with her, with your wife, and with whomever else you're fucking, Manton. Good night, gentlemen. I feel like getting a lot drunker."

"Those Americans are always so hotheaded and impulsive," Binky blandly observed, watching Kit stalk from the room. "Don't understand the rules over here."

"He just doesn't like to lose," Joe Manton smugly noted.

"Plan on taking up where you left off?" the duke casually asked. "Seeing how Angela seems to be at loose ends again."

"Naturally," Joe murmured. "I told the American two months ago he couldn't have her," he added, making sure everyone understood Angela was once again in his territorial preserves. "I should think he'll be leaving England soon."

*K*it had only one drink at the bar and suddenly found himself standing on the porch outside the club with his topcoat on and a rash inspiration stirring his brain. When the doorman said, "Can I help you, sir?" Kit paused for a restless, moody moment and then said, "Have my carriage brought up."

When his driver arrived, he gave him the direction, stepped into the carriage, and then mildly debated the presumption of what he was about to do. "Mildly" being the operative word.

He was drunk, after all; presumption was a given. The rest—principle, expediency, scruple—were all shut away with his reason.

Madame Centisi, dressed in her trademark gray silk gown, greeted him with deference; everyone in the demimonde knew of Kit Braddock's serious pursuit of pleasure. Of late, an informal tally was being kept by the madams, and he was definitely in that rarefied spendthrift rank generally reserved for maharajas and royalty. Madame Centisi invited him into her sitting room, offered him a drink, which he refused, and perceiving he wasn't there to visit, said, "What can I do for you, Mr. Braddock? Are you interested in one of our fine-looking men?" She thought he preferred women, but ennui struck everyone, she realized.

"Actually, I'm interested in watching one of your customers," he said.

"I'm not certain I can accommodate you, Mr. Braddock," the gray-haired proprietress respectfully replied, looking and sounding more like a country curate's wife than a brothel owner. "My customers expect complete privacy. If word got out of such a practice—"

"I understand," Kit gently said, understanding, as well, that everything was for sale in the brothels of the world. "I'd be willing to pay you well for the privilege. You tell *me* what you need to be comfortable with my request."

"How do you know the lady's here?" she asked, knowing full well whom he was interested in; she was always attuned to society tattle. She'd been surprised herself when the Countess de Grae had walked in; she wasn't a woman in need of men.

"An acquaintance saw her enter"—Kit looked down at his wristwatch—"forty minutes ago. Perhaps

I'm too late," he added, restraining his temper at recall of Angela's heated sexual response.

"You're not," she said.

"Blond, petite—a noted beauty," he said. "Are we talking about the same lady?"

"The Boucher room," she murmured.

He immediately offered her enough money to forgo time-consuming negotiations.

Madame Centisi's dark eyes widened appreciably at the staggering amount, and concealing her choking surprise behind a delicate cough, she said, "Would that be cash?"

Sliding his hand into his jacket pocket, Kit pulled out his money clip and stripped free five large bills. He set them on the table between them, then swiftly rose. "I'm in a hurry," he softly said.

She escorted him to a concealed door under the stairs and led him up a hidden staircase to a narrow passageway that connected all her rooms on the main floor. Stopping at the third archway, she put her finger to her mouth to indicate silence and carefully pulled back a small velvet curtain on the wall. Stepping aside, she beckoned him forward and then made to leave.

He caught her by the arm, motioned for her to stay, and looked through the small square opening that offered a broad view of an opulent room.

Angela, fully dressed, was sitting on a gilded chair near the fire, raising a glass of champagne to her lips.

The strapping young man she'd hired to entertain her was seated on the fireplace fender stripped down to his trousers, a wineglass in his hand.

"I'm sorry to be so uncomfortable with this," Angela uneasily said. "I'm not usually so prudish, but I don't know you and . . . well, I'm not certain—"

"—you want to?" the dark-haired man said with a smile.

She delicately lifted one brow. "You've heard this before."

He nodded and, picking up the champagne bottle from the iced bucket nearby, leaned over and added two more inches of wine to her glass. "It's easier after a few glasses of champagne. Did you have a fight with your husband?"

She giggled, the champagne she'd already consumed at Violet's adding whimsy to his question. Waggling her head vaguely, she smiled at him. "Years ago. That's not my excuse tonight."

"You had a fight with your lover?" he gently queried.

"Ah," she sighed in a theatrical fashion, and Kit realized she was feeling the wine. "That must be it."

"Did you pick me because I look like him?" He was relaxed in his undress, at ease in a role he'd performed hundreds of times.

"No . . . because you don't look like him."

"Then you won't want to call me by his name," he teased. "Some women do."

"Really." Her eyes opened wide in surprise. "Have you been doing this long?"

"Not long enough. I enjoy it. Helene pays well, you ladies are a pleasure to be with," he said, smiling at her across the firelit space, "and I like to accommodate hot-blooded women," he finished in a whisper. Standing up, he half swiveled to set his glass on the mantel and then, turning back again, quietly said, "I'm ready whenever you are."

"Oh," Angela softly gasped, startled, his erection plainly evident beneath the soft wool of his trousers.

"Let me take your slippers off," the man suggested. "That shouldn't be too alarming." And kneeling at her feet without waiting for an answer, he turned back the hem of her skirt and petticoat, folding the fabric over her knees so her legs were exposed. Smiling up at her, he very gently removed her high-heeled slippers. "There," he murmured, lightly stroking her silk-stockinged instep. "That didn't hurt, did it?"

"No." Her voice was no more than a whisper.

In the concealed corridor Madame Centisi lightly touched Kit's arm and motioned to him that she was leaving.

Holding up his hand, he mouthed the word "wait" and turned back to the drama being enacted in the firelit room.

"Now we'll slip your garters off," the dark-haired man murmured, slowly sliding his hands up Angela's white silk stockings until his fingers closed on her lacy garters. "Relax," he whispered, touching her hand that lay on the chair arm, smiling up at her as he knelt at her feet. "I'll give you pleasure."

He slipped off one garter and then her stocking, moving with whispered words and gentleness to remove the second garter and stocking, and then he bent his head and kissed the soft flesh of her inner thigh.

Madame Centisi squeaked in surprise when Kit whipped around quickly and bundled her down the passage. As soon as they'd moved past the room Angela occupied, he curtly said, "Get him out of there."

"I can't," the plump matron protested, trying to keep her balance as he rushed her down the stairs. "What could I possibly say? She's already paid for Steven's time. She'd wonder what was going on."

When they reached the bottom of the stairway in the hidden recesses of the house, Kit grasped her arm firmly, deterring her from exiting. "Will another five thousand get him out of there?" he growled.

She quickly nodded. For that price she'd carry him from the room herself.

Releasing her, he pulled his money from his pocket and counted off ten bills. "Here's an extra five thousand," he brusquely said, "not to hear anything. I'll be visiting this evening with Countess de Grae."

She took a deep breath, debating. There was a hot-spur violence in his utterance.

He held out the money.

After a second more of hesitation, she took it.

"Move," he said. "Quickly."

When Madame Centisi went into the Boucher room to recall her young employee, she was so nervous, her stammering excuse realistically suggested an emergency. As soon as Angela's companion walked out into the hall and saw Kit, he said after a swift survey, "You must be the lover. You don't look like a husband."

"Forgive the interruption," Kit said, his clipped words only marginally polite, not responding at all to the comment.

"You're not going to hurt her, are you?" The man in evening dress looked angry.

"No, not that it's any of your concern."

"I think maybe you've hurt her already. . . ."

Kit's gaze swiveled to Madame Centisi.

She saw the impatience, the implacable authority separate from the power of his wealth, and taking the young man by the arm, she said, "Come."

The young man shrugged; he understood the limits of his vocation and the monetary factors motivating his employer.

"Have tea sent up with that item," Kit reminded Madame Centisi, "and tell the lady's friends I'll have my driver bring her home." He nodded his dismissal.

And he was left standing alone in the hallway.

22

Genuinely relieved to have been interrupted by Madame Centisi, not sure she could have gone through with the amorous transaction, Angela was slipping a stocking back on when Kit walked into the room.

Turning and looking up at the sound of the door closing, she went motionless, shocked at the sight of Kit leaning against the door, languid menace in his stance.

Reaching behind him with leisured deliberation, he turned the key in the lock and slipped it into his trouser pocket.

"What are you doing?" Already sensitive to the antipathy in his gaze, the sound of the lock sliding shut was unnerving.

"Enjoying the view," he casually said, pretending to misunderstand. "That muscular young man was very good with you."

"You've been watching?" Instantly provoked, Angela bristled at his audacity and the insolence of his tone.

"Don't sound so shocked," he said, moving into

the room. "Surely you're aware of the possibilities in houses like this." He unbuttoned his jacket. "I don't imagine you came here expecting a piano recital." And shrugging out of his satin-lapeled jacket, he tossed it onto a chair.

"What do you think you're doing?" she inquired, thin-skinned and testy at his presumption, hastily brushing her skirt and petticoats down over her bare legs.

"I'm taking over from your young stud," he coolly replied, unclasping the pearl buttons of his white silk waistcoat. "You must have come here to be serviced. I think I still recall what you like."

"I'll pass," she tartly replied.

"But, then, no one's asking you." His voice was velvet soft.

"Why not accommodate one of your choice courtesans?" she sneered. "You've been devoted to them of late, I understand."

"Really?" he murmured, stopping for a moment in his unbuttoning, gazing at her, one eyebrow raised in mocking query. "Are you keeping track of me?"

"It's common gossip," she snapped, sitting bolt upright in her chair, her eyes bright with anger. "You have no discretion."

"Unlike you," he sardonically noted, renewing his unbuttoning. "I'd say the Prince of Wales is rather high profile."

"I don't care to argue with you," she peevishly said, "over so fruitless an issue."

"Nor do I when I find you so readily available. How have you been lately?" he urbanely inquired as if they were meeting over tea.

"Heartbroken, unhappy, and filled with gloom. How have you been?" she sarcastically challenged.

"Equally devastated," he murmured with a faint

smile, pulling his watch chain through the button hole.

"You must put a pall on the courtesans' nights."

"No one's complained," he softly said, slipping his watch free and dropping it on top of his jacket. "And you didn't seem to mind that young man kissing your thigh," he went on, smiling without warmth. "You were definitely ready to fuck him, darling. So, tell me—who's been soothing your abject sorrow in the country?" he mocked. "Your old beau Manton?"

"You're intensely irritating," she said, indignant and moody, taking exception to his casual disrobing. "And you needn't continue undressing. Even if I was in the mood to make love to someone tonight, it wouldn't be you."

"If you don't want to confide in me about your love life," he gently said, as if she'd not snapped at him, "I understand, but Manton already told me you'd renewed your friendship." He shrugged out of his waistcoat, the diamond studs on his shirt front twinkling with his movement; then he dropped the garment beside his jacket.

"He *told* you?" Her expression was incredulous.

"He was vastly pleased to give me the news."

"He's a liar," she curtly said.

"You didn't have tea with him today at the Ritz?"

"Yes, I did, along with Violet and Georgiana. Did he fail to mention that?"

"He did say his wife would be leaving soon for a holiday. He was looking forward to your entertaining him in her absence."

"You men are all alike," she resentfully declared. "Women exist on some personal scorecard. Or as a triumph of ownership."

"I'm just a temporary player, darling, no score-card, no ownership. I'm interested only in tonight."

He surveyed the room with a practiced eye, comparing it to the scores of others he'd frequented lately. "I've been living in these places the last few weeks. So, tell me, Countess, would you be more amenable for a price? I've plenty of money. How much do you want to oblige me in bed?"

"How dare you!" She flushed pink in affront.

"I've already paid Madame Centisi fifteen thousand pounds to look the other way tonight. I'll dare just about anything. Don't bother putting those stockings on. I want them off."

"And if I don't oblige?"

He laughed softly. "But you always do, *mon ange.*" And he pulled his tie loose at his collar.

"Tonight will be the exception."

"I don't think so." His voice, for all its blandness, held a distinct hint of reprisal. "Fifteen thousand pounds buys quite a lot in these brothels." Discarding his tie on the pile of clothing, he walked over to the wall on his left and moved an armoire in front of the peephole. "I prefer not having spectators," he said, turning back to her.

"A locked door and now this need for privacy. Should I be alarmed?"

"Not alarmed, but certainly cooperative."

"And if I'm not?" She hadn't moved in the chair.

"Did I mention I'm drunk? It makes me short-tempered."

"Are you threatening me?"

"Probably not." He shrugged. "I'm not sure . . . maybe I am," he indecisively murmured. "But I'll be *fucking* you," he said, his voice husky, "in this"—he cast a swift, narrowed glance around the room— "flamboyant purple boudoir." He sighed. "So that's probably a threat."

"Violet and Lucy talked me into coming," she quietly said.

"Did they pick out Steven for you, too?" he asked, his voice brittle with derision.

"I didn't know his name."

"But you found out how his mouth felt on your cunt," he said, the flash of his smile chill. "We can be as anonymous if you like. A fuck's a fuck."

"It always has been for you, hasn't it?" He smelled of whiskey and vice . . . of fatal temptation despite her wish to despise him. "How did you find me?"

"Binky saw you. He was at Madame Jordan's down the street. Your scarf caught—he saw your hair."

"Bloody hell." She sighed into the perfumed air.

"The wages of sin," he sardonically murmured, walking the few feet to the bed and dropping onto the purple satin counterpane.

"And of this incestuous London society," she said, clipped and disgusted.

"In which your reputation has a certain unsurpassed glory." His voice was soft; his temper showed in his eyes. "Olivia was pleased to give me an accounting of your conquests at Bertie's last week."

"So you're sleeping with her again?" Angela coolly said, angry at herself for caring.

"Not likely. I prefer my skin in one piece. She backed me into a corner at Alexandra's tea."

"You at tea?"

"Chambers made me go," he said with blunt directness. "Some Siamese prince with a good harbor was the guest of honor."

"And Olivia couldn't get you off in some secluded nook?"

"Not for lack of trying. When I refused, she decided I was pining for you and thought to disabuse me of the notion you were doing the same for me.

"She said you'd fucked Lew Archer after every race he won. You were his inspiration that championship year. I should have known, with his smiling face in all the newspapers.

"And she thought I'd be interested to know the Prince of Romania almost gave up his throne for you. Now, that's a fuck. Then there was a royal house in some Greek state she went on about where both father and son were enamored of you. Did you do them both at the same time?"

"Olivia's not exactly the font of truth."

"Near enough. Which one didn't you fuck?" There was mockery in his voice, and a different sound, too—an undertone of charged constraint.

"I'm not arguing with you about my past," she coolly said. "We've been over this before."

"Steven must have been looking forward to the evening with a seductress of such note. Too bad."

"Are you really going to insist on this?" She never should have listened to Violet. "It's not very gentlemanly, even for you."

His gaze from under the fringe of his lashes was unruffled. "I'm not a gentleman, darling. I told you that a long time ago. As for insisting, I don't think it'll come to that." He spoke very softly without undue inflection. "Just consider me a substitute for Steven. Tell me what you want. That shouldn't be so hard."

"I want to leave."

"Later."

"You won't let me leave now?"

"No."

"In that case, unless you intend to force yourself on me, it's going to be a long, uneventful evening."

And leaning back in her chair, she crossed her arms over her waist and shut her eyes.

He smiled—the sight of her stubbornly unyielding pose in this house of pleasure a charmingly incongruous sight. "Should I call for another woman?" he silkily inquired.

"Madame Centisi doesn't have women."

"She'll find me one for fifteen thousand. You could watch us."

"I'll keep my eyes shut," she replied, doing just that.

"You can listen, then."

"I'm sure I'll be entertained."

"Not as much as I," he noted, "but there's a degree of titillation in voyeurism, I suppose." And he pulled off his shoe and dropped it onto the floor.

The second shoe followed a few moments later, the sound of the thud as it landed on the carpet magnified in Angela's ears.

"I've never been monkish, and the last few weeks . . ." He exhaled softly. "I'm going to need my nightly quota of sex." Pulling off his stockings, he gazed at the primly seated lady dressed in seductive black lace, the juxtaposition of pose and costume strikingly erotic. "Maybe I should have two women."

She heard the soft snap of his embroidered suspenders as he slid them over his shoulders, and then a hushed silence fell, the unbuttoning of his trousers inaudible, only her imagination fabricating the successive step in his disrobing. The swish of fabric sliding down his legs was distinct, as was the ringing impact when his trousers landed on the chair, the door key in his pocket striking the wooden back with a soft ping.

And now his shirt, she thought, finding her imagination creating his image from memory, each stud pulled loose from his stiffly starched shirt front a crisp, clear sound in her ears.

He swore once and she stole a peak. His diamond cuff link was stuck halfway through the layers of his cuff. His shirt hung open, his tanned skin framed by the pristine whiteness of the fine linen, the sculpted muscles of his torso and chest starkly defined in the lamplight. Wrenching the cuff link free, he slid the shirt from his shoulders, and the impact of his muscled strength struck her viscerally. Only his white underwear remained.

Squeezing her eyes shut against the heat infusing her senses, she recalled how those hard muscles felt under her hands when he moved inside her, how they flexed and flowed and stirred. Searing memory recalled in graphic detail the sensational pleasure he offered. She clenched her arms tightly around her waist.

The soft linen of his abbreviated trunks had revealed a rampant erection.

And she was starving for him.

Noting the flush on her cheeks, the new rigidity in her body, he allowed himself a faint triumphant smile. Countess Angel had come there tonight to assuage her desires. In his expert opinion, it was just a matter of time until she did. Unbuttoning his underpants, he slid them off and tossed them so they joined the heap of clothing. "I'd rather have you, Angel, than Madame Centisi's wares. Look. We're waiting for you."

"I don't want to look." Her voice was a small, suffocated sound.

"Do you think I'll still fit?"

She could feel her body opening at his words, as if her senses knew the extent of the pleasure he was so casually promising.

"How can it hurt to look?" he murmured, offering sex in a caressing tone.

And when she slowly opened her eyes, her gaze was inexorably drawn to his splendid erection.

He was seated on the side of the bed, leaning back on his hands, his engorged penis was arched taut against his belly, following the narrow trail of reddish hair running up his stomach. The tracery of pulsing veins stood out in high relief, the ridged head broad, swollen, reaching waist high in all its flaunting glory.

"Come and see us."

She shook her head, but her gaze hadn't moved from the ostentatious display. He knew exactly how to communicate with her susceptible longing.

"Last chance. You might find it frustrating . . . watching," he said. Gently grasping his erection, he ran a practiced hand down its length, and she caught her breath as its size surged. "Sure, now?" he gently queried, aware of her rapt attention.

The pulsing in her vagina was spreading a carnal heat upward; she could feel her nipples hard against her corset, the swollen weight of her breasts tingling, a dewy moisture dampening her drawers. It took all her concentration to whisper, "I'm sure."

"Should I have one woman or two? Any preferences?" he lazily inquired.

"I'd prefer you let me go."

"Sorry. I'm paying more than you are, so I get my way. Two, I think. It's still early." And rising from the bed, he moved toward the door.

"No," she whispered.

He stopped, gazed at her. "No, *what*?"

She swallowed, opened her mouth to speak, shut it again, and finally said so softly, he barely heard the words, "Don't call for the women."

He turned, retraced his steps, seated himself on the bed again. "Are you interested, then?"

"Don't do this to me," she whispered.

"Why shouldn't I, after what you did to me? Are you?"

She didn't answer at once, but he waited.

"Yes," she finally breathed, her eyes not meeting his.

"Look at me and say it," he brutally insisted.

Her gaze came up and held his for a stark, direct moment. "I'm interested."

He smiled, held out his hand.

And she came to him because she wanted him so desperately, she was willing to do anything he wished.

He had her undress for him while he sat and watched her, giving quiet orders, saying no, do that next, or leave that on until later, or come here and let me help you, telling her what he was going to do to her until she was as wet as if he'd already made love to her. He untied her black satin corset for her because she needed help taking it off, and he merely said with mild disfavor when her corset had been discarded on the froufrou of yellow silk petticoats at her feet, "No chemise? Planning ahead, darling? It saves time in places like this, doesn't it?"

Nude save for her drawers, she was trembling with desire, unable to participate in casual repartee so coolly. "I'm sorry," she whispered.

Everything about her ready sexual response offended him; she would have been trembling for Steven or Manton or any other man, he thought, thin-skinned and moody. And suddenly, hot-tempered at the image, he wrenched open the tie on her lacy drawers so they fell at her feet, and jerking her close, he put his hands on her waist and hoisted her onto his lap, her thighs straddling his.

"Up," he brusquely ordered, slapping her bottom lightly so she rose to her knees. "Are you ready for a fuck?"

She was quivering helplessly.

"Manton must not have done a very good job this afternoon. You're like a bitch in heat. Tell me."

"Please, Kit, don't."

"It's only four letters. Tell me," he growled.

It wasn't love he was talking about, she knew, and shamed and humiliated at her longing, she whispered, "I want a fuck."

"How much do you want it?"

She wanted him with an almost will-less desire, an insatiable craving. "Desperately," she said, her voice almost imperceptible.

"Your hot cunt's always been one of my favorites," he drawled, guiding the tip of his penis to her drenched vulva, sliding the crest over her warm, slippery cleft, teasing her like a stallion a rutting mare until she whimpered and moaned and tried to draw him into her. But he held her up, his palm under her buttocks, his holding her there an act of authority. "It's my game tonight. My rules, my pacing, my directions. You're my Tuesday-night fuck, and I'm not interested in speed."

She stared at him, her eyes glazed with sharp desire, her lascivious secretions oozing down his penis, her body so close to orgasm, she was rigid under his hands.

"You need some training in orgasmic restraint."

"From you?" Her eyes were hot. "A world-class libertine?"

His fingers dug into her buttocks. "I saw you with Steven."

"Then we're talking about something else, and you don't own me."

"I own you tonight." He jammed his fingers inside her, hooked them into the front of her pelvic bone and pulled her up so she was almost raised off her knees, so their eyes were level, so she could see the icy rancor. "I'll be fucking you all night. Not Steven, me."

"I hate you."

"Really? Is that what this dripping cunt means?" He pulled his fingers out so abruptly she lost her balance. Catching her, he held her with a cupped palm under her bottom. Raising his other hand, he placed his drenched fingers across her mouth. "That's not hate," he whispered. "You're ready for cock." And he covered them and her mouth with his in a rough, hard kiss that tasted of sex and craving.

She didn't hate him. He knew and she knew, and deep down in that part of her that wanted to erase the sadness from her life, she wished she did.

He ate at her mouth through his fingers and she bit his fingers that smelled and tasted of her body and he said, "Jesus fucking Christ," and jerked them away.

"Are you going to hit me or fuck me?" she said with a flaunting sexuality. "You can't decide tonight, can you?"

His eyes were cool green for a hovering moment, and then his hands spanned her waist, lifted her, guided his erection to target point, and he pressed downward on her hips with a rough, brutal force.

Her eyes closed, and before he was completely submerged, she began to climax, her scream echoing in the sumptuous purple Boucher room on Half-Moon Street. He paused, sunk hilt-deep, his hands hard and unyielding on her hips while her orgasm washed over her, and once the fluttering had stopped and her keening cry had died away, he lifted her, gliding her newly sated body up his rigid length with deliberation, then back down again in a compelling, sensuous rhythm.

She was warm, slippery, docile in his hands, the woman he'd been dreaming of for weeks.

He was filling her body, her soul, every crevice

and groove, with melting pleasure, and leaning over, she kissed him, shameless in her need for him, ravenous for all that he could give her—challenge and contention washed away by a deluge of bliss and breathless desire.

"I've missed you," she whispered, squirming her hips at the base of the downstroke, striving to keep him deep inside against his upward leverage.

"I can tell," he said, raising her effortlessly, knowing this was what he'd been searching for in all the brothels, this indefinable rapture, both carnal and deep-felt.

"Did you miss me?"

He waited until their rhythm had brought her up to his eye level again, and holding her poised on the tip of his erection, he smiled. "I even missed you sober." And he kissed her then with a warm, nuzzling sweetness.

"I'm glad you came here." Her whisper tasted of his whiskey as she glided down his hardness again with a voluptuous sigh.

"Thank Binky."

"I'm going to kiss you all night," she said with a tantalizing throatiness.

"I'm going to make love to you for a thousand years."

"I'll never last that long." Another orgasm was slowly building.

"I'll make you—"

A sharp knock sounded on the door.

"Just a minute," Kit called.

"No," Angela whispered, her heated senses too close to climax.

"They're bringing tea."

"Not now."

"You have to do what you're told tonight, Angel.

Shut your eyes." Wrapping her legs around his waist, he rose from the bed and, supporting her weight with his hands, grabbed up his trousers with the key, then began walking to the door.

Each stride drove him upward as she clung to his shoulders and hips, her legs locked around him, her thighs stretched wide, opening her body to even deeper penetration, to each upthrusting stroke. He held her firmly in place so she couldn't move, so he could force himself deeper, so she could feel the solid placement of his footsteps in the hot, throbbing center of her body.

She didn't argue anymore; she could hardly think, overwhelmed by profligate sensation, every thought save that of her imminent orgasm relegated to obscurity.

She began to peak as he reached the door.

Quickly extracting the key with his fingertips while he balanced her against the wall, he unlocked the door with his left hand, pulled it open, kicked it wide with his foot.

After a brief nod to the serving girl, indicating a nearby table, he leaned into Angela, refitting his hands under her bottom, pressing her back against the tapestry-covered surface so she felt his hard length slide in a profound distance more. "Now," he whispered, "you should feel this," and bracing his feet, he pushed up into her with all the strength of his powerful legs.

Her explosive scream startled the servant, who dropped the tea tray onto the table with a clatter, and averting her eyes as she'd been taught to do in her various duties at Madame Centisi's, she scurried from the room.

Kit didn't move for a very long time after the door closed. She'd come for an orgasmic eternity.

Her eyes finally opened; she blushed under his gaze. "I'm embarrassed."

He seemed to find the idea quaintly amusing. "You were enchanting."

"The girl—" She blushed again.

"It doesn't matter," he said with the flat, dispassionate voice he used discussing what some people referred to as the profligacy in his life. "I could screw you in the entrance hall and no one would stop me."

"Please don't." Her voice was tentative, her eyes wary. His mood was wildly capricious tonight, and there were stories of him, Violet had said, that were blatantly exhibitionist.

He smiled. "You're so modest."

"I'm sober."

"And I'm not. You don't want an audience?"

She buried her face in the warm hollow where his throat met his shoulder.

"It's the purple bed, then," he said with a faint smile, and carrying her to the huge tester bed, he eased her down without dislodging himself. Moving her upward, the driving pressure of his erection riveting adjunct to his hands, he placed her in the center of the bed.

"It's my turn now," he murmured.

"And mine, too," she said with a smile.

"It's always your turn."

"Do me a favor."

"Now?" he said, a flicker of disbelief volatile in his gaze. "Could this wait?"

"Lift up, so I can take my Dutch cap out."

"Why would you want to do that?"

"It's been moved; I can feel it." Her nose wrinkled in distaste. "It doesn't work for us anyway."

He removed it because she was right and he was capable of caution, drunk or sober. He did it quickly because he'd been politely indulgent long enough; his turn was overdue. "You're at my mercy now," he whispered.

"Or you at mine."

His smile was lush. "No complaints."

"It's like we're home," she murmured, holding her arms out to him.

Sliding between her legs, he invaded her slowly. "Now we're home," he said, and they both felt the shuddering desire, the warmth, the gratifying sorcery of his languorous penetration, and when he was buried deep inside her and he was as close as anybody could be, she whispered, "I love you," when she knew she shouldn't, when it would only complicate her life and his, when she should know better than to talk of love in a place like this.

He'd been drinking her out of his life for many weeks. "You feel like heaven," he said, "or a thousand nirvanas."

She hadn't expected him to offer her more. It was enough, she told herself, for him to want to be with her tonight. "I can give you pleasure," she murmured, flexing her muscles in a delicate small tremor that eased him in deeper, that squeezed in a tiny, exquisite spasm.

"I noticed," he whispered, smiling down at her. "Will there be a charge?"

"Nothing you can't pay."

His languid rhythm was matched by hers at first, the sleek penetration and withdrawal melting rapture, their bodies rocking together leisurely as though they had all night to taste the pleasures of love. He kissed her and she him, their lips savoring, nibbling, a thousand coquetries of tongues revealed. And then the tempo changed as he caressed her breasts and suckled them until she moaned and writhed and flowed wet around him. The pitch shifted again when their bodies grew hot and sweat-sheened, when raw passion overrode all else as if they were in the grip of some erotic spell. His eyes changed and the deep sound of his voice, and he adjusted his grip on her with a restless, volatile suddenness.

He drove in deeper then and deeper still, wanting to put his mark on her, each plunging stroke merciless, fierce, uncurbed. And she whimpered in his hold like some helpless female mating out of instinct and seasonal heat, wanting to be covered and penetrated, wanting him to plant his seed in her.

His thighs forced hers farther apart as he rammed into her, his hands hard on her hips so she couldn't move, so she couldn't get away, so he could invade her, subdue her, make her his.

There was no conscious thought, no intellect or will, only need and sensation and a hot-blooded urgency. She welcomed him into her body, arching up to meet him, holding him tight as he penetrated to the very deepest depths and pressed himself hard against her womb.

Even as he was driven by savage impulse, even in extremis, the most elemental principles still functioned in his brain, and when he felt his orgasm begin to crest, he started to withdraw.

Whimpering, breathless, she clung to him, her arms and legs gripping him more tightly. "Stay . . . ," she pleaded. She wanted all the savage fury for herself, she wanted his hard, powerful body, she desperately wanted his love, and since she couldn't have that—not in this present world of pretense and faithlessness—she wanted his seed in her . . . in the deepest recesses of her heart . . . she wanted his child.

"No." His voice was hoarse with restraint.

"Please," she implored, her arms locked around his neck, her legs vise hard at his waist, her body so near orgasm she was quivering.

Braced to withdraw, he knew he could easily break her hold if he wished; he understood less why he didn't.

"I want all of you inside me," she whispered.

He was shuddering on the brink, she was hot around him, the enchantress of his lustful dreams, pleading to be the repository for his semen. His gaze flickered up in a skittish, swift glance, and he saw their reflection in the mirror tilted above the headboard. She was small, pale-skinned beneath him, her body overwhelmed by his, engulfed, impaled—an animal coupling . . . dominant male and a thousand images of yielding, fruitful womanhood. And in some barbaric remnant of his mind overlooked in the evolutionary process, suppressed under the cultivated veneer of sophistication and breeding, existed a brute animal instinct that responded to her plea. He wished in some primordial way to possess her totally. He could see his hands slide beneath her bottom and lift her.

She gasped.

He tightened his grip.

With his eyes intent on the mirrored image, he watched his leg muscles flex, saw himself plunge in, a man separate from his worldly self, functioning at the most primitive level, impelled by naked lust. Her pliant flesh gave way to him; he could feel the reluctant yielding, he could feel her spine relax under his hands, her response as hot-blooded and wanton as he remembered. And then her words of love echoed in his ears, familiar words from his time at Easton, a sweet siren song to his hard, driving rhythm.

He was staying, she joyously thought, his benevolence the equivalent of reward or compromise—maybe even love. Her want of him filled her mind and soul and body to bursting. She stroked his shoulders, his arms, the taut muscles running down his back, the soft hair curling at the base of his spine. He was elusive and terrifyingly remote, ruthless, pitiless in walking out of her life. And she loved him utterly.

He was devouring her, eating her alive, thrusting and plunging, his harsh breathing like an animal sound in the silken room. The reflection in the mirror excited him, alarmed him; he was almost hurting her, he easily could if he wished. He wondered in a flickering moment why he responded to her with such brutality, the insanity of total conquest incredible when he had never done more than play the game with all the rest. Then his breath caught, and insanity or not, he was past the point where decision making functioned. His back arched, his eyes shut, and he gushed into her.

She met him in a wild, delirious coming, a kind of turbulent paroxysm that convulsed her body and stirred her soul. They were connected now in the most intimate way imaginable, and she felt warm down to the marrow of her bones.

In the shuddering aftermath they lay collapsed, savage impulse gone, bliss melting through their senses, torrid flame no more than a luscious glow. Kit kissed her lightly on her cheek and earlobe, on the upturned corner of her mouth; he gently unwrapped her legs from his waist and placed her feet on the bed. "You're very convincing," he murmured, licking her hot cheek.

"I'm stronger than you are." Her smile was sultry with allure.

"Maybe you are. I hope I won't regret this."

"*I* don't," she whispered, tracing the perfect curve

of his upper lip with the pad of her finger. "I want you to fill me."

He was rigid still inside her despite his orgasm, which she well knew, and at her words his erection swelled. "Round one, then," he said with a lazy smile. It didn't matter now; it was too late. He stroked her throat, a caress, a gesture of possession. "How much do you want?"

"All of it," she said, moving her hips in an enticing rhythm, slippery and wet around him, sensual female to his carnal hunger.

"You always were greedy." He moved in her, a small fluid distance.

She slid her hands over his broad shoulders. "And you were always accommodating."

"How long can you stay?" He stirred in her again.

"As long as you need me," she whispered.

He stopped moving. "You probably shouldn't say that."

"I know."

They both knew better, but for a finite time they were relinquishing reason.

"I deserve you," Angela said. "I've been working hard."

"While I've been practicing for tonight." He hadn't been working hard; he'd been handling Chambers's minimum needs and then consoling his melancholy with vice.

"I didn't think you needed more practice."

He smiled. "I'll show you the new improvements."

And they explored the heated boundaries of passion and lust and impatient desire on the purple-swathed bed in Madame Centisi's exclusive house of pleasure, both starved for each other, their bodies in ravenous sync, the long fast of their separation over.

23

After the first stark craving was gone, after the bedclothes had been crushed and ruined and tumbled to the floor, after they'd experimented with a glorious number of diverse positions, he kissed her rosy cheeks, her smiling mouth, unlaced her arms from around his neck, and, rising from the bed, went to the small table holding the basin and pitcher to wash himself.

Lying in a cocoon of pillows, she took pleasure in watching him, his long-limbed body incongruously both lean and muscled, the synthesis of power and lithe grace honed to perfection by the strenuous years of sailing and by this—his second avocation.

His smile when he looked up and saw her gazing at him quirked with amusement. "You're next on my list," he said. "How hot do you want your water?"

"I adore being taken care of by you." He was the most beautiful man on earth. Her body was aglow with sensual heat, her skin attuned to his merest touch, her throbbing vagina unsated in his presence, lascivious.

"I'll give you tea next."

She raised her eyebrows slightly. "Is this a ritual in these establishments?"

"I thought you might enjoy it." He was rinsing the soap away, the silken skin of his penis gleaming wet, glistening in the lamplight, his erection lush to behold.

"That looks delectably clean." Her body responded to the sight with a kindling heat.

He heard the sultry tone in her voice. "It's for you."

"Hurry, then, because you've been gone long enough." She could never have enough of him, he was the drug to her addiction.

Pouring away the water, he refilled the basin from the small sink and, carrying the steaming water over, he set the bowl on the bedside table. "You smell like a strumpet."

"I wouldn't know. That's your specialty. Do you wash them, too?"

"I don't stay long enough. Lie still, now." She was reaching for his erection, but he moved away so her fingers only brushed the luxuriant auburn hair at his crotch.

"You'll be getting it soon." He stood just out of reach.

"Let me touch it now."

"No. Put your hand down." He waited until she obeyed, pouting but compliant. "You look like May." He grinned. "Just your pout," he clarified. "The rest of you could bring an army of pious monks hard-ons."

She wrinkled her nose at him. "I don't know why I can't touch you."

"Because I want you clean before I put this stiff prick up your tight little pussy, and if you touch me—" His eyebrows rose in lecherous curves.

"You need me," she whispered, content.

"I need this," he said, sliding his middle finger

down the damp hair of her Mount of Venus, down the slippery cleft in it. "Now, don't move." His voice was suddenly gruff, as if he were mad at her or at himself.

He bent her right leg at the knee and then her left, bringing her feet up to her bottom so her thighs fell apart, so she was wide-open, so he could see how plumply she was swollen, how soaking wet she was. And she saw how much he wanted her in his eyes. "I should lock you away," he muttered.

"I want only you."

He laughed softly. "At least for tonight." And picking up the soap, he smiled down at her. "You're better than all of them, *mon ange.* Don't let anyone ever tell you you're not." His familiar impudence had returned, and as he lathered the washcloth, he asked her of Violet as though they were meeting over lunch at the Ritz. Then he parted her with his fingers and smoothed the soapy cloth over her engorged flesh.

She moaned, a breathy, small sigh of pleasure, the slippery pressure luscious on her pulsing tissue, and when he forced the cloth deeper into all her folds and crevices, she squirmed under his hands. His fingers were sunk deep inside her, the slick friction of the soap silk on silk. She moved against his stroking fingers, lifted her pelvis, her deep, insistent craving for him insatiable.

"Please, Kit, don't make me wait."

"I'm almost finished. You have to wait." His voice was calm, but the low timbre vibrated like a growl.

"I don't want to."

"You never do. Hush." And he rinsed the washcloth and wiped away the soap with swift, economical movements. Then she felt his finger go inside her and she lifted to meet it. His other hand came up to hold her still, his wet palm cool on her stomach. "I'm just checking how clean you are."

"Clean enough to eat," she murmured, smiling at him, and then she moaned as he slid in a second finger and gently searched the front wall of her vagina, with riveting results. His fingerpads pressed lightly, and a spasm of pleasure vibrated through her body, so acute and salaciously carnal, she wondered if you could love someone for that feeling alone. The thrilling heat scorched through her body, up her spine, down her legs, throbbing deep inside her, and squirming, she reached to recapture the sensation. Exerting pressure on her mons with the heel of his hand. Kit's fingertips pressed up on the sensitive nub of tissue.

And she came, quivering, pulsing, her eyes shut tight against the exquisite rapture. Hot-spur, instantly, she came.

Pausing only a moment while she caught her breath, he resumed his delicate massage, his fingers deft, skilled, her body tantalizingly imprisoned between his hands. The same shocking sensations that had just come to climax in her body promptly reappeared, even more compelling and profound. She climaxed within seconds again, and then once again in quick succession, and he sat beside her after that waiting for her to reenter the world.

"What did you do?" she whispered, dazed.

"Did you like that?" His green eyes were amused.

"Just slightly," she murmured, stroking his hand that still lay on her stomach. "You're a gift from the gods."

"I can't take credit; the Chinese discovered that subtlety a long time ago."

"And you read Chinese. How nice for me."

His grin was indulgent. "And I'm always ready to help you out. Are you rested enough for tea?"

She looked at him as intently as she could, still

half-stupefied by orgasmic glut. "Do I have to be rested for tea?"

He shrugged. "I had Madame Centisi fetch something from my flat."

"For me?"

He nodded and, offering her his hand, pulled her upright. Sliding off the bed, he picked her up gently, as a still-sleepy child would be eased from her cot, carried her to one of the chairs by the fire, and settled her comfortably. He built the fire up so she wouldn't be cold, although the room was warm already and her body heated from his artful skills. He brought the tea tray over then, set it on the table between the two chairs framing the fire, and poured two cups of tea from the silver pot while she decided she must have done something very good lately to have been given him as a reward.

"Milk or lemon?" he said, looking up.

"Milk and sugar. I need my strength."

"Good idea," he said, gazing at her from under his lashes. Scooping three spoons of sugar into her cup, he poured in milk, stirred it, and handed the cup to her, offering her a plate of iced cakes with his other hand.

"You think of everything. How did you know I like pink cakes?" She took the largest one, the delicate pink frosting rippled with silver dragées.

"I know everything you like," he said, setting the plate back down.

"Smug men annoy me." Her voice was teasing.

"But you fuck them anyway," he softly said, self-assured, recognizing the look of longing in her eyes.

"Only when I'm locked away with one." He was sinfully beautiful, she thought, and fully aware of women's interest in him. She wished she didn't want him so badly.

"Do you want to leave?" He dropped into the chair opposite her, his brows poised in winged query.

"Do you want me to go?" She gazed at him over her teacup.

"Of course not." He smiled. "I've an investment here."

"Are you getting your money's worth?"

"So far." Leaning over, he picked up a small red lacquer box from the tray, opened the lid, and offered it to her. "Tell me what you think of these. They're to replace the ones I threw away."

"But you left Easton too abruptly to give them to me," she said, gazing at the two gold balls in their silk cushioned bed. They tinkled when she lifted them out, the sound like tiny bells.

"I had them engraved," he said, ignoring her comment.

She turned the small globes in her fingers. "To Love," she read on the first. "To Pleasure," on the other. And the goldsmith's mark was stamped beneath each engraved sentiment.

She smiled. "Do they go with tea?"

"They do now. Give them here." And leaning over, he held out his hand.

He had beautiful hands, like the rest of him, she thought, slender, long-boned, graceful, despite their strength.

He held his hand out palm up, the muscles of his arm flexed, and when she dropped them into his hand, his fingers curled around them loosely.

He didn't move or speak for a time as he lounged back in his chair, and uncertain of his mood, with his assessing gaze so remote, she found herself blushing. She could feel the heat on her cheeks.

"You're very small in that chair." He spoke softly,

the hand holding the balls draped over the gilded wood of his chair arm.

"I can't say the same for you."

He smiled. "You look chaste and innocent when you blush like that. Even your breasts turn pink." And he moved then as she flushed a deeper shade of rose, half rising from his chair, going down on one knee in the space between their chairs, parting her legs with the gentlest of pressure on her inner thighs. "Have you tried these lately?" The shiny globes rolled on his open palm.

"You threw mine away." Her answer pleased him; she could see the sudden warmth in his eyes.

His hand on her thigh moved, stroked upward, sending his personal signal to her body. She could feel herself spreading wide to receive him.

"I'd forgotten how small you were."

"I hadn't forgotten anything about you."

His mouth quirked. "I've been drinking a lot," he said, sliding one golden sphere into her vagina, placing the second one in with slightly more pressure, the deft, smooth motion of wrist, hand, and fingers executed with virtuoso artistry. "How's that?" With the faintest pressure his fingers slid over her swollen, wet vulva, blockade to the metal balls. He stroked the plump, pulsing flesh; heated pleasure spread through her body, setting off outlying ripples of bewitching sensation, making her unaware of anything but her sexual craving. Then he suddenly pressed upward, and a spiking rapture shuddered through her body.

"They seem to be fine," he blandly said.

"I'm going to die by morning." Her hands were trembling, the waves of delirium rippling with increasing intensity outward from the engraved balls lodged inside her.

"No, you won't." It was as if he knew how much

and when and to what degree she would respond, while all she could do was want him shamelessly.

"Let me feed you," he softly said, watching her visible arousal.

"I don't know if I can eat right now," she whispered, unconsciously rocking to maintain the ravishing sensations.

"Try." Taking a cake from the plate, he offered it to her, the soft tinkling of the bells inside her body silver-toned in the stillness.

She shook her head, an irrepressible need for him electrifying her senses. Was it possible, she wondered, to die of sexual excess? "I want only you." Her eyes were heated, restless.

"I like the bells," he softly said, scooping up a dab of frosting from the cake in his hand, reaching over, smoothing it over her nipple.

She shuddered at his touch, her nipples sensitized to the merest tactile contact.

Setting the cake down, he steadied her with a hand on her wrist—a small authoritarian restraint— and lifting up another measure of frosting, spread it with infinite care over the entire susceptible surface of her aureole. He kissed her then to appease her whimpering cry. "I knew you'd like the bells," he whispered, lifting his mouth from hers. "I should keep you as my musician in residence."

She heard him through the panting rhythm of her breath and the lyric sound of the bells, the velvet upholstery silken against her stirring, gorged vulva, her mind drifting away. Her body was reduced to an eager, willing sexual vessel, libidinous sensation flooding every cell and nerve and millimeter of skin, her world narrowed to a finite focus. An unbearable sexual hunger drummed through her senses, her all-consuming desire abased to the most minimalist needs. Sex and

Kit or Kit and sex or Kit alone because he was sex incarnate.

He covered her nipples with tantalizing, languid strokes, the slippery frosting smoothed on with a perfectionist's attention to detail. Then kneeling, he spread her legs and moved between them, easing himself in carefully, sensitive of the metal balls suspended within her, not wishing to unduly stretch the distended flesh holding them in place.

Bending, he took a sweet frosted nipple into his mouth, and when he sucked gently at first and then less delicately, her breath caught in her throat, the stabbing pleasure almost too much to bear. She grew jewel hard in his mouth and her hands came up to hold him close, her fingers laced through his hair. She whimpered when he released her nipple, but he merely moved to her other breast and she sighed, held her breast up with both her hands and offered it to him. His tongue stroked gently, circling the slippery aureole, sliding the frosting in glistening paths over the swollen plump flesh.

She was oozing pearly fluids of arousal, the golden balls slipping inside her in a river of succulent need, her senses suspended on the very brink of orgasmic release. After nibbling and teasing the taut bud for excruciating moments, he drew her nipple into his mouth, fastened his lips firmly on the swollen crest, and sucked as if he were in need of the ripe, swollen tip for sustenance.

Her climax exploded deep inside her, and while she still trembled in orgasmic fever, he moved his hand downward, sweeping gently over her stomach, coming to rest with precision over her pulsing labia. He pressed upward, forcing the golden balls higher, and another climax began, surging over the remnants of the first, the spasm so intense she jerked under his hands. He was suckling her still, milking her ripe breast, his hand hard on her cleft, holding her body in thrall.

She died away in quivering helplessness.

Gently removing the balls with long-fingered finesse, he set them aside and, rising from his knees, dropped back into his chair. Lounging quiescent, he leisurely surveyed her with a connoisseur's eye. She lay utterly replete, her eyes shut, her head thrown back, her arms limp on the padded cushion, totally vulnerable to the feelings he provoked.

It gave him pleasure to indulge her voluptuous senses, and in the less gracious reaches of his mind, her defenselessness offered him a measure of revenge —for all his suffering the weeks past. Vengeance, though, figured less than the more gratifying tumult of emotions pervading his mind. She was still the only woman he'd ever loved; his matched pair, the soul mate of his life; she was unparalleled carnal bliss and the keeper of his heart. He wondered how he'd been able to disavow those feelings since leaving Easton. He wondered how he could live in the future, knowing that.

But her eyes opened then, and her mouth formed a welcoming smile, and he smiled back at her.

"Have I told you lately how much I love you?" she whispered, a beautiful houri lounging on purple velvet, pale-haired and flushed pink from sensual delights.

"Not lately," he murmured, sprawled in the chair opposite her, all lithe grace, toned muscle, and male beauty. "Thank you."

"You have to tell me you love me. Even if you don't mean it."

"I love you, Angel. How could I not?"

"You say it so easily."

"No, I say it with great difficulty sitting in this room only recently vacated by Steven."

"I suppose I can't explain that to you."

"Probably not."

"I've missed you every day since you left, and now that I'm with you again, I find myself infinitely more needy." She shut her eyes briefly, gripping the chair arms as if struggling against the sensation. "It's as though I'm addicted to your touch, your body, the sound of your voice."

"And this," he added, sweeping his fingertips up his arousal, aware of the focus of her gaze, constraint coloring his voice.

"And that," she softly agreed, watching his fingers stroke his erection. "I feel as though I should apologize."

His mouth curved into a smile. "I don't know if he's been apologized to before."

"Would you mind if I did?"

"I don't remember your being so polite."

"I need you too much to be difficult."

"How fortunate for us," he said, understanding the meaning of her word "apology." He pushed his grand, perfectly formed penis away from his belly and toward her, so it stood rigidly upright.

She moved from the chair as if drawn by an over-powering sexual allure and, slipping between his outspread legs, knelt before him. "Does he like frosting?" she whispered.

"Only pink frosting," he replied with a grin.

She touched his penis delicately, tentatively, as if some arcane mystery were concealed within it that would explain her unquenchable hunger. And it moved under her brushing touch—a vital life force with a mind of its own. Sliding her finger down the silken skin, she examined the bulging veins, the curl-

ing hair at the root, the full globes resting on the purple velvet chair.

Shifting on the chair, he groaned as she lifted the
heavy weight of his testicles and stroked the velvety
skin. It gave her a sense of power to see him respond
to her caresses. She watched his erection swell, the
enormous head inch upward, the pulse quicken in the
prominent veins.

And he observed her with rapt attention as she
grasped the base firmly in her hand so it jutted upright
and then stroked the shiny red crest with the first
globule of frosting. She took great pains to spread the
pink icing evenly, carefully smoothing the sugary confection over the bulging arc of the head, then around
and under the sensitive ridge as if she were being
graded on coverage.

He held his breath against the shocking intensity.

"There." She observed her handiwork, her craving for him in her voice and heated eyes. "My own
large pink lollipop."

It took him a moment to answer, carnal urgency
paramount in his mind. "Don't take too long. . . ."

"Are you in a hurry to make love to me?" she
whispered.

He made a sound in his throat, a low growl.

"You can't come in my mouth," she said, her
plump breasts brushing against his legs, her eyes gazing up at him, blue innocence, her mouth the merest
breath away from the frosted crest. "I want you to
come inside me."

"We'll see," he said on a suffocated breath, the
ridged muscles of his torso tense with constraint.

He sucked in a harsh breath when her tongue
flickered over the tip, leaving a faint path in the icing,
her tongue curling into her mouth, tasting with a leisurely appraisal.

"You'll be tasting more than that if you don't hurry," he said, his voice thick with self-discipline, his body barely in check, a substantial amount of frosting covering his erection.

"Aren't you a master of orgasmic brinkmanship?" she teased.

"Don't push, Angel," he growled.

And as her tongue gently licked away the sticky sweetness, he clutched the chair arms, absorbing the searing pleasure, curbing his sharp-set lust. Then her mouth closed over the distended crest completely, engulfing the sensitive underside, sliding the hard length of him deep into her mouth, and he wasn't sure he could last much longer.

When all the frosting was licked and sucked and swallowed, she lifted away, rested her arms on his thighs, and, looking up, said in a voice husky with need, "When I hold you in my mouth, I can feel you inside me."

Her red lips were rimmed with pink sugar, sleek with moisture, her mouth only inches away, a receptacle for his passion if he chose. "That's it," he muttered, and pushing her back onto the carpet, he followed her down in a sweeping dive, pinning her under his body, his knee already spreading her legs apart with a rough, impatient force. He invaded her, slipping inside her glossy passage with an intoxicating familiarity that stirred sweet, reckless memory. Aeons beyond impatience, frenzied, no longer coolly detached if he'd ever been, he drove into her, forced her, filled her, crushed her into the floor.

And she wrapped herself around him and welcomed him, panting at the plumbing depth of each powerful stroke, surging up to meet him with breathless longing, wanting him beyond her power to comprehend.

Lifting one of her legs so he could penetrate more deeply, he held her thigh hard against his hip, his lower body pounding into her, ramming her, his grunts savage accompaniment to each headlong thrust.

"Come in me," she whispered, her hunger for him suffocating, saturating.

"No," he growled, already beginning to ejaculate. "No," he rasped, pouring into her with a shuddering turbulence, filling her fertile, hot, temptress body when he knew he shouldn't, when any green, rank youth knew better. "No, you little witch," he whispered, feeling the top of his head lift away, the last drop of himself spilling inside her.

"Fuck," he muttered, leaning his forehead against the carpet, gasping for air, the pounding of his heart audible in his ears, sweat dripping in his eyes. He already wanted to screw her again. "We have to talk about this," he raggedly said.

He was her love of the ages. She didn't dare say yes. "Not right now."

"Later, then." His voice was muffled.

She drew air into her laboring lungs. "Later," she whispered.

And when he could breathe normally again and his heart was no longer thudding in his chest, he lifted her and carried her to the bed.

They gently kissed and touched each other as if they had to store away the finite sensations against another bleak, cold time. And they made endless love till night gave way to dawn—with fierceness and frenzy, with bittersweet languor, with great tenderness.

With desperation.

As she lay in his arms with the light of morning rimming the heavy draperies, she wished they could stay forever in this luxurious room, locked away from the world, isolated from all the problems that assailed them.

And when he asked her again to marry him, as she knew he would, and promised to protect her from Brook and the shibboleths of society, she cried like a child. She begged him to stay with her, she pleaded, she'd do anything, she said, to keep him.

Anything but marry him, it turned out.

For the same obstacles, the same impediments, the same gilded prison enclosed her.

"I can't live like that," he finally said. "To have only a part of you. I'm sorry." He couldn't, at base, share her, no matter how tenuous her husband's presence in her life. And he left the bed and dressed while she watched him with tears coursing down her face. "If you ever want me, tell Chambers," he quietly said. "He can reach me anywhere in the world. But it's marriage, *mon ange,* or nothing. I'd die away a piece at a time, living as your friends do in their sham world." And she clung to him when he kissed her good-bye, until he finally unclasped her arms from around his neck and said, "Don't go soft on me, now, tough girl. We'll both live."

But he didn't know if he actually meant it, and walking away from her was the hardest thing he'd ever done in his life.

*M*adame Centisi knocked on the door after a time and told Angela that Kit's driver would take her home. So she wiped her puffy, red eyes and blew her nose and told herself people lived without love or happiness. And she dressed as if she were going to her doom.

When she climbed into Kit's carriage, his scent

surrounded her, and she broke down and sobbed so loudly, Kit's driver wondered what his master had done to her.

She didn't sleep at all that night; she wrote pitiful notes to Kit begging him to come back, pleading with him to stay. But she tore them all up as she wrote them, and burned them one at a time like some pagan rite of death because she couldn't ask him and he wouldn't stay anyway.

It was pointless.

24

Kit walked around London that early morning from the West End to the City and back again along the river, where the sun came up in glorious splendor as if the universe wasn't aware that his existence was dimmed and gray and bordered in black.

When he finally let himself into his flat, he sat in his study and drank his breakfast, and when Saskia came in at nine and saw him, she said, "You need some good news, I think."

He looked up with bleak, empty eyes. "I'm sorry," he said, "but there isn't such a thing as good news."

"The *Desiree* will be finished in ten days. Guaranteed."

He sighed instead of smiled. "Are you coming with me?"

"As a friend?" And she waited for his answer with more trepidation than she would have thought possible.

He hesitated so long she wondered if he'd heard her, and then he finally said, "Yes, as a friend."

"Thank you, no," she gently replied. "I think it's time for me to see what Paris has to offer."

"Can I come and visit you sometime?"

"Of course," she said to the man who'd given her back her life. "You're always welcome."

He smiled very faintly, as if her answer had given him a minute measure of hope. "Stay at least until I sail."

"If you want me to."

"I'd appreciate it." He rotated the cut-glass tumbler of whiskey in his hands, looking down at it briefly with a grimace. "I saw her tonight."

"I could tell."

He sighed. "I feel like ripping my heart out to stop the pain." He smiled grimly. "Or better yet, rip out Greville's heart and have an end to it."

"It's a thought, darling," Saskia said, so close to death on several occasions by her husband's hand, she viewed revenge with an unconventional honesty.

"I haven't reached that point yet." He traced the cut pattern on the glass with deliberation. "Cold-blooded murder requires a certain frame of mind, I suppose."

*A*ngela was obliged to see her mother that morning. She couldn't think of a suitable excuse to extricate herself from the commitment. But she made Violet come with her. In her utter dejection she wasn't capable of listening to her mother's lectures alone.

"My, you're looking fatigued, my dear," her mother ungraciously said immediately as she entered the room. Poised ramrod stiff in her usual chair by the window, she exuded a cold chill. "Haven't I repeatedly warned you that all your activities at Easton will wear you out?"

"I'm fine, Mother," Angela blandly said, checking the time on the porcelain clock near the door. She'd stay half an hour, no more.

"Violet, I depend on you to help me talk some sense into Angela," the dowager Countess of Ross declared. "She spends too much time and money on her tenants," she punctiliously went on. "I'm sure they don't appreciate it. Will you girls have tea or chocolate this morning?"

They both opted for chocolate, and as the dowager poured from the silver pot before her, she said with a frown, "Brook's sister told me some awkward news. I find the fast set you associate with so unworthy of you, Angela. Gwendolyn was quite upset."

"Gwendolyn is a shrew, Countess," Violet asserted. "Everyone knows it.

"That may be, but her news is still alarming. She spoke of an engagement ring?"

"I'm not going to discuss anything Gwendolyn said, Mother," Angela replied, gritting her teeth against an overwhelming urge to scream. "She's not an authority on my life."

"I only hope, Angela, that you at least understand the seriousness of provoking Brook," her mother sternly admonished. "Lady Orme recently saw the queen, and she reminded me that Wales is only barely in his mother's good graces. You can't afford to antagonize your husband."

"Perhaps Brook should think instead of the danger in provoking me, Mother. I may not give a damn about Bertie or the queen."

"I won't have you swearing in my presence," her mother chided. "You sound like your father." A large, austere woman, the countess had suffered her first husband's wildness with resentment. "And how can you even consider jeopardizing the royal family? Have you no sense of obligation to your class?"

"Brook is very much a scoundrel, Countess," Violet interjected. "He's unpleasant in countless ways. Surely the queen would take his character into consideration if a dispute arose."

"What does she know in her isolation at Windsor except what she's told?"[23] the Countess of Ross rebuked. "And what she hears could bring shame on our family. I won't have it, Angela. Do you hear?"

"Mother," Angela said with a small sigh, "don't order my life about today. I'm very tired."

"I would hope you'd at least have some consideration for your sisters and me," the countess went on as though her daughter hadn't spoken. "Think what the disgrace would mean to Millie and Dolly. Not to mention the Sutherlands. They're devoutly concerned with propriety."

"Edward is quite normal, Mother, and as for Millie and Dolly, I'm sure they'd wish me some happiness."

"You've always been so selfish, Angela," her mother crossly said. "With never a care for anyone but yourself. I blame your grandfather in part. He spent much too much time with you before he died. I find you remarkably like him at times. He never did give a whit for good manners."

What she really meant, Angela knew, was that her grandfather had erred in leaving his entire fortune to his granddaughter instead of to his daughter-in-law as trustee. "Grandpapa only wanted Easton to prosper," Angela quietly said, the litany of her faults all to familiar.

"I'm sure there's no need for the outrageous expenses you contract for that old pile of stone. As for your farming—heavens, Angela, don't other estates survive without every new outlandish agricultural practice?"

"I'm sure they do, Mother. And I'm sure you're right about everything else, too," she wearily said, much too disheartened to defend herself against her mother's unceasing attacks.

"Then you'll contrive to be pleasant to Brook," the Countess of Ross insisted.

"I don't want to see him ever again, Mother. I'm sorry, you're going to have to deal with it," Angela firmly replied, adamant on that point, fatigue or not. "He terrifies the children, and I won't have it."

"I'm sure they're just too young to understand his manner."

"No, they're too young to have to suffer him."

"Well, I'm sure I don't understand why you can't be civil to him," the countess righteously maintained. "Others arrange their lives without such hysteria."

"I'm not hysterical, Mother. I'm simply not going to put up with Brook or his sisters any longer. It's been eighteen years, and I think it's time to reduce their presence in my life."

"Your steppapa would be very disappointed in your attitude, Angela. I'm pleased he's not alive to hear such selfishness."

"I'm due to depart on the one o'clock train for Easton, so I'll be leaving," Angela remarked, her feelings too strained to endure her mother long. "Thank you for the chocolate," she politely added, pushing away her full cup. "And if you see Gwendolyn again, tell her to mind her own business."

"I most certainly will not. She's a relative, whether you like it or not."

Violet stood first, and Angela smiled at her in gratitude. "I'll see Angela to the train, Countess. Dudley sends his regards."

"Isn't he always so gracious?" Angela's mother said. "I'm sure you're very happy you married him. Unlike Angela, who can't seem to appreciate the duties of a wife."

"Dudley and I get along famously," Violet replied with a silky mockery. "He appreciates my money."

"And he should. As I'm sure Brook appreciates Angela's. You see, dear, other women make the necessary adjustments."

"Yes, Mother," Angela said, smiling with only the most intense effort. "I'll bring May your good wishes."

"For heaven's sake, she's only two. What does she know of such things? Remember what I told you, now. Duty above all."

Angela suddenly felt nauseous.

She turned and walked from the room, leaving Violet to say her good-byes.

"I'd faint, too," Violet said when she joined her out in the hall, "or vomit, I don't know which. My lord, she's frightful. And you're not recovered from last night," she kindly added. "Why don't you take a later train and sleep at my house for an hour or so?"

"I just want to go home."

"Do you think he might change his mind?" Violet asked, conscious of Kit's appearance last night, of his renewed marriage proposal.

"No," Angela quietly replied. "He can't, no more than I. At least at Easton my life has purpose. I can't wait to see it again."

*K*it's purpose of late was devoted to arranging supplies for his coming voyage. He also spent a morning buying presents for May. He bought her jewelry—a bracelet and locket and a small rendition of a rabbit in enamel and gold—wishing he could buy her mother something as well. He did finally, anyway, just as he was leaving the shop. He bought Angela South Sea pearls, ropes and ropes of them, and had them put in a chased gold box with a note. "Every pearl is a kiss from me. I wish I could give you more, but there aren't enough in the world." He sealed the note quickly against his impulse to expose more raw feeling, said, "Send it out," and left the shop.

He stood out on the pavement in the chill November air, while shoppers walked around him and stared with open curiosity at his motionless figure. He wanted to travel north and get Angela and take her away. Now, this instant, with or without her consent, with or without her husband's consent, without the damnable queen's consent. And it took a very long time before he was able to overcome that rash impulse.

The toy store he went to next distracted him momentarily, and when he was finished with his purchases, May had enough toys to keep her entertained for a decade. Following the directions he'd received from the toy-store clerk, he went to a seamstress last and arranged for a new wardrobe for Peter Rabbit. He would be the best-dressed fuzzy rabbit in the world. Then, satisfied that he had shown prudence and good judgment in dealing with his sense of loss, he went to the nearest pub and drank himself into oblivion.

His nights were the most difficult, because he no longer had the activities pertinent to his departure to keep him busy. He generally stayed home drinking; he couldn't bring himself to be sociable and accept the invitations he received. Saskia was his solace, friend, and confessor, and she paid him back perhaps in small measure in those days for all he'd done for her.

He left finally two days early for Plymouth because he was anxious to go. He said good-bye to Saskia at his flat, kissed her gently like a sister on the cheek, and murmured, "Thank you for saving my sanity. I'll miss you in the Pearl River trading," he added with a smile. "You're my best cutthroat negotiator."

"Who knows? If I become bored in Paris, I might sail with you again sometime."

"You have an open invitation. Tell Chambers and I'll come back for you."

*W*hen Kit's presents arrived at Easton, Angela wore all her pearls to bed that night and dreamed impossible dreams. Peter Rabbit was dressed and undressed endlessly in the coming days, and the nursery looked like a miniature toy store. Now that the agricultural college had opened, Angela spent long days at the school, talking to teachers and students, involving herself in hundreds of details, sitting in on classes, overseeing her new investment.

Fitz came home on a flying visit one weekend for no apparent reason. "I just missed you," he said, and when he left, he held his mother longer than usual and cryptically murmured, "Don't worry about me."

She'd smiled at him when he'd spoken. "You're doing a very fine job of taking care of yourself. Soon you won't need me to watch over you at all."

He'd hugged her again and then carried May on his shoulders down the drive to the gate, where a carriage waited to take him to the station. Angela and May had walked back in the wan afternoon sunlight, talking of their plans for Christmas, when Fitz would next be home.

The letter came three days later, and when she could breathe again and the short-circuiting synapses in her brain had quieted, she thought back on her son's strange behavior and decided she should have known.

I've left for South Africa, he wrote. *Don't worry about me. I'll be out of the way and de Grae can't touch me. You won't have to protect me down here. I'm traveling with Reggie Carlton, who's going to be stationed in Port Elizabeth. I can stay with him.*

South Africa? Angela nervously contemplated. Where the country had been on the brink of war a dozen times the last year. Everyone knew since the Jameson Raid, when the British force was captured in the Transvaal, that it was just a matter of time until the Boers and the British government declared war. Fitz was trying to help her by running off to South Africa, but good lord, he was only seventeen, much too young to risk his life; he was her only son. Even if the war didn't erupt to endanger him, some exotic disease could take his life. Africa was called the white man's grave for very good reason. De Grae was by far the lesser threat of the two. At least against Brook she had the means to defend her son. Money was always an effective weapon with her husband.

Quickly checking the date on his letter and the postmark, she saw that Fitz had still been in Cambridge two days ago. There might be time to stop him. Calling for Nellie, she immediately began making her travel plans.

Even as she was issuing directions to Nellie and Bergie concerning May's care in her absence, she knew she'd have to ask Kit for help. If Fitz had sailed already, the *Desiree* was the only vessel that could overtake him. Not another ship had the speed.

*A*fter reaching London that evening, she discovered from the Lawton House staff that Fitz had stayed overnight there two days previously. Even if she wished to avoid asking Kit, with Fitz's two-day advantage she had no choice. Immediately setting out for Kit's flat, she woke Whitfield only to discover Kit had already departed for Plymouth.

She arrived at Chambers's home a brief twenty minutes later, and when he came down hastily dressed in trousers and a robe to find her pacing in the entrance hall, she said without preliminaries, "Forgive me for the intrusion, but I need to reach Kit *immediately*. Whitfield tells me he left for Plymouth."

The countess was obviously distraught, and though Kit hadn't confided in him, he'd left instructions should Angela call that Chambers was to reach him anywhere, anytime. Additionally, since Chambers paid Kit's bills while he was in England, he was aware that two very large jeweler's bills had been for items delivered to Easton. "He may be at The Gull in Plymouth," Chambers declared. "Although it's possible he's already sailed," he apologetically added. "Mr. Braddock was scheduled to go out on the tide tonight. Is there something *I* could help you with?" No one made calls at this hour unless some crisis existed.

"Thank you, no," Angela replied. "I need to see *him*. Please accept my apologies again for waking you."

But Chambers dressed after Angela left and went down to his office to send a telegram himself. He knew Kit would want to hear of Angela's appeal.

Angela's own message to Kit sent from the nearest

telegraph office open at that hour briefly explained
her predicament:

> I need your help to find Fitz. He sailed for
> South Africa. Wait for me in Plymouth.
>   Angela

Kit received the two telegrams from the same mes-
senger as he waited dockside for the last supplies to be
loaded aboard the *Desiree*. Chambers's missive was a
simple notice of Angela's visit. He appreciated his
banker's sense of responsibility. Folding the paper
away, he opened the second telegram with measured
hope and skittish nerves, already aware of its sender.
But Angela wasn't asking for him, only for his help,
and after a moment of debate he wasn't certain he
wished to wait for her. His crew was ready to weigh
anchor. Henry Watson was on hand to see them off.
He had a chance to leave a doomed and bittersweet
love affair behind, and he was more familiar with gratifying himself than gratifying others. He didn't know
whether he was benevolent enough to be accommodating, and certainly, in Plymouth, any number of
ships were available for hire.

"Is it bad news?" Henry asked when Kit crushed
the telegram in his fist.

"I'm not sure," Kit quietly said, shoving the slip
of paper into his pocket. "How much time do we have
before we lose the tide?" It was a rhetorical question;
Kit knew the tides better than most.

"Four hours," Henry said. "Maybe a little less
with that new keel."

Kit looked up at the full moon as if gauging his
time, took the telegram out of his pocket again,
straightened it out between his fingers, and reread the
message. Angela had sent it two hours ago.

He could have been gone two hours ago.

She hadn't asked for a reply.

She had no way of knowing when he'd left.

Hell and damnation, he silently swore, tossing the telegram away.

But when a gust of wind started rolling the scrap of paper toward the end of the quay, he lunged after it, grabbed it, and exclaimed to Henry Watson, who was politely controlling his curiosity, "Please tell the crew to settle in for the night. We'll leave on the morning tide."

And he walked back down the moonlit quay toward the small hotel he'd just quitted.

*A*s it turned out, Angela wasn't able to leave immediately because Brook was at Lawton House when she returned from the telegraph office. Her butler nervously said, "He's in the Chinese drawing room, my lady. He was quite adamant about staying until you returned."

"You had no choice, Childers. I understand. The earl rarely does as one wishes." And she forced herself to deal with her difficult husband even as a crushing anxiety burdened her mind.

"I saw the lights on and realized you were in town," Brook drawled, exceedingly drunk and smiling as she entered the drawing room.

Brook's smiles were always alarming. "It's late, Brook. If you wish to discuss something, I'd prefer a morning call. I'm about to retire."

"Won't wait till morning, my dear," he lazily said. "Damned creditors getting damned impertinent. Need a bit of your fortune to set things to rights."

"I can't help you tonight," Angela said, not moving from her position by the door.

"That Lofton chit sent me a childishly sweet note wondering if Fitz would consider writing to her," Brook softly said. "She's apparently in love. I was thinking, too, perhaps May should come and spend some time with me," he silkily went on, his lounging pose as idle as his smooth tone. "I'm sure the courts would approve if you don't want to accommodate me. Father has a right to see his daughter, I'd think."

"How much do you want?" she said with disgust.

"Seventy thousand would help for a time." His smirk was triumphant.

"Call on my banker in the morning," Angela abruptly said. "I'll give him instructions."

He was immediately sorry he hadn't asked for more, she'd consented to readily.

"Childers will show you out," she declared, interrupting his drunken contemplation. Opening the door, she called for her butler, who was standing at attention in the hall. The Lawton House staff always saw that the countess was protected when the earl was about. The earl's reputation was well-known.

And she left her very costly husband and swiftly traversed the hall to her study. Brook's appearance required a note to her banker and, additionally, a late-night call on Violet before she could leave for Plymouth.

*A*ngela was ushered into Violet's boudoir by a sleepy footman and greeted by her friend, who had risen from bed when she heard of Angela's arrival.

"What brings you out at this hour?" she asked with concern, such a late-night visit unusual. Angela wasn't on her way home from a party; she was dressed for traveling.

"I've a favor to ask of you."

"Of course. Sit down and tell me," Violet offered, moving toward chairs near the fire.

"Fitz sailed for South Africa with Reggie Carlton," Angela said, her voice trembling. "I'm just terrified something might happen to him."

"He's gone?" Violet's shock raised her voice an octave.

"He sent me a letter," Angela explained. "He left two days ago. And you know how ghastly everything's been down there."

"How terrible for you. Let me call my cousin Chester in the War Department. He'll know what to do."

Angela shook her head. "I'm going after Fitz. And I need you to take care of May for me. I wouldn't even ask, except Brook accosted me just minutes ago at Lawton House, asking for money again and threatening May if I wouldn't agree. I'm not sure she's safe at Easton with just the servants. Brook can be intimidating."

"Not to me."

Angela smiled for the first time that night. "And I'm grateful. So would you go to Easton tomorrow and bring May back? She knows you; she's comfortable with you. Bring Nellie and Bergie down to care for her. And I don't want to sound melodramatic, but May can't be allowed outside without two footmen as escorts."

"I've plenty of footmen," Violet noted, her gaze following Angela's nervous promenade. "Don't worry; she'll be safe from Brook. Consider it done. Now, how are you going after Fitz? In the *Shark*?"

"I'm hoping Kit will take me in the *Desiree*. It's faster than the *Shark,* faster than anything on the seas."

"I thought he left. No one's seen him for days."

"I'm not sure, but I talked to his banker tonight and he may still be in Plymouth. I'm taking a train down tonight as soon as I leave you."

"Do you think he'll do it?" Violet had seen Kit one night at Marlborough House, and he was dangerously moody.

"I hope so. He's my only hope of overtaking Fitz."

"At which point you may have additional problems. The boy may be headstrong, like you. Can you make him return?"

"Once the captain realizes how young he is, he'll understand Fitz shouldn't be sailing off alone into a possible war zone."

"Do you want me to call Admiral Hartley to find out what ship he sailed on?"

"Reggie's father said they left on the *Adelaide* out of Portsmouth. I've already talked to everyone who would know his plans."

"Have you packed?"

"I've a few things in the carriage." Angela glanced at the clock. "My special train is waiting for me. Tell May I'll be back soon."

25

It was shortly after sunrise when Angela arrived at The Gull. On watch for her in the small downstairs parlor, Kit met her at the door as she alighted from her carriage.

"Thank you for waiting," she said, almost collapsing from relief, having worried all night that she'd miss him.

"You're exhausted," Kit kindly said, careful not to touch her. "Come upstairs; I'll have some food sent up and you can tell me about Fitz." He'd had all night to debate his options, but no simple answer had resolved itself in his mind, and he was still indecisive.

She told him briefly all she knew from those she'd talked to, and then she asked him to help her overtake the *Adelaide* and bring Fitz back.

"Please, Kit," she implored, "I'm willing to beg on bended knee if necessary. Fitz could be killed. I couldn't bear it if he died. *Please*, you have to help me."

Her eyes were filled with tears, her face a mask of anguish, her voice so stricken, he wanted to hold her close and soothe her pain and tell her he'd do anything she wanted.

But he'd barely survived the emotional devastation of the weeks since he'd left her. He must have drunk enough whiskey to float the *Desiree*. Was it fair for her simply to arrive and expect so much of him?

A kind of vengeance may have prompted his decision, or a brutal quid pro quo. Or maybe something more carnal and elemental.

"I'd be willing to help you," he said, his voice utterly without inflection, "but I have a condition."

"Anything," she exclaimed, her eyes suddenly alight through her tears.

"You have to stay with me for four months," he quietly said.

She looked at him with cautious bewilderment. "What do you mean . . . stay with you?"

"Sail with me to the Pearl River. The trip takes four months. We can bring Fitz back to England, if he wants, before we leave; you'll want to pick up May, anyway. Or Fitz can stay with us if he likes. That's it."

"And I'd sleep with you," she softly murmured, her gaze direct.

"Of course. Very much of course." He made no apology.

"You can ask that of me at a time like this?" Indignation quivered in her words.

"You're asking me to open my wounds again. So this is in the way of a business arrangement. I'll give you what you want; you'll give me what I want. And maybe I'll survive the bloodletting." This from the man who'd opened twenty-two trading depots around the world.

"You're cold and unfeeling."

"No, you are. You've made my life a living hell."

The silence was tense with restraint, a simmering anguish vibrating in the small chamber.

"I'm sorry," Angela said, not understanding that Kit Braddock had indeed been spared unhappiness until he'd met her—he'd been a golden child, much loved and adored, a youth of wealth and beauty and accomplishments, a man with the world at his feet.

What had he ever known of misery?

"Very well," she agreed. "I'll do anything to save my son." There was insolence in her answer. And then her effrontery altered, chameleonlike, and she said with humble gratitude, "Thank you."

He was merciful regardless of his proviso, and she was indebted to him.

"When can we sail?" she said in a flashing heartbeat more, her voice animated, her face bereft of gloom, the familiar vivacity glowing in her eyes.

And he smiled despite himself.

"Now," he said, and offered her his hand.

*B*ut he didn't trouble to hold her to their bargain as they raced south—tactful, perhaps, or gallant out of respect for her anxieties over Fitz, or afraid himself of future personal heartache.

He studiously avoided her, staying on the bridge, having his meals brought up, not going down to his cabin to change and wash until she was sure to be sleeping.

And he left orders for the lady to stay below.

Angela willingly obeyed because she appreciated his honorable intentions, and she also knew better than most how arduous and critical the task of piloting when the engines were roaring at full steam in storm-tossed seas.

They traveled through heavy winter weather,

fighting to stay on course under the onslaught of gale winds forcing them east—on watch for the *Adelaide* after the third day out. Angela paced as best she could in the pitching cabin, tense and anxious. She recalled all the stories of fevers and epidemics on troop ships, her mind obsessed with a multitude of morbid thoughts; she checked and rechecked the maps Kit had thoughtfully sent down, grilling the stewards on their progress whenever they came to her cabin with meals.

Kit stayed at the wheel save for short snatched naps, his brain too agitated to sleep for more than a few brief minutes at a time, the same inauspicious thoughts looping through his mind: the uncertainty of overtaking a vessel with such an advantage in time; the possibility of the storm driving them off course; the doubtfulness of sighting the *Adelaide* at night; or the *Adelaide* having been blown off the shipping lanes by now.

The *Desiree* signaled two ships they passed in the night, but neither were the object of their search. One had sighted the *Adelaide* the previous day and gave them her course bearings. Kit had a message immediately sent down to Angela. *Tomorrow we should overtake them,* he had written.

He asked for additional speed after that—if his crew could manage it without blowing the engines, he qualified—and the men in the engine room responded with a five-knot increase, driving the pressure gauge into the danger zone.

The *Desiree* pounded through the night.

 The next day Angela asked permission to come up on the bridge, too restless and impatient to remain below any longer.

"If you stay out of the way," Kit brusquely said. "I can't vouch for my politesse." His gaze swept over her. "Have you slept?"

"Not much," she replied, noting the deep shadows under his eyes, the dark red stubble on his cheeks. "I can't ever thank you enough for taking me."

"We haven't found him yet," he gruffly said, bracing himself for an oncoming wave. "Save your thanks. Now, sit over there and hang on."

She sat without taking affront at his curtness, the bridge bustling with crew and commotion.

Vessel on the starboard bow," Kit's first mate called out that afternoon, the dim shape of a ship faintly visible through the driving rain.

"Approach her," Kit said, "and if it's the *Adelaide,* send out a signal man when we're within a hundred yards."

A small cheer went up as the vessel's name came into view, and despite orders, Angela couldn't sit still. Moving up to the bridge window, she pressed her face against the glass, trying to see through the storm. "Can we board in these seas?" she asked.

"*We* can't," Kit said, his gaze trained on the port bow of the *Adelaide,* "but *I* can."

"You won't let me go?"

"Be reasonable, Angela. There are eight-foot troughs out there."

"Maybe we should wait; we could follow them into calmer seas."

"I'd rather not. We're four days out already, even sailing at high speed. It's another four days back." He exhaled, his weariness evident. "If this storm continues, we may have to trail them all the way to the cape, and I don't want to take the time. They're expecting me in Pearl River. I should have gone weeks ago."

She looked up at him quickly.

"I'm not blaming you," he said, his expression as composed as his voice. "It just happened. But I have to be there as soon as possible. Do you think Fitz will be frightened by a crossing in this weather?"

Angela shook her head. "He's been sailing all his life, but Violet wondered if he'd come back with me. I hadn't considered that problem until she mentioned it."

"Don't worry about that."

The simplicity of his reply was reassuring. As was the brief message he had his signal man send to the *Adelaide* requesting permission to board.

After wrangling for some time with the *Adelaide*'s captain, who tried to discourage their mission in the high seas, a small boat put off from the *Desiree* manned by the eight strongest crew members and Kit. It was a heart-stopping sight as the lifeboat pitched and tossed on the towering waves, the sea lifting and dropping it like so much flotsam, the sailors rowing with all their strength in the depression of the wave and hanging on to their useless oars as they were flung up onto the crest.

Slowly, with Herculean efforts, the men brought the lifeboat closer to the *Adelaide,* the rail of the larger ship lined with spectators riveted to the sight of the heroic passage.

Then Angela made out the figure of her son with a life vest on, clinging to the gangway on the side of the ship, three other men in a human chain holding him secure.

With relief, Kit had seen Fitz emerge through the deck rail not sure himself, despite his assurance to Angela, that her son would come willingly. He'd intended to bring Fitz back to her, but now, at least, it wouldn't require any coercion.

He waved up at Fitz on their approach, signaling him to make his way down the wave-washed stair, as their small boat converged perilously close to the troop ship. In the storm-tossed seas, they could be smashed against the ship's sides if they came too near or be driven under the hull if the force of a wave propelled them downward. He gave Angela's boy high marks for courage; it was a hazardous undertaking at seventeen. It was a danger at any age.

Their boat rolled and pitched, inching closer until a mere six feet separated them from the *Adelaide*. The fear on Fitz's face was evident at this range, all the men in the human cable lining the stairway equally frightened. Kit shouted to the man on the seat beside him, his voice muffled by the screaming wind, and at the man's nod he balanced himself precariously on the unsteady seat and gunwale for a split second before leaping across the heaving sea—arms outstretched to catch the steel ramp.

Angela screamed, her voice echoing in the small contained area of the bridge, and then she shut her eyes, not daring to see if he had cleared the dangerous distance.

"He's caught it," someone quietly said, but the statement was cautiously uttered, and when Angela opened her eyes again, she understood why there was no elation in the tone.

Kit hung suspended from the last step, his body dangling over the churning sea, the ship rising and plunging, his form minute against the vessel's enormous gray bulk.

His legs swung once in an abbreviated pumping arc, then once again in a wide sweeping curve, and with a powerful surge he heaved himself up on the ramp, the cohesive flow of muscle and tensile strength grace in motion. He squatted on the step for a second, catching his breath, while everyone on the bridge of the *Desiree* cheered. Then, coming to his feet, he mounted the slippery gangway to the waiting boy.

Angela saw him bend close to Fitz's ear and speak to him. When her son nodded, Kit waved the other men away. Then they were alone, two small figures against the backdrop of the towering ship and nature's raging assault.

He should have worn a life jacket, Angela thought, noticing for the first time that Kit had none. But then the two men began descending the companionway, and any superfluous considerations vanished from her mind.

As they maneuvered down the tilting stairway, Kit seemed to be talking to Fitz. But whatever he was saying wasn't finding favor, for Fitz was emphatically shaking his head. At the base of the stairs, holding the boy firmly with his hand on his wrist, Kit motioned the boat and his crewmen away from the side of the *Adelaide*, carefully watching their laborious progress until they'd put enough distance between themselves and the ship to leave a twenty-foot trough of heaving green sea.

Then, wrapping his arms around Fitz, without warning, Kit jumped clear of the ship, taking the boy with him. Terrified, Angela shut her eyes again, praying to any god who would listen to save them from danger.

"He's got him," the first mate said.

Almost hysterical with relief, Angela saw Kit's dark head and Fitz's fairer one, bobbing like corks in the angry ocean. Swimming strongly, Kit pulled Fitz to the small boat and bodily heaved him over the side, hoisting himself up behind.

They were safe.
And Angela burst into tears.

*F*itz and Kit were laughing when they came on board, thoroughly drenched, water streaming down their bodies, immune to the discomforts of the storm. Looking up, Kit saw Angela standing at the bridge door, and he pushed Fitz forward.

He watched mother and son embrace, his expression shuttered, the merriment gone from his eyes, and then he turned to his crew and individually thanked them, shaking their hands, talking to each man.

Off to one side of the men, Fitz apologized to his mother. "I never should have gone, Maman," he said. "I'm sorry, don't cry," he soothed, awkwardly patting her shoulder. "I'm fine. Did you see me when we jumped into the sea?" His voice was cheerful and vibrant, his peril no more than an adventure now that it was over.

"I definitely saw you," Angela said, brushing away her tears, smiling up at her son towering over her. "You were both very brave."

"He just pulled me in," Fitz admitted with a chuckle. "Kit," Fitz said, touching Kit's arm to gain his attention, "tell Maman how I screamed when we jumped."

"It was just the shock," Kit graciously said, turning away from his men. "He was fine once we hit the water."

"Did you thank Kit?" Angela prompted. "We both owe him enormous gratitude."

"All the way back, Maman," Fitz affably replied. "That troop ship was a hellhole." He grimaced. "Thanks for coming to get me, Maman," he gratefully said. "And thanks, Kit," he added with a grin, "for the exciting swim."

"Next time we'll pick better weather," Kit replied with an answering smile. "Why don't we get out of the rain now?" He motioned a crew member forward. "Afgar will show you below. And if you'll excuse me," he added with a sketchy bow to Angela, "I'm going to see that we get the *Desiree* about and set on course for England."

Kit didn't appear for dinner that evening. Their steward offered his regrets. The captain was still busy on the bridge, he explained. So Fitz and Angela ate alone and then visited afterward in the salon. Fitz explained that he had thought his leaving would help. She wouldn't have had to defend him, then, against his father.

"Your father can be managed," Angela quietly said, so pleased to have her son back, she wasn't inclined to chastise him.

"I'll be with you the next time you see him. I'm old enough to take care of you now," he flatly said, as though he'd come to terms with his fear of his father in the past few days.

"I'd like that," Angela softly said, seeing her boy grow up before her eyes. "I'd like that very much."

"Don't cry, Maman." Fitz leaned over and put his arm around her shoulder.

"I'm not crying," she said, sniffling and brushing away the wetness in her eyes. "I'm not crying at all."

$\mathcal{26}$

Very late that night Angela heard her cabin door open, and sitting up at the sound, she saw Kit's form silhouetted in the threshold. The light from the hall formed a pale nimbus around him, briefly illuminating her stateroom as well before he walked in and quietly shut the door.

"We sailed out of the storm," he said, walking over to a chair and sitting down.

"I noticed," she said, reaching for the light by the bed, her hands trembling, cognizant of the bargain they'd made. As the soft golden glow of the lamp flared high, she saw him clearly, slumped low in the chair, lethargy in his pose, his eyes dark shadows in his lean face.

"I thought I could be chivalrous," he softly said. "But as you see." He shrugged, exhaustion etched on his features. "I won't keep you long."

He opened the brass buttons on his jacket slowly, as if it were an effort to coordinate his fingers, and shrugged out of it with a small, repressed sigh.

"You haven't slept at all, have you?" Angela said, aware of the effort it took for him to move.

He looked up at the sound of her voice as though recalling where he was, his expression polite but quizzical.

"Have you slept?" she repeated.

"I think I did." Lifting his foot onto his knee, he untied his shoe, pulled it off, dropped it, and sank back in his chair, girding his body for the next effort. "You must be tired, too," he said, his voice raspy with fatigue. "I apologize for my intrusion."

"Don't apologize. You brought Fitz back to me. I'm eternally grateful."

He smiled for the first time. "He's a brave kid."

"And safe, thanks to you." She felt a great wave of warmth and affection for the weary man seated across from her. He had quite literally braved the raging elements for her. "Let me help you," she suggested, throwing the covers aside and rising from the bed. "Pretend I'm one of your harem girls serving as your valet. At the rate you're going, you'll fall asleep before you do what you came here to do."

His gaze held hers for a stark moment in the small stateroom in the middle of the dark Atlantic. "You don't mind my being here?"

"I owe you an enormous debt. Tonight is an occasion for celebration. I have my son back."

He always marveled at her resilient spirit—a determining factor, no doubt, in surviving a marriage such as hers. He was smiling faintly when he said, "Do you know how to do harem duty? I'm not sure I can move much tonight."

"I've undressed a few children over the years," she said, kneeling at his feet. "You're just a larger version," she added, smiling up at him. She began by untying his second shoe.

"A woman of multitudinous talents," he contentedly murmured, gazing at her through half-lidded eyes, his senses enticed by her submissive pose, by her innocent beauty in the voluminous gown a nun would wear. He lazily reached down to finger the lace on the high-necked collar of the gown. "You weren't expecting me," he said, slipping the first button at the neckline free. "This is very prudish for you."

"I was cold."

He laughed softly. "I should have come sooner. Unbutton my trousers and I'll warm you up."

His voice had altered. She recognized the undertone of command, the amused impudence. "What do harem ladies say to your orders?"

"They say thank you," he said, his smile shameless. "I think I'm waking up," he added, running a raking hand through his longish hair.

If he wasn't, certainly his erection was, Angela realized, as her fingers unclasped the utilitarian navy-colored buttons of his fly; she could feel its hard, stiff presence. Her body responded as it always did to Kit Braddock's sexuality, a flame leaped deep inside her, an ache of longing began pulsing through her senses, and she felt curiously anxious and shivery, like an untried virgin. "It's been a long time," she whispered, her fingers trembling at her task, not sure she could as casually deal with a renewed intimacy. He always overwhelmed her with his extravagant sexual allure, made her feel famished.

Kit's hand closed over hers, holding it over his wool-clad erection. "You'll do just fine, Angel. He remembers you."

"I haven't been with a man for—"

He put the fingers of his other hand over her mouth. "I don't care," he murmured. "Finish what you're doing." And he lay back in the chair and watched her shaking hands struggle with the remaining buttons, with his belt buckle.

He saw the heated flush warm her cheeks and move down her throat and disappear into the opened neckline of her prim white nightgown. "You should take that off next," he said when his trousers were open, when she was trying to unfasten the small mother-of-pearl buttons on his underwear. "I'll do this."

She looked up, not understanding.

"You look warmer now. So you can take off that damnable virgin's nightgown."

"How would you know what virgins wear?"

"I saw one once. Any more questions?"

"I don't know why I have this immense craving for you," she seductively murmured, taking measure of the erection he'd freed from his clothing. "You're rude and insufferable."

"And I'm willing to die for you. Do I get some points for that?"

So succinctly put, she realized her own anxieties were all out of proportion to the simple act of love. Quickly slipping the nightgown down her shoulders, she let it drop to the floor, and standing before him in all her lush, voluptuous beauty, she whispered, "You get me for that."

"Damn right I do," he said, heaving himself out of the chair, pulling his white sweater over his head with one quick jerk of his wrist. "Lie down right there, *mon ange,*" he said with a smile, indicating the rumpled bed, "and we'll see to our business arrangement."

He had his trousers and underwear stripped away in seconds, and wide-awake suddenly, he was ready for action, his hard, powerful male body mesmerizing in its graphic force. He came into her violently the moment he settled between her legs, and they met in a wild, feverish fusion of body and soul, as if they were allowed at last, with the crisis past, to give into their breathless longing.

He knew exactly what she liked, and even weary to the bone, he was willing to give her those delectable, gratifying pleasures. She came twice, then three times before she touched his mouth with hers and said, "You needn't be gallant anymore." She drew him into her scented body with that special sorcery that had captured him from the first and matched him passion for heated passion, stroke for stroke, holding him so tightly inside her, he shuddered from the violent feelings.

This time she didn't have to beg him to stay in her, as she had the last time they were together. He was too tired to make that supreme effort; he wanted too much to stay inside her sweet, blissful warmth. And as the convulsive intoxication broke over him and he was spilling into her, he marveled how a single woman in all the world could mean so much.

He kissed her gently when it was done, his body utterly exhausted, sated, drowsy. "I'll leave in a minute," he murmured, rolling away. But his eyes drifted shut even as he was speaking, and he fell asleep in her arms.

He'd been awake for days, Angela realized, gently stroking his silken hair, his head resting on her shoulder a solid, comforting weight. He hadn't slept because she needed him to save Fitz, and kindhearted, he'd obliged. She loved him without measure at that moment—for his generosity, for his indomitable courage, for his tenderness and passion, for all he'd been to her in the past, and she wondered in that isolated stateroom in the darkness of the ocean if anything of herself was left, she wanted so much to be part of him.

He was essential to her life, a blind necessity as indispensable as breath itself, and in a stark, clarifying moment she realized that she no longer wished to live her life for other people, dutiful and obedient to society's custom.

She wanted to be Kit Braddock's wife, if he'd still have her.

She wove romantic scenarios in her mind as she lay there holding him close, imagining the phrases she'd use to tell him, how he'd smile with tenderness and say he wanted her for his wife. They'd talk of their future life together, of their hopes and dreams, of all they'd do together. Smiling to herself, she composed the perfect blissful conversation.

But her announcement when it came wasn't wreathed in scented words or lyrical garlands of prose. Bolting out of bed at five in the morning, she barely reached the small adjoining bathroom before she vomited. When she looked up to see Kit standing in the doorway, she weakly said, nausea churning her stomach, "I think I'm pregnant and it's all your fault for coming in me at Madame Centisi's."

"As I recall, it was you who wouldn't let me go," he mildly disclaimed, his gaze less mild than his voice. "And after that, it didn't matter much."

He looked splendidly nude, like some glorious, perfectly proportioned Hellenistic statue, which wasn't entirely fair when she was feeling so awful. "You're going to have to marry me now," she whispered, pale and wan and queasy.

He stood absolutely still, gazing down at her seated on the marble floor. "Are you proposing?" he gently asked.

"It's your duty," she murmured, her smile unfolding sweetly, her nausea suddenly vanishing in the curious way of morning sickness.

"My duty?" he said as if the concept were alien, offering her a drink of water to rinse her mouth, sitting down beside her. "I'm not sure I'm dutiful." Lifting her into his lap, he murmured with a grin, "What else is in it for me?"

"A baby, a son and daughter, and a desperately enamored wife," Angela replied with a beatific smile.

"Hmmm," he playfully murmured, gazing at her with theatrically narrowed eyes. "Let me think about it."

"You can't," she disputed, unabashedly Angel Lawton, who had always gotten what she wanted. "I need someone to hold my hand every day when I retch."

"Every day?" he said with mock horror. "Maybe we should reconsider this proposal."

"I'll *make* you marry me."

His brows rose in roguish sport. "How exactly will you do that?"

"I'll chain you to my bed," she declared, malapert and cheeky. "And just to get away from my rapacious demands, you'll finally agree."

He smiled. "You don't have that quite right, darling. I don't usually look to get away from rapacious women. But the other idea's intriguing. I've never been a love slave."

"You can't tease me anymore," she challenged, deliciously pouty and captivating. "I want you too much. And we're having a baby."

"You're that sure?" His gaze slowly surveyed her voluptuous form, lingering on her breasts and stomach for a searching moment.

"I haven't had my courses since Madame Centisi's," she frankly said. "I thought it was just nerves at first, the stress of, well . . . us . . . and then of Fitz leaving and all the apprehension and uncertainty. But throwing up in the morning now . . ." She lifted her brows and smiled. *"Bonjour, Papa."*

He didn't smile back. "How do I know it's mine?" His voice was temperate, but he was clearly waiting for an answer.

"Because I've been in deep mourning since you left."

"Except for your night out with Steven." He spoke in an incredibly soft tone. "Were there other nights like that, I wonder?"

"You don't believe me?"

He shrugged almost infinitesimally.

"You don't!"

"I may."

"Even if I'd been with other men—which I wasn't—I'd never be so irresponsible as not to use protection. Do you think I was *acting* that night at Madame Centisi's?" Her eyes were sparking with tiny fragments of anger.

The memory of that night was both tender and painful. He wasn't sure he could separate the emotions.

"Answer me, damn you."

"No, you weren't acting," he softly said—the rest he'd have to deal with himself. "Forgive me for . . . questioning you."

"You'll see," she said, "in eight months," her smile restored as instantly as it had vanished, the thought of having Kit's baby filling her with joy.

He smiled back this time, the possibility of fatherhood a pleasant conceit when he let it actually settle into his consciousness. "Does this mean Pearl River is off?" he asked, a teasing light in his eyes.

"If you can get me back in four months, that's plenty of time."

"Do you want the baby born in England?" His tone had changed.

A flickering uncertainty briefly altered her expression, and then her smile returned. "I hadn't thought," she replied. "I'm sorry. But as long as you love me desperately, singularly, excessively, and you vow never to look at another woman again in your entire life," she said in a cheerful rush of words, "we can have the baby wherever you want."

She didn't speak of Brook, Kit noticed, and not wishing to alter her buoyant mood, neither did he. Her husband could be handled by the lawyers. With enough money they could even manage the queen. "Why don't we decide later?" he said.

"Do you love me?" she asked, suddenly winsome and apprehensive.

"I've loved you from the very first night I met you. And I'll love you till my last breath on earth." He touched the anxious arch of her brow and smoothed it with a gentle finger. "Yes, I love you, *mon ange,*" he said very, very softly, "with all my heart."

"Tell me everything will work out," she whispered.

"I'll see that it does." He'd care for her against the apocalyptic hordes.

"But what if . . . you know . . . the divorce could be . . . lengthy and . . ." She stumbled over the words, the hindrances and obstacles daunting. "Maybe the courts will be— He *can't* have this baby," she fearfully murmured.

"No," Kit firmly said, resolute and sanguine about Brook's claim to this child. "I won't allow it."

They told Fitz the next morning of their plans to marry once the divorce from Brook was final.

"Good," her son said. "You should have done it long ago."

And when Kit began telling Fitz of the coming

child, Angela tried to stop him, but he said, "Hush, he'll know soon enough. I want to tell him now."

Fitz looked at his mother as Kit related the news, smiled her grandfather's familiar warm smile, and said, "May's going to be ecstatic, too."

"You don't mind, then?"

"Why should I mind? I've minded more that you've suffered so long with Brook. And there was nothing I could do." His eyes turned shiny with tears. "I couldn't make him leave you alone."

Kit touched the youngster's shoulder and gruffly said, "We'll both see that your mother doesn't suffer anymore. I'll expect your help."

"Yes, sir," the young man quickly said, blinking to clear his eyes. "You just tell me what to do."

"We're thinking of going to Pearl River first during all the initial haggling. It might be useful to be out of the country while the lawyers and bankers negotiate."

"China, sir?" Fitz said with excitement. He glanced over at his mother, his expression glowing. "Kit said China, Maman. Can we go?"

She and Kit exchanged warm glances. "Sounds fine to me," Angela replied.

"It's settled, then," Kit said.

They made plans for their future on their journey back, discussing where the baby would be born, where they'd live—some months at Easton, some on board the *Desiree,* part of the year in San Francisco, where Kit had a home. They talked of their first Christmas together, and Angela made lists of presents for the children. Kit only smiled and said, "Get whatever you want."

When she asked him what he wished to eat for

Christmas dinner, he said, "*You,* first—the rest doesn't matter."

"In that case, I'll add an item or two to our private menu," she replied with a smile.

They spoke of children's names, too, considering various ones until Angela realized the conversation had lapsed into a monologue, to which Kit was responding in blandly neutral terms.

"Say what you think," she prompted.

"I don't want to argue."

"We'll have to, eventually. The baby isn't going away."

He looked at her for a considering moment. "I have no strong preference for a girl's name, as long as it's not Priscilla," he said with a small smile. "But if the child's a boy, I'd like it named Billy, for my father."

"Why would you think I'd argue about that?"

"I didn't know if you would, but it's not negotiable . . . so if you were about to"—he negligently shrugged, discounting his willful inclinations—"sorry."

She understood he wanted a son named for the father he'd never known; they decided her father's name would be included as well.

"Do you think because we both grew up without our fathers, we found this special love?" Angela asked one night as they lay in each other's arms, the sound of the engines and the sea muted background to their content.

"We found this special love, darling, because I pursued you relentlessly and dragooned you into my bed." He didn't believe in mystical fate.

"Into *my* bed," she said with a grin. "And I'll never let you go."

"That'll work out, then, because the mother of my child stays with me."

"Now I'm just the mother of your child?" she teased.

"No, you're the mother of my child—among other things."

"What other things? You make it sound like a laundry list."

"Well, first, you're the hottest little piece on God's green earth, and that's real high on my list, although it's definitely not a laundry list. Also, I find you a perfect breakfast companion, not to mention lunch and dinner." Unlike Priscilla, he thought—thank you, God. "You happen to run an estate anyone would envy; I'm definitely marrying you for your stable, and you're enormously bright. Did I mention I like to make love to you twenty-four hours a day?" When she smiled at him, he kissed her for a very long time and then said, "Where was I?"

"Telling me how wonderful I am."

"Let's see. . . . Your children, of course, are perfection, thanks to your nurturing care. And if ours is as wonderful, I'll be content." His gaze swept her bounteous form, still rosy from their lovemaking. "Your breasts are even more lush now. Motherhood becomes you." His voice had turned silky. "I think I'm going to have to kiss them again."

"You know what happens to me when you do that." Just the thought of it had her body melting inside.

"I know," he murmured, touching her nipple with the pad of his finger, watching it swell. "That's what I'm here for. . . ."

27

Four days later, when they landed at the Chelsea warehouse, each of them had immediate tasks to accomplish before sailing again in the morning. Fitz and Kit were to arrange extra supplies now that Angela and her family were traveling to Pearl River. Kit had to see Chambers as well—a meeting of some import with his marriage plans entrain.

Angela was to go to Lawton House, tell the staff of her coming absence, have their clothes packed, and then go fetch May, Bergie, and Nellie from Violet's.

When she entered Lawton House, Angela was immediately apprised of Brook's reoccurring calls in her absence. He'd come to the house daily looking for her. Such industry on her husband's part suggested a pressing matter—which always concerned money. He rarely called otherwise. She was thankful to be leaving the country for a time. Let the barristers deal with him; she'd prefer never seeing him again.

As her maids hurriedly packed clothes for May, Fitz, and herself, she wrote a brief note to her mother, informing her of her divorce and marriage plans. It served no purpose to see her in person. They wouldn't agree on the divorce; they'd rarely been in sympathy on any issue.

It took some time to pack all the trunks: May's favorite toys had to be selected; Fitz's books and sailing gear brought together; her own clothing chosen with an eye for an expanding waistline. But eventually the luggage was all sent off to the *Desiree,* and after saying good-bye to her staff, Angela set off for Violet's to pick up May and her nursemaids.

The afternoon congestion in the streets caused her minor delays, but carriage traffic often made driving through London an uneven affair, and she was absorbed in assembling a last-minute list of necessities that still had to purchased for the journey. So when her carriage stopped briefly on several occasions, she didn't pay attention. But she did take notice eventually when the cobblestones of the city gave way to an unpaved road. Gazing out the window, she scrutinized her surroundings.

The cityscape had been displaced by homes and gardens; they were driving through an outlying district of London she didn't recognize. Tapping on the carriage roof, she slid the hatch cover back and shouted to her driver, "You're on the wrong road, Burton. I want to go to Eaton Square."

She heard the crack of the whip in response, and their speed increased, spiking a rush of fear through her senses. Rapping on the carriage roof, she shouted again, ordering her driver to stop in her most imperious voice. But the carriage only sped faster, and an ominous dread settled in her stomach.

Her husband had to be involved.

No one but Brook would resort to abduction. And if he was deranged enough to kidnap her, he was truly past the point of rational dealing. Gripping the door handle, she decided to jump from the carriage regardless of the speed, her husband's desperate act prompting serious alarm. But the handle didn't move when she pressed it. Putting her entire weight on the metal latch, she tried to release the catch, tears of frustration welling in her eyes, a building panic assailing her mind.

It wouldn't open.

She was locked in.

And the windows were too small to afford escape.

Falling back onto the seat, she shivered at her plight, the racing carriage taking her away—worse—carrying her to her husband. Since the episode when Brook had beaten her, she'd never again dared be alone with him. She'd always seen that servants or friends were about, someone to call on for help. That wouldn't be the case this time. So she forced herself to access her options logically.

She wasn't expected back at the *Desiree* for some time, she thought with a sinking feeling. Lawton House considered her abroad for four months. Violet didn't even know she had returned to London. It would be hours before any alarm went out, she apprehensively reflected. A sense of foreboding flooded her mind.

Her only real hope was to buy off Brook. But even that usual option held a new ambiguity. If Brook was willing to settle for money as in the past, why was he going to such extremes?

So you've finally returned," Brook casually said hours later, when Angela was ushered into his presence at a small country house she didn't recognize. "My men were despairing of results in their vigil. But I told them you'd come for May eventually. She's fine, by the way; they've been watching Violet's too."

"Why go to such trouble, Brook? Wouldn't a knock on the door have done as well?" She spoke in a temperate voice, although her apprehension deepened at the sight of her husband. He was drinking and disheveled, his eyes malicious.

Lounging back in his chair, he gazed up at her as she stood in the center of the room, where she'd been deposited by two burly men. "It's come to the point, my dear, when we have to discuss money with serious intent."

"Haven't I always given you money, Brook? Surely this dramatic abduction wasn't necessary." If she kept her spine absolutely rigid, she thought, maybe she could control her trembling. His face was pale and terrible to look at, like a lunatic mask.

"It's simply not enough, Angela." Lifting his liquor glass to his mouth, he drank it dry. Filling it again with a swift, unsteady movement, he waved it in her direction, slopping liquor onto the carpet. "To our new financial arrangement," he said with a boastful flourish, his evil smile striking terror in her soul.

"Which is?" she queried, almost numb with dread, but forcing herself to respond, not willing to show her fear.

"I'm going to have *all* your money," he softly said, his voice like a whisper from hell.

The extent of her peril struck her like a blow. If she agreed, he no longer needed her; if she didn't, he'd take pleasure in abusing her until she consented. "Why don't we discuss it over dinner?" she said, hoping to gain time to plan an escape. "I'm sure we can come to some agreement."

"How cool you are, my dear."

"We've managed to arrange our married life for

years, Brook. I'm sure we can arrange this as well." It took enormous effort to speak in a conversational tone, to maintain her composure under his malevolent stare.

"There's really nothing for you to arrange anymore," he bluntly said. "*I'll* be arranging things from now on."

"I see. Am I free to go, then?"

"Not until you sign a few papers."

"You'll need witnesses, won't you?"

"I *have* witnesses. Any other questions?" he sarcastically asked.

"When may I leave?" The overwhelming objective in her mind.

"We'll see," he said with a sinister intonation. "You're free to go upstairs right now. I don't need you until morning." And he waved her away with a dismissive fling of his hand.

When she exited the room, the two men guarding the door followed her up the stairs and kept watch on her as she looked into the rooms lining the short hallway. She selected the last room because it offered possible escape into the unkempt rear garden. But when she shut the bedroom door and went to the window to gauge the drop to the ground, she realized the distance was dangerously high.

A light supper was brought up to her by one of the men, a simple plate of bread and cheese, but she ate it all with relish, despite her dangerous plight. With her pregnancy she was constantly hungry.

She sat up that evening, trying to conceive of a plan to deal with her husband. Perhaps he'd be less unyielding in the morning, when he wasn't drunk, and they could come to some agreement on the money he needed. Perhaps she could simply sign his papers and be on her way, she optimistically reflected; time enough to counteract his coerced signature once she was free of him. Or maybe his witnesses would offer some means of negotiating her release if their sympathies had a price. But whatever measures were required, she'd have to rely entirely on her own resources. Kit wouldn't be able to find her; *she* hadn't even known of this house.

*A*t midafternoon, with all the new supplies loaded, Kit left Fitz in the care of his first mate and set off for his meeting with Chambers and the lawyers he'd been instructed to assemble. On docking, Kit had sent Chambers a note with a brief overview of their plans.

En route, Kit made a flying trip to his flat to inform Whitfield of his altered itinerary before sitting down with Chambers and his lawyers to go over the methodology and protocol of a British divorce. They discussed procedure in some detail, and when Kit explained Brook's threat to implicate the Prince of Wales in the divorce should Angela force the issue, the men visibly blanched.

"If you'd prefer not being involved in these proceedings," Kit bluntly said at that point, "let me know now. I need an aggressive team that's not afraid of any threat of sanctions. And I don't care if the queen herself has to be called to testify. Do we understand each other?"

They all nervously nodded, cognizant of the money he was willing to pay to expedite this divorce. Chambers had already filled them in on the finer points of their financial remuneration.

"And I'm offering a fifty-thousand-pound bonus for each of you if the divorce is final in six months," Kit said. "Are there any more questions?" He sat at the head of the long table, well dressed, assured, perfectly aware of what his money could buy.

"Will the countess be willing to testify?"

"No, I don't want her in court." He spoke in a voice of authority, a man familiar with having his orders followed. "Do what you have to do to keep her from appearing."

"She may be subpoenaed."

"Then see that she's subpoenaed only for evidence and not as a witness. She's in delicate health," he quietly added. "I've already explained the circumstances to Chambers, and if any of the details become public, I will personally see that you all burn in hell." Kit smiled as though he'd not just threatened all their lives. "I don't mean to be difficult, but on that issue the lady deserves her privacy. Are we agreed?" His smile was full of charm, but his gaze surveyed the men with an uncompromising directness.

He calmly waited for each individual's nod of agreement or embarrassed response before he stood. "We concur, then," he said with a nod. "In that case, I wish you all well." A brief, cool smile appeared, a flash of white teeth. "Chambers is my voice on nuances of detail," he went on, turning to his banker. "You know how to reach me on issues of greater importance."

"Yes, sir." Chambers's round face was flushed, his sparse gray hair standing on end. He'd been working frantically since receiving Kit's note.

"We should be abroad for four months. Good afternoon, gentlemen," Kit said to the table at large. "My best wishes in dealing with the Grevilles."

When he left the large paneled room, it seemed as though a rush of energy had left a vacuum in its wake, and in the hushed silence one barrister hesitantly said, "He realizes what he's asking for, doesn't he?"

"He's willing to pay whatever it takes," Chambers quietly said, his tone subdued like his well-cut black frock coat. "And to that purpose I assembled you men. He wants the best." The unspoken concluding phrase—"that money can buy"—was understood by everyone.

"A preemptive offer of a cash settlement to the Grevilles would be our first step," one of the men said. "What do you suggest in terms of an offer, Chambers? You know Mr. Braddock's finances."

"He's flexible on the amount. He's more concerned with accelerating the process. Why not study the Grevilles' income and revenues, talk to the estate trustees, and make them an offer they'd vigorously recommend to the earl? Greville's been losing rather heavily in the clubs lately, I'm told. Perhaps an additional sum to cover his losses would be tempting. I leave it up to you. The amount is incidental to Mr. Braddock."

None of them had ever been given carte blanche before, and reading their expressions with the experienced eye of a financier who often made decisions on the basis of personal trust, Chambers steepled his fingers and added a caveat. "Keep in mind, gentlemen, that I serve as Mr. Braddock's conscience on this undertaking, and though his personal feelings are deeply involved in this situation, mine are not. I won't have his need for haste taken advantage of. You will all be extremely well paid. Don't become greedy." He carefully folded his hands on the tabletop and gazed at the men with bland geniality. "I'll expect a preliminary report by this time tomorrow."

Shock registered on the faces of a half-dozen barristers of high station.

"And if you can't accommodate me," Chambers mildly said, "I know several men who would be more than happy to draw your fees and bonus." He stood up, indicating the meeting was over.

*W*hen Kit returned from Chambers's office, the afternoon was turning to twilight and Angela hadn't yet returned.

"Maman and Lady Lanley are probably deep in all the news of the town," Fitz said when Kit expressed his concern. "They can talk for hours."

Kit hoped he was right, but he hardly thought Angela would linger at Violet's so late. "I'll go coax her away, then," he casually said, not wanting to alarm Fitz, although his own warning signals were on alert.

Violet hadn't seen Angela when he stopped by, and she instantly whispered, fearful and distraught, "I hope he hasn't harmed her."

"Good God. He's been here?"

"No, nor has Angela, but if she was coming for May, she would have been here by now. I'll come with you to Lawton House. Let's not frighten May and her nursemaids yet. Can you wait to see Baby May once we've—" Her voice broke off as Kit grabbed her by the arm and pushed her from the room.

The news at Lawton House was more alarming. Angela had been there early in the afternoon and left with her driver and carriage hours ago. Neither the carriage nor the driver had returned. "The countess was on her way to Lady Lanley's, sir," Childers gravely said. "Did she tell you of the earl's late-night visit prior to her departure on the *Desiree*?"

She hadn't.

"I was given a note to deliver to her banker the following morning, sir. Which, may I presume to say, usually means she's been obliged to advance more money to Lord Greville."

"What time did she leave here?" Kit sharply asked.

"Approximately one o'clock, sir."

Over four hours ago—a very long time if she was in danger, Kit nervously thought. "Could someone see Lady Lanley home?" he asked. "Violet, if you don't mind, I'll leave you here," he added. "Give me the earl's address and those of his family. I've a few calls to make."

𝒯he earl's apartment in Mayfair was deserted, Kit quickly assessed. No light, no servants, no sign of anyone in residence. The doorman explained that Lord de Grae had been absent from his apartment since morning, his servants sent on holiday. Highly unpleasant news, with Angela's recent disappearance.

Kit's next stop was Greville House, where he was left to wait in the entrance hall. The butler came back to him with a cool refusal. Lady Greville wasn't at home to Mr. Braddock.

Since she obviously was in the house or the butler wouldn't have received his orders, Kit back-armed the startled man aside and took the stairs in a run. Banging open each door on the main-floor hallway, by a process of elimination he eventually reached the east sitting room, where Brook's sisters were settled around a well-ladened tea table.

Looking up with resentment at his abrupt intrusion, Gwendolyn irritably exclaimed, "How dare you burst in!"

"Where's your brother?" he curtly demanded. "Either you give me the information, or I'll have the city constables and Scotland Yard on your doorstep in ten minutes."

"Rowland!" Gwendolyn screamed.

"Don't bother. I left him on the floor in the entrance hall. Just answer my question."

"Why should I tell you anything, Mr. Braddock?" she petulantly replied, looking down her long nose at the man who matched the description of her sister-in-law's newest lover.

"Let's just say it would be more pleasant if you did."

"Are you threatening us?" Beatrice exploded.

"As a matter of fact, I am, and I'm in a damned hurry. I need your brother's direction." His voice went very soft. "And I need it now."

"Don't be ridiculous," Gwendolyn snapped. "We know who you are. My brother wants nothing to do with you."

"Look," he said with exasperation, wishing he could threaten them physically and be done. "I don't really have time to wait for a constable to get here. If you're attached to that rather hideous Poussin over there," he went on, unclasping a small gold pocketknife from his watch chain, "you might want to tell me your brother's direction."

"You're mad!" Gwendolyn cried, watching him move toward the large painting on the wall.

"Not like your brother, but at the moment, equally dangerous. I intend to find out where he is. Why don't I start with this corner," Kit said, indicating a figure of a shepherd on a bucolic background. And he opened the blade of the knife with cool deliberation.

"He's at Wickem House, Mr. Braddock," a voice from the doorway declared.

Kit turned to see an elderly lady standing at the door. She was small, slender, still dressed in her bonnet and pelisse; her eyes were grave. "I just returned from a hastily called meeting with our trustees. They were told by your Mr. Chambers a preliminary answer was required by morning. You're being very generous."

"He's taken Angela. Did you know that?"

The dowager Lady Greville looked stricken at the news, and when she spoke, her voice shook with emotion. "I was afraid of something like this. Please hurry."

Kit was already striding toward the door, his knife put away. "How far is Wickem?" he demanded. And when she gave him the directions, his heart sank; it was impossible to reach the place in less than three hours. He couldn't bring himself to say thank you, although he appreciated her information. At the moment he wished all the Grevilles at the bottom reaches of hell.

He brushed by her and ran.

$\mathcal{K}$it stopped at Chambers's house on his way out of town to borrow his best bloodstock and weapons. Mounted within minutes, he spoke rapidly to Chambers in a clipped, curt delivery, detailing his instructions as the grooms readied three more horses with tack and strung them out on a long lead. "I need a message sent to Fitz—nothing dire—just tell him Angela and I were delayed and will be back in the morning. Have some of your influential friends at Scotland Yard telegram to whoever is in charge of Wickem's police. A constable should be dispatched immediately to Wickem House. The countess must be taken from the house—make that very clear," he deliberately added. "She's to be kept in their care until I arrive. Don't mention any names to the police save Greville's, just in case . . ."

Chambers nodded, understanding the words left unsaid.

"I should be back in the morning with the countess," Kit said, his quirt hand raised high, his gaze intent on the groom tying the last knot in place on the lead. As the groom stepped away, Kit brought the quirt down sharply. His mount sprang forward, Kit jerked on the lead rope, and Chambers's best racers swept out of the stable yard.

28

Early in the evening Angela heard the distinct sound of bicycle tires coming up the drive. Running to the side window, she strained to see the newcomers. But they stopped just short of her line of vision.

Their arrival precipitated a reaction in the occupants of Wickem House. Within moments she heard rapid footfalls on the stairs, then steps moving quickly down the hallway toward her room.

She recognized the heavy tread of Brook's guards, and apprehensive, she stood waiting. Bursting into the room, in an obvious hurry, they advanced on her while she looked for an escape route, her heart pounding deafeningly in her ears.

She tried to run when they lunged at her, but they caught her between the wall and the armoire and clamped a hand over her mouth even before she was picked up off her feet. Although she kicked and tried screaming through the muzzling hand, they held her securely, gagged her, tied her arms and legs, placed her on the bed, and left her trussed without a backward glance—the entire procedure accomplished in short, utterly silent minutes. Almost immediately after her bedroom door shut behind them, Angela heard the pounding on the front door.

Was it possible help was on the porch? The local constables always rode bicycles. Hope warmed her heart.

*B*rook, bolstered by brandy, resentment, and his inflated sense of self, answered the door, prepared to send the local policemen promptly on their way.

"We're looking for the Earl de Grae," the taller and senior of the two constables said.

"I'm de Grae. Why am I being bothered at this hour?" he inquired with a haughty gaze.

"We were told to inquire of a lady here, sir. The Countess de Grae."

"To what purpose? She's my wife."

"Merely a question of identity, my lord," the younger man replied. "A routine matter. We have instructions to bring her back to the village."

"She isn't here," Brook brusquely said.

"Could we have a look around?"

"You most certainly could not." His face turned red with blustery affront.

"We wouldn't disturb anything, sir."

"You won't disturb anything because you're not coming in," Brook snapped.

"We *could* get a search warrant, sir," the elder constable quietly threatened, offended by drunken, arrogant peers.

"Well, then, damn well get one. You're not coming into my house otherwise." And the earl slammed the door in their faces.

*O*nce the bloody constables leave, get my wife down here," Brook brusquely said to his two henchmen, who were standing out of sight in the back hall.

And when Angela was untied some minutes later and brought into his presence, he said with intense irritation, "We seem to have a problem here."

"You had visitors," Angela noted, pleased to see his agitation.

"Someone sent the constables looking for you."

Kit, she thought, comforted by the information, knowing deliverance was at hand. "Perhaps you should rethink your plans," she remarked, feeling more secure. "Apparently your whereabouts are discovered. It's just a matter of time now, isn't it?"

"Luckily time isn't an immediate problem," the earl briskly said. "I'll have the papers here in an hour." He'd sent one of his men to wake the local solicitor with the change in plans. Instead of a morning meeting, Haversham would have to bring the papers immediately.

"Why should I sign anything for you, Brook?" Angela inquired, heartened by the possibility of rescue. "Maybe you should just take your two burly thugs and leave."

"You don't understand, Angela," her husband softly said, enmity glowing in his drunken gaze. "We're not negotiating any longer about whether you'll allow me your money. Either give it to me or I'll kill you."

His words sent a cold chill down her spine. He'd never openly and deliberately threatened her life. "I don't have a choice, then," she calmly said, hoping to assuage his disordered mind—at least until the man with the papers arrived. Perhaps he might turn out to be an ally.

"Damned right, you don't. As soon as my man

gets back with old Haversham, I'll be very rich. Sit down where I can keep an eye on you. He should be here soon."

"I'd rather stand," she said, wanting to be ready to run should the need arise.

He hit her. It was an open backhanded blow to the side of the head that knocked her down. "Do as you're told!" he screamed, his face pale with rage. "I told you to sit down!" He kicked out at her, missing in his frenzy. And then he turned away to pour himself a drink with a casualness as strange as his sudden violence.

With Brook's back turned, Angela stumbled to her feet and ran for the door, but she was caught short of the exit, his hand closing on her just as she touched the doorknob. Gripping her by the arm, he hurled her against the wall. "Bloody independent bitch," he growled, swaying slightly on his heels, watching her crawl behind a chair as he lifted the half-full glass to his mouth. After draining the liquor, he tossed the glass aside, shoved the chair out of his way, and reached for her. Miscalculating again in his drunkenness, he lurched upright empty-handed. Quickly coming to her feet, Angela faced him across a small table she'd pulled in front of her, her gaze intent on his swaying form, his riding clothes wrinkled as though he'd slept in them, his face flushed from drink, his nostrils flared like an animal in pursuit.

How had her life reached this point? she thought, trembling with fear.

"You need to be taught a lesson," the earl muttered, brushing the table aside, advancing on her like a madman, his face contorted with hatred.

When he came into range, Angela kicked out with all her strength, connecting with flesh and bone. As he stumbled away, writhing in agony, she shot past him, making for the door.

Jerking it open, she raced across the entrance hall to the front door only to find it locked. Frantically searching for the key on the side table, she whimpered in frustration and fear, unable to find it. Turning away like a cornered animal, she ran toward the ground-floor hall.

But halfway across the foyer, one of the thugs materialized from the shadows of the back hall. Veering away, she leaped for the stairs.

At that moment Brook's bellow exploded as he burst through the parlor door, forcing more speed into her headlong flight. Sprinting up the first few steps, she envisioned refuge if she could lock herself in a bedroom. Kit was on his way. Then her foot caught in her skirts and she stumbled, scrambling feverishly to jerk away the impeding fabric. The skirt tore, she lost her balance, and fell into a sprawl halfway up the staircase.

Brook grabbed her, hauling her around by the arm. "I don't like to be kicked," he snarled, his fearsome eyes like burning coals only inches away. She shivered, struggling to push him away even as his hands closed on her throat and began squeezing. Gasping for air, she frantically clawed at his fingers, his arms, his demented face. But the pressure of his fingers inexorably tightened.

"Hey, boss, you need her to sign," the huge man standing at the bottom of the stairs calmly said, as if he weren't watching a lethal struggle.

Brook hesitated, rage dominating his mind, a bloodthirsty frenzy convulsing his senses.

"Haversham's on his way."

The words finally seemed to register. The earl twitched as if coming to his senses. "You've a reprieve," he demoniacally whispered, his hands still clamped around her neck. "While you're waiting, think of how I'm going to kill you," he murmured, beginning to drag her up the stairs, his fingers clenched so tightly, she was still being choked, unable to get air into her lungs, not sure this time she'd survive his wrath. She was deadweight, helpless, nearly unconscious as he jerked her up the stairs by her neck, one step at a time, huffing and puffing, red-faced, sweating, swearing vengeance in a raving prattle.

She lost consciousness before he reached the top.

29

Twilight gave way quickly to night as Kit raced south, the early-December temperatures chill, the wind bringing odd gusts of rain from the northwest, his fevered brain anguished, in torment, not knowing if Angela was safe. Had Chambers found the men to authorize the telegram? Had the constables removed her from Wickem House? Was she away from her brute husband? If not, the consequences were too unbearable to contemplate.

He'd kill him, Kit vowed, if Angela was harmed. There was no question in his mind of principle or ethics. If de Grae had hurt her, he was going to die.

Riding full out, he discarded the first mount at the stable in Beechton, shouting for an ostler as he leaped onto the second horse, and spurred him on. Chambers's bloodstock was superb, strong and fleet, and the pounding rhythm of the galloping hoofs on the road echoed his own precipitate urgency.

On that cold, dark winter night, burdened by his terrible fears, he prayed for the first time in his life, talking into the rushing wind, as if the pagan spirits of the night would serve as messengers to greater gods. It was a desperate call for help from a desperate man. He couldn't lose the woman he loved. She was his sun, his moon, his heart and soul, his entire happiness.

And after he'd pleaded for favors from all the conventional gods, he asked Devaraja last to bring him hope. Perhaps Kit knew him best, for the Buddha on Earth had carried him through a dark, tormented time in Java once, when he hadn't known if he was going to live. "If you bring your merciful help to this cold, distant land, I'll build a road to your lost temple at Kedu," he promised, "so your people can worship you. Please hear me. I need you to save my love from a demon who plagues her."

He didn't know if anyone heard; he wasn't completely sure whether anything but sanguine means would bring him peace. And he whipped his horse to more speed because he would accomplish his mission, with or without divine help. Brook Greville had lived too long.

But the most tormenting fear on the long ride that night was not knowing Angela's fate . . . or that of his child. Each minute seemed an hour, each mile an endless road to nowhere. She had to be safe. Their life together was just beginning. They'd talked about names for their child and how large a family they wanted. They'd made plans for Christmas—their first of many, they'd happily thought. He loved her more than he'd ever thought it possible to love another human being.

His vision blurred momentarily before he blinked away his tears. Dammit, they needed a rail line to this outback village, he angrily thought. If there'd been a railroad, he could have saved Angela three hours of fear.

While Kit was racing toward Wickem, Alfred Haversham was being rousted out of his bed by a rough, uncouth man who'd brushed by his servant after the door was opened to his pounding, tramped upstairs, and frightened the local solicitor and his wife half to death. "The earl wants you at Wickem House now!" the huge man had growled, and pulled the old man from his bed while his wife had huddled against the bed curtains in terror. Immediately the ruffian had left with her hastily dressed husband, Mrs. Haversham had called for her manservant and sent him posthaste for the constable. Nobles may have their place in the world, she heatedly thought, dressing herself with shaking fingers, but the Earl de Grae had overstepped his bounds if he thought he could take her husband away in the dead of night like some common vagrant. The daughter of a well-to-do squire, she took affront at being treated so shabbily. It was time patricians like de Grae understood that she and her husband were as influential as he in this small village. Earl or not.

Angela regained consciousness on a bed in a strange bedroom that swirled and moved and finally stilled, but her mind wouldn't so readily regain its reason. She found herself unable to think or plan or deal with her situation in any familiar ways. She shut her eyes again, hoping a brief respite would settle her thinking. Her entire body ached. She couldn't move her head without excruciating pain, so she surveyed the chamber when she opened her eyes again with a slow, continuous shifting of her position, understanding even without her usual sharp clarity of thought that she was in the deepest peril. Her husband couldn't let her live once the papers were signed, for she'd be sure to contest them. He intended to kill her. He almost had.

Such a despondent prospect cast her into a mopish pessimism. But only briefly, because her abiding hatred for her husband inspired her to continue her struggle until she no longer could.

She had no intention of relinquishing her life to a cowardly bully like Brook without a fight.

She smiled faintly on the bed in the unknown house, her resolution renewed. Perhaps the time to give up hadn't yet arrived, she reflected. Her grandfather, for one, wouldn't look kindly on her surrendering his fortune without a struggle. And certainly she wouldn't want Gwendolyn or Beatrice to benefit by so much as a penny. Which thought stirred her to a wider smile, and she experimented with a small movement of her legs. Definitely a manageable level of pain, she decided.

If she wished to muster some defense against Brook, she'd have to get up. Lifting her left arm even a moderate distance elicited a gasp of pain. So she wouldn't use her left arm, she decided, reminded of all the times she'd been thrown from her horse going over dangerous fences.

She'd survived those and numerous other tumbles in her years of hunting. She was going to survive this, too, but in her present, unregenerate mood, she wasn't so certain Brook would. She'd have his blood for this beating.

*B*rook Greville was pacing in the downstairs parlor, watching the clock with nervous agitation, going to the window and the front door a dozen times, waiting for his man and Haversham to return. He'd lost within a day the seventy thousand Angela had given him at the gaming tables, and his creditors were clamoring for payment, threatening his trustees with foreclosure. The bulk of his property was entailed, but if his creditors foreclosed, he'd lose several smaller estates and all his liquid assets, furniture, paintings, family heirlooms, his stable, the Greville plate. While his wife continued to live in luxury. Not likely, he thought, raging at the injustice. Where the hell was Haversham with the papers for her to sign?

*W*hen her guard came to bring Angela downstairs, she was prepared. She'd redone her hair, pinning her pale curls high on her head so the horrendous bruises on her throat were plainly visible. Somehow the pearls Kit had given her had survived Brook's attack, and the two strings of them she wore at the neckline of her green wool gown gave her courage and hope, as if Kit were with her in spirit. When she walked into the parlor a few moments later, she was the same Angel Lawton who had met the Grevilles years ago and faced down the ranks of barristers and trustees with an imperious presence remarkable in a seventeen-year-old girl.

"I'm here against my will," she said, her voice strong and plain. "In case any of you have doubt. My husband is quite mad."

"That's enough, Angela," Brook growled, moving toward her with menace.

"Will you choke me again, Brook?" she coolly said. "What if I had died before I could sign your papers?"

Alfred Haversham nervously cleared his throat. "This is highly irregular," he stammered, gazing at the deep-purple marks ringing Angela's neck. "I wasn't informed of the countess's reluctance. I don't care to be involved—"

"Bloody shut your mouth, Haversham," Brook barked. "Nobody asked for your opinion." And he waved one of his men toward the small elderly man.

"If this is done under duress, Brook," Angela pointed out, "it won't stand up in court for a minute."

"You let me worry about that," her husband snapped. "The papers are on the table," he said, pointing to a small writing desk against the wall. "Just sign them."

"For the record, Mr. Haversham," Angela said as she walked by him toward the desk, "I'm doing this under coercion."

"I understand," he murmured, fearful of the outcome of this violent night. He wondered whether either of them would be alive to give evidence of the circumstances. The earl seemed unconcerned with the gross irregularities, as if they were both incidental to the process.

As Angela sat down, her husband came to stand by the table, his fists clenching and unclenching in his agitation, his mind further disordered by the complications that had overtaken all his careful planning. He shifted from foot to foot, his riding boots gleaming in the lamplight. The fortune he'd been waiting for so long was almost within his grasp.

Taking up the pen, Angela dipped it into the inkwell, glanced at the papers, and then set the pen back down.

"Sign it!" the earl screamed, slamming his fist on the table.

"I won't," she said, because she wouldn't docilely give in to a madman who was going to kill her anyway. And picking up the single sheet of paper, she ripped it in two.

"No!" the earl shrieked, bending to pick up the separate pieces. And a second later he turned on her with such fury, she jumped up and recoiled without regard for pain or bruises. Clutching at her hair as she twirled away, he wrenched her back, his free hand raised high to strike her. She screamed.

Her cry rose simultaneously with the vivid noise of crashing glass coming from the rear of the house.

The earl's arm fell, and turning to the man nearest the door, he said, "Go check that. And you," he snarled at Haversham, "don't move. See that he doesn't," he ordered his other henchman. "Now, sit down," he commanded Angela, forcing her back into the chair with a painful jerk on her hair. "And sign that damned paper, torn or not."

Angela took her time seating herself, hopeful the breaking glass meant rescue.

"Hurry, dammit," her husband ordered.

As she took up the pen, the south window in the parlor exploded in a shower of glass, a stone garden bench hurtling into the room, followed a heartbeat later by Kit leaping through the smashed window. His booted feet crushed the glittering shards; his revolvers were instantly trained on Brook and Haversham's guard. "If you so much as blink, I'll kill you," he said into the abrupt silence.

"Move away, Angela," he quickly added, wanting to distance her from her husband, knowing there was a third man returning any moment. His boots crunched on the glass as he advanced into the room, waving the burly guard toward Brook.

Haversham trembled where he stood, the events of the evening terrifying, worlds removed from his ordinary existence.

Walking toward Brook and his ruffian, his revolvers leveled at the two men, the hammers cocked, Kit said, "I'd be tempted to kill you now, Greville, if I didn't have a conscience." Although he'd never shot a man in cold blood, the bruises on Angela's neck were stark motive to deviate from principle. But a gunshot would bring the third man back immediately from his survey of the broken rear window. Those few moments of reprieve while he was gone would help them in their escape. Slowly backing up, Kit murmured to Angela and the elderly man, "We'll go out the front door."

Both were white with fear, and just as they began to move, Angela abruptly came to a standstill, her horrified gaze on the smashed window.

"I've got him, boss," a deep voice said.

The second guard stood outside at the window, a pistol pointed at Kit.

Brook smiled. "Drop your guns, Braddock, and now we'll see who shoots whom. Maybe we'll have you dig your grave first," he said with a wicked smirk. But he cautiously waited until Kit discarded his pistols before he bullied Angela, dragging her toward the table. "Sign," he ordered.

Leaning over the table, Angela quickly scrawled her name on the torn sheet and then, straightening in a quick wheeling twist, the steel-pointed pen still in her hand, she drove the naked steel directly at Brook's face. The sharp spike plunged into the hollow under his eye and sank in. His scream richocheted round the room.

Angela had already taken half a step in flight when he shrieked, "Shoot them!" and jerked the pen from his face.

In those tumultuous seconds Kit had dropped into a crouch, scooped up a revolver from the floor, and dived for Angela. The whistle of a bullet slid over his head in the arc of his dive. Catching Angela around her waist with his right arm, he rolled a half turn to his left and dropped, taking the brunt of their fall on his broad shoulders.

He had already taken aim at his target, and the first round took out the man at the window, who fell openmouthed into the room, his surprised scream arrested in death.

In the split second it took to fire again, the man at Haversham's side went down before he managed to pull the solicitor in front of him as a shield.

Kit saved Brook for last.

Feral impulse prompted Kit in the disposition of his shots. He wanted unthreatened time to watch the bullet sink into de Grae's flesh and tear it apart.

De Grae had swept up Chambers's other revolver from the floor, Kit observed. Good. He would have shot him, anyway, but now there was unimpeachable justification. Kit took particular note of the pleasure he felt as he pulled the trigger, as if there were virtue in destroying such a vile man.

It gave him great personal satisfaction to see the shock on de Grae's face when the thirty-eight cartridge struck him, blowing away half the earl's head. His body crumpled to the floor, lifeless.

Finally, Kit thought, lying on the floor with Angela held tight to his side, the smell of gunpowder in the air, the loud report of gunshots still echoing in his ears, his adrenaline pumping at ramming speed.

It was done.

Setting his weapon aside, he sat up, lifted Angela into his lap, and held her close. "I didn't have a choice about killing them. He would have killed us." His voice was without inflection, as if he had to conceal the satisfaction in his soul.

"Don't apologize," Angela whispered, shivering in the aftermath, her mortality blinding her with its closeness, the events a horrendous flashing moment in time.

"You saved our lives," Mr. Haversham tremulously exclaimed, visibly shaking, clutching at a chair back to support himself.

"We're going to need some constables," Kit calmly said, coming to his feet with Angela in his arms, Chambers's revolver left lying on the carpet. He rapidly surveyed the carnage. "His family will have to be notified."

Haversham swallowed hard, released his grip on the chair, and stood under his own power. "I can handle that, Mr.—"

"—Braddock," Kit offered. "Thank you. As you can see, the countess has been through an ordeal," he went on in a conversational tone that Chambers had heard on more than one occasion when tasks were being delegated. "I'd like to bring her back to London as soon as possible." Angela's face was ashen. "If you could manage all the local procedures, we'd appreciate it."

"Certainly. Alfred Haversham at your service, sir," the elderly man said with a bow. "He was a terrible man," he added, shaking his head. "My deepest regrets, my lady, for any disservice I unknowingly did you," he apologized. "I had no idea . . ."

"I understand," Angela said, trying to smile at the remorseful man. "Don't blame yourself. You couldn't have known."

The tread of feet in the entrance hall interrupted their conversation, and for a brief moment apprehension struck them all. Kit quickly gauged the distance to his revolvers, debating whether he could reach them in time with Angela in his arms.

"Haversham?" someone shouted.

The old solicitor broke into a smile. "Our local

constable," he said. "We'll take care of all the administrative details."

"If you could find us a driver for the countess's carriage," Kit politely suggested, "we'd be grateful."

In the next half hour everything was set to rights, a driver was found, the team harnessed, the bodies taken away, the necessary reports arranged by Haversham and the constable. And as the countess's carriage pulled away, the local men discussed the steel-cold nerves of the American who'd shot three men in the time it took to draw a breath. "Didn't even work up a sweat, he didn't," Haversham said with wide-eyed awe. "And then looked at the bodies afterward without blinking an eye at the mutilation. Head shots every one. Exactly the same—all three of them—right above the eye, left side. Would have thought, looking at the corpses, that they'd been lined up in a row instead of every which way in the room."

"He did everyone a service, I'd say," the older constable said. "A man's not a man who beats his wife."

"I shouldn't say it, but I'm glad he's dead," Angela murmured as they drove away, gazing at the house that could have been their dying place. "Does that make me a terrible person?"

"You're not even remotely terrible," Kit said, holding her in his lap, trying to cushion her bruises against the roll of the carriage. "De Grae was the evil one. While you were the brave impetus to our salvation. You gave us a chance when you wounded de Grae."

"I had that chance because you came for me," she murmured. "Thank you for finding me."

For finding you in time, he thought, feeling the brush of guardian-angel wings in the very close equation of distance and time. "I wish I could have arrived

sooner," he gravely said. "And saved you from this."
He gently touched the livid bruises on her throat.

"How *did* you find me?" She hadn't even known
of the estate.

And he told her then of his search for Brook, of
his visit to Greville House, of the dowager's help.

"I owe her my life, don't I?"

He sighed, debating whether to be grudging and
disputatious when she was still recovering from so
much. "You do in part," he neutrally said, understanding the critical significance of the dowager's aid.
But he wouldn't forgive the dowager countess for allowing her son to continue so long in his depravities.
Someone should have stopped him years ago. She was
to blame in some measure for Angela's torment.

As was the iniquitous code of society that allowed
deceit, duplicity, and pretense to taint so many lives in
the hollow name of class honor.

"I won't go to the funeral," she firmly said.

"No one would expect you to."

"Is it really over?" Her voice had a spiritless pas-
sivity, as if she'd suffered too long.

"It's over," he gently said.

"What will I tell May and Fitz?"

"Fitz should be told the truth. Gossip will embel-
lish the lurid details, anyway, regardless that Haversham tells me he can control some of the disclosures.
But May's too young. When she's older, you can decide."

"And this new baby?" She smiled up at him with
sweet hope in her eyes.

He was encouraged by that first smile; she'd
seemed almost despondent since the killings. "This
new baby will have no idea there's evil in the world,
darling," he softly said. "I promise you."

—

They didn't sail for the Pearl River immediately, for there were legalities having to do with Brook's death that required Angela's presence in England, but once all the papers had been signed, all the death duties and settlements from the marriage contract filed in court, they were free to leave.

They made plans to marry quietly in the chapel at Easton over Christmas with only the children, family, and a few close friends in attendance, for society would view such haste after a husband's death with disapproval, regardless of the fact that Brook had tried to kill her.

"Screw society," Kit succinctly said with endearing charm and an insolent smile. "As if I want to see Joe Manton at our wedding."

"Or Olivia," Angela sweetly rejoined.

"You see," he said with a shameless grin, "the advantage of a very private ceremony."

"At least I won't have to fight off Olivia."

"Or I your most devoted lover," he replied with unabashed impudence.

"You promised me never to look at another woman," she reminded him. "And don't you forget it. I'm green-eyed jealous and getting fatter every day."

"More to love, *mon ange.*"

"Promise me."

"I said I wouldn't."

"Wouldn't what?" she demanded, wanting all the words.

"Won't ever look at another woman. Satisfied?"

Her smile was pure sunshine.

And he laughed and pulled her into his arms and tasted the sun.

30

Kit's mother and the Braddock-Blacks all came to the wedding, the telegraphed invitations responded to with dispatch. Joining the party at Helena, Montana, Kit's mother traveled east with Blaze and Hazard Black's family in their private train that ran on Etienne Martel, Duc de Vec's rail lines. Since his marriage to Daisy Black, the duc had wasted no time buying up rolling stock in America.

After a four-day journey by rail to New York and six days more for the Atlantic crossing, they arrived at Easton on December 20, joining Angela's half sisters and their families. The house was beautifully decorated for the holidays, the scent of bayberry and pine awash in the rooms, wreaths and garlands draped and hung on walls, mantelpieces, railings, doors, window frames, huge vases of holly, red and white roses, feathery sprays of Angela's hothouse pale-green orchids adding color and sweet fragrance to the rooms. The house was filled with family, thirteen children adding to the tumult: Angela's two; Millie and Dolly's five; Trey and Empress Braddock-Black's four, the youngest a two-year-old boy; Daisy and the duc's two young children, a four-year-old girl and a boy just learning to walk.

It was pandemonium but of the pleasantest kind.

"I like your family," Angela had said the first evening after she'd met everyone and dinner was over and she and Kit had retired near midnight to the quiet of her rooms.

She was sprawled on the bed, while Kit, in his shirtsleeves, was divesting himself of his cuff links and studs, dropping them into a tray on the dresser. "No one stands on ceremony," she added. "There's such warmth . . . and your mother doesn't mind I'm not an eighteen-year-old virgin."

"I told you she wouldn't," Kit replied, half turning to smile at her over his shoulder. "She trusts my judgment. What were you two talking about after dinner for so long?"

"How sweet you were as a child."

He grinned into the mirror. "Mama has a convenient memory. I was a holy terror."

"Apparently an adored holy terror," Angela said with a fond smile. "I know your entire history from age one through six. Tomorrow I'll hear the next installment."

Kit groaned softly. "I'll tell Mama to leave you alone."

"I like hearing about you. And I like your mother, so you needn't interfere," Angela affirmed. "She's going to help me arrange the music for the wedding in the morning." After meeting his mother Angela had immediately understood a measure of Kit's charm. Blond, beautiful, and gracious, Bianca Herbert-Braddock was utterly delightful. In the short time Angela had known her, she felt closer to Kit's mother than she ever had to her own. "She's agreed to play for the ceremony, too. I'm very excited."

Kit was also pleased. No one played the piano as well as his mother, and if she hadn't fallen in love with his father, she would have had a distinguished career. "But I loved him more," she'd always said. "I didn't want to tour, and then you were born, and I wouldn't have ever left you."

"Make sure mother plays my favorite piece—Chopin's Nocturne in E flat major—at the wedding," Kit said. "She knows the passages I like."

"Whatever you say, darling."

He turned around at the lush, purring resonance. "You must want something," he softly said, his gaze amused, "when you're so agreeable."

"Just a slight favor, if you're not too tired," she murmured, pink-cheeked and tousle-haired, her shoes kicked off, her gown half-unhooked so it fell off one shoulder.

"The same slight favor you requested this morning and then again before dinner?" he queried, one brow slightly raised in whimsical challenge.

Her smile was coquettish, enticing. "I seem to have this insatiable craving since I've become pregnant."

His voice dropped into a husky whisper. "I may have to curtail my schedule the next few months if you're going to require all this personal attention."

"How gratifying," she sweetly said, lifting her skirts and petticoats in a frothy sweep of grape chiffon and silver tulle, so he could see she wasn't wearing any drawers.

He smiled as he took in the delicious view. "I bought you some little bibelots the other day. Would you like an early Christmas present?"

"I'd like *you* right now."

"I come with them."

Her smile was instantly joyful. "Yes, then . . . yes, yes, yes."

Walking into his dressing room, he returned a few moments later with a satinwood box the size of a small jewel case. Sitting down on the bed, he handed it to her. "Merry Christmas, darling," he said. "I wasn't sure what you had."

Lifting the lid, Angela gazed at a stunning array of sparkling jewels in every color of the rainbow—necklaces, bracelets, brooches, earrings, rings. Her eyes lifted to his and she smiled. "So you bought one of everything."

"Do you like them?" he casually inquired. "Look at that turquoise-and-diamond bracelet. The bird on the clasp is interesting."

"They're all very beautiful. It's too much. You shouldn't have." She smiled. "I have a feeling I'm going to be saying that a lot with you."

"It gives me pleasure to buy you presents."

"You're too extravagant. I don't need all this."

"Sell them and build a new wing on your school, then, except for that small item there," he said, pointing to a velvet box in the corner of the jewel case. He was planning on giving her a new building for her school as a Christmas gift, but he was saving that for later. The jewelry was a frivolous offering.

"Why shouldn't I sell this?" she queried, lifting the blue velvet box.

"Open it and you'll see."

Lifting the lid, she said, "Earrings?" in a questioning tone, her gaze mildly perplexed. Two very small gold clips that looked like ear clips lay inside the box, one decorated in green enamel, the other in red, a tiny bell attached to each.

"Christmas bells," Kit said.

"But not earrings."

"No."

"And these wouldn't be a readily salable item."

"Not here, I don't think."

"But they would be—" And she raised her brows in query, a faint smile lifting her mouth in understanding.

"—in Kenya," he softly noted.

"Which means these didn't come from Cartier's."

"I had them made for you."

"I adore personal gifts."

"I thought you might."

"And you're going to show me now where these go."

He smiled. "If you'd like me to."

"What do *you* think?"

"I think you're about to say 'hurry.' "

"How astute," she said, with a captivating grin, handing him the small velvet box.

Lifting the satinwood jewelry box from her lap, he placed the lid back on it and set it aside. Dropping the velvet box onto the bed, he unhooked the remaining clasps on her gown with dispatch and slipped it off. Her petticoats and corset soon joined her evening dress in a heap on the floor, and laying her against the heap of pillows, he said with a teasing glance from under his dark lashes as he took the first clip from the box, "Am I moving fast enough?"

The tinkle of the bell reverberated in the quiet of the room, the delicate intonation as sweetly pure as Angela's gratified nod of approval. And as Kit nudged her legs apart with the pressure of his palms on her inner thighs, she gloried in the delicious sensations suffusing her body. He was God's answer to pleasure.

Gently opening her labia, Kit clipped the small green ornament onto her inner lips, midway down the flaring curve. The spring clasp was lightly contrived, so it kept the ornament in place without undue pressure. And when the second red clip was attached, Kit stroked the sleek, plump flesh holding the fragile enameled trinkets. "The very loveliest of tinseled adornment, Angel," he softly murmured, flicking the tiny bells. "You're nicely bespangled for the season. Can you feel them?"

Angela sighed in a half moan of pleasure, the tingling pressure on her throbbing flesh exquisite.

He touched the bells again so the sensation trembled through her pulsing tissue. "Merry Christmas," he whispered.

Her lashes lifted and her eyes held a heated, glittering flame. "You're my very best Christmas present," she whispered.

"And you're mine." Bending close, he kissed her until she felt as though she were dissolving into nothingness. "Be a sweetheart, now," he softly said, his mouth still close to hers, "and walk over to the mirror while I undress. See if you like the sound."

"Later," she murmured. "Afterward . . ."

But he lifted her from the bed, the bewitching jingle silvery in their ears, and setting her down, he turned her to face the cheval glass across the room. "Go, now," he quietly ordered.

Gazing at him over her shoulder, Angela playfully murmured, "Then I'll expect you naked by the time I come back. Patience isn't one of my virtues tonight."

"As if it's ever been," Kit replied with a teasing grin, already tugging his shirt from his trousers. "I'll be ready," he added. "Walk."

The dangling bells chimed as she moved across the room, the tone dulcetly aphrodisiac, as if the sound were softly calling attention to her alluring, wet cleft, to the tantalizing seat of her desire. To the welcoming sweetness between her legs.

She stood for a moment before the mirror, searching to see if any visual evidence of the bells existed. But nothing showed in her pale, curvaceous image, and when she stood very still, no one could tell how lustful she was, how urgent her sexual need, how her body burned and throbbed, how it tingled at the site of the small gold clips.

"Are you coming back?" Kit said, his deep voice velvet soft.

The voluptuary bells rang breathlessly vivid in her ears when she turned, and she almost climaxed at the suggestive ring.

"That's a delicious sound," Kit softly said. "Are you advertising your availability? Because I'm interested." He indolently crooked one finger as he lounged on the bed, nude, powerfully aroused, beautiful as sin, his green eyes unabashedly sensual. "Come here."

The music of the bells accompanied her as she moved toward him, toward his covetous gaze, her arousal so near to orgasm, she didn't know if she'd reach the bed in time. She ran the last few steps into Kit's waiting arms, and rolling her underneath him, impatient and wild with longing, he entered her immediately, wanting her as much she wanted him.

And the tiny bells played in melodious counterpoint to their heated passions, the music of pleasure, of eagerness and craving, of sweet, luscious love.

It was the beginning of a wonderful Christmas season.

*C*hristmas was particularly lavish in terms of festivities, joyous spirits, and presents. The staff, tenants, and village participated in the seasonal activities, too, so Easton was the scene of numerous parties, the merrymaking including everyone from the youngest babies to the elderly. Presents were distributed to one and all, Fitz and May helping Angela as they'd always done, the great hall filled with tenants and staff and an enormous decorated tree. The services in the chapel on Christmas Eve were enchanting, the Christmas songs sung by children from the village, the grade-school mistress beaming her approval as she directed her young students.

And when Angela and Kit presided over the festivities of Christmas dinner, each guest special and specially loved, the children seated for the grand occasion with the adults, they smiled down the long table at each other, feeling grateful and blessed. Then Kit winked at her and, standing, raised his glass in toast.

"To our first of many Christmases," he said, his gaze that of an enamored man as he smiled at his beloved. "Joy, peace, and love."

Hazard stood next. "To family," he said, his gaze sweeping the convivial group, his eyes resting last on his beautiful wife. "And to good fortune," he softly added, thinking of the many joys they'd shared.

And everyone stood around the table that Christmas Day to toast the season with heartfelt words. Even the children entered into the fun.

It was the very best Christmas Angela had ever had.

𝒯he night before the wedding the men had a bachelor party for Kit at Stone House.

"Without women," Kit had instructed. "And I'll have to leave early. But don't let my departure stop the rest of you from drinking," he'd added, not wishing to hinder anyone's merriment because his wife-to-be needed him in her bed.

But regardless of Kit's stricture on no women, Trey and Etienne had arranged for some dancing girls, anyway, with the help of Carsons and Sutherland. It wasn't a bachelor party without females, they'd all agreed.

Later that night, when the scantily clad women made their appearance with the musicians, Kit turned to Trey and said with a smile, "Your work, no doubt."

"It's strictly a cultural entertainment," Trey replied with a broad grin. "They're Egyptian dancers."

But none of the men were truly interested in more than the women's dancing, the assembled group unique in terms of other wealthy men. Unlike most of their contemporaries, who accepted the double standard as a way of life and endorsed the practice of extramarital sexual activity as their right, the men at Stone House were in love with their wives. So they applauded the extraordinary skill, talent, and beauty of the exotic dancers but declined any more personal involvement.

Etienne, who spoke the dancers' native language rather better than they spoke English, was forced to explain no discourtesy was intended in the men's polite rejection of their sexual overtures. Yes, they were very beautiful, he agreed to their beautiful, pouty query. And very alluring . . . while they danced divinely. No, the men didn't prefer young boys, he explained as they continued to question the motive behind the men's refusals. Would the women perhaps accept some added money as a token of their esteem? he asked, and with that offer the women's smiles returned.

Sometime later, after the dancers and musicians had been dismissed with a last word of thanks, whiskey glasses were refilled and the discussion turned to Kit's activities in England. No one in Montana had heard from him since the telegram he'd sent after his victory at Cowes, and despite the general conversation of the past few days, some pertinent facts had been left unexplained. So Kit gave a more male version of the events transpiring since August.

"About time you settled down," Trey quipped after Kit's brief narrative concluded. "You've held out long enough." Of the same age, Trey had already been married for several years.

"Aren't you pleased you didn't decide on Priscilla?" Sutherland said with a smile.

Kit's eyes widened fleetingly in alarm. "I must have momentarily lost my mind."

"She's marrying old Congreve, you know," Angela's brother-in-law went on. "His wife dropped dead, and damned if he didn't propose the next day. It's all supposedly hush-hush. The engagement won't be announced for six months."

"A perfect match," Kit mockingly noted. "She acquires his money, and he gets an opportunity to look at her young body—he's not capable of more. But she always has the stable boys."

Various eyebrows rose in curiosity.

"I overheard one of them make a personal remark to her after one of our rides in Hyde Park, and rather than take offense, she flirted back. I'd say those young bucks might be first on her list once old Congreve leaves the honeymoon bed," Kit said with a cheeky grin.

"So very convenient," Carsons softly murmured.

"And not likely to be believed should they ever step out of line. I'd give her two weeks after the wedding, tops."

"New blood in the Congreve family wouldn't be amiss," Sutherland sardonically noted. "Congreve's heir and grandson are both overbred and sickly."

"No doubt a consideration in Priscilla's ready acceptance of the old rogue's suit. If she produces a spare heir, her future is assured."

"Lord Congreve was old years ago," the Duc de Vec casually remarked. "He must be at least seventy."

"At least," Carsons noted. "My grandmother knows him."

"But he's rich—the only criteria of consequence for the Pembrokes," Kit drawled.

"Speaking of which, we spent some of your money on another railroad line in California," Hazard interjected, marriages between old rakes and necessitous young females a familiar tale. "Etienne made them an offer they couldn't refuse. We have four equal shares of five thousand more miles of rail line north of San Francisco."

"Thanks, Etienne," Kit said. "Now that I'm going to have children, I'll have to get serious about making money." This from a man who'd casually amassed a fortune in the last decade.

And the discussion turned on investments, the Braddock-Black extended family a fine-tuned business operation with investments around the world.

The men drank the bourbon Hazard had brought over and talked of railroads, the Braddock-Black newest copper mine, the China trade, coffee and sugar plantations, the state of South Africa's diamond mines. It was a convivial group—relaxed, knowledgeable, genuinely fond of each other. And Angela's brothers-in-law considered how starkly different the Braddock-Blacks were from Brook de Grae.

Carsons brought up the subject of Brook's death two drinks later, his consumption of bourbon having reached the stage where curiosity had the better part of discretion. "Brook was a real bastard," he said. "Glad you shot him. He wasn't alone, I heard."

And Kit explained what had happened without undue emotion. He didn't mention the pleasure he'd taken in killing the man. After a brief description of the events, he said only, "He deserved to die."

Hazard and Trey glanced at each other when Kit calmly uttered those words, a look of understanding passing between them. Vengeance had been a requisite of the warrior's code in Hazard's youth, and he and Trey on several occasions over the years had protected their Montana properties from encroachment by force. Even in 1896 justice on the northern plains was often personal, unofficial, explicitly violent.

"You did the world a service," Sutherland said. "De Grae was out of control."

"Angela had suffered long enough," Kit quietly declared, and glancing at his watch, he set his glass down. "My orders are very plain," he added with a faint smile. "And it's almost eleven. No need to curtail your drinking, but I promised to be back to the house by eleven."

"I'd just as soon see Daisy, too," de Vec casually said, rising from his chair. Although he and his wife had been married four years, they were virtually inseparable. Since she thought she might be pregnant again, he knew she'd be feeling tired by this hour of the night. She wouldn't mind an excuse to go to bed.

"It's going to be a long day of festivities tomorrow," Hazard pleasantly noted, rising too. "I'll walk back with you."

The other men decided to join them as well, and they all strolled through the parkland to the house, the winter night crisp and cool, the moon brilliant in the starlit sky.

*A*ngela had taken note of the approaching hour as she entertained the women over champagne in the drawing room. Waiting for Kit to appear, she rested on a soft cushioned sofa and listened to the women talk. Kit's family was enchanting—bright, interesting, not prone to gossip as so many of her friends were.

They'd talked at length about the stock market. Blaze and Empress were serious investors; Daisy was their partner, too, but less involved on a daily basis, her legal duties for the Braddock-Black companies taking priority. After listening to Blaze and Empress explain the methodology that had resulted in their successes, Millie and Dolly had become enthused and were bent on starting an investment group of their own.

Kit's mother, it turned out, kept busy as sponsor for ten promising young musicians. She was going on to La Scala after the wedding for the debut of one of her young sopranos in *L'Italiana in Algeri.*

The women had shared anecdotes of their children in the course of the evening, children always a topic of conversation when women assembled. The next generation of Braddock-Blacks were increasing in number.

"I might be pregnant, too," Daisy had said when Angela had spoken of how well she felt now that her morning sickness had eased. And they'd compared symptoms and sensibilities with a familiar, warm intimacy. Daisy and Angela were the same age; they discovered they'd once been at Newport the same August when Angela had brought the *Shark* over for the races; they shared a common interest in helping their people as well—both women deeply involved in philanthropy.

When the drawing-room doors opened to the men shortly before eleven, they brought the smell of fresh night air into the gilded drawing room, and the sweet scent of whiskey.

"I'm on time," Kit proclaimed, striding into the room, casting a glance at the clock and grinning. "So the wedding's still on. Not that I was under any pressure," he sportively added with a wink at Angela.

"You were allowed a small grace period," Angela dulcetly murmured, her eyes alight with merriment.

"How very kind," Kit whispered, standing very close, his gaze frankly sensual. Dropping onto the sofa beside her, he placed her slippered feet in his lap. "I'm really looking forward to this wedding," he murmured, running his palms over her ankles. "And the honeymoon," he huskily added.

"Your mother," Angela softly remonstrated, casting him a warning look, pushing her skirt back over her ankles.

"She's not looking." His voice was hushed and low, his grin lush. "She's talking to Millie. Did you miss me?" As Kit leaned over to kiss Angela, wives made room for their husbands on the Louis Quinze furniture.

"You're back early," Blaze said to Hazard as he sprawled next to her on a couch.

"Kit had his orders, apparently," Hazard replied with the understanding smile of a long-married man. "And de Vec missed Daisy, as he always does. So I decided to join them because I missed you as well," he softly added. "The rest came along. Did you women enjoy yourselves?"

"Probably not as much as you, since we didn't have any dancing men," Blaze lightly teased.

Hazard shrugged. "The dancers didn't stay long. Kit and de Vec were clearly anxious to get back."

Blaze leaned closer to Hazard. "Daisy thinks she's pregnant again."

"Ah, that explains de Vec's mood."

"He's changed her so much," Blaze pleasantly said. "Look."

Daisy sat on her husband's lap, her arms around his neck, her head resting on his shoulder, openly affectionate even in the midst of so many people.

"She's learning from him. He's a man without rules," Hazard noted. He'd always worried about his daughter's emotional reserve in the past. Even as a child, she'd been cautious about showing her feelings. With de Vec she'd become warmly demonstrative. "He's good for her," Hazard quietly said.

Empress and Trey were holding hands, seated beside each other on a small settee. And he whispered something that made her blush and giggle.

"No secrets, now," Kit sportively noted, looking up at Empress's giggle.

"I was telling Empress about the dancers," Trey said with a grin. He'd mentioned she was much better.

"What dancers?" Angela asked.

"It was Trey and Etienne's idea. Absolve me," Kit replied. "They left early, anyway."

"A token, no more," de Vec casually murmured, stroking Daisy's arm. "A bachelor party requires a naked female or two."

"We were very tame tonight," Hazard remarked. "We mostly talked business." At fifty-six, Jon Hazard Black was still lean, fit, handsome. The son of an Absarokee chieftain, he'd seen the world change drastically in his lifetime, the traditional Absarokee way of life almost vanished, the style of their entertainment tonight indication, perhaps, of the altered nature of their present, assimilated world.

Blaze touched her husband's hand, recognizing the small earnestness in his voice. She'd known him first when the word "tame" was inapplicable to him.

He turned to her and, taking her small hand in his, gently stroked her wrist, their hearts so much in accord after years of a loving marriage, they understood each other's thoughts.

"What time will the guests be arriving tomorrow?" Carsons asked, filling himself a glass of whiskey from a small table set with liquor decanters.

"The private train arrives at one," Angela answered. "Bianca has graciously agreed to play for Bertie and the others during their brief wait, and since it takes Kit no more than fifteen minutes to dress, he's going to help entertain our guests until the wedding at two. Now, if everyone will excuse me, I'm going to sleep."

"And I as well," Kit quickly said, rising from the sofa and offering Angela his hand.

*D*id you ever think he'd marry?" Trey asked after they'd left. "Pardon me," he added nodding to Angela's two half sisters. "But we've known him a long time."

"I was beginning to give up hope," his mother interposed. "And when he wrote to tell me he was selecting a bride on the marriage mart like a head of cabbage, I was truly alarmed. How nice he met Angela."

"How nice for Angela," Millie said. "We're all so grateful she's happy again. Her husband had become quite unsound. It was a matter of concern to us all." She didn't say "We're glad Kit killed him," but her sentiments were obvious.

Hazard, Trey, and Etienne exchanged glances, thinking they wouldn't have allowed Angela to suffer so long.

"De Grae's father was difficult, too," the duc de

Vec quietly said. "He had to be subdued once at the Jockey Club in Paris. The man didn't hold his liquor well."

"Brook had a similar problem," Carsons noted.

"Kit took care of it," Trey calmly remarked.

"And all is happily resolved." Hazard's expression was as bland as his voice. "Have Kit and Angela decided on a honeymoon?" he casually inquired, turning the conversation to a less emotionally fraught topic.

*B*ertie came to the wedding, too, and Souveral and Violet with smiles and teasing comments and special gifts to commemorate the joyful occasion.

Bertie gave them a rare lacquerwork box that had belonged to a shogun of Japan, the scene depicted on its lid the romantic "Tale of Genji." Souveral and Violet had composed a charming narrative poem to commemorate their passionate courtship and had it bound in a precious medieval book cover.

May was a flower girl, both serious and delighted with her task of strewing rose petals, and Fitz was Kit's best man. Violet served as Angela's matron of honor and wistfully talked of finding happiness herself.

"There's hope, darling," Angela had whispered just before they'd walked into the flower-bedecked chapel at Easton. "We both know it now."

Kit, waiting at the altar, turned to watch his bride, resplendent in embroidered blush velvet, a coronet of roses in her hair, come down the aisle to him, and he blew her a kiss.

Smiling at him, she broke with tradition, ran down the aisle, and threw herself into his arms.

The curate coughed politely, Kit whispered, "Behave," with a grin, and Angela kissed him twice more before standing demurely at his side, because it was her chapel and her curate and her wedding.

They promised to love and honor and care for each other.

Faithful unto death.

When it was Kit's turn to repeat the vows and he said "faithful," he smiled down at her and added the word "forever"—this man who had never understood the need for faithfulness.

Smiling up at him, her eyes filled with love, she promised him as much.

They were married on the first day of the new year.

Eighteen ninety-seven was a new beginning for them all—their small family, their future child, a man and a woman who'd found each other in the tumult of the world.

Epilogue

"The doctor downstairs said I'm punctual. Did I time that right?" Kit teased, coming into Angela's bedroom with the Cowes Regatta silver race cup in his hand. "We crowded on every shred of sail."

"Actually, *I* timed it right," Angela said with a smile, lying in bed, very pregnant and in labor. "I wanted to let you finish the race first—" She suddenly gasped and clutched the bedclothes.

Without regard for the prestigious prize, Kit tossed aside the silver cup that nations and teams and wealthy men coveted and ran to his wife's side. "Oh, lord," he whispered, taking her hand, overwhelmed with helplessness at the sight of her anguished expression. "We need more doctors," he hastily said. "We don't have enough. Where's the midwife? She should be here. I should go and get them," he went on in a rush, powerless to arrest his wife's pain.

Then the contraction passed, Angela's nails loosened from his flesh, and he gently stroked her hand. "I'm terrified," he murmured.

"That wasn't too bad yet," she whispered, taking a deep breath.

"Jesus, Angela," he skittishly said. "I never realized . . ."

"It's a beautiful day for our child to be born," she calmly said, looking out on the sparkling sea outside her windows, her pain gone, placid reality transiently restored.

"You're very calm about this," Kit cautiously noted, tense and anxious and not at all sure it was a beautiful enough day to counteract his wife's distress.

"Just stay with me," Angela murmured.

"Always," he gently answered. "But give me some guidelines on this, darling," he softly appealed. "When do the professionals come on the scene? I hate to see you in pain."

"I'll tell you when."

He exhaled, nodded his head, and said, "They'd better be good."

"Do you want a boy or a girl?" she asked, lying back on her pillows, smiling at him, the months since their wedding the happiest of her life.

"Neither right now. I'd like a rain check to reassess the misery you're going through. Why didn't you *tell* me?"

"I *want* your child," she softly said. "Our child. I'll be fine. And when I'm not, you can call the doctors for the chloroform. Now, kiss me and tell me you love me."

He did with tenderness and devotion and a full heart. "You're my life," he whispered. "My joy, my contentment."

"My true love," she murmured.

He nodded. "My only love . . ."

Their son was born that languid August evening at Eden House, Cowes, announcing his arrival into the world with a noisy squall.

His new family was exultant.

He had pink fuzz on his head that made him look like a beguiling putto and newborn blue eyes already touched with green and a gurgling coo tht instantly charmed.

Later that evening May said, "I'm three now, I can hold him, see?" as she struggled to lift her brother's pudgy weight from the cradle while Kit stood near in case she lost her precarious grip. "He likes me," she added, gathering him up into a crushing embrace.

But Billy didn't seem to mind the stranglehold. He smiled up at his sister with a cheerful gurgle.

"He's talking to you," Fitz said, seated at the foot of his mother's bed, still dressed in his race clothes, his youthful face wreathed in smiles.

May tipped her head to one side, listening intently. "He wants to go sailing," she declared. "That's what he said. Can we go, Papa?" she eagerly asked.

"If your mother agrees," Kit said, all the treasures of his world in this bedroom overlooking the sea.

Angela put her hand out to him, wanting to feel his touch, and he walked over and took her small hand in his and smiled down at her with boundless love in his eyes.

"We can go tomorrow," Angela replied. "But you'll have to carry me."

"I'll carry you anywhere," Kit said, bending low to kiss her cheek. "Even to the ends of the earth."

She smiled up at him as she had that night on the terrace of the yacht club, lush, delectable, the instant angel of his heart.

And he carried her one day in the following year down a wide, broad avenue hacked out of the jungle and paved with stone to a small temple in a steaming green clearing. The building was an exquisite jewel of Javanese architecture, all rich gold leaf and lush sculptures and tall, flamboyant spires.

He told her then how Devaraja had helped them that night at Wickem.

Suddenly understanding the significance of the new road, she said, "Perhaps we should include his name with those of our second child."

"Really?" Kit said, surprised and pleased.

"Is it too soon for another child?" she inquired with an irresistible smile.

"Considering your amorous appetites, darling," he said with a grin, "I'm surprised it hasn't been sooner."

"You don't mind?" A flirtatious lilt underscored her words.

He laughed. "Not likely, *mon ange.* I'm more than willing to do my part. You tell *me* when we've reached our quota."

Notes

1. Although *The Tale of Peter Rabbit* wasn't published until 1902, the story first appeared in a picture letter Beatrix Potter wrote to Noel Moore, the young son of her former governess, in 1893. Beatrix remembered the letter seven years later and expanded it into a little picture book with black-and-white illustrations. It was rejected by several publishers, so she had it printed herself, to give to family and friends. At this time Frederick Warne agreed to publish the tale if the author would supply color pictures. The book was an instant success. Since Baby May adores Peter Rabbit so, I'm taking liberty with the date and assuming Angela could have been one of the friends who received an early picture letter and a form of privately printed book. It was very common for the upper classes to have their manuscripts privately printed.

2. Although it had been customary after a meal for men to remain at the table for port and cigars after the women departed to the drawing room, the Prince of Wales's preferences had changed the practice in the

Marlborough House set. In the Duchess of Warwick's memoirs she states

> I think it was the introduction of cigarette smoking immediately after dinner by the Prince of Wales that killed the claret habit. After the first whiff or two it was difficult to tell good wine from bad, and champagne speedily took the place of Bordeaux. Men began to follow the example set by the Prince, of leaving the dining-table almost immediately after dinner to join the ladies.

3. The drive for women's legal rights in England began in earnest with debate over the divorce bill of 1856–57. Protection of married women's property and equal access to divorce for men and women were the two most delicate and dangerous issues on the agenda of the women's reform movement in mid-Victorian England. The demand for equal access to divorce on grounds of adultery by either husband or wife struck at the very foundation of the double sexual standard. The demand for the placing of a married woman's property under her own control struck at the heart of the economic aspects of a marriage contract and threatened the strategic manipulation of marriage to advance family property interests. In the 1857 debate all that could be achieved was two modest proposals that protected property of separated and deserted wives. Although these amendments to the Divorce Bill left untouched the husband's full control over the property of his wife among normal cohabiting married couples, they succeeded in salvaging something. But in the course of the next twenty years the Married Women's Property Act was amended in 1870, 1874, and 1882, and wives were at last granted full control

over their own property. Although the top 10 percent of society, including almost all of those represented in Parliament, were already marrying under the settlement arrangement, by which the wife kept control over her own property through trustees—as Angela did—debate over women's rights was still fiercely contested.

4. According to custom, when the Prince of Wales was going to visit a household, the guest list was submitted to him for approval, and he would add the name of a particular friend or friends if he chose or cross out a name if he wished. During the time of his liaison with Daisy, later the Duchess of Warwick, the great houses were requested always to invite Lord and Lady Brooke when the prince would be present. Conversely, during the long feud between the prince and the Churchills, the Prince of Wales let it be known he and the princess would boycott any house the Churchills entered. Only two people flouted his power—Louisa, Duchess of Manchester, and John Delacour, a close friend of Randolph Churchill, who when reprimanded by the prince said, "I allow no man to choose my friends." On another occasion, Daisy Warwick relates in her memoirs, the influence of the great families was also apparent. The Prince of Wales had added the name of a particular friend to the list submitted to him by a hostess, in this case a person whose standing was open to criticism among the elect of society. A letter couched in perfectly appropriate terms came by return from the hostess. She said that she did not know the prince's friend, whose name had been added to the list; she asked at the same time that she might be relieved of her post in the royal household. The prince wrote back at once to say that he regretted the hostess did not know his friend, that it was of no conse-

quence, and that he hoped she would not resign her position.

5. Many amorous rendezvous took place at country-house weekends, and the creaking of floorboards in the halls at night was commonplace. In one instance a gentleman, worried about which door to open for his amorous tryst, had asked the lady to put her sandwiches (which were placed by each bedside in the case of sudden hunger after the five heavy meals of the day) outside the door. Unfortunately, the German chargé d'affaires, Baron von Eckardstein, passed that way, couldn't resist, and ate the sandwiches. When Romeo came tiptoeing along the corridor, he saw an empty plate and, fearing that it was intended as some kind of warning, fled. An absolute necessity in the game of illicit rendezvous was knowing the correct door to open in the dead of night in a strange house. One time Lord Charles Beresford, who was a great ladies' man, tiptoed into a dark room and jumped into the vast bed shouting "Cock-a-doodle-doo," only to find himself, when the light was suddenly lit, between the Bishop of Chester and his wife. Oops. If a hostess approved of a liaison, however, rooms could be discreetly allotted side by side, saving trouble and embarrassment. In Warwick Castle, for example, home to Daisy Warwick, one of the long-term mistresses of the Prince of Wales, the prince's room was immediately adjacent to Daisy's boudoir. So very convenient.

6. Neither Queen Victoria nor the Prince of Wales believed in any form of democracy. And on the occasion of debate over extending the vote in 1884, the queen wrote to Mr. Gladstone:

No one is more truly liberal in her heart than the Queen, but she has always strongly deprecated the great tendency of the present Government to encourage instead of checking the stream of destructive Democracy which has become so alarming. This it is that, she must say justly, alarms the House of Lords, and all moderate people. To threaten the House of Lords that they will bring destruction on themselves is, in fact, to threaten the Monarchy itself. Another Sovereign but herself must acquiesce in any alteration of the House of Lords. She will not be the Sovereign of a Democratic Monarchy.

7. In England in the thirty years from 1827 to 1857, only three petitions for divorce by wives were successful. Before the 1857 Divorce Bill, only the smallest of cracks had been opened in the wall of traditional belief in the double sexual standard, as a result of which wives were virtually denied access to parliamentary divorce. When debate began over the 1857 bill in Parliament, marriage separations amounted only to about twenty a year, while there were only three or four parliamentary divorces a year. Demand was clearly minimal, opponents declared. Even with the passage of the Divorce Bill of 1857, within three years the number of divorces rose from 4 to 150. By 1914 that figure rose to 800 a year. But the number of people involved remained statistically minute. England still remained basically a nondivorcing country. In the United States, in contrast, divorce laws were unique to each state, and two thirds of the divorce suits were instigated by the wife. In 1886, 25,000 divorces were granted in the U.S.; in 1906, 72,000—about double the number reported for that year from all the rest of the Christian

world. Between 1887 and 1906, 945,625 divorces were reported. Clearly, a radical difference in culture related to divorce law existed between England and America.

8. Daisy Warwick, who served as inspiration for Angela de Grae, was reckless and tempestuous as well as beautiful, and on hearing that forty-year-old Mina Beresford, the wife of her lover, Charlie Beresford, was pregnant, she turned tantrumish. Since Lady Beresford's virtue couldn't be doubted, this meant that Charlie, having sworn to be true to Daisy, had embraced his wife. Daisy was outraged; she accused him of infidelity! Unfortunately, his wife opened the letter and a sensational scandal ensued. Daisy's imperious demand came to mind when I was writing the dialogue between Kit and Angela in this scene. I didn't think Daisy Warwick would have minded asking her lover to give up his harem, either.

9. As early as 1838 a German gynecologist, F. A. Wilde, had recommended a cervical rubber cap specially molded by taking a wax impression. Wilde's modest and forgotten recommendation of a cervical cap was ultimately to find wide usage in Europe and the United States. Dr. Henry Allbutt may have been responsible for the introduction of the rubber cervical cap into England. His publication of a medical pamphlet in 1884–85 drew condemnation from the General Medical Council, and the case occasioned so much publicity, it increased the demand for the improved contraceptive device. A refinement of the cervical cap, the Mensinga diaphragm, had reached Holland from Germany by the early 1880s, but apparently not England. Because the Mensinga was popularized in Holland by Aletta Jacobs (she opened the

world's first birth-control clinic in 1882), it's been nicknamed the Dutch cap ever since. The first mention of the Mensinga diaphragm in England appears in Mrs. Besant's *Law of Population,* 1887 edition.

10. A variety of spermicides have been used over the centuries, the earliest surviving recipe from the Egyptian Petri papyrus of 1850 B.C. suggests crocodile dung made into a paste with honey and natron. Some recipes over the centuries have been practical potions—rock salt, a very powerful spermicide; alum, vinegar, and lemon proved effective as well; others, such as lizard and snails, crocus and mint, are more magical than useful. In the late nineteenth century one of the preferred spermicides was a combination of quinine and cacao-nut butter. Recent research has shown, however, that quinine's spermicidal power is low. Casanova's (1725–98) memoirs also describe a direct forerunner of the modern Dutch cap. He mentions cutting a lemon in half, extracting most of the juice, and using the disc as a cervical cap, an ingenious and effective method that would have a spermicidal effect as well.

11. Casanova liked to vary his methods of contraception, and though he often wore a condom, many of his partners inserted little gold balls instead. He was very particular about them. They weighed sixty grams, measured eighteen millimeters in diameter—and cost an exorbitant amount. But they were worth it, doing service for him for fifteen years and never letting the sperm through by becoming displaced. His own account reads:

> It is sufficient for the ball to be placed at the base of the temple of love when the loving

couple carry out the sacrifice. But, says the friend, movement may displace the ball before the end of the libation. This is an accident which need not be feared, provided one exercises foresight.

Small metal balls have been used in the Middle and Far East for centuries. During the Chinese Ming dynasty, one novel describes a "Burmese Bell" made of copper and containing the semen of a lascivious Burmese bird, which was supposed to act as a sexual aid. And Richard Burton added the following note to his *Arabian Nights* translation:

> When Pekin was plundered the harems contained a number of balls a little larger than the old musket-bullet, made of thin silver with a loose pellet of brass inside somewhat like a grelot; these articles were placed by the women between the labia, and an up and down movement on the bed gave a pleasant titillation when nothing better was to be procured.

12. The first known published description of the condom is to be found in the work of the great Italian anatomist, Fallopius, who in his *De Morbo Gallico*, first published in 1564, two years after the author's death, described a linen sheath. He invented it as a protection against syphilis. The prophylactic linen glans condom of Fallopius (1564) gradually became a full covering using the ceca of various animals. The earliest sheaths of contraceptive form were undoubtedly used for that purpose by the eighteenth century. The actual word "condom" didn't appear in print un-

til 1706. It turned up in a poem, "A Scot's Answer to a British Vision," which states:

> *Sirenge and Condum*
> *Come both in Request.*

By the third decade of the eighteenth century mention of condoms is extensive in literature, medical tracts, handbills, advertisements. But making condoms was a painstakingly slow business, as the following entry in Gray's 1828 *Pharmacopoeia* indicates:

> The intestina caeca of sheep soaked for some hours in water, turned inside out, macerated again in weak alkaline ley changed every twelve hours, scraped carefully to abstract the mucous membrane, leaving the peritoneal and muscular coats; then exposed to the vapour of burning brimstone, and afterwards washed with soap and water; they are then blown up, dried, cut to the length of seven or eight inches, and bordered at the open end with a riband.

Widespread, common use of the condom, however, had to await the vulcanization of rubber, first successfully carried out by Goodyear and Hancock in 1843–44. This lowered cost so materially that the condom immediately won a place for itself.

13. In the winter of 1896, Daisy Warwick planned to help the world become a better place by introducing her socialist editor friend William Thomas Stead to the Prince of Wales. There is always a sense of whimsy about Daisy's serious endeavors, and having just suffered a concussion while out foxhunting, she had to

supervise this important meeting from her invalid couch. Stead, the son of a northern Congregational minister and editor of the *Pall Mall Gazette* and the *Review of Reviews,* was considered a firebrand radical. In 1885, in a striking display of action journalism, Stead had bought a thirteen-year-old girl in order to expose the traffic in virgins for prostitution. His intimate accounts of the episode week after week in the *Pall Mall Gazette* anticipated the shocked exposures commonplace in twentieth-century journalism. The hostile reaction to his exposé, directed not at the vice operators but at Stead himself, who affronted a prudish society deliberately blind to unpleasant truths, was essentially Victorian, and by a legal technicality Stead was sentenced to three months in prison. The Prince of Wales, while polite for Daisy's sake, had no common meeting ground with a man like Stead. And while the lunchtime conversation was amicable, touching lightly on current topics, politics, and diplomacy, Stead wrote later that the prince reminded him of "the type of Society hostess who contrives to give the impression to every one that she is much interested in what he is saying, and five minutes afterwards forgets all about it."

14. In the time period in which *Brazen* is set, young girls were routinely coerced into unwanted marriages, the notion that parents knew best a recognized Victorian precept. In her memoirs Consuelo Vanderbilt, an American heiress forced into an unwanted marriage, relates the events leading up to her acceptance of the Duke of Marlborough's marriage proposal (a proposal offered, by the way, after he told Consuelo that he was in love with another woman but that the upkeep of Blenheim required her Vanderbilt money):

Driving home my mother observed an ominous silence, but when we reached the house she told me to follow her to her room. Thinking it best no longer to dissemble, I told her that I meant to marry X not the Duke of Marlborough, adding that I considered I had a right to choose my own husband. These words, the bravest I had ever uttered, brought down a frightful storm of protest. I suffered every searing reproach, heard every possible invective hurled at the man I loved.

We eventually reached a stage where arguments were futile and I left her then in the cold dawn of morning feeling as if all my youth had been drained away. My life became that of a prisoner with my mother and my governess as wardens. I was never out of their sight. Friends called but were told I was not at home. Locked behind those high walls—the porter had orders not to let me out unaccompanied—I had no chance of getting word to my fiancé. I could not write, for the servants had orders to bring my letters to my mother. There was no one I could consult; to appeal to my father, who was away at sea and who knew nothing of my mother's schemes, would, I knew, only involve him in a hopeless struggle against impossible odds and further stimulate my mother's rancor.

Later that day Mrs. Jay, who was my mother's intimate friend and was staying with us at the time, came to talk to me. Condemning my behavior, she informed me that my mother had had a heart attack brought about by my callous indifference to her feelings. She confirmed my mother's intentions of never consenting to my plans for marriage, and her resolve to shoot X should I decide to run away with him. I asked her if I could see my mother and whether in her opinion she would ever relent. I still remember the terrible answer, "Your mother will never relent and I warn you there will be a catastrophe if you persist. The doctor has said that another scene may easily bring on a heart attack and he will not be responsible for the result!"

Still under the strain of the painful scene with my mother, still seeing her frightening rage, it seemed to me that she might indeed easily suffer a stroke or a heart attack if further provoked. In utter misery I asked Mrs. Jay to let X know that I could not marry him.

Several months later, she writes,

I spent the morning of my wedding day in tears and alone; no one came near me. A footman had been posted at the door of my apartment and not even my governess was admitted. Like an automaton I donned the lovely lingerie and gown. . . . I felt cold and numb as I went down to meet my father and the bridesmaids who were waiting for me.

15. A poignant entry in Daisy Warwick's memoirs suggested the line in *Brazen*:

The chief folly of those of us who belonged to the Marlborough House set was to imagine that pleasure and happiness were identical. I cannot remember one friend of mine who was really happy, though each was always just going to be so. They had their hours of bliss—I recall many joys, both theirs and my own, but we were never able to cling to happiness. Each of us knew that disillusion must follow. Nobody felt quite safe—how could we, recognizing that, in the feverish search for pleasure, any woman might lose her lover, any man's mistress might be lured away.

16. Although condom decoration has taken many forms and colors, the last word must go to the English. In 1883 Frenchman Hector France described a visit to Petticoat Lane. Along with canaries that turned gray in the rain, he was delighted to find "French letters" (condoms) for sale, bearing the portrait of none other than Queen Victoria. Aware of the queen's inordinate sense of self-importance, I found the citation irresistible. I had to mention it in my story.

17. I particularly like the account of the only advice Lady Moncreiffe of that Ilk gave her girls when they left the Highlands to enter London society: "Never comment on a likeness." This was a tactful rule to remember when admiring Edwardian babies. Harry Cust is one example of the phenomenon that motivated Lady Moncreiffe's worldly counsel to her daughters. Harry Cust, it was said—who was poetic, golden-haired, Adonis handsome, wellborn, and irresistible—left his mark on a great many noble English families, his brilliant sapphire eyes shining up from any number of cradles in the years of his amorous adventures—when the husbands of those mothers had very dark eyes. And yet, by bitter chance, his wife, who had forced him into marriage with the ruse of a sham pregnancy, would be one of few women who

came under his spell who did not bear his child. That's another interesting story.

18. I found the description of a dinner with Queen Victoria amusing. Daisy Warwick relates,

> Just before my eighteenth birthday, my mother surprised me with the news that we were all commanded to dine and sleep at Windsor, that I might be inspected as a future daughter-in-law. So to Windsor we went in state. Before dinner, which was to be at eight-thirty, we all assembled in a draughty corridor —it was long before the days of central heating—and there waited for three-quarters of an hour talking in low voices. Suddenly doors were thrown open, and a very little lady ran in, bowed with grace right and left to the whole company, while we stood at attention, and then sped into the dining-room with Princess Beatrice hurrying after her. When we took our places, the Queen as usual had Princess Beatrice on her right. Lord Beaconsfield sat next to the Princess and my stepfather sat at the Queen's left.

She goes on to describe the conversation, then continues. . . .

> Queen Victoria reminded me in appearance of my old nurse, Susan Forster, who was living at the age of a hundred, but when Her Majesty smiled her ingenuous, charming smile, the whole face lit up and became beautiful. The Prince of Wales inherited his mother's smile. Dinner was served in hot haste. In half an

hour, the Queen got up as abruptly as she had
arrived, and seemed to run from the room, so
rapid was her walk, followed as before by
Princess Beatrice. Now we streamed into the
corridor in her wake, and the Queen went
from one to another, talking intimately with
each in turn.

19. In 1870 the Prince of Wales was first implicated in
a divorce case, cited as a corespondent. A provincial
paper managed to get hold of the eleven letters he'd
written to the wife being sued for divorce—Lady
Mordaunt—and published them. When the prince
was subpoenaed as a witness, this caused utmost distress to Queen Victoria. But the prince decided to
waive his plea of privilege and went into the witness
box. He was questioned by Dr. Deane, Lady
Mordaunt's counsel, and in a very firm tone denied
that there had been any improper familiarity or crimi-
nal act between him and Lady Mordaunt. But the
public wasn't satisfied. Edward was greeted with
hisses when he arrived at the theater and when he appeared on the racecourse at Epsom; even when the
Princess of Wales was with him at the Crystal Palace,
the crowd expressed its disapproval in the same way.
At other times he was received in absolute silence. *The
Times* chided him in a leading article and advised him
to follow in his father's footsteps. Other newspapers
took up the theme. There was talk of abolishing the
monarchy and setting up a republic, since the cost of
maintaining the Crown was too high. (An age-old
complaint, apparently.)

In the course of the succeeding years two further
scandals followed. The Aylesford Affair implicated the
Prince of Wales once again in a divorce proceeding,
indiscreet letters of his having fallen into the wrong

hands. Randolph Churchill, as a means of protecting his brother, threatened to expose the compromising letters, saying if they were published, the prince would never sit upon the throne of England. Lord Aylesford was eventually persuaded not to seek a divorce, and scandal was averted. But the bitterness over the unsavory affair lingered for years.

Then again, in 1890, a scandal over gambling came to public attention because the incident led to a lawsuit. The Prince of Wales was subpoenaed and under cross-examination admitted that he had had a long close friendship with the man accused of cheating at cards and had been present at the incident. The moment the case ended, the floodgates opened for widespread criticism of the prince's way of life. Nonconformists held meetings all over the country and were quite unrestrained in their attack. The Welsh Baptist denounced his "immoral habits." The Wesleyans "bitterly regretted that the Heir to the Throne should be given to one of the worst forms of gambling." *The Times* "almost wished for the sake of English society" that the prince would follow the example of Sir William Gordon-Cumming and sign a declaration that he would never touch a card again. The *Review of Reviews,* estimating that 880 million prayers had been said for His Royal Highness since his birth, indicated that the only answer from the Almighty seemed to be a baccarat scandal. The "Wee Frees" removed the prince's name from their prayers. When he arrived to open a new hall in Camberwell, he was met with a banner inscribed "Welcome to our Prince—but No Gambling."

Nowhere in the world was he spared. The American press, the newspapers on the Continent, the cartoonists; all joined in. One German paper, in a cartoon, showed the great door of Windsor Castle decorated with the Prince of Wales's feathers, but the familiar motto was altered from *Ich Dien* (I serve) to *Ich Deal.* The prince also received a rebuke from his nephew the kaiser, who in a personal letter expressed his displeasure that anyone holding the high position of colonel in the Prussian Hussars should "embroil himself in a gambling squabble and play with men young enough to be his son."

Queen Victoria was acutely distressed. She wrote to her son again and again: They were sharp, scolding letters. She asked him to give up playing cards and eventually extracted the promise that he would never again allow baccarat to be played in his presence.

As Queen Victoria lamented in a letter to her daughter, "It is a fearful humiliation to see the future King of this country dragged through the dirt just like anyone else."

20. In the years after her marriage Lady Brooke gradually became aware of the poor opportunities of the young village girls who left school at thirteen to do the rough work of farm and household, when they could get it, for a general servant's wage of one shilling a week. There existed in every village a number of delicate or handicapped girls who found this work impossibly strenuous and remained unemployed, a burden on their families or on charity. Daisy Warwick came to realize that these girls had often one talent actually encouraged in the dreary curricula of the elementary schools, that for intricate needlework. To take advantage of this skill, and to provide some employment for the delicate, Lady Brooke set aside one of the many rooms of Easton Lodge for a needlework school, with one teacher to supervise a handful of local girls, who had trudged sometimes three or four miles, in all weathers, through the acres of parkland from the

neighboring villages. She paid the girls two shillings and sixpence a week during the preliminary three years' training, and ten shillings when they became fully proficient, wages that quickly created a big demand for places among frail and healthy alike. Her project proved immediately successful, although it didn't hurt to have royal connections. Princess May of Teck, later to become Queen Mary, ordered her trousseau to be embroidered at Easton, after which it became the smart thing to do. As orders poured in, Daisy bravely rented a shop in Bond Street to deal with the expanding production. The notice over the shop, "Lady Brooke's depot for the Easton school of Needlework" provoked malicious innuendo among society, who despised trade and made spiteful play with her "taking up shop" where, word had it, she served behind the counter. Having no business experience, Daisy ran the shop at considerable cost to herself, and the needlework school lived expensively on. But in its small way, this fumbling attempt to provide employment instead of alms showed a growing awareness of the desperate situation and narrow opportunities of the very poor. Daisy Warwick also made over one of her farms to become a technical school, providing the only secondary education in the area with a special bias toward science and agriculture. This coeducational boarding school, trying particularly to attract pupils from the public elementary school and to combine secondary education with practical training for country life, was probably the most important and interesting scheme Lady Warwick ever started. In making Bigods School coeducational—an unusual step for a secondary school—Lady Warwick had to fight not only the usual rural distrust of schooling, but the ingrained reluctance of country people to educate girls.

Over the next few years this project was to cost her a considerable sum.

In contrast, at the same time, Queen Victoria was expressing her opinion that education had been carried too far, and that "it ruined the health of the higher classes uselessly and rendered the working classes unfit for good servants and laborers."

21. When the fight for women's legal rights began at midcentury in England, the two issues of women's property rights and equal access to divorce were the main thrusts of the drive. Married women's property was secured by 1882. Equal access to divorce, however, remained elusive until 1923. So Angela's concern over petitioning for divorce without her husband's approval was very real. Although women could petition for divorce on desertion and cruelty by the nineties, the judicial interpretation still didn't give wives full legal equality with their husbands. Only in 1884 did an act of Parliament end the powers of the Matrimonial Causes Court to use the threat of imprisonment to force a wife to cohabit with her husband. And not until 1891 did a judge reverse the 1840 ruling in the Cochrane case. Until that 1891 reversal, a husband had the right to confine his wife to prevent her from eloping. An additional act of 1895 empowered magistrates to grant to battered wives both maintenance and custody of children up to the age of sixteen.

It wasn't until the end of the century that legal support for the physical control of husbands over their wives finally ended.

22. In the late nineties both Havelock Ellis and Sigmund Freud were beginning to be published. Ellis's *Studies in the Psychology of Sex* quickly found a readership. Ellis assaulted almost every aspect of the

nineteenth-century sexual heritage. For Ellis sexual indulgence didn't pose the threat to health or character that preoccupied many earlier writers. Rather, he described it as "the chief and central function of life . . . ever wonderful, ever lovely." Ellis equated sex with "all that is most simple and natural and pure and good." He asked his readers: "Why . . . should people be afraid of rousing passions which, after all, are the great driving forces of human life?"

The writings of Freud best symbolized the new direction that sexual theorizing took in the twentieth century. Whatever subtlety or complexity his theories possessed took a backseat to the concepts that infiltrated society's imagination: the notion of infantile sexuality, the drama of sexual conflict in the family, the case histories of female patients who seemed to suffer from the denial of their sexual desires, the idea that the sexual instinct permeated human life. Above all, readers absorbed a version of Freudianism that presented the sexual impulse as an insistent force demanding expression.

23. When Queen Victoria's consort, Prince Albert, died in 1861, she went into mourning from which she never completely returned. She essentially retired from London, to Windsor or Osborne House or Balmoral. She kept her husband's suite of rooms at Windsor Castle exactly as they had been at his death, and every evening Prince Albert's clothes were set out for him to wear and his medicine bottle and a spoon placed in readiness for his use. She continued her royal duties from her semiretired state but made only rare public appearances. No more than a half-dozen times in the course of her forty widowed years had she bothered to take part in the opening of the new session of Parliament, which was one of the Crown's duties. The Court

was dull, stodgy, and partially insulated from the events of the world. An interesting aside in this self-imposed retirement, however, was the close companion of the queen, a tall, handsome Scotsman, a servant gillie named John Brown. He occupied a privileged place in the queen's life after the death of Prince Albert. Familiar in his manner to her, he insisted on being treated with deference and respect, but in turn was offhand and rude to almost everybody. This merely amused Queen Victoria, who often quoted the things he said. She took him everywhere with her, even on her annual trips to the Riviera, and gave away miniatures of John Brown set in diamonds as a special mark of her favor. The man called her "Mrs. John Brown."

Immediately after his mother's death, the new king had all the tartan removed from the drawing room at Balmoral and the statue of John Brown taken down. King Edward wanted no reminder of him. His relationship with Queen Victoria had caused the most embarrassing gossip over the years. I've often wondered if a tiny portion of the queen's motivation for remaining retired from society for forty years might have had to do with her wish for privacy in this very close relationship between servant and queen. If the gossip was true—and one clearly wonders, when marble statues are erected to servants—Queen Victoria adhered to her own very comfortable double standard. While scolding her son for sixty years over the style of his indiscretions, she conveniently chose to overlook her own.

Dear Reader,

Several years ago, when I first read about Daisy, Countess of Warwick, I was touched by the heartrending sadness she'd suffered over an unhappy love affair. Fate was very unkind to her, for when she finally found the great passion in her life, it was impossible for her to marry the man "she loved best in all the world." I wished at the time that I could have given her the man she loved.

Now, with literary license and revisionist history, *Brazen* offers her—in the guise of Angela de Grae—the happiness she deserved. Daisy Warwick (Lady Brooke, before her husband came into his title) was a remarkable woman of spirit and independence, struggling against the strictures of her era. She wasn't perfect; she made mistakes. She was a product of her class and background. But of all the woman in her privileged set, she was the only one who seriously questioned the inequalities of life.

In her memoirs she states: "When they write my obituary notice, it should be the record of a woman who feverishly designed many things for the betterment of human lives, while the 'Green Gods' sat smiling at the puny efforts of an imprisoned soul trying to find a way of escape."

And Daisy Warwick at her best is expressed in her account of an interview she had in 1896. A woman reporter for a ladies' paper asked her, "What is your opinion as to the opening of public careers to women?"

"I do not know why people should always make such a distinction between men and women," Daisy said. "There are certain persons in the community who are capable and public-spirited and have leisure to serve the community. Why should you ask whether they are men or women? If they can do the work, let them do it. Woman have quite enough against them without anything being added by the kind forethought of the other sex. I have never found any objection made to taking part in any work because I was a woman."

"Except taking services in your parish church," the interviewer interpolated. "That you would never be allowed to do."

"Who knows?" Daisy replied quickly. "When I want to do that, possibly the door will open."

She was a woman of great optimism.

I hope you like Angela. I think Kit Braddock is a perfect match for an independent women.

Best,

Susan Johnson

P.S. I enjoy hearing from readers. If you'd like a copy of my newsletter written on a between-books schedule, write to:

P.O. Box 37
North Branch, MN 55056

About the Author

Susan Johnson, award-winning author of nationally bestselling novels, lives in the country near North Branch, Minnesota. A former art historian, she considers the life of a writer the best of all possible worlds.

Researching her novels takes her to past and distant places, and bringing characters to life allows her imagination full rein, while the creative process offers occasional fascinating glimpses into complicated machinery of the mind.

But perhaps most important . . . writing stories is fun.

The legendary Kuzan Dynasty lives on in

Sweet Love, Survive

by Susan Johnson
On sale July 1996

Thrill to Susan Johnson's
next historical romance

Breathless

available from Bantam Books
in Winter 1996

*Here's a sneak peek at this sizzling love story
from the acclaimed mistress of the erotic
historical romance. . . .*

When he first heard the soft footfall in the passageway outside his stateroom, he glanced at the clock mounted on the ship's overhead beam as if to substantiate the odd sound to the moment.

Two o'clock.

He came fully awake.

A woman was on board his yacht.

He immediately recognized the tiptoeing gait as female but then Beau St. Jules had vast experience with tiptoeing rendezvous in the middle of the night. As he had with women of every nuance and description, his amours rivaled—some said surpassed—his father's distinguished record. The Duke of Seth's eldest son wasn't called Glóry by all the seductive ladies in London for the beauty of his smile alone.

That celebrated smile suddenly appeared on his starkly handsome face as he threw his legs over the side of his bed and reached for his breeches.

A female stowaway on his yacht. How serendipitous.

Entertainment perhaps, for his voyage to Naples.

Creeping down the dimly lit passage, Serena hardly dared breathe. She'd waited until all sounds of activity had ceased on the yacht save for the night crew above decks. And if she hadn't been famished she wouldn't have risked leaving her hiding place in the small closet filled with female attire, the scented fabrics reminding her poignantly of her mother's fine gowns.

Long ago . . . before her mother's death.

Before her father's spiral into drink and gambling.

Before her own servitude as governess to the despicable Tothams.

A small sigh escaped her as she moved toward the galley she'd seen when she'd stolen aboard the yacht at Dover late last night. How far removed she was from that distant childhood—without funds, in flight from England aboard a stranger's yacht, hoping to reach Florence by the grace of God and her own wits.

Her stomach growled as the delicious scent of food from the galley drifted toward her. She eased open the door and the more urgent need to eat drove away any remnants of nostalgia or self-pity.

She was adding a crusty loaf of bread to the cheese and pears she held in the scooped fold of her skirt when a voice behind her gently said, "Would you like me to wake my cook and have him make you something more substantial?"

She whirled around to find a gentleman lounging against the door jamb. His smile flashed white in the subdued light, mitigating the terror his voice had engendered although his state of undress, clothed as he was in only breeches, gave rise to another kind of fear. He was powerfully built, the light from a small oil lamp casting his muscular body in shadow and plane, his virility intense at close range.

"Have we met before?" he softly asked, wondering if he should know the young lady. The blur of women in his life occasionally made it difficult to recall specific females.

"Not precisely," Serena replied, hesitant, not certain of his mood despite his soft voice. "I saw you in the parlor of The Pelican last night."

"Really," he said with genuine surprise, shifting slightly in his stance. He rarely overlooked women of such striking good looks. She had glorious golden hair, huge dark eyes, a slender, voluptuous form and a sensuous mouth he was definitely interested in tasting. "I must have been very drunk," he added, half to himself.

"You may have been," she said, repressing an odd flutter induced by the graphic display of rippling muscle as he moved. "You didn't come aboard till almost dawn."

"Really," he said again, his voice mild. "Are we sailing mates then?"

"I'd be happy to *pay* for my passage."

His gaze raked her swiftly, pausing for a fraction of a second on the food gathered in her skirt. "But you prefer not taking conventional routes."

"My ship left without me after I'd already paid for my passage." Her eyes suddenly filled with tears.

"Please don't cry," he quickly said. "You're more than welcome aboard the *Siren*." He was uncomfortable with distrait women and she was obviously without funds if she was reduced to stealing aboard his vessel.

"I can . . . reimburse you for my passage," she said, swallowing hard to stem her tears. "Once we reach Italy." The tuition money she'd sent to Florence should cover her fare.

"Nonsense," he murmured. "I'm sailing there anyway." He smiled briefly. "How much can you eat, after all." Easing away from the jamb he stood upright, his height suddenly formidable to her upturned gaze. But his voice was bland when he said, "Why don't I find you some better accommodations and real food. Do you eat beefsteak?"

"Oh, yes." Serena salivated at the thought, her last meal a frugal breakfast in London two days ago. "Yes, definitely."

"Why don't you make yourself comfortable," Beau suggested. "The second door on the right should do," he quietly added, moving back into the passageway to allow her egress from the galley. "I'll join you directly once I get my cook awake."

He didn't reappear for some time. Instead a young lad with hot water and towels appeared in his stateroom, followed shortly by another servant with a decanter of tokay and cookies. He was allowing his beautiful passenger time to wash and refresh herself while he gave directions for a sumptuous meal to his French chef he'd cajoled out of bed with a sweet smile and a lavish bribe.

Some sauteed scallops first, he'd requested while the young Frenchman had sulkily rolled out of bed. "She's very beautiful, Remy, and not quite sure she can trust me."

"Nor should she," the slender young man muttered

standing motionless beside his bed for a moment, still half-asleep.

"But your luscious food will set her mind at ease."

"So I'm supposed to help you seduce her," the Frenchman grumbled, his chestnut hair falling into his eyes as he bent to pick up his trousers from a nearby chair.

"Now, Remy, since when do I need help there," Beau murmured, his grin roguish. "I just want her happy."

"Then maybe you should serve her oysters first," Remy said with an answering grin as he stepped into his trousers. "And save the scallops for lunch for tomorrow when her passions are sated."

"She wants beefsteak too."

Remy groaned. "You English have no subtlety. Served bloody, I suppose."

"With your mushroom and wine sauce, *s'il vous plait*," Beau pleasantly added, "and I'll add another fifty guineas to my offer."

"Make it sixty and I'll give her floating islands for dessert as well. Women adore them."

"You're a treasure, Remy. How would I survive without you?"

"You'd be skin and bone with all your fucking, no mistake."

"And I'm deeply grateful." Beau's voice was amused.

"I suppose you need this all within the hour so you don't have to wait too long to make love to this female you've found."

The young Earl of Rochefort grinned. "After all these years you read my mind, Remy darling. An hour would be perfect."

But he gave no indication of his designs when he entered his stateroom a few minutes later. "My cook is grumbling, but up," Beau said with a smile, walking over to a built-in bureau and pulling out a crisply starched shirt from the drawer. "So food should arrive shortly. Are you comfortable?" he politely queried, slipping the shirt over his head.

"Yes, thank you," Serena looked up at him from the depths of a soft, upholstered chair she'd almost fallen asleep in. "The cookies were delicious . . . and the wine."

"Good." Glancing at the crumbs remaining on the plate, he gauged the amount of wine remaining in the decanter with an assessing eye.

"I'd like to thank you very much for your hospitality." The lanterns had been lit by his servants and Serena's fairness was even more delectable bathed in a golden light. And her eyes weren't dark but aquamarine, like the Mediterranean.

"My pleasure," he casually said, dropping into a chair opposite her. My *distinct* pleasure, he more covetously thought as he gauged her lush beauty tantalizing. How would she respond, he wondered, to his first kiss? "Where had you booked passage?" he asked instead, gracious and well-behaved. "Perhaps I could see that your money is returned."

"Do you think you could?" She sat forward, her eyes alight with hope.

And for the briefest moment Beau St. Jules questioned his callous pursuit of pleasure, her poverty so obvious. But in the next flashing moment he soothed his momentary twinge of conscience by deciding a generous settlement once they reached Italy would more than compensate for his dishonorable intentions. And who knew, he considered in a more practical frame of mind, she might not be so innocent despite her enchanting delicacy. She'd stowed away after all—not exactly the act of a proper young lady.

"I'm sure I could. How much did you lose?"

"Fifty pounds," she said. "I'd been saving for years."

Good God, he thought, briefly startled. He gambled thousands on the turn of a card. "Let me reimburse you in the interim," he suggested, reaching for a wallet lying on his desk.

"Oh, no, I couldn't possibly take money from you."

He looked up from the purse he was opening, not because of her words but her tone. A small reserve had entered her voice and her eyes, he noted, held a distinct apprehension. "Consider it a loan," he calmly replied, gazing more critically at her, trying to properly place her in the hierarchy of female stowaways—a novel category for him.

Her navy serge gown was worn but well-cut, her shoes equally worn but impeccably polished; her exquisite face and radiant hair couldn't be improved on in the highest ranks of society. Was she some runaway noble wife dressed in her servant's clothes or someone's beautiful mistress fallen on hard times?

"I'm a governess," she deliberately said.

"Forgive me. Was I staring?" His smile was cordial as he counted out a hundred pounds. "Here," he said, leaning across the distance separating them, placing the bills in a neat stack on a small table beside her chair. "Pay me back when you can. I've plenty. Do you care to divulge your name?" he went on, noting her necessitous gaze, willing her to pick up the money, wanting the distrust in her voice to disappear.

"Why?" Her blue-green gaze rising to his was cool, guarded.

"No reason." He shrugged—a small lazy movement, deprecating, indulgent. "I was just making conversation. I have no intention of hurting you," he softly added.

Her expression visibly relaxed. "My name's Serena Blythe."

Definitely an actress, he thought. She couldn't be a governess with a name and face and opulent body like that. "Have you been a governess long?" he casually asked, waiting to decipher the fabrications in her reply.

"Four years. When my father Viscount Amberson died I was forced to make a living."

He felt his stomach tighten. A *viscount's* daughter? Did she have relatives? he instantly wondered, the kind who would exert all the conventional pressures? And then as instantly he decided any young lady so destitute must be on her own. "I'm very sorry."

She sat very still for a moment, thoughts of her father always painful, and then taking a small breath she said in a controlled tone, "Papa gambled his money away. He wasn't very good at cards after his first bottle."

"Most men aren't."

She glanced at the bills and then at him and he could almost feel that small spark of elation he suddenly saw in her eyes.

"Are *you*?" she mildly inquired.

"Best hand wins the hundred pounds?" he softly suggested, one dark brow raised in query. "Although I warn you, I'm sober."

"It would legitimize my taking the money." She smiled for the first time, a lush yet curiously girlish smile, enigmatic like her.

Twenty minutes later when the first course of oysters arrived, she was five hundred pounds richer, the tokay decanter was empty, an easy bantering rapport had been established and Beau had only deliberately let her win two hands. The rest she'd won on her own. She was either very good or very lucky. But she was definitely beautiful, he cheerfully noted, lounging in a comfortable sprawl across from her, his cards balanced on his chest, his gaze over the colorful fanned rims, gratified.

As was his mood.

The chill in her voice had disappeared, the guarded expression in her eyes replaced with animation. And when she smiled at him after a winning hand, he found it increasingly difficult to refrain from touching her.

She ate the oysters with relish.

She drank more wine when another decanter arrived and she said, "Thank you" so sweetly and gracefully when only the empty oyster shells remained on her plate, he almost considered giving up his plans to bed her.

But then she leisurely stretched and smiled at him. And

all he could think of was the plump fullness of her soft breasts raised high for that slow lingering moment with her arms flexed above her head. Even the plain navy serge couldn't disguise their delectable bounty.

"Did you make your gown?" he inquired to mask his overlong gaze with politesse. "I like the lace trimmed collar."

Leaning back against her chair, she delicately touched the white lace. "It was my mother's. I outgrew all of mine."

He swallowed before he answered, the thought of her outgrowing her girlish gowns having a profound effect on him after just having observed the voluptuous swell of her breasts.

"We could probably find you some additional dresses on board."

"Like the ones in the closet under the stairwell?"

"You were hiding there?"

She nodded. "The scent was luscious. Very French."

"I'll have my steward put together a wardrobe tomorrow," he blandly said, not about to discuss French scents or the reason they were there.

"Whose gowns are they?"

He gazed at her for a brief moment, gauging the degree of inquisition in her query but her expression was open, innocent of challenge.

"I'm not sure," he evasively answered. "Probably my mother's or sisters'. Which meant the more garish gowns would have to be culled out before offering the lady her choice. His light of loves had a penchant for seductive finery.

"I often wished I had siblings. Do you see your family often?"

He spoke of his family then in edited phrases, of their passion for racing and their winning horses, of their stud in the north, how his younger brother and sisters were all first class riders, offering charming anecdotal information that brought a smile to her face.

"Your life sounds idyllic. Unlike mine of late," Serena

said with a fleeting grimace. "But I intend to change that."

Frantic warning bells went off in Beau's consciousness. Had she *deliberately* come on board? Were her designing relatives even now in hot pursuit? Or were they explaining the ruinous details to his father instead? "How exactly," he softly inquired, his dark eyes wary, "do you plan on facilitating those changes?"

"Don't be alarmed," she said, suddenly grinning. "I have no designs on you."

He laughed, his good spirits instantly restored. "Candid women have always appealed to me."

"While men with yachts are out of my league." Her smile was dazzling. "But why don't you deal us another hand," she cheerfully said, "and I'll see what I can do about mending my fortunes."

She was either completely ingenuous or the most skillful coquette. But he had more than enough money to indulge her and she amused him immensely.

He dealt the cards.

And when the beefsteaks arrived some time later, the cards were put away and they both tucked into the succulent meat with gusto.

She ate with a kind of quiet intensity, absorbed in the food and the act of eating. It made him consider his casual acceptance of all the privileges in his life with a new regard. But only briefly because he was very young, very wealthy, too handsome for complete humility and beset by intense carnal impulses that were profoundly immune to principle.

He'd simply offer her a liberal settlement when the *Siren* docked in Naples, he thought, discarding any further moral scruples.

He glanced at the clock.

Three thirty.

They'd be making love in the golden light of dawn . . . or sooner perhaps, he thought with a faint smile, reaching across the small table to refill her wine glass.

"This must be heaven or very near . . ." Serena murmured, looking up from cutting another portion of beefsteak. "I can't thank you enough."

"Remy deserves all the credit."

"You're very disarming. And kind."

"You're very beautiful, Miss Blythe. And a damned good card player."

"Papa practiced with me. He was an accomplished player when he wasn't drinking."

"Have you thought of making your fortune in the gaming rooms instead of wasting your time as an underpaid governess?"

"No," she softly said, her gaze direct.

"Forgive me. I meant no rudeness. But the demimonde is not without its charm."

"I'm sure it is for a man," she said, taking a squarely cut piece of steak off her fork with perfect white teeth. "However, I'm going to art school in Florence," she went on, beginning to chew. "And I shall make my living painting."

"Painting what?"

She chewed a moment more, savoring the flavors, then swallowed. "Portraits, of course. Where the money is. I shall be flattering in the extreme. I'm very good, you know."

"I'm sure you are." And he intended to find out how good she was in other ways as well. "Why don't I give you your first commission?" He'd stopped eating but he'd not stopped drinking and he gazed at her over the rim of his wine glass.

"I don't have my paints. They're on the *Betty Lee* with my luggage."

"We could put ashore in Portugal and buy you some. How much do you charge?"

Her gaze shifted from her plate. "Nothing for you. You've been generous in the extreme. I'd be honored to paint you"—she paused and smiled—"whoever you are."

"Beau St. Jules."

"*The* Beau St. Jules?" She put her flatware down and

openly studied him. "The darling of the broadsheets . . . London's premier rake who's outsinned his father, The Saint?" A note of teasing had entered her voice, a familiar, intimate reflection occasioned by the numerous glasses of wine she'd drunk. "Should I be alarmed?"

He shook his head, amusement in his eyes. "I'm very ordinary," he modestly said, this man who stood stud to all the London beauties. "You needn't be alarmed."

He wasn't ordinary of course, not in any way. He was the gold standard, she didn't doubt, by which male beauty was judged. His perfect features and artfully cropped black hair reminded her of classic Greek sculpture; his overt masculinity however, was much less the refined cultural ideal. He was startlingly male.

"Aren't rakes older? You're very young," she declared. And gorgeous as a young god, she decided, although the cachet of his notorious reputation probably wasn't based on his beauty alone. He was very charming.

He shrugged at her comment on his age. He'd begun his carnal amusements very young he could have said but circumspect, asked instead, "How old are *you*?" His smile was warm, personal. "Out in the world on your own?"

"Twenty-three." Her voice held a small defiance; a single lady of three and twenty was deemed a spinster in any society.

"A very nice age," he pleasantly noted, his dark eyes lazily half-lidded. "Do you like floating islands?"

She looked at him blankly.

"The dessert."

"Oh, yes, of course." She smiled. "I should save room then."

By all means, he licentiously thought, nodding a smiling approval, filling their wine glasses once more. *Save room for me—because I'm coming in. . . .*

When the dishes were cleared away by the servants and coffee and fruit left, they moved to a small settee to enjoy the last course. She poured him coffee; he added his own brandy and leaning back, took pleasure in watching her slice a pear and leisurely eat each succulent piece.

"Your employers didn't feed you enough, did they?"

She turned to look at him, all languid grace and beauty. "You wouldn't understand."

His lashes lowered fractionally. "Tell me anyway."

"I don't want to," she retorted, suddenly disquieted, all the misery still too fresh. "I don't want to remember anything about those four years with the Tothams." And despite her best intentions, her eyes grew shiny with tears.

Quickly setting his cup down, he took the dessert knife from her grasp and the remains of the pear, wiped her fingers on a lavender scented napkin and holding her small hands in his, softly said, "It's over. You don't have to go back."

When a tear slid down her cheek, he gently drew her into his arms and held her close. "Don't cry, darling," he murmured. "By the time we get to Naples, you'll have won a fortune from me. And then the Tothams can go to hell."

She giggled into his chest.

"And I'll see that the portrait you paint of me is seen at the Royal Academy. Should I pose nude as Mars? That should draw attention."

She giggled again and pushing slightly away from him, gazed up into his smiling face. "You're incredibly kind," she whispered.

Her lips were half parted and only inches away. It took all his willpower to resist the temptation; her sweet vulnerability, her sadness affected even his disreputable soul.

"May I kiss you?" she whispered, her feelings in turmoil, the warmth and affection he offered inexpressibly welcome after so many years of emotional deprivation, the feel of his arms around her a balm to her lonely heart.

"You probably shouldn't." He was trying to be honorable. She perhaps didn't understand what a kiss would do to him.

"I'm not an innocent." She'd been kissed before although against her will, by the Tothams' repulsive son when he'd dared transgress his mother's commands apropos servants. It was immensely satisfying to offer a kiss of her own accord.

Beau shut his eyes briefly, her few simple words permission for all he wished to do. And when he opened his eyes, he murmured, heated and low, "Let *me* kiss *you* . . ."

She was lost then, a true innocent despite what she'd said, her notion of a kiss eons distant from Beau St. Jules's kisses.

He made her feel lusciously heated, melting, his mouth delicate at first, offering butterfly kisses on her lips and cheeks, on her earlobes and temples, on the warm pulse of her throat. And then his mouth drifted lower, following his fingers as he unbuttoned the top three buttons at her neckline, drew her collar open and kissed her soft pale skin.

She kissed him back after that and a new tremulous feeling flared deep in the pit of her stomach. Pleasure inundated her senses, her heated blood, the warming surface of her skin and most of all, gloriously in her spirit where she felt overwhelmingly happy. "You make me feel wonderful," she whispered, too long in the wasteland to want to forego such blissful sensations.

"You make me feel . . . impatient," he murmured, lifting her into her arms, moving toward his bed, his mouth covering hers again, eating her tantalizing sweetness.

"Maybe I shouldn't," she breathed moments later when he lowered her gently to the bed.

"I know," he murmured, brushing his mouth over hers. "I shouldn't undo these buttons," he whispered, unclasping another pearl button at her neckline. "Tell me I shouldn't."

"It's highly improper," she gently teased, touching his strong jaw with a trailing fingertip, smiling up at him.

"But I have this powerful carnal urge." His voice was deep, low, rich with promise.

"Should I be frightened?" Her heart was racing, her senses in tumult.

"Are you usually?" he silkily inquired, amused at how well Miss Blythe played the game.

She didn't know what to say for a moment. "No," she finally replied, trembling, eager for his touch. "I'm not."

And then the man known by salacious repute as Glory lived up to his name.